the thought of you

a sapphire creek novel

Georgia Coffman

Cover design by Kate Farlow, Y'all. That Graphic

Story coaching by Nancy Smay, Evident Ink

Proofreading by Amanda Cuff, Word of Advice Editing

playlist

"Famous Friends" – Chris Young & Kane Brown
"What's Your Country Song" – Thomas Rhett
"Bluebird" – Miranda Lambert
"Pretty Little Poison" – Warren Zeiders
"To Be Loved By You" – Parker McCollum
"The Good Ones" – Gabby Barrett
"Red" – Taylor Swift
"Dance Like No One's Watching" – Gabby Barrett
"I Can Do It With a Broken Heart" – Taylor Swift
"I Hope You Dance" – Lee Ann Womack

prologue

ADDIE

My mother's awake.

Not only that, but she's fully dressed and pilfering in the kitchen like she's... cooking. Is she making me a celebratory breakfast for my first day of school?

"Good morning, Rain." I slide onto a stool at the counter.

It's been six years since she first required me to call her by her chosen name, Rain, and while it was a difficult transition, the name freely rolls off my tongue now.

"Oh! Hi, honey." She turns with a mug in her hand.

I glance at the spot where the coffee pot used to sit, and it's still vacant. "The coffee pot broke yesterday, remember?"

"Shoot. That's right." She slumps against the sink and blows out a frustrated breath.

"I'll grab one on my way home from school later." I add that to the list of things I need to do around here, right after adjusting our budget now that she's quit yet another job.

Rain's eyes lock onto the backpack in my hand, and her shoulders perk upright again. "Does school start today?"

"I thought that's why you might be up already." My voice trails off into a question as I skim the kitchen. No red light on the stove to indicate it's on, no steaming eggs in a skillet, and no celebratory breakfast to be found.

"I'm just getting home, actually." Rain wiggles her eyebrows, and the mischievous gleam in them nearly blinds me.

"Rafe kept you out all night, huh?" I say, trying to match her enthusiasm, but it proves to be difficult with so much disappointment weighing me down.

Then again, it's my own fault for expecting anything more from my mother than this show of cluelessness.

I know better.

"Not Rafe." She shakes her finger back and forth. "I met someone new."

"I see," I practically squeak in yet another attempt to meet her halfway.

"Don't give me that look." Rounding the corner, she shoots me a pointed stare. "I thought you agreed with me that I need to have fun."

I hoist my backpack onto my shoulder and say, "I was talking about a different kind of fun, like taking up a hobby or learning a foreign language."

"Dating is a hobby. And it has its own language."

"I meant something like knitting. Something that keeps you out of trouble."

"One time!" she bursts on a laugh. But she's the only one amused. "I got into trouble *once*, and as I've told you, I didn't know Garfield illegally sold guns."

"With a first name like Garfield, you should've known there was something off about him."

"If I did, do you really think I would've gone out with him? You know how I feel about weapons."

"I had to beg Leon to drive me to bail you out. He was *so*

thrilled with the favor that he's never let me forget it. Brings it up all the time, right in between his distaste for the bright color of our house and our lack of lawn ornaments."

"He should've been happy to take his rusted old wagon out of the garage for once. In fact, he owes me a thank-you." She smiles deviously.

Quietly, I back away toward the door, and she follows me, much to my chagrin.

"Speaking of driving…"

"Please don't start." I throw the door open and race out of it.

But she chases after me. "It's just hard to believe you're not on my side about this."

I release a sound somewhere between a scoff and a snort.

"You could sell the car, Cloud. Imagine the good we could do for the environment with that money."

"By that logic, we should sell the house and everything in it," I toss back as I jump down the porch steps, my never-before-worn shoes bright and ready to be shown off, as is my shiny new car.

"You sound just like your father," she calls out as I pluck the driver's-side door open.

"Probably because he's the one who practiced with me," I mutter under my breath.

My father and I both predicted she would be appalled by his expensive birthday gift to me over the summer. It's why he coached me through rebuttal statements like he and I do for my debate team meets.

Why does she continue to bug me about this car, anyway? At the end of the day, I will always win. It's my name on the title, and I have decided to keep it.

I'm sixteen, with countless extracurriculars, and I need a freaking car. With Dad living three states away, Rain has been the only one left to drive me around for school and fun with the girls, and she's always been late.

Now that I have my own ride, I can finally make it to the previews of movies for once.

"Have a good day!" I lift my hand to wave, but my mother's already halfway back inside. As I slide onto the pristine leather seat, I ramble to myself, "I'll have a great first day as well, Rain. And oh my gosh—you like my outfit? Great to hear. Daphne helped me pick this out from her boutique last weekend, no thanks to you. I so appreciate you asking about me, Rain. As always, it's been a gigantic pleasure talking with you."

My heavy sigh pushes through my flaring nostrils with the pent-up frustration of the last six years—ever since she and my father divorced.

During that time, I've had to deal with the finances. I've had to do most of the grocery shopping and first-day-of-school planning. I've had to keep up with the house and call the exterminators, plumbers, and lawncare experts.

I do it all because my mother is too busy with her "hobby" of dating and her second favorite love affair—nature.

Before he moved from our quaint little town of Sapphire Creek, Georgia, my dad would ask if I needed his help with anything. "Is your mother taking care of you?" he'd ask. "I'm willing to lend a hand when she's not there," he'd say.

And I'd always shake my head no. He divorced her for a reason, and I didn't want to bring him back to the scene of his near insanity.

After he moved to Louisiana and remarried, he stopped asking, and I could finally stop lying to him.

The school comes into view, and I exhale, my muscles instantly relaxing into the leather seat. Relief seeps into my bloodstream as I turn into the parking lot and enter the parameters of my happy place. I scan the empty spaces for my best option—a spot where everyone can see me exit this killer car for the first time.

This car will get me noticed for something other than being a nerdy teacher's pet.

This car will make me cool.

I might even secure a date to the homecoming dance before the final bell rings this afternoon, and I can cross it off my to-do list a whole week early.

My heart thumps with grand plans of arriving to school today as a new Addie Lockhart.

This is *my* year!

But the splash I make isn't quite the one I was hoping for. Instead of a glamorous arrival, I open the door of my car and drop my foot into a puddle of muddy water.

"Ah!" I shake my foot and sling droplets every which way, but it's no use. The grimy water has seeped all the way up my sock. Brown stains already form around my ankle, and before I closely inspect the crime against my once white shoes, I already know I'll need to change.

The whole fabric of the canvas shoe is ruined.

As class president the last two years and running, I've tried and tried to convince the administration to fill in these stupid holes in the parking lot. I figured getting it done would be child's play, but they always turn me away like I'm asking them to solve world hunger.

Screeching tires coming to a halt pull my attention away as a Jeep skids into an empty parking spot a few yards away.

Owen Conrad.

Class clown. Baseball player extraordinaire. And major thorn in my side.

The guy never takes anything seriously, and he teases those of us who do—mainly me.

I climb out of the driver's seat, my feet as far apart as possible on either side of the puddle.

In three squishy steps, I open the back door in search of any other shoes I might've stowed away.

I cringe when I realize I do have a dry option, but the freaking boots might be worse than just keeping my sopping wet shoe on for the rest of the day.

"Looking good, Lockhart," I hear just before the Jeep door slams shut to my left.

Owen saunters around the side, his jeans hung low on his narrow hips and his wavy hair damp, presumably from a recent shower. "When can I take this epic ride for a spin?"

Huffing, I sink onto the edge of the backseat, the corner of the boot box digging into my hip as if to point and laugh at me. "I will be the only one behind the wheel of this Volvo."

He throws his back door open and reaches his long baseball-throwing arm inside. Then he slings a backpack onto his broad shoulders like it weighs nothing. The thing moves so effortlessly, I assume it is, in fact, empty.

"That's cool. I don't mind riding passenger," he says with a wink.

I'm no flirting expert, but I know Owen. His dirty mind only thinks in innuendos.

As always, I ignore him and pluck the shoe off my foot, frowning as people toss nods and low whistles of admiration toward my car and me. Maren and Nathan greet me as they breeze by, hand in hand, and I offer only a faint wave and a lazy smile in return.

"Need a hand? You look lost."

I blink and find Owen next to me. "I need help, but this is totally out of your wheelhouse."

"Try me." He shrugs, showing no signs of humor.

I don't trust it, though. Humor is his whole personality.

Caroline passes by, her blonde hair loose and perfect for the day. We've been friends since we were toddlers, and even though her popularity status far outweighs mine, we've remained close.

She'll have the answer.

I call out to her, and she bounces between Owen and me, her blue eyes sparkling like diamonds behind thick eyelashes.

"What's going on?" She glances between us, then focuses her attention on me when she asks, "Are you already plotting the senior prank? You've come to the master." She smacks Owen's chest, and he squares his shoulders with pride.

It's true. He is the pranking mastermind, but we have more important matters to address at the moment.

"Do you have an extra pair of shoes in your car I can borrow?" I ask, my words rushed as I lift my dirty shoe. "Major crisis here."

Caroline's hand flies to her mouth. "No way!"

Her outraged response is warranted and appreciated, but when her eyes droop in the corners, I know she will not be saving me today. I search the parking lot for Maren, but she's long gone. I continue scanning for anyone else I could pester for a clean pair of shoes, but I come up empty.

And I'm running out of time. This was supposed to be the beginning of a new era, where punctuality could finally make it on my list of qualifications on my resume. I'm a firm supporter of such a quality, despite my mother's belief that clocks are for the weak. She constantly argues with me that time is a human construct developed to control and stifle us, and only the strong rebel against it.

"I have a pair of my sister's shoes in my Jeep from camping last weekend, but they're a size six." Owen hooks a thumb over his shoulder, and again, he actually appears genuinely concerned. I don't think I've ever seen anything but a smirk on his face and amusement in his eyes.

"I need an eight. Thank you, though." I force a smile and blow out a frustrated breath as Caroline waves to someone over my shoulder.

"I'm sorry," she offers with a squeeze of my hand, then skips away toward her boyfriend.

Owen saunters off in the same direction, where he high-fives a friend.

And I dig into the box behind me for the embarrassing

monstrosities—green rubber rain boots with bright yellow ducks on them. Astronauts can spot them from Mars, and I have to wear them on my first day of school.

Why my mother thought these would be an appropriate birthday gift for me this summer is beyond my comprehension. I would have been too old for these even at ten, which was when I started budgeting and paying our bills.

Sighing, I quietly accept my fate and make the switch, grimacing more and more with every inch of my foot, ankle, and shin these boots cover.

I try to stand tall, but is such a thing possible with these on my feet? They don't match with anything, except perhaps a baby onesie, but they certainly don't go with the pastel pink sleeveless dress I'm wearing over a white top.

"Cute, cute, *cute* boots."

Oh no.

Please, Lord, *no*.

"Why didn't I think to wear my ducky rain boots today? Oh, right, because I'm not four."

I steel myself against the evil voice that belongs to none other than Emmy Salinger. I've been the object of her terror for the last two years, ever since she got her headgear off, but now I've actually fueled her fiery rampage of insults by wearing such hideous boots.

"Good to see you too, Emmy," I toss back, my tone as sweet as freaking honey because I'm a polite Southern woman in the making, damn it.

"Yvonne, come get a load of this!" she calls out to the second most awful human in our class.

Was it me who threw out a few of their homecoming maid ballots last year? Sure was. I'm not proud of committing fraud, of course, but I can't say I didn't enjoy the looks on their faces when they realized they both had lost.

My stepmother has done an excellent job of teaching me to take the high road, but even I have my limits.

From the looks of it, though, I played the fraud card too soon.

Yvonne rushes over to witness my humiliation, stars in her eyes like she's struck gold. She takes one peek at my boots and points and laughs alongside Emmy.

Their eruption of mockery feels like it echoes across the parking lot, catching the attention of a few passersby. It seems that the whole student body is laughing at me, when in reality, it's mostly just the evil twins.

In a blink, I feel like I'm in a teenage drama where the overexaggerated cartoonish bullies become warped, slow-motion figures. They loom over me, and shadows emphasize their soulless features.

I slump against my car, wishing I could hop back into it and drive away to Florida, where I could change my name and be someone else.

With a deep breath, I reach into my car for my heavy backpack full of fresh notebooks just waiting to be filled with ideas and valuable information. I square my shoulders and prepare to strut into the school for homeroom, my skin thicker than ever, but I freeze.

Owen reappears and drapes his arm around Emmy's scrawny shoulders.

"When we go shopping this weekend, can you get me boots like hers?" Emmy asks him with a point of her manicured nail at me.

He simply nods in return without sparing me or my shoes in question a glance. If Owen senses her nasty sarcasm, he doesn't show it.

He whispers something else in her ear, then nuzzles his nose into her neck, which makes her giggle. The high-pitched sound could wake hibernating bears.

Are they... together? When did this happen?

And here I thought Owen had a decent side to him beyond the goofy jokes and careless façade. When he offered his sister's shoes to me, I assumed there was a tender part of him, but obviously, I was so very wrong.

He's exactly what I've always thought about him—a spineless jock with absolutely zero standards.

I can't wait for him to disappear to the other side of the world to play baseball far from here. I only hope he takes his precious Emmy with him.

That way, after high school, I'll never have to deal with either one of them again.

chapter
one

ADDIE

Present day...

Karma is a relentless bitch with an excellent memory.

That has to be the only reason I'm currently being tortured.

I must've done many things karma deems awful, because I barely had time to finish my shower.

I snagged the sleeve of my sweater on a nail sticking out of my porch railing.

And I was only able to inhale half my dinner, during which, I nearly choked.

It's all because of karma—and Owen freaking Conrad.

My foot twitches on the gas pedal as I fight my natural instincts, begging them to let me drive over the speed limit.

It's homecoming week—aka one of the busiest times of the year for us as high school teachers—and I have to get to the float site to chaperone the sophomores. We can't leave the students to their own devices, not with tools at play, per the rules of our educational system. I follow and respect the rules.

It's why I agreed to fill in for Owen, the flake who doesn't take his professional duties seriously.

We're all hands on deck around the clock until next weekend. This requires hours outside of the classroom. This requires dedication and focus, and we must access the responsible parts of our brains to make this a success.

But clearly, Owen doesn't comprehend any of that. He doesn't seem to care about the importance of this at all. He wouldn't catch a care if it was hurled at him from his beloved pitcher's mound.

The irritating former baseball player, in a twist of fate, is now my frustrating co-worker.

I clutch the steering wheel as my tires roll to a stop in front of a dated barn with fading red paint on the outside.

I hop out of my car with a huff and race through the open sliding barn door, where I school my features against the oncoming grimace from the faint smell of must and a few other substances I don't care to identify.

"I'm here," I say, my breathless voice on edge as I tuck the dripping strands of hair behind my ear.

Gemma rushes up to me, her purse slung over her shoulder and eyes wide. "Thank you for coming so quickly. I don't know what happened to Owen. He texted to let me know he's running late, but that was twenty minutes ago."

"He's probably drooling over a baseball game, or distracted by a butterfly," I toss back. It might be a cheap shot behind his back, but then again, it's no different than the jabs I make to his face, which most around town consider to be quite handsome.

I might be the last living woman in Sapphire Creek who's immune to his charms, and it's a hill I'll proudly die on.

"See you at school tomorrow." Gemma ducks out of the barn to pick up her kid from her mother's, leaving me alone with thirteen teenagers.

And a harmonica.

"What the…" I mutter as a few distinct notes of a bluesy song drift above the chatter of the sophomores.

I hug my arms around my midsection, blinking and taking stock of the students milling about the open space until I find the source of the music. A lanky kid with curly black hair is hunched onto his heels in one corner with a harmonica perched on a holder around his neck like headgear.

While playing perfectly, he also never misses a beat in stapling the chicken wire to the boards set up around the perimeter. I like this multitasking kid.

A trailer sits in the middle of the room like a centerpiece on a table. Built onto it is a grand float decked in our school colors of black and gold. We're playing the Badgers next weekend for homecoming, so the sophomores had the idea to decorate a badger trapped in a kennel to amp up excitement for a win.

I didn't need to assist in their creative process, either, not like I have for other classes. I'm happy to help, though; it's what I do.

It's why I'm here tonight.

Since I became an English teacher at Sapphire Creek High School, I've been called on a lot to lend a hand, and I'm usually stoked to be the go-to girl. I just prefer to dry my hair before being thrust into chaos.

The sophomores currently alternate between stuffing tissue paper into chicken wire and each other's noses. I'd speak up to halt the nonsense, but they're making such great progress this far in advance. I'll let them have their fun for just a little while longer.

I step outside and suck back a healthy breath, enjoying the early evening air as the sun slowly sets, a stretch of fields between me and the horizon. Bursts of yellows, oranges, and pinks paint the sky, and the kid's harmonica from inside pauses just long enough for me to hear the crickets singing their own tune.

But that's not all I hear.

Sniffling sounds from my right, and I strain to follow its trail. The harmonica starts up again, nearly drowning out the crying altogether. I keep walking around the barn until I find a young girl crouched against the side of it between two barrels. There's no telling what the brown stains on the outsides of them are, and I have no desire to think too hard about it.

The girl glances up as she draws her knees to her chest and wraps her arms around them. "Who are you?"

"I'm Miss Lockhart, the junior English teacher. I'm filling in for Ow—I mean, Mr. Conrad." It's been only a month of working together, and I'm still getting used to calling him by anything formal. It so doesn't fit him. "What's your name?" I ask, clearing my throat.

"Beth."

A whiff of whatever animal must have died in these barrels assaults my nostrils. I mask my features with a brave face and lower myself next to the girl, wedging myself into the mix like peanut butter smashed between two crackers.

"I'm fine," she mumbles and picks at her cuticles. It's an all too familiar move.

"If that were true, you wouldn't be out here all alone."

"Am I in trouble or something?"

"No."

We stay silent for a minute as I mentally conjure my fifteen-year-old self and all the emotions that came along with it. Whenever I felt like this, it was because a boy I liked had crushed my little heart, or because the mean girls were doing what they did best. Either way, I didn't want to talk about it until I was ready.

So, I give Beth the space she might need.

A few seconds pass before she takes a deep, shaky breath and peeks over at me. "I ran into the door of the cafeteria today. Everyone saw, and I've been the butt of every joke for hours. There's actually a meme of it going viral as we speak. It's *brutally* embarrassing."

I purse my lips and sink farther onto the ground, the cool

breeze drifting through the damp strands of my hair and causing a shiver down my spine.

"Please don't tell me this will pass by tomorrow when they get distracted by something else or that they're only making fun of me to ignore their own insecurities. My big sister's already tried. She thinks I'm crazy dramatic for my 'high school drama.'" She throws up air quotes, then swipes under her eyes. "She just graduated from college a few months ago, and suddenly, she's the queen of everything."

"Well, your sister is wise and also pretty right about this. The first part, anyway." I sigh. "It doesn't mean this sucks any less. In fact, it sucks a lot."

Beth releases a watery exhale bordering on a laugh.

"I served as a punching bag for other kids' insecurities plenty of times," I say honestly, although the words are difficult, even after all these years. "If they weren't picking on me for my lopsided braids, it was my nasally voice or my two left feet. I don't know how many times I tripped just standing upright. I wasn't very balanced in any sense of the word." I shake my head as I recall how hard it was to navigate my mom's cooky ways, my dad's new life, plus the never-ending "high school drama."

One side of Beth's lips tilts upward. "How did you deal?"

"My stepmom convinced me to sign up for dance classes before high school started."

"And it helped?" She tilts her head to the side, her skepticism as clear as the red paint on her nails.

I nod. "With enough practice over time, I became rather graceful on my feet. Didn't trip over any rugs or table legs. Not as often, anyway. I'm still human, of course."

This earns me a soft but unmistakable giggle.

I dip my head, my chest lighter than before as I add, "But mostly, it helped me with my confidence. The kids at the studio were supportive and encouraging, and they opened up a whole world for me. I stopped caring so much about the jokes and comments at school, but again, that's not to say it didn't suck."

"It feels like I'm alone. Even my own friends abandoned me today."

"I'm sorry, Beth." I frown. I had my fair share of run-ins with the evil twins, but I don't know how I would've gotten through any of it without my friends. "We can stay out here as long as you'd like, but I think it'd make a bigger statement if you held your shoulders back and your chin up while you marched in there to show them you're not made of glass. You're stronger than that."

"I don't think I am."

"Just takes a little practice." I wink, and a hint of a smile makes her lips twitch. "What do you say? Should we practice?"

She blows out one more breath, then nods.

"Good, because showing them they don't bother you is the best kind of revenge."

"What's another kind? I'm open to options." Her attempt at a full grin falters before it reaches her eyes, but I appreciate the effort. It helps me know I'm alleviating the suck factor of her situation at least a fraction.

My answer comes out quickly—a little *too* quickly, in fact. "The other kind is waiting for your bullies to grow up, marry for money and status instead of love, and miserably stomp around town with permanent frowns on their Botoxed faces."

She blinks. "Weirdly specific, but I like it. I think."

I smile, thankful she doesn't push the topic so I don't accidentally tell her that's exactly what happened to Emmy Salinger, who's *Emily Winchester* now. "Let's get inside, because this smell is going to make me pass out. How are you not getting sick over this?"

"I'm used to it. I live on a farm." With a shrug, she follows me around the corner of the weary structure toward the sliding door, where she pauses to dry the last of her tears on her cheeks with the end of her shirtsleeve.

My heart cracks, but the way she raises her head high keeps it from breaking altogether.

"Ready?" I ask.

"Only one way to find out." She plasters on a smile, and I wave for her to lead the way inside.

"Alonso, stop it already!" One of the kids shooshes the harmonica player. She then taps on her phone and shifts a Bluetooth speaker to the side, which plays even louder music than the harmonica.

"Walk much?" One of the guys snickers as Beth inches by, and the kid next to him joins in on the laughter.

Beth's steps falter only slightly, but she doesn't crumble. She makes a beeline for an open spot on the other side of the trailer and dives into the work.

As hard as it is to get through this phase, I find comfort in knowing she'll be okay, because I was.

"Let's keep it at a reasonable volume," I call out.

This grabs their attention. It's safe to assume they hadn't noticed my arrival before this moment, given how wide their eyes grow.

"I thought Mr. Conrad was going to be here tonight," one says, but it's more of a question. It's laced with disappointment too.

"He told us he'd bring his cornhole set for us to play," another student chimes in and nudges the first boy with his elbow. "I was going to show Ray what's up."

Irritation pinches my nerve endings, and my eye twitches. I'm exhausted and flustered to the hundredth degree, but I'm the one who showed up—the second-rate, non-fun adult compared to the cool guy who acts and talks just like them.

"Mr. Conrad couldn't be here tonight, unfortunately. Last-minute obligation," I say through gritted teeth. What I truly want to tell them is that they idolize the wrong teacher. They don't know me yet, as they won't have me in English until next year, but they should learn now that Owen's the *wrong* teacher.

But I'm a professional. I'm above childish antics and drama.

I'm responsible, and some day, when these teens grow up, they'll appreciate me.

"But if you work really hard over the next hour, you can leave early," I chirp, and it seems I speak their language.

The group dips their heads practically in sync, and they don't make much of a peep for the next hour. The snickering boys don't even make another crack at Beth. Not one that I hear, anyway, and I do strain to listen.

With the music turned down and the tissue paper dedicated once again to the actual float instead of their nostrils, I dig my phone out of my massive tote and call Owen for the third time tonight. But just as the previous two times, I'm greeted by his voicemail.

And my blood pressure rises, as if it's not high enough already.

I'm the one who loses sleep over school functions.

I'm the one who takes my job, this community's traditions, and general human decency seriously.

I'm the one who... I peer down, and my jaw drops to my chest in horror as I fold my arms across my unsupported breasts.

In my efforts to arrive as quickly as possible to relieve Gemma, I forgot to put a bra on.

Owen Conrad is going to fucking pay for this.

chapter
two

OWEN

I CUP my hand around Huck's soft head and bounce him with each slow step, comforting the little guy in the best way I've learned over the last few months.

He seems to appreciate an easy rhythm as his tears dry on his plump cheeks.

"That's right, little man. Slow and steady wins the race," I whisper as I pace the living room with him resting in the crook of my arm. "You'll hear a lot of wise, wise words that are not at all clichés from your favorite uncle." I chuckle as Huck makes a few incoherent sounds. I point to the TV, where an old baseball game flashes back at us. "Did you see that?" I ask him, as if the seven-month-old understands. "Did you see the way he slid into third?"

The TV is on mute so as to avoid riling up the little guy, who does not yet enjoy loud noises, but I imagine the commentators. The cheers. The crack of the bat against the ball.

But he'll learn to love it. All in good time, if I have anything to say about it.

Baby steps.

"Someday, I'm going to teach you how to play baseball," I

continue as the boy's big brown eyes stare back at me. His cheeks are still red from his tormented fit earlier, and my heart cracks as I add, "We're going to play catch and Jenga, and I'll teach you how to swim too. Your mom's great at many things, but she's a terrible swimmer. I've tried to teach her, but she's rather stubborn. Prefers to lie out on a towel with the tip of her toes in the water, instead."

Huck blows a spit bubble, which slides down his chin, and I'd like to think his smile is because he genuinely understands me and how much he's loved.

Instantly, my mind fast-forwards to ten years from now, when I'll tell him stories of his mother that she won't otherwise share. Of our childhood with our twin sisters. Of his grandma and grandpa raising four unruly children.

I imagine Huck laughing at the silly games we played and the pranks we pulled. Well, I did most of the latter, which I will, of course, teach him too. He's not even a year old yet, but I can tell he's got jokester blood in him.

Most of all, I picture the little guy with family surrounding him, always. He might not know his own father, but he will have the support and love of a big-hearted family, that's for damn sure.

The only other thing we take almost as seriously as our loyalty to one another is Jenga. My family takes the game more seriously than heart health and trimmed lawns. We've been playing ever since I suggested it at eleven years old. At the time, I just wanted the twins, Laurel and Lottie, to stop fighting, and Jenga was the only distraction in the house that we could all play. Whit was too young to join us back then, but she's definitely made up for lost time ever since, kicking our asses more often than not.

On the TV, the player takes a swing, launching the ball into the outfield, and at about the same time, the door swings open. My youngest sister storms inside like a tornado, her large bag swinging from side to side as she unties the flannel shirt from her waist.

Once she slumps it all into a pile on the middle of the couch, she flips her wild hair to the side and practically leaps toward Huck like she hasn't seen him in months, when it's really just been a couple of hours.

It's what I love about her as a mother—her affection for her son is out of this world.

"How are my two favorite guys?" She beams as she peppers kisses along the back of Huck's head.

"What about Dad?" I joke.

"He's my favorite grandpa." She pats my shoulder as she side-steps us and makes her way to the kitchen. "I got back here as quickly as possible. Was Huck okay? His belly seemed to be bothering him earlier."

"The gas coming out of this tiny body was killer," I say. "I'll just remember a mask next time."

Huck giggles like he appreciates my joke. He reaches his tiny hand up to grip my thumb, and my knees buckle. The heart *certain* people at work don't believe I have swells until it crowds my chest.

"Shhh," I coo as Whitney rifles through the kitchen cabinets. I rock Huck from side to side until his grip on my thumb loosens, and his eyelids flutter, teetering on the cusp of sleep.

According to Whit, he didn't nap as long as usual today, but he needs to eat before he tuckers out for the night.

"Easy," I say, projecting my voice toward my noisy sister the best I can without jarring him.

"I am trying..." She climbs onto the counter and pulls a sippy cup from a jungle of other tumblers on the shelf. She keeps producing them like a long string of ribbons a magician pulls out of his sleeve. As she arranges each one next to the other on the counter by her knee, she huffs. "To get these," she finishes as she lands back on her feet and plucks a cup from the row. "Dad probably put these back there. No one else in this house can reach so far back."

I continue rocking the swaddled bundle in my arms. It's true. The only men who frequent this house are Dad and me. And Huck. But even though he seems to be growing fast, we still have plenty of time before he's tall enough to reach those cabinets.

A few minutes later, Whitney tests the milk's temperature on her arm, and once she's satisfied, she brings a full bottle over. "Thank you for coming by so last minute. Mom and Dad had some housewarming party to go to, and I've had to stop bothering with the twins. I can always count on you, though."

I squeeze her shoulder, fortunate for the opportunity to live nearby, thanks to the recent changes I've made to my life.

"Lottie always insists I call her to help, but when I do, she practically chews my head off. She's focused on the studio, which is great, but she's becoming worse than Laurel in constantly reminding us how *busy* she is."

I chuckle at her playful eye roll. I know exactly what she's talking about when it comes to this facet of our twin sisters.

"I swear, all Laurel talks about is *how busy she is*, and I always think to myself, we could've accomplished so much in all the time it took for her to describe every excruciating detail of her jampacked schedule." She scoffs, and it's not as playful as the eye roll. "She's in med school—we fucking get it."

"Language," I whisper and cover one of Huck's innocent little ears.

"Relax. He doesn't even know the difference between fuck and fofo."

"What is fofo?"

"Exactly." She blows loose strands of hair from her forehead. "As I was saying—thank you for coming. I wasn't going to go to the thing earlier, but after I saw the grade on my essay, I needed all the help I could get."

I was on the phone with her while on my way over, during which she mentioned "the thing" was a happy hour poetry slam at an artsy bar here in Savannah. The essay was for the English class she needs to retake this semester since her first attempt ended with too many absences because of morning sickness, doctor's appointments, and what she refers to as her "cankle crisis."

Huck's eyes blink open again as if he can smell his dinner like I would a ribeye grilled to perfection.

"You're only a month into this semester; you should really start off on the right stanza." I snort as I slide the eager, wiggling baby into her open arms.

"You're hilarious," she deadpans as she positions the bottle into Huck's ready mouth.

"It's what I do best," I joke, but there's a layer of sad truth to it too.

I've been the funny guy ever since I can remember, and while it's an easy, natural gig for me, it can be a double-edged sword at times.

"What you do best is being a big brother." She lifts her tired yet sparkling eyes to meet mine, and my chest swells again. This time, it fills with pride. "Thanks again for coming over. I hope I didn't spoil your evening."

"You don't have to keep thanking me, sis. In fact, next time you do, I'm taking back one of your wins. I'll cross it right off the board."

She gasps. "You wouldn't."

We've only recently started playing Jenga at family dinners again, and what started as a short-term solution to the twins' bickering as kids has officially become the longest-standing Conrad tradition.

"How was the thing?" I ask her.

"It was actually more fun than I thought it would be." Her yawn stretches through time and space. Between school and Huck, plus family dinners and the soreness in her back, she doesn't get enough rest—not exactly the sleepless college experience she expected when she enrolled. "Got to hang out with some of my classmates, and I didn't realize how much I needed to be with other people my age."

I clutch my chest. "Ouch. And here I thought you just went because you had to."

"I did have to. For many reasons," she says with a lazy smile on her pale lips. "As much as I love you, most of our conversations and hangs lately have involved Huck's spit-up, explosive diapers, and busted eardrums from trying to talk over his screams."

"I fail to see the downside. I live for that stuff." Again, my attempt at a joke is undercut with a hint of truth.

I might've moved back to Sapphire Creek because my ACL injury ended my professional baseball career just over a year ago, but that wasn't the only reason. The biggest one is staring back at me with his wide, innocent eyes.

Whit shakes her head as Huck drains the last of the bottle. "We both need a life."

Humming, I raise my hand and bring it an inch from her nose. "You are breathing." I skim the backs of my knuckles against her cheeks. "And you are warm. Definite signs of living." I crack a grin, and she tsks.

"You're going to make some woman very happy and equally annoyed someday," she says on a laugh.

"She'd be lucky to be on the receiving end of my huge—"

She holds the bottle up with her fingers spread out from behind it. "Don't be gross."

"Jokes. My huge *jokes*. What did you think I was going to say, you perv?"

"I'm serious, Owen." Her lips sink into a frown, and I brace myself. "You've been hiding away since your surgery, rehabbing your knee like a maniac in between working and trying to sell your house in Atlanta, and I've been cooped up in here with this little guy for what feels like an eternity. We should get out more and *live*."

She's right. I have spent the last year transitioning from a career in professional baseball to teaching Physical Education to high school freshmen in Atlanta. When the same position opened up in

Sapphire Creek, I jumped at the chance to move back home and be closer to my family.

When I learned it was my old baseball coach who was retiring, the deal was even sweeter, as I received the added bonus of taking over my hometown's team too. Principal Weathers chomped at the bit for me to coach and practically offered me the job before my interview had even begun.

I've focused on nothing other than the steps of my plan ever since. It's not as detailed a plan as something Addie Lockhart— aka control freak extraordinaire—would be proud of, but it's better than anything else I've come up with in my entire adult life.

It's fucking drained me too, not that I can let any of it show to Whit or the rest of the family.

With Huck ready to be burped, Whit slips him into position over the cloth on her shoulder and pats his back. Afterward, it doesn't take long for the little guy to pass out, his mouth slightly open.

We both stare at him in the crib, his tiny arms resting above his head as he peacefully sleeps, until my leg cramps, as if to announce, "It's time to go."

I haven't been stretching and exercising it as much as I should, not since school started last month, and unfortunately, the ramifications of it have tortured me more and more lately.

At the door, I pull Whit in for a quick hug and squeeze her shoulder. "I'll check in with you this weekend to see about that life you mentioned."

"You know I wouldn't change a thing, right? I was just... talking before."

"I know. We both just need better balance," I offer. "Also, you're doing great."

"Thank you," she whispers, and it's thick with emotion. Seems like she needed to hear that more than I thought.

"Talk soon, okay?" I level her with my sincerest expression, my lips firm in a tight line. "As always, call if you need anything. I mean it."

"You always do."

In my truck, I check my phone and sigh. A missed call and a text from Gemma. Three calls and twice as many texts from Addie.

LOCKHART

Are you still coming to float?

You were supposed to be here an hour ago.

I had to fill in, and I don't have the time. GET YOUR ASS OVER HERE.

The rest of the messages describe the evil she'll impose on me, and mixed in are a few colorful words that must never be repeated.

So, it's pretty much a typical day at the office.

I rub the exhaustion from my eyes. Then I back out of the narrow driveway and inch away from my sister's duplex, settling into my seat for the thirty-minute drive back to Sapphire Creek.

My phone glares at me from the passenger seat the entire drive, like Addie does during faculty meetings and school functions.

She's never going to let me forget that I'm over an hour late to my float shift, especially not after the basketball fundraiser debacle. It's bad enough I was so late to that, but this second strike might end me altogether.

Addie doesn't offer three strikes.

She barely ever hands out a single one to those she likes, and I am not on that list. On the contrary, I'm on her shit list, alongside litterers, puppy kickers, and jerks who take longer than two minutes to order in a drive-thru.

I made up the last one, but knowing the tightly wound hard ass, I'd bet it's true. Then again, there's no chance she's the type to enjoy greasy fast food.

I check the time again as I near the city limits. There's a chance I'm able make it to the last twenty minutes of float, so I drive directly to the barn, zipping past the widespread golf course on the edge of town. The streetlights cast a glow over the large mossy oaks at its entrance, which are merely a blur as I slow my truck to the legal speed limit.

My foot itches to press on the gas and floor it, as I'm losing precious time, but this is not the moment to get pulled over. Addie would have a field day with that.

I trace the square downtown, driving around each corner with my thumb tapping on the steering wheel faster and faster. Half the shops and restaurants have shut their lights off and locked their doors. A few people mosey along the sidewalks and cobblestone alleys, bags in hand from what's probably their dinner leftovers.

Reaching the barn on the opposite side of town feels like it takes twice the normal amount of time, and when I finally throw my truck into park next to Addie's car, a sigh of relief escapes me with a *whoosh*.

She's still here, which means there's hope for me yet.

I hop out as Addie emerges through the creaky sliding door, holding one arm across her chest. The woman is usually peculiar, but the way she folds her second arm high across her breasts like she's holding her shirt up is extra odd.

"I made it!" I announce with my most charming grin. During my baseball days, this grin was an important aspect of my brand. It could turn the droopiest frowns upside down, and many fans would even rave on their socials about how quickly I could transform their dreary days into sunshine.

I'm not above using it to my advantage with Addie, even though history has made it clear that it has no effect on her.

"I'm sorry I'm so late, but I had—"

She storms past me, her arms still secured around her chest as she rushes to her car and yanks the door open.

I follow her hurried steps and call out, "Are you all right?"

She slams the door shut and whirls around with both hands on her hips. "No, I'm actually not all right, Owen," she clips, hissing my name with the sneers of a thousand cartoon villains. "You're not just late; you missed the shift altogether. I had so much to do tonight, but I had to drop everything and rush over here to cover for you."

"What did you have to do tonight—organize your damn yarn for your weekend knitting circle?" I toss, seamlessly falling into normal patterns. It's been like this with her for months—years, really.

"I nearly swiped a mailbox on my way, and I was here for a whole thirty minutes before I realized I'd forgotten to put a damn bra on."

On instinct, my gaze drops to her chest, but her sweater reveals nothing. If she hadn't told me her tits were going commando, I wouldn't have known.

"Don't look at my chest," she screeches and wraps her arms around herself again.

"Relax. There's nothing to see."

"Excuse me?" Grimacing, she lurches backward like she's dodging a punch. "Just because I don't have plastic balloon boobs like your baseball groupies, it doesn't mean there's *nothing* here. There's plenty."

"I just meant your sweater is thick enough. There's nothing scandalous for you to worry about."

She shakes her head, and her humorless laugh echoes in the night, the sharp edge in her tone striking me in piercing waves.

Well, that wasn't the right thing to say, either.

Fuck.

"You are unbelievable." She throws her hands up. "You make me do your job, and instead of thanking me, you come here to insult me. But you know what? I expect nothing else from you. In fact, thank you for your consistency. At least I can count on you for your unwavering sense of rude and careless behavior. Isn't that comforting?" she deadpans and jerks her door open again.

"Now, wait a minute. It's not what you—"

The slam of her door cuts me off, and the roar of her gurgling engine signals the end of our *non*-conversation.

It wouldn't have made a difference to explain to her my complicated personal situation, anyway. No matter how badly I'd love to dispel all the unsavory things about me clogging her brain, what's the point?

She's hated me since we were teenagers. Back then, my biggest problems were getting my math grades up, winning the state championship with the baseball team, and deciding on the date of the next bonfire party at Josh Rivers's house.

I only saw Addie at one of those parties.

For her, *I* was the biggest problem. That's what it seemed like, anyway.

I was too much of a loose cannon. Too unreliable and goofy. I think she called me cheeky once, and while I thought it was a compliment at the time, it most certainly was not. She snatched my uneaten Little Debbie and threw it into the trash on her rampage out of the cafeteria that day. I don't even remember what I did to set her off.

Since then, I've done a million other things she considers heinous, so it's hard to nail down the exact reason for her distaste of me, not that I've ever asked. She's never given me the chance.

It's been ten years since high school. We've lived separate lives during that time, and now that I'm back, I've basically picked up where I left off.

I'm still the biggest problem for Addison Lockhart.

ADDIE

THE WIND DECIDED to rearrange my hanging line—again.

A pair of leggings and a few socks decorate a rose bush in my backyard like the most unique Christmas tree in all of Georgia.

I rush down the steps of my deck and delicately untangle them from the branches, wary of any flying critters. The last time I gathered my clothes from the line I've draped across my deck, a bee zipped out of my black dress and gave me a scare.

I skim the rest of the yard to ensure I've gotten them all, and with a huff, I mutter, "This cannot be my long-term fate."

I had no intention of going this long without a proper dryer, either, but once again, I missed Judd. He came by to fix it, as promised, but I wasn't around to let him into my house. I delivered a box of his favorite donuts to him as an apology with a note to beg him to come back soon.

Judd's usually busy with his auto shop, where my friend Austin works, but Judd is also rather handy in unclogging a vent hose. I'd find a *YouTube* video and do it myself, but when Judd mentioned over the phone that it might need to be replaced altogether, I washed my hands of the issue.

I'm good, but I'm not fix-a-damaged-dryer good.

But I haven't been home much over the last few days, so I still have no dryer, which is why I'm now completing a scavenger hunt around my yard for my clean clothes.

They *were* clean, anyway.

I lay the rescued items across the top of my loaded laundry basket, hoist it onto my hip, and head back inside.

I've just set the basket on the floor at the foot of my bed when the front doorbell rings.

With extra pep in my step, I race out into the hall, through the living room, and yank the door open.

"Your wish is my command." Maren holds up a brown bag in one hand and a wine bottle in the other.

"I only asked for a glue gun." My lips twitch.

"Yes, but since I've known you for most of my life, I figured you could use some Skittles and wine."

"Bless you." My mouth instantly salivates. I imagine this is how dogs feel in the presence of juicy meat or peanut butter.

As she enters my living room, she asks over her shoulder, "How bad has this week been for you?"

"Not bad. It's been great. Full of opportunities and fun." Some might call their items on a to-do list *tasks* or *chores*, but I refer to them as opportunities—rungs on a ladder to success.

"You're stressed." My best friend sets the goodies down, and I help myself to the contents of the bag.

"When am I not stressed?"

"I'm starting to think that while the rest of us need water to survive, you're gulping back lists and calendars to thrive." Next to the coffee table, Maren reaches a hand toward the stack of photos and gasps. "Oh my God. What are these?"

"They're for our reunion Saturday. I'm going to put a few copies on each table so people can reminisce. They can also take them home, since I have multiple of each. They're kind of like nostalgic party favors." I point to a separate stack and say, "Those are ones of Caroline, you, and me."

She skims through the pile and holds one up. "Oh, my pageant days with Caroline."

"Your hair was a fire hazard," I playfully tease as I take the picture from her.

In it, we're around twelve, and the circumference of Maren's hair is bigger than a beach umbrella. The curls are glued together with an ungodly amount of hairspray. I stand between the two in the picture, my jeans and T-shirt remarkably plain next to their sparkling dresses. Their coordinating puffy sleeves hide part of my face on either side, but our matching smiles are wide and excited.

The three of us remained close, even after Caroline moved to New York ten years ago. She's in town for the class reunion, and even though I had plans to enjoy many a stress-free girls' nights with her and Maren, I have not had the time I expected I would, not with all the last-minute arrangements to be made for homecoming and our big reunion this weekend.

Maren continues sifting through the photos while I rummage into a Skittles bag and scoop up a handful. "You should've printed this one in a much larger size." She presents a picture from a legendary bonfire, which features many classmates sticking out their tongues. Owen is front and center with his shirt stretched over his head.

I roll my eyes. "I could not, in good conscience, draw any more attention to Owen with a larger print."

"I'm surprised you printed it at all."

I furrow my brows. *Why did I?* "It's a memory, that's all," I say, but my voice is faint.

"This one definitely deserves a larger size." Grinning, she shows me the one from spirit week during our senior year. A few guys wear gold bandanas around their heads, and several girls are decked in black-and-gold shirts with the letters SCHS filled in with glitter.

It's been ten years since this picture was taken, and this week, it's all coming full circle.

With a sigh, Maren arranges the photos back into a neat pile on my coffee table, just as they were before she arrived. "Let's get to work. I have an early morning."

As the owner of a coffee truck, every morning is early for her. Even so, she's here to help me this late in the evening. Giving up on rest and sleep equals true friendship, which is why I've already made a note to stop by her house tomorrow with a bouquet of air fresheners. She mentioned earlier that she's run out of her favorite scents, so it's only fair and proper for me to return the favor with a nice gesture of my own.

I hop up from the couch to follow her into the other room, but a glimpse of the top picture on the stack gives me pause. It's the same picture from the bonfire, with Owen's abs on display.

I was the one who snapped the shot.

It was the one time I'd gone to one of those parties, and since I'm not in the picture, there's no proof of my presence. I made no impression on these people back then other than to be the one who organized and documented their fun.

And I'm still doing it.

As our senior class president, the opportunity of hosting the reunion ultimately falls on me. I've worked tirelessly all summer to get the Buchanan House ready for us. I've stalked online sites for sales on décor, I've gone back and forth with caterers on a menu until I was dizzy, and I've spent all week trying to bring it all together.

We're under budget too.

I've done it all with little support from our class's beloved VP —Owen Conrad.

But even if he were around to help, he'd only be in my way. Getting things done has been my thing since I was young. I'm good at it, and more than that, I enjoy this stuff as much as I do dance and Skittles.

In the kitchen, Maren pours two glasses of wine, and I make my way to the dining table, the bag of Skittles tightly clutched in my hand. "Thanks for coming over tonight," I say as she hands me a glass. "And thanks for this."

I savor a sip, and my eyes nearly roll into the back of my head. It's probably not as good and flavorful as the wines from faraway places like Napa Valley or Italy, but right now, it's the best wine I've ever had.

It hits the spot like cold lemonade on a hot day.

Maren plugs in the glue gun, then holds up a black vest with a ribbon of gold sequins hanging off one end. "What is this?"

"Another unfinished project for my outfit tomorrow." I sit in front of a pair of white shoes just begging me to bedazzle them for spirit week.

Tomorrow is black-and-gold day. Principal Weathers wanted to assign that day to Friday, but with the homecoming parade at one, and most students needing to wear dresses, cheerleading uniforms, and such, I convinced him our school colors deserve a whole day.

I point to the vest, which is my next order of business tonight, and say, "I ran around town in search of one like it, but it's true what they say—why ask someone else to do what you can do better?"

"Totally." She sips from her glass, nearly draining it, and I know she gets it. She's also good at sewing, like me, but neither one of us knows how to knit, contrary to Owen's buffoon-ish assumption about my friends and me.

With the kitchen table covered in a plastic tablecloth, I bring the untouched shoes over for us to decorate. She tests the glue gun, and I spread out a handful of sequins to stick to the shoes.

To my side, I tap my phone to play a song for us, then switch to my messages, where I find a text from my mother.

Squeezing my eyes closed, I release a rough exhale. I'm not surprised she asked me to lunch on a weekday—on the day of the homecoming parade, no less. It's not the first time, and much to my chagrin, I don't imagine it'll be the last.

Rather than respect my life choices, she lectures me, claiming the tension in my body and the negativity in my aura are the products of me being trapped by "the system."

My mother and her free spirit don't confine themselves to a regimented work schedule, or to a single home address. According to her, the world—and beyond—is her home.

But there's one important thing her text indicates. The fact that she's inviting me to try green beans means she'll be in town. Is she coming to the chili dinner on Friday night? I'd ask her, but what's the point? Anytime she's told me of her plans in the past, they've always changed at the last minute, so I stopped asking a long time ago.

I skim past her message without responding and locate the thread I need. "I texted Caroline to come over too, but she hasn't responded."

"She's probably with Austin."

I lift my head, my eyebrows shooting into my hairline. "Oh?"

She shrugs. "They've been spending a lot of time together this week."

Maren takes minimalism to a frustrating level when it comes to her expressions. The fact that she's so nonchalant about this flabbergasting bit of news could be because it's not shocking or interesting at all.

On the other hand, it could still be epic gossip, but Maren's pursed lips are sworn to secrecy.

Could she know something? I've barely seen Caroline all week, and when I have, I've been flustered and preoccupied. I've practically redecorated the Buchanan House three times in an attempt to get it *just* right.

After all, we're going to remember our reunion for years to come. Even if Owen thinks I'm ridiculous for the lengths I've gone to, which he's obnoxiously mentioned multiple times the last few days, I know I'm doing important work. It's my responsibility to ensure Saturday night is memorable for all the fun times rather than for it being lame.

"Are you surprised?" Maren asks as she finishes gluing a line of sequins along one side of a shoe. She picks up the other and begins the same task over again to match the first.

"They didn't get off on the right foot last weekend," I say as I recall the morning I ran into Caroline at Bready or Knot downtown, and she introduced herself to Austin.

I had to remind her that he was in our graduating class, and he was less than amused or forgiving, which is putting it nicely.

I pull the thread through the sequined ribbon, sewing it to the edge of the black vest. "I figured he'd avoid her like the plague this week."

Maren snorts. "Doesn't he avoid everyone?"

I hum in agreement. Austin Kyle is a friend, one I've grown relatively close to since high school, but the guy is grumpier than Leon, the eighty-year-old man living across the street, who calls to scold me about my hedges not being trimmed to his liking. Last week, he called to inform me my trash bin was still on the curb, and I should've brought it up my driveway already.

When I first started living here alone after college, I gave him my number in case of emergencies. In hindsight, he and I have very different definitions of the concept.

"The other night, when I asked Austin to drive Caroline in the parade tomorrow, he turned green." I shake my head, picturing his scrunched face like I'd twisted his arm into a pretzel.

"He's going to do it, though, right?"

"He is, but I think it's only because his mother was standing next to him when I practically begged. There was no one else to drive her."

As our class's homecoming queen, Caroline was in the top five people I needed to secure a ride for in the parade. She's giving a speech on the courthouse steps to conclude Friday's afternoon festivities, so I might've actually cried had prickly Austin not agreed to lend his truck and time for one of the highlights of homecoming.

Then again, I'd worked too hard to let him worm his way out of helping. I was ready to promise him a kidney, but thankfully, his mother's excitement over the idea was enough.

He loves her more than anyone, so he basically had no choice.

"Are you sad Nathan isn't coming this weekend?" I peek over at her, but she doesn't visibly react at the mention of her high school boyfriend.

"So, it's not just a rumor, then?"

"He RSVP'd with his attendance, but I heard he's stuck on a job somewhere in Wyoming that's taking him longer to complete than he previously thought."

"Hmm" is all she offers.

But I know just the thing to crack this nut—if I continue pressing, she'll eventually cave.

"You didn't answer my question," I say as I bring the ribbon around the bottom corner of the vest, careful not to make eye contact as if she were a deer I stumbled upon in the woods.

"You prying little shit." With a sigh, Maren drops the shoe to the table with a thud. "Would it have been nice to see him? Sure. For nostalgia's sake. But he'll be back soon to visit his parents, and since they live right next door, odds are I'll see him then, not that I'll be glued to the window waiting for that day." She scoffs, and a giggle accidentally escapes me. "Oh, since you think that's so funny, why don't we talk about Owen?"

"Whoa." I hold a hand up as if it's a white flag. "I only asked about Nate because I care."

"That's why I'm asking about Owen."

"There's nothing to talk about when it comes to that dick-headed butt munch."

"Such strong words imply strong feelings," she sings sarcastically. "Especially when those words are a decade old."

"Strong feelings of hate, maybe, and don't you dare give me shit about some mythical line between love and hate."

"Not love. Just lust." The evil grin she wears stretches all too proudly from cheek to cheek, and I vehemently shake my head. "Come on. You complain about the guy more often than you use your car."

"Because he's the bane of my existence," I remind her, although I shouldn't have to. That much should be as clear as freaking day. "My life was great before the Devil spit him back into town."

She tongues her cheek.

"I'm serious," I assert.

"Fine, but you have to admit he's good-looking. It's an objective fact."

"He's cuter than Leon, and that's as far as I'll go."

She dips her head and laughs. "Okay, you don't have to admit it, but he's changed since high school. I'm telling you this as your friend and nothing more. I think you'll be happy to see I'm right. If you would just give him a chance, then maybe your blood pressure won't be so high. It's not healthy."

"My mother claims I should eat fewer Skittles to fix my health problem."

"She's not wrong."

"It's my one guilty pleasure. Let me have this." I put an end to the discussion by popping a few pieces of my beloved candy into my mouth.

Just like I will never abandon my obsession with Skittles, I refuse to let even one of my best friends sweet-talk me into changing my mind about Owen. I'm not biting on that thread unless it's to chew his stupid head off.

chapter
four

ADDIE

"Reporting for duty." Austin stands on the inside of the old bread factory and stuffs one hand into his pocket. In the other, he holds up a bag of Skittles. "And here's this."

"You magnificent flannel-loving cactus," I say, but my voice isn't as enthusiastic as I'd like it to be.

The guy might be prickly and frustratingly curt, but he's definitely a kind and generous friend. It's why he answered my SOS and rushed over here.

He deserves a proper thanks, but my boiling blood is too close to the surface.

"You still promise to let the band practice at your house while Hunter's garage is getting painted, right?" Austin arches a brow.

Oh, right.

Our conversation all comes rushing back to me.

That's how I'd planned to thank him for giving up his evening to help me. His band plays at the Tap every Sunday night, and they practice on Wednesdays, which works well for me because that's when I volunteer at the dance studio.

"Sure. Whatever you need," I say, completely distracted, but I'd bet not even broody Austin can blame me.

The homecoming parade is tomorrow, and the freshmen have yet to finish their float. While the other classes successfully stuck to their schedules I arranged, the freshmen took my hard work and chucked it out the window like littering jerks with their empty cans or fast-food wrappers.

We have zero room to mess around tonight, which is why I brought in reinforcements. Austin's already here, and Maren, Caroline, and Owen should arrive soon too.

Together, we can finish this in our allotted time slot.

I retrieve a plastic tablecloth from my tote bag of wondrous things and drape it over the rusty table before I let him throw my precious Skittles onto it.

Maren pops in, two lavender boxes in her hands, and my stomach growls at the sight. It's not subtle, either. It sounds more like a croaking bullfrog in summer.

"Easy," Maren teases. "I brought cookies for everyone. You have to share."

"We'll see," I joke back, even though there's a touch of truth to it. I'm starving.

I open each box, and with a deep inhale of the homemade treats, my stomach growls louder.

"How many kids are coming tonight?" Austin points to the cookies. "There are enough cookies here for a small school of juvenile bass."

Maren and I both stare at him.

"The younger ones tend to swim with each other in groups, unlike the more solitary adults," he clarifies with a clipped tone.

"I have no idea how I survived my whole life without knowing that," I deadpan.

"You're welcome," he throws back with a grunt.

Maren hooks a thumb over her shoulder and inches toward the door. "On that fascinating note, I need to run."

"You're not staying?" I frown.

"I have so much work to do if I have any hope of making it to homecoming stuff tomorrow." She holds her hands up in a prayer-like fashion. "I'm sorry."

"You're forgiven. Now, go, you beautiful human with fantastically talented baking hands." I wave her off to go be the extraordinary girl boss she is.

"Let me know what you think about the spicy pear cookies. It's a new recipe."

"Since she's leaving, can I go too?" Austin nods in the direction where Maren disappears.

"You don't have to work."

"You don't know that."

I tilt my head in doubt, then hand him a cookie. "Eat this. The sugar should balance your bitterness."

I bite into my own sugary heaven and groan when it melts in my mouth. It's almost enough to fix my mood. The fall spices complement the sweetness of the raisins, and the flavors coat my tongue in a blanket of seasonal glory. If I didn't care so much about the students, I'd hide one whole box away to take home for myself.

They'd deserve to miss out on the treats after the stress they've put me through this week, but alas, I'm not evil. I close the boxes and pat the cookies like they're good little pets.

Then I throw my tote onto the table and rifle through it, skipping past an extra bra I tossed in here in light of last week's wardrobe malfunction.

Among the first aid and sewing kits, I locate the hand sanitizer, rub a small blob into my palm and around my fingers, then sip from my water bottle. I face Austin again, who frowns at my appearance.

"What's with the getup?" He waves a finger over me.

In truth, it looks like Sapphire Creek High School threw up on me.

The array of blacks and golds are admittedly disorienting. The tie-dyed headband around my head matches my T-shirt. Long pigtails emerge over each shoulder, cascading over the black vest I lined with gold sequins.

Beyond that, my shimmery leggings are tucked into knee-high socks with glitter covering them, and on my feet, I wear the canvas shoes I decorated with Maren last night. This morning, I painted two black lines under my eyes too, but I washed them off before leaving my house, deciding such additions sent the whole outfit from enthusiastic to psychotic.

"Spirit week." I shrug, as I figure it's obvious.

But knowing Austin Kyle and his clueless ways, he probably thought this was some change in trending fashion. When we were in high school, he was *not* the type to be aware of spirit week, let alone dress up for it.

I study the dim space as a dust bunny skips across the concrete floor like a tumbleweed, and the faint smell of something unknown drifts in and out of my senses. We have got to find more suitable—and odorless—places to build these floats in the future. It can't be that hard to locate some proper, unoccupied buildings, right?

Since it's just Austin and me so far, I use the opportunity to make a note for future me to search for open floorplans with less rancid smells. "Ugh!" I hit the end of the pen on the table, but when I try to use it again to write, it still does nothing.

I toss it over my shoulder and dig into my bag for another, because even my backups have backups.

"Are you... well? You're a bit... twitchy." The brute doesn't scare easily, but Austin is suddenly pale as he appraises me like I've grown three zombie heads.

"Just peachy," I grind out, opting to bury the curse words inside my body as I shove my notebook back into my tote. "Why wouldn't I be just *peachy*? Why would the fact that the freshmen aren't anywhere close to finishing their float bother me? I'm cool.

I'm confident. I'm perfectly well, my dear, sweet Austin." The mix of sarcasm and disappointment in my voice echoes across the dusty old factory, and my heart races.

Why don't they care as much as I do? Do they not realize this is part of their class legacy? This is a piece of our town's history in the making, and the only thing they seem to award their attention to is the fact that Junior is grounded for taking his dad's truck without permission, Maple got her braces off, and her best friend Frances was voted the freshmen homecoming maid.

It's all exciting, but they have no idea how monumental things like the float are for the community. These are the things and experiences they'll fondly remember down the road. These moments are the stitches in the quilt that makes up high school, but they're treating this quilt like just another grimy cloth abandoned in an attic somewhere.

"I don't suppose now is a good time to let you know Judd will be out of town Saturday and Sunday to visit his brother."

I whirl around, my eyelid convulsing like a volcano just erupted in my head. Austin isn't kidding. I should've known he wouldn't joke about it—the guy wouldn't know how to kid if he were tossed into a pen full of comedians.

I just wish he were the playful type, because if Judd is out of town this weekend, then he can't fix my dryer. *Fantastic.*

Masking my frustration, I slide the drill off the table and hand it to Austin. "The others should be here soon. Let's get to work, shall we?"

The whirring of the drill quickly descends upon us and mildly distracts me from my busy mind. It's as overcrowded in there as peaches in a mason jar. But the unpleasant screeching from Austin screwing boards along the outside of the trailer is no match for my overpowering thoughts.

Each one slams into me as if I'm physically pushed.

Once he pauses the drilling, I continue working as I absentmindedly say, "The parade is tomorrow. I've already arranged for designated drivers to haul the floats to the high school in the morning, one being the big gorilla from the gaming club in Judd's garage. The rest are scattered around town, and I'm putting more trust in these happy helpers than I do my dentist."

No sound comes from Austin. I don't even glance up to see if he's listening.

"I've worked and re-worked the order of participants as people have dropped out, and others have been added. Is it finalized? Or will there be more changes to deal with at the last minute? There are always stressful changes in the final hour, especially with something of this caliber," I ramble.

Austin powers up the drill again. Once he ceases, his sigh echoes across the space, and I sigh too.

"Most of the town will be there," I say. "All those eyes will be on the school—and me. It *has* to go well."

The pressure is so on, but I'm no stranger to it. Pressure and me? We're best freaking pals.

"Are you talking to me?" Austin asks, and I finally peer over at him from the opposite side of the trailer.

This makes me laugh for the first time today.

The crunching sounds of cars pulling up the gravel path drift over us, followed by low chatter from the approaching students.

Before they barrel inside, Austin strides over to me, his voice low when he asks, "You'd tell me if you weren't all right, wouldn't you? Or is this one of those things where I need to *read between the lines* or ask you to blink twice if you're in some sort of trouble?"

"I'll be fine," I whisper, but he doesn't immediately break eye contact.

Only when the kids scramble inside does he step away, a broody shadow firmly in place over his expression.

He's worried about me, and while it's much appreciated, it's not necessary. This is not my first rodeo. I will make it to the other side of homecoming week with a triumphant victory, just as I have in years past.

This might be the first time so much responsibility has fallen on me, but it's what I do. It's all part of my ten-year plan—more responsibility means more trust, which means more clout, which gives me a better shot at a promotion when one becomes available.

I'm going to be principal someday.

My body runs on autopilot as I idly stuff tissue paper into the chicken wire in order to give the freshmen a fighting chance to get this done, when Owen finally arrives.

He strolls in here fifteen minutes late smelling like the inside of an old gym bag that got wet, dried, then got wet again.

My senses are attacked by a whiff of him before I see him, and I make a mental note to add "all chaperones must shower before school functions" to my list for future me.

Owen smacks Austin's shoulder and adjusts the bill of his baseball cap over his forehead, the unruly strands of his dirty-blond hair curling over the tops of his ears.

His black T-shirt clings to what some women around town call his lickable biceps. The sweatpants he wears rise over his hips and rest along his tapered waist. He's casual, yet most women in Sapphire Creek—including a few around the teacher's lounge— would say he's still a mouthwatering slab of hunk they'd love a bite of.

I don't share in their ridiculous observations. Owen Conrad is just a man. Of course, if his personality were appealing in the slightest, I might view him as a decent-looking man. He's definitely not an ogre, even if he does currently smell like one, but that's as nice as I'm going to be on the subject.

"So great of you to join us," I chirp, infusing my voice with honey-sweet sarcasm. "You're late, but at least you made it before we all left this time."

"At least you remembered to, you know..." He twists his thin lips as he points across his chest and nods toward what better not be my breasts.

Except he's totally referring to my breasts.

What was I thinking by telling him about my lack of bra last week? Clearly, I wasn't thinking at all when I overshared, and I cannot believe he's bringing it up now in front of the students and my friend.

On the other hand, I *can* believe it. The guy's maturity level is that of a gnat.

Caroline pops in and stands on the other side of Austin, whose eyes crinkle in the corners as he stifles a grin with his palm.

When I glance back at Owen, he's still looking at my chest, his lips now twitching like he's fighting a laugh.

"What?" I clip.

Owen points at me again. "You got a little something on your ti—I mean, your chest." He clears his throat and glances over my shoulder at some of the freshmen who poke at each other, completely oblivious to us.

I peer down and find three pieces of tissue paper clinging to the sequins on my vest.

"I can help you with those." The goon stalks toward me with outstretched hands, a smirk the size of his ego stretching across his clean square jaw.

I swat Owen away and hiss, "You are so unprofessional."

His gaze travels over my body and up to my mouth as amusement blinks in and out of his expression, alternating between it and something I can't decipher.

I can usually read him easily—he's not exactly a complex specimen—but this look is new.

Rustling distracts me from getting to the bottom of this mysterious element clouding Owen's light eyes, and I drag my attention to the root of the interruption.

"Hey! Those are not for you." I march toward the students rifling through my bag of Skittles, and I wave my hands over them like I would shoo away a swarm of flies. "You can have the cookies, though."

"This is a huge bag of Skittles. Literally thousands, so plenty for us all." Maple crosses her arms over her chest in an equally bold and very naïve move. Chucking the braces has done something extra special to her confidence, aka teenage snark.

"*Literally* refers to an actual fact, so it does not apply here." I blink over her and Frances, who sidles up next to Maple like we're in a standoff on the set of *Grease*.

God, they remind me so much of the evil twins I graduated with—Emily and Yvonne. They never ignored an opportunity to sling spiteful comments my way, and I was certainly an easy target. The backbone I now carry was only in the incubation stages back then.

But unlike the ornery PE teacher behind me, I *am* a professional. No haughty teenager, whether or not she reminds me of someone I once despised, is going to make me stoop down to her level.

"Let me give you a more accurate example of the word's correct usage." I exaggerate my contemplation with a double tap to my chin. "You *literally* have two hours to finish this float. If you don't, you *literally* won't be allowed to attend the dance on Saturday night. So, you should get to work *literally* right now."

Several grumbles of outrage ensue as an overpowering presence casts a shadow over me.

The smell he dragged in with him is less potent now, and when his forearm brushes against mine, my skin pricks.

Is Owen offering his support, like a united front type of situation? Or is the jerk after my Skittles for himself? I can't be sure.

Maple scoffs. "The only reason I'm even here is because my dad made me. What about the rest of our class? They didn't show up. Why don't they have to be punished?"

"Plenty of your classmates have helped as much as they could. Let's be considerate of their obligations outside of school, shall we?" I say, carefully riding the delicate line of oversharing and being direct.

Instinctively, I flick my gaze over to Austin, who gives a simple but meaningful nod.

He never came to float when we were in high school. He had too many responsibilities at home, plus his part-time job at the auto shop. I had my own worries too—it's how our friendship was first forged during our senior year.

"Miss Lockhart, this isn't fair!" Maple whines, stepping forward like she's the leader of the entire unruly pack as she garners their support.

This has gone far enough.

I open my mouth to put an end to this, but to my surprise, Owen beats me to it.

"What isn't fair is that the other classes have managed to show up on time for their float shifts and complete the tasks without resistance or disrespect." He naturally towers over the students, not only because he's tall, but also because the fourteen- and fifteen-year-olds are still growing into their sneakers.

"We're not float scientists. How are we supposed to finish it in two hours?" Frances chimes in as Maple's backup.

Owen holds his large hand up, revealing strong fingers and a thick wrist. "I'm so glad you asked, and we'll get to that. First, how about we apologize for talking back to Miss Lockhart? Then we can get down to business."

"Sorry," the pair mumbles, averting both their gazes.

They clearly don't mean it, but it's enough to unravel the knots of frustration in my shoulders—for now.

I clap my hands to get the rest of the students' attention. "Follow me." I spend the next few minutes assigning various jobs, plus handing out supplies to paint the boards and reminding them what it's supposed to look like. I save what I'm sure is considered the worst for last. "Maple, I have something special for you." I thrust a broom into her hands.

"Cleanup?" One corner of her lips raises in protest.

"A very important job," Owen says. "Thanks so much for being amenable."

Wide-eyed, I slowly face him. I have so many questions, starting with how the hell he knows how to properly use the word *amenable*. I figured his IQ didn't reach high enough to house a word like that.

Once they're all occupied, he and I shift to the side of the room across from Caroline and Austin, who appear rather cozy tonight. Was Maren right? Have they struck up an unlikely friendship... or more? All those girls' nights I'd planned never happened this week, and I've been so out of the loop.

"I, um..." I lick my lips, the impending positive words of appreciation aimed at Owen already sour before they leap out of my mouth. "Thanks for sticking up for me. They can be extra savage sometimes," I manage.

As he turns his eyes to me, my breath hitches. I've never been this close to Owen, and for the first time, I notice the hazel streaks in his irises. They burst like fireworks among the green chaos.

And my heart does something terrifying... it freaking flutters.

OWEN

My throat constricts from the way Addie looks at me—as if she's seeing me for the first time. It hits me in the chest differently than when we fight.

This is... intimate, in a weird, unsettling way.

Without another word from either of us, she joins Caroline on the other side of the room, while I stand frozen, my tongue in a knot. It's alarming when she's nice to me, which has happened a total of once.

This was it. This was the one and only time she's been decent, and she stumbled over the phrase *thank-you* like a baby first learning to talk.

Instead of any pleasantries, Addie Lockhart usually gives me a specific kind of lip twitch that reaches all the way up to her eyes like a smile might. It's an inherent, instinctive response of unadulterated irritation.

It's one she seems to reserve just for me.

I definitely don't catch this particular bounce in the corner of her mouth when Paul, the music teacher, practices his clarinet in the teacher's lounge, or when Justine, the librarian, drinks a glass of diluted apple cider vinegar every other afternoon. Both should warrant a twitch from Ms. Better Than Everyone, but according to her, *I'm* worse than Music McGee and Smelly Cider.

I check to ensure the students are diligently working, then make my way toward the rest of the chaperones. It's like I'm back in high school with my old classmates, although I remember much less stench. Part of the smell could be coming from me, though. I didn't have time to shower before I got here after basketball practice, since I was already late, and I'm pretty sure my sister all the way in Savannah can smell me.

"Threatening them with a ban from the dance is as sinister as it is genius," I tell Addie. "Is it even a real possibility?"

"All that matters is that they think it is." She shrugs, and her stone-cold poker face is positively bone-chilling.

"You should coach basketball with us," I say as we huddle off to the side and away from the students grumbling over how badly this "blows." At least they're working, though. "If you could get them in line like you do these kids, we'd undoubtedly make it to state this year."

She still doesn't look at me as she clips, "I'm not surprised such a concept is difficult for you."

"And why is that?"

"Discipline is usually learned with age, and you have yet to graduate from the juvenile stage." Addie finally cuts her eyes at me, and they are lethal.

There's a chance she might actually combust. She's been due for an explosion for weeks, likely from the second I stepped back inside the city limits over the summer.

I give her a once-over and arch a brow. "It's hard to take you seriously as a *mature* adult when you're dressed like this."

"It's spirit week. Of course, I dressed up. It's part of the job, which I take seriously, unlike you." She waves a dismissive finger over my boring clothes.

"I painted my chest. Want to take my shirt off so you can see for yourself?"

Something flashes across Addie's eyes, and while I can't make sense of it, I'm going to go out on a limb and bet it's not good.

Austin steps between us. "What exactly did you need us here for? I never went to our own float shifts, and I certainly don't want to be here for theirs."

Addie shifts her angry attention toward him. "Just think of this as your second chance to right that wrong."

"I made my peace with it around my twentieth birthday." The smartass gives her a sarcastic tight-lipped smile, but the woman of steel doesn't flinch, nor does her frown loosen.

"All I ask is that you two keep an eye on these kids," Addie says quietly and checks left and right like she's crossing the street, presumably to confirm no students are within earshot. They're still preoccupied on their side of the old factory. "At their last shift, Maple led a few of them out back to try her father's moonshine. Not only is that illegal, but this is a school event. We will abide by the law and keep things *professional*." She punctuates the last word with a jerk of her laser focus onto me.

"You're the one keeping candy away from babies." I hold my arms out.

"We'll watch them," Caroline interjects and pats Addie's shoulder in comfort, even though I'm the one who could use the latter. "Hey, remember the time we jumped into the river in October of our junior year? The water was freezing."

"But it was a dare, and we never back down from a dare," Addie adds, her head held high, and I respect the sentiment.

"We sure don't. And we showed those guys what we were made of."

"Damn right. They were too chicken to jump in themselves. *Suckers.*" The corners of Addie's thin lips tilt, like she's treading along the cusp of a smile, but she pauses before it blossoms. "Where did that come from?"

"You seem tense." Caroline shrugs. "Thought putting a nice memory in your head would help."

"It does. Thanks. You are as beautiful as you are creative and helpful."

Caroline curtsies.

"You know what else helps ease some tension?" I wiggle my eyebrows, and over the girls' heads, Austin shakes his in warning. "Some sweaty—"

"Don't finish that sentence," Addie bites out.

"Running," I finish. "Why? What did you think I was going to say?"

For the rest of the night, Addie keeps her distance from me and channels her inner drill sergeant onto the students, instead. I almost feel bad for them until I realize almost two hours have passed, and they're actually nearly finished. Her methods might not be warm and fuzzy, but Addie Lockhart gets results.

Which works for me because I need to get the hell out of here and shower.

Not to mention, I haven't slept for shit this week. In between answering Addie's distress signals for homecoming and the reunion, my parents needed me to set up their Roku. Plus, I had to fix Lottie's toilet at her studio because hiring a professional plumber was "not in the budget," as she told me with unmistakable panic in her eyes. As the person who does the books for her, I couldn't argue.

As with any new business like hers, being tight with the budget is a necessary evil, which means I'm the guy she calls when things need fixing.

And I'm happy to be that guy. It's often better than "the funny guy." Not that Addie sees me as anything other than the "flaky guy."

She and I have been at each other's throats since dinosaurs roamed the earth. She starts it and almost dares me to finish it. I fall for it every time too.

Because, like her, I don't back down from a dare.

As the group begins cleaning up, I follow Austin outside, welcoming the fresh air in place of the moldy conglomeration of smells inside the old factory. Out here, faint giggles from the kids drift over us. Their moods have done a one-eighty since they realized they don't have to be "float scientists" to get shit done in there.

Austin nods in the direction of the door. "You're real smooth with Addie," he deadpans.

"Aren't I? If you need any tips, you can check out my *YouTube* channel called 'How to Make Girls Who Already Hate You Hate You Even More.'"

"She doesn't hate you."

This catches me off guard. The urge to ask him to repeat this statement—and confirm it with hard, undeniable evidence of a recording or a video—dies on my tongue as I simply accept what he says. Austin is one of her closest friends. He knows her well, and I've come to know him over the last few months. The one thing I learned early on is that he doesn't say things just to say them.

I'd never admit it out loud to him or anyone else, but it means a lot to know Addie might not completely despise me.

"Of course, you'd deserve it if she hated you, but..." He rubs his bearded jaw. "Let's just say, there's more to Addie than you might think."

"Kind of like Caroline?" I cock a brow. Those two have been gawking at each other all night. Clearly, there's something going on between them.

"There's more to her than heels and fixed-up hair, sure." He crosses his arms over his chest, retreating into a metaphorical defensive shell.

"You don't have to toy with me. I have eyes, and they see everything."

"What about your nose? Does it smell you? Because the inside of my fish cooler smells better."

I imagine this is what Austin and I might've been like in high school, had we been friends then. To be honest, I barely remember being in the same graduating class as him, and I've since learned why he was so withdrawn.

There's definitely more to people than meets the eye, which is a good thing for humanity where Addie Lockhart is concerned. If she were nothing more than glares and sneers, we'd all be in a world of hurt.

Instead, it's just me who bears the brunt of her sharp tongue and menacing stares.

Two cars pull into the parking lot as the girls waltz toward us.

Austin stares at Caroline in similar fashion to the way my dad looks at my mom, even after all their years of being married. "She's going back to the city after our reunion," he mumbles, but his defeat reaches my ears like a foghorn.

"So?" I counter.

Austin shoots me a warning glare, but it's going to take a lot more to fool, or scare, me.

"Distance is just a number," I sing.

"That's what they say about age."

"It still applies here," I press as I step away to greet the parents arriving for their children.

I pass Addie on the way and inhale a whiff of her sweet perfume, a welcome change to my own stench.

If Austin's right, she doesn't want to push me into oncoming traffic, in which case, things would be very different for us.

The streetlight above us flickers on and off as the sun slowly sets, literally casting Addie in a different light, and I furrow my brows like I do when making the difficult decision between my favorite muffins at Bready or Knot.

Is there a chance for Addie and me to actually be friends?

chapter
six

OWEN

WITH THE LAST of the students gone, this night concludes the last of float-building madness before the big day. After tonight, we don't have to talk about chicken wire and school spirit for another 365 days.

Thank fuck.

And the sooner I can get out of here, the better.

I saunter back inside the old factory to finish cleaning, since Maple was too busy on her phone to sweep, but a commotion stops me in my tracks. Addie tears a bag of Skittles open, and a rainbow shower of the bright round candy explodes in a waterfall around her feet with tiny ticks against the concrete floor. It sounds like the beginning of a flash flood storm.

She yelps as I rush to grab the broom, careful not to crush her cherished Skittles.

As I start to sweep, my phone vibrates in my pocket. "Did you not have enough tonight? You inhaled most of the other bag like it was your last meal. Have you even eaten dinner?"

She twists her lips. "I had a cookie."

"That's not food."

"There were pear slices on it. It counts."

I open my mouth, concern itching its way up and down my throat like nails on a chalkboard. Addie needs to eat a real, balanced meal, and my protective instincts kick in, sifting through my brain for ways to make it happen.

But my phone vibrates with another call.

On a sigh, I rest the broom against the edge of the table and march outside, phone to my ear, on the other end of which is a frantic Lottie. My heart sinks as she talks through uneven breaths.

"I forgot my keys at my house, and I need them to lock the studio."

I pinch the bridge of my nose as my pulse steadies once again. From the panic in her voice, I would've thought she'd broken her arm or something else equally alarming had happened. Her keys are the last thing she should be so panicked over. "Why are they not with your car keys?"

"I didn't drive here today. Mom dropped me off on her way to Whitney's, and I didn't think to take the keys with me. I figured I didn't need them since I wasn't taking my car. That makes sense, right? *Shit*," she hisses as her breaths release in faster puffs, echoing through the speaker.

"Hey, hey," I say calmly, switching gears for her benefit. "It's fine. I'm not too far away. I'll be there with my spare key in a few minutes. Just need to finish—"

"You're a lifesaver! Thank God." She releases a heavy sigh loaded with obvious relief, and I can't help the smile tugging on my lips.

Crisis averted.

My little sister always holds her emotions right at the surface. She's reacted in similar fashion to misplacing her lucky sweater as she did after accidentally backing her car into Mom's at a family dinner last year.

And while this isn't the emergency I initially worried it was, I do need to get to her ASAP before her blood pressure rises any higher.

"I need to run by the square, but I'll be back," I announce to the group. Seems Caroline's taken off already, and Austin has assumed my position behind the broom.

He shrugs with indifference, but I'm not so lucky with Addie. She laughs, but what's supposed to be a humorous sound is one of sarcasm, instead. "How typical of you to try to get out of the dirty work. You swoop in for the fun and cookies, and then you bail before your job is complete."

"You think this was fun? I mean, I enjoyed the free cookies, but I would've rather paid triple the normal price just to *not* be here."

"Other than the fact that this is our job, homecoming is full of traditions. It's up to us to uphold them and teach these kids the value of such things. How would you feel if they grow up and remember nothing special about their high school experience? Do you want that on your conscience?"

Something in my chest stirs over the passionate way she delivers this speech, and a grin pulls at the corners of my lips.

I find myself staring. Not just staring, really. I'm... admiring.

I'm admiring Addie Lockhart for all her intense but cooky and respectable ways.

"What?" She blinks.

I feel Austin's eyes on me too, and my fucking face heats and tingles like I'm... Wait, am I *blushing*?

"You have cookie crumbs on your chin," I quickly say.

From where I stand, I can't actually confirm if she does, but while she's distracted, I use it as a chance to escape.

I don't turn away fast enough, though, as I have the misfortune of glimpsing the way she touches her delicate fingers to her slightly pointed chin. Her nails are painted black, with one finger sparkling gold. She didn't miss a single detail in her festive outfit.

Why do I find that so... cute?

Without a word, I dart out of the old bread factory and jump into my car like my ass is on fire. I drive toward the square, jerking my steering wheel with more force than necessary and heavily leaning into my door with each turn. I drive as if I'm angry at the asphalt.

What the hell was that?

I'm still in a confusing daze as I reach The Boozy Brush and find out Lottie needs more than just my spare key.

Once I enter the studio, I find her in the corner, hunched over the sink washing paintbrushes. "Can you please help me?" she asks over her shoulder.

The pleading look in her wide eyes hits me in the gut, and I can't say no, even though I'm well aware that Addie will never forgive me for this delay.

I told her I'd be right back, but it's not going to happen.

I can't leave my sister high and dry. Addie at least has Austin with her, so she's not alone, not like Lottie would be if I leave.

So, I sidle up next to my little sister, make a show of sliding imaginary sleeves up to my elbows, and assist her in washing the used brushes.

She briefly leans her temple to my shoulder as the sink fills with streaks of greens and reds. "Thank you," she says on a sigh.

Over the last few months, I've been pulled in all kinds of directions, but at times like these, where I know I'm making a difference for my family, my world rights itself. Like my life steadies on its axis.

I couldn't do this sort of thing when I played baseball. I lived in Atlanta, a brutal three-hour drive from here. There were also the practices, games, and traveling. I couldn't show up for my family like this, for all the big and little moments. At times, it felt like I was a forgotten member of the Conrad crew.

Being needed and fulfilling that need provides me a special sense of purpose I never knew before.

Thirty minutes later, I lock up and wave toward my truck. "Come on. I'll give you a lift home real quick."

Lottie's living with our parents for the time being, and Dad should be there to let her in since his pharmacy closed an hour ago.

After I drop her off, I cruise through town, checking the time on my dash repeatedly. This is taking far longer than I anticipated.

A glimpse of the neon sign at Lucy's Diner stops me from heading straight back to the float site. I'm already on thin ice with Addie, so what's another ten minutes?

I pull into the lot by the diner, park, and shoot a quick text in a group thread with Austin and Addie to apologize for my delay.

I get nothing in return from Addie, but Austin tells me they're finished and have left already.

In a separate thread, I text only Austin and ask for Addie's address.

> Also, what's her favorite meal from Lucy's?

AUSTIN

How should I know that?

> You're her friend.

I'm the kind of friend she calls when she needs help with her car, and that's only because I'm a mechanic.

> You must have shared a meal with her at some point in the past.

I guess that might've last happened over the summer.

> And what did she eat?

That's like asking me what we talked about, or what her favorite color is. I don't know the answer to either, man.

I press the heel of my palm into my eye, then text him back, practically begging him to dig deep into the recesses of his stubborn brain to recall her favorite order. It doesn't even have to be her favorite. Anything she does, in fact, enjoy would be helpful.

After five whole minutes, he finally returns with a useful answer—fried green tomatoes and a BLT.

With these new pieces of information in my holster, for yet another inexplicable reason, the stirring in my chest from before intensifies.

chapter
seven

ADDIE

"THANK you so much for your patience as we resolved this matter," the customer service representative grinds out.

She's anything but appreciative after our hour-long debate over dance costumes.

"And thank you for being so helpful, Janice." I force a smile as if she can see me and end the call while I trudge up the path toward my house.

On top of executing the last few months' worth of planning for homecoming, along with the reunion, I'm also a volunteer at the local dance studio. Since her niece was unavailable, Iris, the aging owner, called me to stop by the studio on my way home from freshmen float to discuss the new costumes.

They arrived for the holiday recital this winter, but they're the wrong color. I spent the last hour on the phone with customer service explaining the difference between Christmas red and murder-y red.

We obviously want the former, but the costumes were of the latter.

Janice's cooperation wasn't immediate, but I never give up until I secure what I want.

I'm about to call Iris to inform her of the good news when something catches my attention. I pause on my porch, my stomach rolling and gurgling like a sick kitten as a familiar smell wafts over me. Among the sweet aroma from the rose bushes behind me is the distinct smell of fried, greasy heaven.

But it could very well be my mind and stomach playing tricks on me.

I forgot to eat dinner for probably the third time this week.

On top of my ungodly list of to-dos, I'm actually trying to enjoy this week's festivities.

Homecoming holds some of my best memories from high school. It's one of the rare times in the past when my mother would put aside her quirky—and often unreasonable—beliefs to enjoy an organized sport. She'd meet me at the football game on Friday night, and then we'd walk arm in arm to the cafeteria for the chili dinner, where we'd see how small we could crush our crackers before letting the pieces rain into our Styrofoam bowls of chili.

When the chili would cool down enough, we'd enjoy the food with the rest of the students and their parents.

We were always an average mother and daughter at homecoming.

My buzzing phone jars me from my quick visit to the past. Sable, the vice principal, is calling, and I almost drop my phone in my haste to answer it.

"Addie! What parade updates do you have for me?" She cuts to the chase, which I appreciate. In that regard, we're very similar.

I take a seat on the porch chair next to my front door, my tote in my lap, and I fish out my notebook. "I secured enough officers from the police department to kick off the parade tomorrow, so *check*. Principal Weathers will ride in a golf cart with DeDe and Birdie—*check*." I snap my fingers. "Oh, and I went by Daphne's earlier this week, and she is generously donating a gift basket for our chili dinner raffle. With that added to the list, we have plenty to give away—so *check* and *check*."

The evening breeze picks up into a gust, and I cover my free ear, straining to listen to Sable.

This is my favorite part.

"Well done, Addie. Thanks so much for all your hard work. We would honestly be lost without you," she praises.

And my heart blossoms like each word of affirmation pumps it full of oxygen. Being complimented is an adrenaline rush.

Each *check* is music to my ears.

Every job well done is another point in my favor for that future promotion.

With a deep, steadying breath, I say, "Thank you."

"You are going to make an excellent administrator someday."

I suck back a breath—that's the dream.

"Enjoy the rest of your night. Get some rest, because this weekend is going to be absolute chaos."

My lips sink into a frown. "I'll surely enjoy *some* of this night," I grumble.

But background noise from her end of the phone crackles through, and it's clear she doesn't hear me. "I need to go. My dog knocked over my—"

I pull the phone back and note she's ended the call. No matter. I got the metaphorical pat on the back for my important role in organizing the parade.

Our local police department is rather small, so some schedules needed to shift in order to spare a few officers and their cars for the afternoon tomorrow. *Easy peasy.*

Also easy was convincing our school secretary DeDe to drive the principal and our mascot, Birdie. DeDe was thrilled to be involved, and she never declines an opportunity to thrust her beloved cat into the limelight.

We're the Lions, but since a real lion is out of the question, a cat was our next best option. It was thanks to my creative thinking too, after the school's mascot suit was stolen as a senior prank a few years ago. It was accidentally charred to bits at their celebratory bonfire.

Since we needed a mascot right away but couldn't replace it in time for the next football game, I suggested we use a cat, and Principal Weathers was so tickled by the idea. Finding a suitable cat was the first task he assigned me outside of the English classroom, and we've come a long way since.

Bursts of hope and excitement explode in my previously heavy chest, lightening the load sitting on it. This is why I'm the first to raise my hand for volunteer positions, seemingly impossible jobs, and the grunge work no one else wants to accept.

I have dreams and goals, and being principal is at the top of my list. All these small stops along the route are proudly leading me to my destination.

Even with my new blast of energy, my body isn't on the same page as my mind. I'm still physically drained. I rise from the chair as if a strong force pushes me down, my feet like bricks from exhaustion. To add, my head aches from what feels like my whole life crashing down on me at once.

But then I see it.

I didn't make up the smell.

The most gloriously greasy brown bag rests on a cushioned chair by my front door, and warm relief seeps into every cool crevice of my body. I'm so glad I don't have to check my leftover chicken casserole from last weekend for signs of mold before I tear into it, I could cry.

A fresh BLT and a little box of fried green tomatoes await.

I inhale a deep whiff of my surprise treat, then glance around for signs of the magnificent Samaritan who dropped this off, but I come up empty. It's too late into the evening for anyone on our cul-de-sac to be out and about. Plus, it's a little chilly for the neighbors to be hanging out on their front porches as they tend to do during the summer, but right before I disappear into my house, I catch Leon emerging from his.

I wave and call out a greeting as I drag my tired feet down my steps to get within earshot. He leans over his railing, and the streetlight barely casts a glow over his frown as I rush to say, "I'm sorry to bother you. I know it's late—"

"It's so late, my stories are over." The sound he makes can only be described as a *harumph*.

"I just have a quick question, and I'll get out of your hair."

"You don't need a ride to bail your mother out again, do you?" While I can't see his face, I imagine the deep-set disapproval in his furrowed brows.

"No. As you might remember, my mother doesn't live here anymore." Plus, it's been fifteen years since the incident—let's move on.

That's what I want to say, anyway, but I stick to the matter at hand before we lose control of this conversation.

I hold the bag up. "Did you by chance see anyone drop this off on my porch? There's no note, and I have no clue where it came from."

"I didn't see anything. Like I said, I was watching my stories."

"Right." I offer a smile and back away. "Thanks for your time."

"I hope I won't have to remind you about your trash bin this weekend. According to the HOA, they are to be back in place and out of sight the same day as pickup."

"It won't be a problem, Mr. Leon. I'll remember," I promise, and I scurry away before he remembers how bad my lawn has gotten.

The truth is, I'm always on top of things around my house, but the last month has been trying to kill me. Matters of trash bins and lawns are the least of my concerns.

My stomach gurgles again as I reach my porch. I'm too tired to play detective tonight, but I will resume the investigation tomor-

row. I have to know to whom I should return the favor. It's the
polite, Southern thing to do.

I could enlist Maren's baking assistance for special cookies, or
Caroline could help me shop for something at Conversation Pieces
on the square. Mrs. Marilyn has an endless array of unique items at
her store that scream *thank-you*.

Unless they were the ones who sent the food, which could be
the case. They know I've been stressed and overwhelmed, and they
do a tremendous job of being my friends, even though I can be a
handful. They could've done this, in which case returning the
favor might be more difficult than baked goods and shopping.

I drop my tote onto the floor on the inside of my door and
kick off my shoes, my feet giddy over their freedom. The bag of
goodies crinkles in my tight grasp as I leap onto the couch. While I
basically inhale my dinner, I rack my brain for something appropriate to meet the magnitude of this generous display of kindness.

But I don't recall any of my ideas as I awake the next morning
with a piece of bacon on my chin.

chapter
eight

ADDIE

"I CANNOT BELIEVE I wore my party jeans for this," I grumble under my breath as I sling my wet hair to the side, thankful to have finally reached the shelter of an awning.

Thunder cracks, and a strike of lightning slices the evening sky in half.

My attempt to squeeze the excess water from my hair is painfully futile as I join the growing crowd inside the school lobby, scanning each face for a familiar one.

With the parade complete and wildly successful, I'd planned to enjoy the homecoming football game with my friends and a salty bag of popcorn, my level of cares nosediving into the negatives.

But Mother Nature had other plans.

We got ten minutes into the game before the storm reigned its terror on our town. In record time, mass chaos ensued as we scrambled toward shelter.

I take one step into the school lobby when Principal Weathers hands off a shivering Birdie to me like a football, calling over another clap of thunder, plus the echoing chatter, "I need to find my wife!"

I fold the cat into my chest, holding her tightly as I search for DeDe, but everyone's merely a blur. My clothes cling to me as I shuffle into the cafeteria and shake out my long hair, flinging even more drops of water onto my shoulders.

I'm soaked from head to toe.

My bones ache.

The arches of my feet cry for the relief of a hot bath.

And the twitch in my eye works double-time as my gaze immediately falls onto Owen Conrad.

On the other side of the crowded cafeteria, past the rows of long tables that stretch between us, I find the bane of my existence with very little effort or desire. He hands napkins to someone I don't recognize, which she uses to dab at her running mascara. It's like he's a gentleman. Does this woman know who she's dealing with?

An arrow of kindness and thoughtfulness could spear him in his perfect ass and stick like a tick, but he still wouldn't grasp such concepts.

Maren sidles up next to me. "I lost you out there. You okay?"

I drag my focus away from he-who-doesn't-matter and squeeze my friend's arm. "Fine. You?"

"Almost sprained my ankle trying to get inside, but I had help." She rises onto her tiptoes and glances over my shoulder.

"Who are you looking for?"

Maren plummets back onto the heels of her feet and snaps her gaze to mine. "No one. Just... taking all this in." She shimmies out of her drenched shacket and ties it around her waist, her dark hair falling in stringy tendrils around her face.

"If we get totally rained out, this might be the first homecoming game to do so in the history of this school." I pet Birdie in hopes of comforting her, but her trembles don't subside.

Through the window, another streak of lightning pierces the sky, and I jolt as if it strikes me personally. Birdie practically shoots out of my arms, and Maren helps me calm her down, which is proving difficult with our surroundings.

Everyone is scattered about the cafeteria with more chaos than every lunch during a school day put together. Parents chase their little ones, young couples and groups of friends dip their heads with high-pitched laughter, and Alonso plays his harmonica in one corner, drawing a small crowd like this is the subway in New York. I've visited Caroline up north a couple of times over the years, and the scene in front of me resembles several of the ones I've witnessed while waiting for the train.

"I didn't think the storms were supposed to be here until Monday," Maren says with a groan as she twists the ends of her hair to rid it of excess rain. It's no use, though. We'd need seven blow dryers aimed at us to really make a difference. "The radar showed clear skies for tonight."

"I just hope this is it for the weekend, because I do not have the energy to drag all the tables and the bar from the courtyard inside. There's no room for them all unless they go into the sitting room, but then that would leave zero space for us to move around," I ramble, but it's mostly for my own benefit as I mentally run through my checklist for tomorrow night.

"Not following, babe."

I blink and bring my friend into clearer focus. As I stroke the scared cat in my hands, I clarify, "The reunion. I've set up high-top tables outside for us to enjoy the last of September, but we can't hang outside if the sky is falling."

She rubs my upper arm in a soothing rhythm like she, Birdie, and I took a page out of my mom's whimsical book and are partaking in some calming assembly line. "If it rains, I'll help you with the tables, but there's nothing to do right now. Let's just warm up and enjoy some chili."

She makes a good point—I can't do anything about the rain now, but I can eat. I forgot yet another meal today.

My stomach is officially out to get me, with my organs feeling like they're clawing their way out of my stomach lining.

With the parade at one o'clock, I didn't have time to eat in between lining everyone up to start on time, and Addie Lockhart is punctual as hell.

I managed to successfully rally half the town for the parade, launching every float, police car, and horse into action according to my detailed itinerary. I was so alert and focused that I never even stepped in manure, which was a miraculous feat. Holding horses hostage in the back of the line was not easy, and it definitely didn't happen without a few piles of shit.

I deserve to eat my precious bowl of chili in peace and not think about the fact that my mom isn't here.

She was in town this week, but I never saw her. Now, she's missing our one tradition that's lasted past the divorce.

Birdie sticks her tiny claws into my shirt. She's wrecked. Even drenched, this pitiful thing weighs next to nothing. It would be a good idea to take her home, if I could just locate DeDe in the crowd.

I come up empty as I follow Maren toward the long line of people waiting for their turn at the chili pots. With a snort, I tease, "How are you going to enjoy this chili? You put more effort into taking out the beans than you do eating it."

"Why do people insist on beans in their chili? They're mushy and gross," she hisses.

Her distaste draws a few heads our way, and I stifle a laugh.

"You can't have chili without the beans," Judd weighs in with a husky cough from in front of us.

"The beans give the chili flavor," his wife Mary adds. "Otherwise, you'd basically have spaghetti sauce and crackers."

"Need I say more?" I ask Maren with a lift of my brow.

She holds her hands up in surrender. "Fine, but when you need backup because you believe hot dogs are sandwiches, don't come crying to me."

"They *are* sandwiches," I insist.

"How can you say that? It's like calling a taco a sandwich, and that's just madness." This new opinion comes from a guy behind us.

Bond Nicholas, a fellow high school classmate—he's in town for our reunion.

"There's no comparison between a taco and a sandwich," I argue, angling my body toward him. "Each one is in a separate category, like cats and dogs." I lift Birdie as half of my evidence. "Just because they're both animals, it doesn't mean they're the same."

"Then you can agree hot dogs are of a different category than sandwiches. You made my point for me." He folds his lean arms over his chest. Last I heard, he works for a law firm in Atlanta, but I didn't expect lawyers to be so fit. He must have a set of dumbbells in his office, with a walking pad under his desk too.

I narrow my gaze, internally navigating our argument. I'm normally much better at debating than this, but my head throbs too hard. I need some damn sleep—and food—before my brain resumes proper function again. "Save the lawyer talk for the courtroom, would you?" I toss back at him.

"You're right. It's poor form to work on vacation," he jokes with a low chuckle that is rather endearing.

When he opens his mouth, I instinctively lean in for what he'll say next, but someone behind him taps his shoulder. What ensues is a reunion of sorts as the man behind Bond shakes his hand and tells him how good it is to run into him.

Maren nudges me to move forward in line with her, and the snicker she releases catches me off guard.

"What?" I shrug.

"I was totally invisible."

"You couldn't be invisible if you tried. If your strong cheekbones didn't draw attention to you, your loud—and might I say, snarky—comments would."

"I saw you two at the game together."

"And? Out with it, Maren."

"He's cute, and he's obviously smitten," she whispers.

Even if she talked at a normal volume, I doubt anyone, including Bond, could hear her over the pounding of thick raindrops against the windows of the cafeteria. It sounds like the crackling static of the backup radio stashed in my storm preparation kit at home.

"Is this like that summer before eighth grade when you insisted Spencer Smith had a crush on me?" I ask.

"He did," she draws out. "Why else did he bring you a pumpkin streusel muffin to the park every single morning?"

"Because he always bought too many," I answer, repeating what he'd told me back then.

Maren tilts her head. "Then why did I never get one?"

"You're ridiculous. Why are we even talking about that?"

"You brought it up, and I go where the leader leads." She traps me under her unwavering stare.

I glance over my shoulder, as Bond has now moved out of the line to chat with Owen and the mystery woman. She seems to captivate Bond's complete focus. What's so special about her?

"You should see if Bond wants to get coffee tomorrow. I know a great little place." Maren snorts, clearly referring to her coffee truck. "And if you're extra nice, the owner might even toss in her new iced pumpkin cookies—on the house."

My mouth instantly salivates at the mention of new baked goods from her skillful hands, and it's not just because I'm starving, either. The woman is a mad scientist with a whisk and a bag of flour.

"I will be by your truck right after school on Monday for said cookies, but I'll be coming alone."

"Bond will be back in Atlanta by Monday."

"Exactly. He lives three hours away. I don't have time to date people who live here, let alone guys that far."

"I'm not suggesting you marry him, Addie."

"Then what's the point? How can I date someone if I know from the start that it won't lead anywhere?" I catch Mary's eyes from in front of us and realize I've raised my voice above a hushed whisper.

I'm outing myself, and I should really nip this in the bud before word travels around town that I'm marrying Bond Nicholas. Knowing the insane rumor mill around here, they'd probably drum up some tale about how our whirlwind romance led us to elope in some faraway land like Switzerland.

The people of Sapphire Creek can really get out of hand with spinning wild stories—bless their hearts—but there's nothing to know about my love life other than it's nonexistent. This is a purposeful construct on my part as of a couple years ago, when I decided I'm better off single.

If I were to get back out there, though, I'd be lucky to find someone like Bond. He's smart and has an important job. Plus, he's not bad to look at.

I imagine he'd accept me as I am too.

A crack of thunder practically rattles the building, and Birdie nearly leaps from my hold. As I tuck her back into my chest, careful to ride the line between comforting and crushing her, my gaze catches on Sable's on the other end of the table, where she waves me over.

"I'll be right back," I tell Maren.

"What about food?" she asks as she grabs a bowl from the stacks.

"I'll get some in a bit," I say over my shoulder, already maneuvering through the throngs of people toward one of my bosses. On the way, a strong whiff of the chili spices assaults my senses and hurls a wave of *boos* across my empty stomach.

When I reach Sable, I find DeDe with her too.

"Addie, I'm sure you're tired of holding Birdie, and DeDe has offered to go ahead and take the poor thing home for the weekend." Sable nods.

"I don't mind helping," I quickly say, expelling any doubt of my servitude, then nobly add, "But I think she could use a break. She had quite the scare." I coo as I give our not-so-brave little mascot one final scratch on her head before I slide her into DeDe's waiting arms.

"She could use a rest by the warm fireplace." DeDe makes kissing noises toward her furry companion.

"Couldn't we all," I joke, and it earns me a laugh from Sable.

Is it pathetic to practically gloat right out of my body from my well-received joke? Maybe for anyone else, but I refuse to be ashamed over it, not when fostering goodwill with the higherups can only lead to bigger and better things for me.

More people filter through the chili line, dividing me from Sable and DeDe, and I attempt to get back into place for my own bowl.

The line is twice as long as before—*great*.

Shoulders slumped, my gaze involuntarily lands on Owen again. The mystery woman leans into him, giggling into her palm like he's just so hilarious.

When the storm hit, he led her inside, his jacket slung around her shoulders. What's completely bonkers is that she probably thinks he's so chivalrous, but what about the rest of the town? Who helped Mrs. Marilyn and old Gus inside? *I* did. I'm the one who thought about the whole group and not my arm candy for the month.

"Who are you staring at?" Maren sneaks up on me.

"Hmm? What? Nothing. I'm contemplating a new... paint color." Squaring my shoulders, I rush to add, "The walls of this cafeteria have not been touched up since we were seniors here, and it's just a crime against this building. It's been so good to us, and look how we treat it. It's tragic."

She squints at me, then turns to face Owen. "It's scary how

serious I know you are, but also, that's not the whole truth. What's going on?"

"You're too damn good of a friend and see right through me."

"It's a gift." She shrugs.

"Owen and that girl have been glued at the hip all night."

"And that bothers you because..." She pauses with a question in her tone.

"Because he's always just around for a good time. He never lends a hand. Yet he's Principal Weathers's favorite all because they're both obsessed with baseball. I can play baseball too, I'll have you know. I'm athletic as hell."

"Honey, please don't take this the wrong way. You're good at many, many things. You're good at scheduling and bossing people around—"

I hold a finger up. "I'm a leader."

"Yes, and you're the best in the biz. But the only physical activity you're good at is dancing. Baseball requires a level of hand-eye coordination you do not possess."

I gasp. "I could be good at baseball if I tried."

"The only sliding you do is when you stumble over a parking block."

"That was *one* time, and those things are hazards!"

The corners of her eyes crinkle, and she purses her lips like she's fighting a smile.

Sighing, I give in. It's futile to argue with her when she's so right. I wouldn't know what to do with a baseball bat even if a million dollars were at stake.

"Hey, did you leave dinner on my doorstep last night?"

"No." She pinches her brows together. "Someone left you dinner? That's thoughtful."

"It was, and I'd like to thank the person responsible. There was no note, though."

"I'm intrigued." She leans in. "Could it have been Caroline?"

"Possibly." I scan the room, but there's no sign of her. She's the kind of woman who sticks out in a crowd, so I'd definitely spot her easily. "Have you seen her tonight?"

"Not since the parade. I don't see Austin here, either. Was it him?"

"Doubtful." I chew on my bottom lip as my eyes find Owen for the millionth time tonight. What is up with that? It's like he's the south pole of a magnet, and I'm the north. We're polar opposites, for sure, but the principle of being drawn to each other should not apply here.

But I can't tear my gaze away. He's laughing with Bond, and the girl from before is nowhere to be found.

"Are you staring at Owen again?"

I whip my head to my outrageous friend. "As if," I say, exaggerating the words like Alicia Silverstone in one of our old favorite movies, *Clueless*.

Her soft giggle is mixed with an exhale. "When are you going to admit he's not so bad?"

"A hundred years from now, when I'm a bitter old ghost haunting him and all his descendants."

"That kind of grudge should be directed at musical haters and people who pass other cars on the shoulder, not decent guys who are capable of changing for the better, like Owen."

"I agree with the first part wholeheartedly, but don't start with the Owen bit again. I've heard your heinous spiel too often for one lifetime."

"Heinous, huh?"

"It's downright offensive. You should be on my side, always." I jut my chin up. The last time we argued like this was over who Rory should've ended up with in *Gilmore Girls*.

"There are no sides to take here. All I'm saying is that he might surprise you, if you let him," she says.

"You're right about a lot of things, but you couldn't be more wrong about Owen."

"He's changed since high school, Addie," she presses, and the weight in her voice grows irritatingly heavier. "He's funny and very generous. I see him downtown a lot, helping Lottie at her studio."

"Lottie?"

"His sister. She's the one who's with him tonight."

I blink as the puzzle pieces finally slide into place, and the tight bundle of nerves in my body untangle. "That was his sister? She looks so different than the last time I saw her. I didn't recognize her."

Owen's twin sisters weren't in high school yet while we were students there, so I never got to know them. I'd heard one of them had opened a paint and sip art studio on the square recently, though I haven't had the chance to stop by.

And she's the one who was here with him. It wasn't some bimbo who'd naively bought into his gentleman act.

Why does that information give me such satisfying relief? I shouldn't care who's hanging out with him. His personal life is of absolutely no concern to me.

In fact, the only reason I did care was because the poor woman might've needed saving from wasting time on Owen, but since she was his sister, there's no damsel in need of my brutally honest assistance.

No harm, no foul.

My racing heart has *nothing* to do with him.

chapter
nine

OWEN

"I THINK I'm going to ask out Addie."

I snap my head in the direction of the light, yet very serious, voice. Bond is staring—more like *leering*—at Lockhart, who's on the other side of the room.

"Why? Why would you do that?" I sputter.

"Why wouldn't I? She's as smart as she is fucking hot, especially in those jeans. She's the whole package."

"I know."

Bond turns to me and lifts a brow.

My mouth opens and closes like a flapping door in strong winds. "I mean, she is most definitely smart. Smart as a chimp, that one."

"Did you just call her a chimp?"

"No! *Pfft*. Of course not. She's... fine." Heat erupts at the base of my neck and spreads across my skin like wildfire.

My old friend's face contorts as he studies me, and something like jealousy clenches my stomach. "Are you okay?"

"I've never been *okayer*," I say, punctuating the non-word with a grunt.

Then I walk away before I do or say anything else embarrassing.

There's also the fact that Lockhart would have my balls if she heard me making up words. This bad habit of mine gives the English teacher hives, which she's made clear to me on many occasions.

And Bond wants to ask her out.

The chili I just devoured wants to make its way up my throat, and it's not because I don't want my friend hooking up with the woman who hates me. If this were the case, my uncomfortable feelings would be a lot easier to navigate, that's for sure.

My heart thunders, and the vibrations echo in my head as I put distance between me, Bond, and my sudden nausea. The last time I felt like this was when I suffered from food poisoning, and I might even prefer it if that were the case.

Unfortunately for me, it has nothing to do with the contents of my stomach and everything to do with the idea of Lockhart on a date with Bond.

They're both single and have every right to go out. I'd go so far as to say the tightly wound woman could use a night out, too. The word around the teacher's lounge is that she hasn't been with a guy since Pangea exploded. Not in so many words, but that's the gist I gathered one afternoon.

I wasn't listening out of curiosity, either. It just so happened I was pouring myself a cup of coffee while Justine and Gemma were gossiping—very loudly.

In any case, it would do the rest of us a huge kindness for Lockhart to enjoy some relief of the romantic variety. It seems she takes her frustration out on the rest of us, and that's not healthy.

But that just makes Bond asking her out so much worse for me, for some godforsaken reason I can't make sense of.

The thought of Addie must bring me straight to her, as I come to a stop next to her and a large pot of chili.

She blinks up at me, and for the first time, I notice a smattering of freckles across her nose. They're fewer and farther in between one another across her cheeks, until they completely fade underneath the corners of her deep blue eyes.

The tip of her nose raises higher as she squares her shoulders, and memories of high school slam into me.

Some of the kids used to compare her to the residents of Whoville because of this nose, but I always found it endearing.

In truth, I always thought she was cute, but since I moved back, that word isn't right for her. It doesn't encompass the entirety of the woman in front of me.

"Don't even think about stealing my chili," she clips and waves with her free hand over the spread next to us. "There's plenty to go around, so get your own."

She sidesteps me and makes a beeline for an empty seat at a table, where Maren sets her stuff down. But before Addie reaches her friend, I practically leap in front of her.

And my gaze lands on her sexy-as-hell denim-clad legs.

Jesus—I've never seen such a simple material look so damn good.

This is a bad fucking idea, but the words roll off my tongue like a golf ball racing downhill and right into a bunker.

"You and Bond, huh?" I force a wiggle of my brow, but the movement doesn't feel natural.

Her own eyes widen with horror. "What? Where did you hear that?"

"He told me he asked you out..." I search her expression, but the only thing residing there is confusion—and more horror. "You two will make the cutest darn—"

She cuts me off with an exasperated exhale and sets her bowl down. With a murderous glare, she shoves me backward. "Come with me," she demands and drags me out of the cafeteria, her fingernails digging into my forearm as she leads us into the hallway.

She doesn't stop until she pushes me into a supply closet and shuts the door with more force than seems necessary.

The private room muffles the sounds of the chili dinner and—did I hear a harmonica somewhere? The darkness hides what rests in here, but there's no covering the foul smell of mop water. It singes my nostrils.

I'm still reeling from the surprising strength on such a small person, but Addie is definitely no delicate flower. I shouldn't be caught off guard by her physical strength—it tracks with the rest of her.

"What are you doing?" I ask.

She flicks the light switch on and jabs a finger into my chest. "What are *you* doing? You can't spew rumors about my personal life in front of half the town, especially not with our *bosses* present."

"I thought—wait. Rumor?"

Oh, fuck. Bond said he's *going to* ask her out, didn't he? As in, he has not yet done so, and I have made a complete ass of myself.

What is wrong with me tonight?

My skin crawls like she dumped a bottle of whatever chemicals are in here on me. I shift, as if it's possible to escape the feeling, and my shoulder bumps into a shelf. When I shift again, I nudge a mop from its resting place by the door. It nearly falls, and we reach for it at the same time.

Our hands are clasped around each other.

Our eyes lock, and my face does that weird fucking heating thing again akin to blushing.

Her hand is soft over mine.

If I turned it over, gluing our palms together, my hand would engulf hers like a baseball in a mitt. I have the faintest thought that she'd even appreciate the safety of my firm hold, but that would be insane. As a matter of fact, it would be crazier than a bear and a kangaroo sharing a beer.

Addie's made it clear she doesn't like me in any sense of the word.

She's the first to break our eye contact, with a strangled clearing of her throat.

I stiffen, careful not to knock over anything else, but it's hard not to when the space is so cramped. I'm too large for this closet. "Did you bring me in here to kill me?" I ask her, and I'm only halfway kidding.

"I brought you in here for the same reason politicians take great measures to hide their personal lives from the public—to ensure their reputations are free of scandals before they win elections."

"You're running for president? I didn't know. That's amazing. You've got my vote." I smack her shoulder and give it a squeeze. "My life will be so much easier once you move to the White House. *Huzzah!*"

Her sigh of exasperation echoes between us like she's using a megaphone, and I glimpse the adorable lip twitch.

Until she shrugs me off and snaps, "I want to be principal someday, you buffoon. And I can't risk a stain on my impeccable reputation, which includes dating random guys who live in Atlanta."

A wave of confusion washes over me, and I'm officially lost on this train to Looneyville. What the hell is she talking about?

As if she reads my mind, she explains, "Dating someone from out of town implies I might leave Sapphire Creek, and that'll never happen. I can't risk a rumor floating around that it might be the case, which it isn't."

"Okay?" I blink.

"No scandals."

"I'm going to stop you right there because dating Bond Nicholas would not be scandalous. It would be as boring as watching grass grow."

"Bond is perfectly nice and wholesome and respectful. If he lived in town, I might even consider him, if he were to even ask me out."

I stick my finger in my open mouth and make a gagging sound.

"Of course, such sentiments are lost on oafs like yourself."

I drop my hands as annoyance pinches my nerves. "You know what? You and Bond would be great together. You can compete for the title of the world's most boring people. *Congratu—fucking —lations.*"

"Boring is better than being irresponsible and careless."

I lean in until her heaving chest brushes against mine. "Guess it wouldn't bode well for your reputation to be caught in a supply closet with your buffoon-ish co-worker, then, would it?"

I'm sure a haughty comeback is on the tip of her tongue, but I don't get to hear it.

Her full and pouty lips fall into the shape of an *O*, and her eyes clear as if my loaded question doused the fire in them.

But she doesn't move. Instead of fleeing from here and away from me, she stands tall with her mouth zipped into a firm line. Our labored breaths fall into sync, and thick tension fills the empty crevices around us, making my fucking head spin.

As I peer down at Addie, her lean body nearly flush against mine, I do something I should've done years ago. "Why do you hate me so much?" I whisper, and as I wait for her answer, my damn stomach churns.

I might as well be standing at the edge of a plane's open door, ready to freefall without a parachute.

Addie licks her lips, and my gaze drops to them. I witness the tip of her tongue sliding across her plump bottom lip in slow motion, and my throat dries.

She's still a little tan from the summer. Spending afternoons at the river with her friends, where the sun's rays gently kissed her skin, did her a lot of good.

But it did nothing to curb this hostility she aims at me day in and day out.

"You dated Evil Emmy in high school. She terrorized me for four years, and you dated her of your own free will. That says everything about your judgment and character," Addie finally says, but her voice is hesitant and unsteady.

My chest sinks. "I didn't know. I'm sorry she treated you so badly."

She dips her head, her mumbling incoherent.

"But that was a thousand years ago, when I was sixteen and dumb, and we only dated for about five minutes. I broke up with her when she tried to get her hairdresser fired for getting loose hair in her eye during a trim."

"She hasn't changed much, either. Last week, she scolded Mrs. Goodwin at Bready or Knot for her lemon raspberry muffins being *too lemony and raspberry-y*."

"You can still hate her if you want, but it's hardly enough to hate me too all these years later. Unless you hold the record for the most severe grudge in history. What's the real reason?" I insist, although I don't know why. Nothing good will come of this, but something inside me screams to unearth the truth.

"Where do I begin?" Addie narrows her eyes until the blue in them turns gray, and her nostrils flare as some of the fire from before sets her body ablaze again. The rage buzzes off the surface of her skin. "Aside from being irresponsible and careless, your total disregard for other people is as astounding as it is infuriating. You're praised and complimented for merely breathing. You're completely ridiculous, and I hate your hair."

"Is that all?" I deadpan, and while the insults should hurt worse than a punch to my gut, I can't help the chuckle swirling in my chest, ready to explode.

I mean, my hair? She hates my fucking *hair*? How am I supposed to not laugh at that?

"Most of all, I hate that you just do whatever you want whenever you want. You are selfish, Owen."

"And you're jealous of that."

"Exactly." Addie pales. "Wait—no. That's not what I meant."

"I think you meant it. You can't stand those things about me because you wish you were like me. Spoiler alert, angel—you can be."

"I can't."

"It's not easy, of course, but I could definitely help you loosen up." I smirk.

"Not in a million years." She folds her arms over her chest, and her hands brush against my abs in the process.

My muscles tighten from the small contact, and my blood boils.

Her smart mouth drives me wild, and it's mere inches from mine. I could kiss some sense into her... or it would just give her yet another reason to despise me.

"What about a million and one years?" I venture, dropping most of my amusement. "I'm a patient guy."

Her head is angled upward, her eyes on mine, but it doesn't feel like she's actually looking at me. Her expression sinks into one of sadness. "I don't get to be reckless. We already have one of those women in my family, and the last thing I want is to be like her."

The dark shadow passing over her smooth features pierces my chest, and the urge to dissect every piece of her fucking rips at me.

So many questions bounce against one another in a tornado of curiosity in my head, but she doesn't give me a chance to voice them before she yanks the door open.

Instead of disappearing through it, though, she twists around again. "Do you really help your sister with her new business? Or do you show up just to drink all her wine?" She tilts her head to the side, her skepticism loud and clear.

My eyebrows draw together. "I actually help. I take care of the books, and the other day, I even fixed her bathroom."

The only thing she offers in return is a hum. It's not a sarcastic or a mocking sort of hum, either. It's almost as if she's... surprised. Dare I say, impressed, even.

The soft sound lingers long after she's disappeared, like a sweet scent on a pillow.

chapter
ten

ADDIE

I FLEE into the hall in a daze of turmoil.

It's not because I'm worried anyone saw me shoving Owen into the closet, nor is it because I fear I overshared once again. I didn't say much, but if I would've stayed in that closet for one more second, I would've spilled my guts about my mother.

I float past the rows of yellow lockers like I'm rising outside my body, because one very important question nags at me—did he mean it? I'm not referring to his claim of being a patient guy, either. For some reason, I know he meant it.

It's the other thing Owen said that sparked a thrill down my spine. The thing about helping me loosen up. Wouldn't that be a welcomed change of pace?

But there's no chance in Hell I could allow myself to cross such a sacred line with Owen Conrad.

Right?

"There you are!" My mother slides in front of me, a burst of bright colors decorating her top, which flows over her bell-bottom jeans. The soaked hem of her pants flares over clogs similar to ones

I've seen the Dutch wear. They look new. A gift, perhaps, from one of the men begging to lock her down.

But according to Rain, birds aren't meant to be caged; they're meant to fly.

She slips her arms around my waist, wrapping me into a hug just like her lavender scent, thanks to the organic concoction she's raved about for years.

It smells of love and nostalgia and comfort.

Whatever out-of-body experience I just had comes to a halt like a pin to a bubble. *Pop*! There goes whatever insanity had consumed me regarding Owen.

"Look at how long your hair has gotten." She swoops a chunk of my dark auburn strands into her grip and places it over her own hair, the clunky bracelets rattling together on her wrist. "Now that it's so long, we look more alike than ever."

I school my cringe, but it's a painful effort.

She drops my hair and shakes my shoulders until I see four of her. "You look like you've spent the last week in my van, smoking Nigel's good stuff."

"Nope. Not me. I don't do partake in such things." I glance around for witnesses. It will be a miracle if I leave here without my name on people's gossiping lips. "I'm just surprised, is all. I didn't think you were coming. You weren't at the game earlier."

She flashes me a devastatingly gorgeous smile. "If you'd ever answer my calls or texts, you'd know I lost track of time. I know you don't understand that. But you should've assumed I'd be here. You know I would never miss homecoming with my favorite girl."

The makings of my own smile form, but I freeze when I sense him next to me.

His cologne washes over me like a tidal wave, and my nostrils flare at the very fresh memory of my beaded nipples brushing against his hard chest.

"Lockhart, I..." Owen's mouth closes when he realizes he and I are not alone. "Hi" is all he says to Rain, but it comes out as more of a question.

She lifts a brow, and my blood cools near freezing temperatures. For some reason, it's like I'm on display, as if my mother caught me with my panties around my ankles next to a boy.

Not that such a thing has ever happened, but had it, knowing her, she probably would've applauded me and tossed condoms at me like confetti.

Dad was always the sensible and responsible one.

"Who might you be?" she sings.

Her slow perusal of Owen makes my stomach recoil. I'm dizzier by my two worlds colliding than by the bold patterns of her outfit.

"I'm Owen, the PE teacher." He glances between us. "You two could be twins. Are you sisters?"

Rain's laugh erupting from her matches the thunder outside, which is still going strong, and I wince. "Aren't you a treat, Mr. PE." She nudges me with her elbow, and she doesn't remove her sparkling gaze from him as she says, "I'm Lockhart's mother, Rain."

"Her real name's Cynthia," I correct and clamp my mouth shut, but my mother doesn't flinch.

Instead, she tilts her head toward me and tells Owen, "This one's always so caught up in the semantics of society. I've tried and tried to paint her life with more color, but she insists on coloring inside the lines."

"So glad you two could get acquainted," I chirp through gritted teeth and step between them, angling my body toward my mother. "Ready for chili?"

"Only if it's the next item on your checklist." She snorts, and my temples throb.

Over my shoulder, my gaze lingers on Owen's, which darkens with each step I take after her.

His eyes—his bold, searing green eyes—follow my every movement as I hook my thumb into the pocket of my jeans and spin on my wobbly heel.

As I lead Rain toward the cafeteria, my shoulders lock into position just underneath my ears. Something like embarrassment nibbles at my nerve endings. It's the same feeling I had when I was ten years old and had been at lunch in the cafeteria with some kids from my class.

It was around the time my father had moved out, and my mother quit her salary-paying job. Soon afterward, she asked everyone to call her Rain. I went to school the next day and declared my name would be Cloud from then on. She was Rain, so I wanted to be like her.

Rain and Cloud—we'd take on the world and pave the way for rainbows. That's what we'd decided together.

Except when I announced my new name at school, the kids pointed and laughed at me. It went on for what felt like an eternity, until the only safe place I could escape to was in the library underneath one of the computer desks.

Their mocking laughter followed me all the way there. It was the haunting kind of sound that stays with a person.

I hid in the library every day for a while after that incident. I stowed myself away among the fictional, magical places I could get my hands on, my pointy nose buried in the pages of the books on the shelves around me.

I wanted reality to be as magical, but I quickly realized it wasn't possible. I needed to be practical, like my father. He was settled and happy, and his way of life was safe.

I learned early on that I needed to live the opposite from my mother. My life may not have turned out whimsical and adventurous like hers, but I have something priceless—stability. Everything on my lists and calendars makes sense.

Schedules are easy to follow, and logic is on my side.

I still take trips to see my friends and get a taste of the world, and when I can't, I escape into books. It's all the magic I need.

With a hot bowl of chili warming my palms, I follow my mother to a corner of the cafeteria toward an empty table by the windows. Maren has disappeared. In fact, many people have cleared out, presumably opting to get home sooner rather than later. I haven't heard an official announcement from the principal or football coach, but it's safe to say the game won't resume tonight.

The rain has let up now, but the lightning still blinks across the sky with warning of more storms ahead of us.

Rain curls her ankle under one knee on the chair next to me. "You didn't tell me you were seeing anyone."

I nearly choke on my bite of chili. "I'm not."

Her lips curl around her spoon.

"I'm not," I repeat more firmly.

"So, the sexual energy between you and Mr. PE was just my imagination?"

My throat closes as if I'm having an allergic reaction. "You do have a wild imagination," I manage.

She hums, clearly not buying what I'm selling, even though it's the truth.

There's no energy of any kind between Owen and me. There can't be. He's wrong for me on every level.

"He and I exist in different realms," I say in a language she might understand.

"Doesn't mean you can't hop from one to the other."

"See? Here's the wild imagination we were just talking about," I tease, itching to shy away from the topic.

"You didn't mind it when I'd tell you outlandish stories before bedtime."

A warm sensation settles in my chest, replacing the usual fight-or-flight reaction that normally overwhelms me when she's around. "They were fun," I say.

And I mean it. Her stories of fairies with powers and beautiful fields of infinite flowers sparked my love of reading and all things literature. It's what led me to the library after a bad day and why I eventually went on to become an English teacher.

She's what also made me realize I need something to ground me, or I'd drift away into make-believe worlds of fairies and unicorns.

She indirectly taught me the beauty of magic and the need for reality.

Rain scoops a large portion of chili onto her spoon and waves it around as she says, "Remember Jazzy?"

"The four-armed princess of Solstice City?"

"Where it was summer year-round."

"I wanted to live there so badly. I thought if I wore my swimsuit every day, I'd be transported there."

She beams, and we settle into a comfortable rhythm of mother and daughter, just as we have in years past.

And even though our relationship is complicated, it doesn't matter right now. In this moment, I'm merely happy to see her. As with any boat that sets sail, it returns to shore eventually.

She's my boat, and I'm her home, nestled safely on the shore.

OWEN

THE LATE EIGHTEEN hundreds mansion rises into the sky as I slump along the uneven path toward the front porch. Ten years ago, the weeds were so high, they obstructed half the house. Vines, and God knows what kinds of creatures, engulfed the structure that resembled something out of a horror movie.

It bore a haunted mask, for sure.

But looking at it now, it's hard to admit it's the same house. It's trimmed, revitalized, and properly decorated for our high school reunion, thanks in large part to Addison Lockhart.

My button-up attire squeezes my damn throat.

This fucking monkey suit isn't me, and neither are my heavy steps as I sulk up to the open door and enter the black-and-white tiled lobby. I wasn't bogged down to this extreme when they wheeled me into the operating room for my ACL surgery.

And it's all because I think I meant what I said.

Last night, when I offered to loosen Addie up, I was... serious.

For a woman as tightly wound as her, I can't stop picturing the different ways she might release such tension. Does she have a battery-powered friend? Does she use her own hands?

The thought that Justine and Gemma might've been wrong about her status kept me up all night. What if she does have a guy? I almost broke out in hives thinking she might allow some chump to touch her.

Bond might become that chump. Addie might've told me she wouldn't accept if he were to ask her out, but it doesn't mean she really won't. She could've changed her mind between last night and now.

Which is why I brought my alcoholic buddy tonight.

The flask practically burns in the pocket of my sport coat, so I answer its call and suck back a healthy gulp. The faint scent of something floral, like one of my sisters' bath bombs, fills my senses. It's sweet and calming, and it gives me a modicum of understanding as to why my sisters rave about that shit.

In the sitting area, I spot Bond and the fraction of Zen the smell gave me vanishes. I throw back the flask for another sip—an extra dose to help me survive the night.

Only a few old classmates have arrived so far, and Addie is nowhere to be found. I'm surprised she wasn't the first one here, to be honest. Guests are here, and she's not greeting them all at the door, which I figured was her plan.

Bond rushes up to me, eyes gleaming like a guy on a mission, and when he utters her name, I realize I did not have enough to drink. "How should I ask Addie out?" he presses.

"Give her a Skittles-covered planner."

"That's what you consider romantic? It's a mystery why you're still single." His sarcasm irritates the shit out of me.

"It's more romantic than wanting to ask a woman out but dragging your feet for two days," I toss back. "Aren't you leaving tomorrow?"

"I'm not leaving for the moon. She and I can have a lunch date before I return to Atlanta, and then I can be back next weekend."

Two dates? He hasn't grown the balls to ask her out on the first date, and he's already planning the second. What a fucking tool.

Was he like this in high school? If so, it's hard to believe we were friends.

I clasp his shoulder with my free hand, the flask warm in my other. I open my mouth to say something sarcastic, but at the last second, guilt nips at my tongue.

It's not his fault I'm currently stuck in limbo with Addie. Why did she and those sinful jeans have to fucking haunt me all night?

"Good luck, buddy" is all I offer before escaping into the lobby, where I find Austin staring at the door.

"Are you waiting for Mr. Buchanan's ghost to float in?" I smirk.

"It'd make this stupid party more interesting, that's for sure," he grumbles.

"We need some music. Good thinking." I smack him on the shoulder.

"I didn't say anything," he says, but I'm already marching toward...

Where do they even keep the music?

My pulse spikes as I launch a full investigation for the damn music just to get my mind off Addie. Bond and Addie. Bond and Addie and what nature calls for.

I ask the bartender and a server, who both point to the corner where a speaker stands. "I knew that," I sarcastically toss over my shoulder at the duo in matching black-and-white uniforms.

With two strides, I reach the speaker and hook my phone up, tap on the song at the top of my list, and bob my head to the quick beat.

"Now it's a party!" I punctuate my outburst with a clap, and more classmates filter into the courtyard, cheering and pumping their fists into the air.

"You always knew how to pick 'em, Conrad," Davis says, pulling me in for a bro hug and a pat on the shoulder.

With the crowd clearly happy, I head back inside, and Austin's still right where I left him.

"Where is Addie? Shouldn't she be here by now?" He drags his heel across a tile in the floor.

I lower the flask and stare at him, then the door. "Do you think something happened to her?"

"Like what?" He furrows his brow.

"A car accident? Or what if she drowned in a pile of calendars and Post-It notes?" My eyes widen. Is that possible? Damn it.

My nerves fire like a swarm of bees released from their honeycomb traps. I scratch at the back of my neck as if I can feel bees on my skin, my neck hot.

How much whiskey have I had? I just *had* to bring the good shit too, didn't I?

I shove the flask back into my coat pocket and grimace as I catch my friend Nate in my periphery. The word around town was that he wouldn't make it this weekend, but then he surprised us all.

"What are we staring at?" he asks, turning to face the door as a few familiar faces enter, but they're not the ones we're waiting for.

"The girls" is all I offer.

"Right," Nate draws out. "Any particular girls, or..."

"Addie," Austin says. "We're waiting for her. She's supposed to arrive with Caroline and Maren."

"Have you seen Maren yet?" I ask Nathan with a wiggle of my brows. "She looks good, man. The single life is treating her rather well."

He responds with an all-knowing narrowed gaze. "Hand it over."

"I don't know to what you are referring." I hold my head high.

Nathan tsks. "You are so fucking drunk, you probably already have a hangover." He continues gesturing with his hand. "I know you're hiding a flask somewhere in this jacket. Give it to me."

"This is not Mr. Mitchell's history class. You don't have the right to confiscate my contraband."

"Don't make me go in there."

"I dare you."

Nate yanks on my lapels, and I hook my arm around his neck. I've always been bigger than him, and this wouldn't be the first time my superior strength is tested against his.

I don't suspect it'll be the last, either.

"Just tap out," I goad him.

"Aren't we a little too dressed up for this?" he sputters as his palm smacks my nose.

"I'm thinking you might be too old for this," Austin grumbles from our side.

"Never," I toss back on a laugh and raise my arm to take him under too, but a new voice stops me.

"Why am I not surprised to find you guys fighting like two monkeys after a single banana?" Addie appears next to us, hands on her hips.

My spine jerks into an upright position like a seat on a plane for landing. Nate pries the flask from me and raises it over his head, his wide grin victorious, but it was a cheap shot.

Had we not been interrupted, I would've made sure he saw stars.

But Addie's more than an interruption. She's a fucking meteor crashing into my nice and easy life.

Her hair... that dress... the blue eyes glaring at me...

I nearly swallow my tongue.

"What's with this music? I had arranged for a violin soundtrack." She swipes her loose hair off her shoulder, creamy skin momentarily distracting me.

"This is more fun than boring violin music." I point up to the ceiling as if that's where the music is coming from.

"Of course, it was your doing." She shakes her head and marches past everyone, a woman on a mission.

I'm right on her heel. "People love it," I insist. "Look at their happy damn faces."

"*Happy damn faces* is hardly a good argument—or even an argument at all."

I wave my arm over the guests bobbing their heads along to the electric tunes of my favorite techno song. "Exhibits A-Z and beyond."

She snatches the phone hooked up to the speaker and shoves it into my chest, then hooks her own phone up.

"Where have you even been?" I ask.

"I stopped by the homecoming dance. Everything looked really good, and the kids were having a good time."

Something warm and fuzzy encompasses my body at the thought of our students enjoying themselves and making unforgettable memories. "I like what you said at float the other night, about these kids growing up and having nice memories of high school."

She taps at her phone one last time and sets it onto the stool next to the speaker. "I look back on high school with a smile because of my friends and all the fun we had. For people like me, school was our safe and happy place."

The same feeling from last night takes hold of my heart like a dog with a chew toy, and the top question on the tip of my tongue is—why did she not think of her home as a safe and happy place?

But her grin catches me off guard. She doesn't appear haunted or disappointed like she did in the closet last night.

When I turn, I realize why she's so damn chummy.

Within minutes of the violin playing a slow melody, four couples have already strolled to the center of the courtyard for a slow dance.

"Motherfu—" The rest of the unsavory word catches in my throat as Bond makes his way over.

And my blood boils. I'm pissed that Addie's right. Her choice in music is better suited for this party, and I fucking hate that she's always so right.

But mostly, I hate the hopeful twinkle in Bond's eye as he reaches us.

"Care for a walk?" He holds his bent arm out for her like we're in a scene of *Pride and Prejudice*.

There's no mistaking how much she loves it, too. Beaming up at him, she loops her arm through his and says, "A walk sounds lovely."

"Give me a break," I mumble, my throat constricting.

"What was that?" Addie cuts her eyes at me.

"Have a nice walk," I forcefully chirp. "Such a nice evening for a wholesome walk. A *walk-some*, if you will. It's refreshing, no?"

"What have I told you about making up words?" Addie grinds out.

"Do it more?" I shoot back with loads of sarcasm.

Her face twists as Bond leads her away, and before I think better of it, my feet carry after them like they're floating on my frustration alone.

In the hall, the tic in my jaw bounces with a vengeance as Bond grazes Addie's upper arm. He's smiling and leering like a teenage boy who's never been in the presence of a hot woman before.

And Addie is fucking *hot*. I've realized it doesn't matter if she's rocking a ridiculous outfit for spirit week or if she's dolled up like she is now—she's a damn treasure. There's no other way to describe her.

When Bond finally slips away, I seize the opportunity by the balls and lunge into the spot next to her. "When's the wedding?" I tilt my head toward Bond. "Please tell me I'm invited. I'm great at the Electric Slide."

"That would never happen," she says, emphasizing the word *never* like her tongue is too heavy.

"Fine. No Electric Slide. I'm good at the Macarena too."

Addie folds her arms over her chest, and her cleavage gently hugs the necklace dangling from her neck. It's rather innocent, but my dick practically punches the zipper on my pants. "Both are great, but I mean, you would never be invited to my wedding, not that it's happening any time soon." She glances toward Bond, who chats with another of our classmates, and she drops her arms back to both sides, much to my relief. "I'm not going out with Bond."

My heart dives into my stomach with the excitement of a kid on the first day of summer. "Oh?" I cock a brow and fight the urge to pump my fist into the air. "Let me guess—you finally admitted I was right about something. That he is, in fact, too boring. I'd love to hear you say it, though. This admission would go straight into a special compartment I keep for such moments."

"You don't need a whole compartment. A small change pouch would suffice since you're *never* right. You're not right about Bond, either." She slides her fingers through the ends of her hair, unraveling the silky curls.

Fantasies of loosening the rest of her curls and unzipping her dress until it drops into a pool around her feet flit in and out of my irritatingly dirty mind.

"You look..." Addie's bright eyes scan my face, then skim over the open collar and drop to my waist, where the tail of one side of my shirt sticks out over my pants. "Sloppy."

Shit. My round with Nate got a little out of hand, and I was too distracted by Addie to check on my appearance.

"Is that what the kids are calling *sexy* these days?" I smirk, tucking my shirt back into my pants as my eyes lock onto hers. I can't tear them away.

"You tell me. You're the one who'd know," she shoots back.

"Oh, because I'm a kid, right?" I deadpan. "Trust me, baby, I'm all man. Feel free to check out my huge—"

"Don't finish that sentence."

"My huge *biceps*. Get your mind out of the gutter, Lockhart."

She squints. "Are you drunk?"

"No," I answer, as sober as a minister. I might've thought I was headed down a drunken path with my flask of whiskey before she arrived, but one look at her was enough to make me fucking sober.

I shift to my other foot, bearing most of my weight onto my good knee. "This dress is..." My throat thickens as I finally drag my gaze away from her hypnotizing eyes and rake it over her deep blue dress. It fits her perfect figure like a glove, and her feminine perfume transports me to a field of roses. "You look... majestic."

"That's how I'd describe a horse, but okay. Thank you." She smooths one hand over her waist, then turns this way and that before waltzing away, the high-vaulted ceiling hovering over us. She stops a few feet away and whirls around. "For future reference, giving a woman a classic compliment like *nice* or *pretty* is perfectly sufficient."

I manage to nod.

And I'm left alone with my racing pulse and the unobstructed view of her ass as she disappears into the courtyard. The hem of her dress sashays from side to side, teasingly rising up her legs with each step, torturing me.

Her hair is especially shiny tonight, and while we talked, the way the light caught the auburn tint of her strands mesmerized me. Not to mention the fucking freckles peppering her cheeks. They were still visible even with her makeup, like the few stars across the sky through the windows. It's daylight, but they're still visible among the scattered clouds.

Admittedly, Addie is right about a lot of things, but she's wrong about the kind of compliment she deserves. The classics might be fine for any other woman, but they're not enough for her. They're too boring to adequately describe her.

This confusing, sexy woman deserves all the compliments under the sun and beyond.

My pulse spikes as I exit the house for some air. My skin is heated like I'm too close to a fire.

In the courtyard, Addie sidles up next to Maren, and I glimpse Addie's blue eyes yet again.

They're light and clear and familiar, and it's not because I've known Addie my whole life. It's because the color of her eyes matches the shade of blue of the sky from the day I was recruited. I'd lain back on the pitcher's mound, alone with the dirt beneath me and the rest of the world buzzing by, and I knew my life was forever changed.

As I continue staring at Addie, the same feeling slams into me and knocks the breath from my lungs.

chapter
twelve

ADDIE

"It didn't rain, and the shrimp delivery wasn't late," I proudly announce to my friends.

Maren holds her flute of champagne up with one hand, while the other remains clasped around a martini glass of shrimp cocktail. "Cheers."

Caroline and I clink our flutes against hers, then sip in sync.

"Are you sharing the shrimp, or is it like Addie's Skittles, which are never to be touched?" Caroline teases.

"I have *one* rule," I say with a shrug.

Maren coughs into her glass like she nearly choked on her sip. "Are you kidding? You have too many rules to count." She hooks her thumb over at me and tells Caroline, "This one avoids first-date kisses, although lately, she's been avoiding dates altogether."

"You're one to talk," I shoot back.

"And she still makes a wish and blows kisses to the clock at 3:33 every afternoon."

I hold a finger up. "That's not technically a rule. It's just tradition."

The crease between Caroline's brows smooths free as understanding visibly dawns. "Is that because of the time you found that half-dollar in front of Quinton's, and they offered you a free banana split because you were their hundredth customer for the month?"

"I'm surprised you believe in something so *woo-woo*." Maren punctuates her comment by ripping a piece of shrimp in half with her teeth.

"It's not *woo-woo*; it's sentimental. Big difference." I sip from my champagne. "It was the afternoon the three of us swore to be friends forever. We made a sacred vow with our hands on that very coin. And it's held us together for twenty-plus years."

"You're going to make me cry." Caroline clutches her chest. "How am I supposed to go back to the city now?"

"You can't," I chirp. "You must stay here forever. I know a certain flannel-wearing grump who'd be perfectly happy if you stayed."

"Happy? Does Austin know the meaning of the word?" she teases.

"He's definitely not happy in his suit. He's been fidgeting with his tie like the dance toddlers in their tights." I snort into my flute.

Caroline's hum drifts over us. "But damn, does he look good enough to eat." A dazed shadow clouds her light eyes, but it disappears as she turns back to us. "Much better than this shrimp Maren's stress eating."

"What is going on with you?" I ask.

Around a mouthful, Maren sputters, "What? I like shrimp."

I squeeze my eyes closed and wince. "I think you just blew shrimp in my face."

"Oops. Sorry," she mumbles as she devours another shrimp whole.

I don't think she even chews it.

I swipe at my cheek. "If I didn't love you to the ends of the earth and back, I'd be more pissed."

Maren slides her empty flute onto the table next to us, and her shoulders sag. When I follow the direction of her gaze, I find Nathan McAllister at the end of it.

Her high school boyfriend and the love of her life, not that she'll admit the latter out loud.

It's been ten years since he left this town—and her—behind. Soon afterward, we heard he got married and had a baby.

And my reserved but sweet friend Maren still watches him like she's wishing on a shooting star, even though all he's done to her is leave a giant crater in her life.

Scoffing, Maren glances back at us. "Nate looks better than ever, and I fucking hate him for it."

"I hate his stupid chest tattoo," I chime in for solidarity. The truth is, the guy's pretty cool, but I'll never forgive him for breaking my best friend's heart. "Like, he should button his shirt all the way to the top and cover that shit up, am I right?"

"Totally." Caroline widens her eyes in exaggeration, clearly playing along for Maren's sake.

"The ass," Maren grumbles and swipes another flute of champagne from a server passing us with a tray.

As if her simple curse conjured him, my eyes find Owen's in the crowd of familiar faces. There are only a few people I don't recognize, presumably because they're spouses and significant others who didn't graduate with us.

But the rest are people I'll never forget, especially since most of them stuck around Sapphire Creek and nearby Savannah. Others moved away for a grand life outside the scope of our small, humble town. Caroline was one of them, as she moved to New York City right after graduation, and she has a life up there to return to.

But that's the thing about reunions, isn't it? We come together for a night to reminisce on old times and catch up on new ones. We relive the highlights of the past and then return to the realities of our present, wherever and whatever that may be.

"Can I steal you away for a second?"

This question doesn't come from the girls. Instead, I'm surprised to find Nate suddenly in the middle of our group.

"I need to talk to you about something," he tells Maren, and she zeroes in on that tattoo peeking out from the open *V* of his button up.

"Sure," she draws out, then holds her glass up. "Just need one more sip."

Nate backs away, and when he's out of earshot, I whisper, "Wonder what that's about."

"Go, go." Caroline nudges her toward him, and Maren almost spills her champagne.

I stifle my giggle behind my palm, but it's no use. Maren catches me and hisses, "Don't you have a fight with Owen to tend to?"

This time, it's Caroline who covers her mouth with her hand, and the crinkles around her eyes give her away—she's laughing at my expense.

"You two are on thin ice," I warn.

Maren clears her throat and steps between us to meet Nate on the dance floor, where he holds his hand out, and she accepts.

Caroline leans into me with a sigh as we watch the ex-couple sway to the music together. "What a blast from the past," she muses. "Remember how in love they were?"

"Disgustingly so," I say.

"Just like you and Stewart were. What happened with him, anyway?" She levels me with her curious stare. "You just told me you ended things, and that was it."

I brace myself. "Let's not ruin a fine evening with horror stories, okay?"

She holds her hands up in surrender and offers a sympathetic smile. "In that case, I'm going to run to the restroom, then find my flannel-wearing grump."

"Go be happy," I say as she playfully shimmies away, and I'm left with a bitter taste on my tongue at the mention of Stewart.

I never told her the truth about him because it's hard to repeat it, even to my close friends. Maren barely knows the whole story—just that it has something to do with my mother since I ended things with Stewart the day after he met her.

"*O.M.G.*" Yvonne snickers. She and Emmy—or Emily, as she goes by now—block my view of Maren and Nate, both their brows hitched into an arch in the shape of a hook.

My skin itches with dread and discomfort.

"I'm pretty sure my grandma has this same dress," Emily taunts, waving a condescending finger over me.

"She must have great taste, then." I square my shoulders, raising my spine as if it's attached by a string, and I'm dragging it up into a locked position.

But even at my tallest—and in my heels—I'm still a couple inches shorter than Cruella and Maleficent.

"Sweet Addie Lockhart." Yvonne rubs her hand up and down my arm. "Some people just don't change, do they?"

"You are still single and as predictable as ever, with this balloon arch and confetti on the tables like we're in middle school." Emily's shrill voice snaps my last nerve like a twig. "You are just adorable, Addie. Bless your heart."

"You're right. Some people never change, and isn't that a shame? Because you two could've been much better women by now if you'd grow up even just a fraction." I start to hurl some insult regarding their fried hair from too many products or the fact that Yvonne has already been divorced twice in the last five years, but someone calls for Emily, interrupting what was sure to be the best ending to the most glorious ass-kicking I've ever delivered.

They saunter away, arm in arm, toward Emily's husband, the uptight city counselor who's seemingly on a campaign tour even though it's not an election year. From what I overheard in the sitting room earlier about some mini mall he's angling for, he's off to an early start with his re-election.

I'd appreciate the ambition if he were married to *anyone* else.

"What did the evil twins want?" Austin sidles up next to me.

"The usual—they're out for blood," I mutter. "It wouldn't be a trip to the past if they didn't sink their fangs into some poor soul."

"Good thing you're no poor soul," he says with a grunt.

I could launch into a scathing rant over the Wicked Witch and her wretched sidekick, but I opt for the high road. As I told Caroline, I'd rather not spoil a fun evening. Yvonne and Emily are not worth the trouble.

With all the hard work I poured into this event, I'm hell-bent on enjoying it, no matter what they think of the decorations.

I angle myself to face Austin. "Did you drop off food at my house the other night?"

"Why would I do that?"

"Because we're supposedly friends," I point out.

"Yes, that," he deadpans and scratches the back of his head. "I didn't figure we were *bring-each-other-food* close."

"I've brought you many baked goods over the years," I remind him.

"You've brought those in exchange for something. It's never without strings."

"So, you didn't drop off my favorite food from Lucy's after float on Thursday?"

"From Lucy's on Thursday?" His cloudy aqua eyes flash like a lightbulb, and it's obvious that he knows something.

"What?" I press. The quiet brute will be the death of me. Half of every conversation we have is me prying information out of this human vault of secrets.

"I'd rather mind my own business." He attempts to shrug me off and walk away, but he should know better by now. I'm never easy to evade.

I fist the back of his jacket and yank him backward. "Austin Kyle—you better tell me what you know, or I will tell your mama you're the one who broke her favorite antique vase last year and not the storm."

"You wouldn't." He glares.

"I'm surprised you got away with the lie to begin with. What storm rattles a house hard enough to shatter a vase but leaves everything else intact?"

"That's none of your concern, *Addison*."

"Use my whole first name all you want, but it won't save you. Only the truth will." I mimic his seething glare, daring him to blink first as I stand my ground.

"Owen," he says simply.

It's like talking to a freaking wooden chair.

"What about him?" I pry.

"He asked me for your address after float Thursday night." He works his jaw back and forth, and his words raise the hair at the back of my neck. "He also wanted to know... your favorite meal from Lucy's," he says, shifting from one foot to the other.

"You're telling me that Owen Conrad dropped off dinner for me?" I blink. I don't think I've ever been more confused. Not even biophysics is this baffling.

Austin only offers an incoherent raspy sound, but it's enough to confirm this phenomenon. There's no other way to describe it.

"Why would he do that?" I ask.

"Why do geese fly in a V-shaped formation? The reason can be complicated, but there is an answer."

"Spare me the lecture," I mumble. It's times like these when I realize as much as we have in common, Austin and I could not be more different people.

"If you change your mind, you know where to find me."

I wave him off and take hesitant steps toward Owen, my mind clambering for an explanation. My emotions run from one end of the spectrum to the other over the short distance to reach him.

As I approach, another guy steps away from Owen to high-five a friend and laugh over something I can't hear. My ears are ringing.

"Dick," Owen mumbles.

Now that, I definitely hear.

I wait for him to finishing tossing back what appears to be... is he drinking water? What happened to his offensive flask of whiskey?

"Who are you talking about?" I ask, jolting him in place as if I shocked him with a taser, not that I'd ever take my distaste for him so far.

"Just stupid Lorenzo." He waves a finger around his glass toward the guy who just left. "Do you remember him? He played baseball too."

"Doesn't ring a bell." I shrug, but the truth is, I'm too distracted by Owen to focus on whether or not I remember "stupid Lorenzo."

"Let's just say he was a jerk in high school," he continues.

"Oh, there were more of you?" I toss back.

He drops his narrowed gaze onto mine. "He was jerkier than I was."

"As a professional teacher of English, I can't allow you to ever repeat that word." I cluck my tongue against the inside of my cheek, my chin angled upward. "But as a woman, I have to say you were the jerkiest jerk of all."

"Is that why you came over here? You're seeking me out to insult me now?"

Fusing my lips together, I tilt my head and study Owen from a different angle, using the twinkling lights above us and what little sunlight is left to my advantage.

He's not wearing a hat tonight. His hair is unencumbered, naturally bouncing back into place even after he runs his hand over his head, the ends swooping over the tops of his ears.

His square jaw is sharp. Yet it's not intimidating like some of the ones I've seen on guys marching down Wall Street. It's definitely not as lethal as the sharp edges of some boulders I've seen near the river.

Owen's jaw is strong, and it's very... him.

And I guess I agree with the rest of the women around town—he's rather attractive.

Has he always been this good-looking? When the gossiping shrews have gone on about his looks, I've usually turned the other way to fight a gag. But now, is it possible that I see what they mean?

"Well?" he presses, still peering down at me. "I'm sure there are better ways to celebrate a job well done. I mean, this reunion turned out great, and it's all thanks to you. You should enjoy yourself, or is that what's happening here? You're celebrating by doing what you love most—insulting me?"

The only part of his rambling that my brain latches onto is the compliment of a great reunion. "Do you really think so?" I whisper, searching his green eyes for any sign of sarcasm, but I come up empty.

"It's *bitchin',*" he belts from deep in his chest.

And a laugh rumbles free from my throat, a sound I've never made around him.

His eyes drop to my mouth, which curves upward, the intensity of his gaze like the heat of the sun.

Goose bumps prick my arms as I clear my throat and say, "Listen, did you... I found dinner on my porch the other night, and I was just... Austin mentioned you might have..."

"I left you dinner," he states evenly.

I stuttered over my words, but he couldn't be more calm and collected, as if he does this sort of thing for people he hates all the time.

"I thought it best to forego a note, since I figured you wouldn't eat it if you knew it was from me."

The sound I release resides somewhere between a scoff and a snort. "That's so not true."

He lifts a brow, and I glimpse a bounce in his cheek like he's fighting a smile.

"Okay, it's true, which begs the question—why? Why did you bring me dinner?" I urge.

"You hadn't eaten," he says, and again, his answer is simple.

It's *too* simple for my liking.

I have so many questions.

"What did you hope to gain from it?" I start. "I've seen you since then, but you haven't mentioned it. If I hadn't talked to Austin, I wouldn't have known it was you, and I wouldn't have been able to thank you."

"Is *this* supposed to be a thank-you?"

"Yes," I clip.

"You're not very good at it."

"Well, I'm not finished, am I?"

"Please. Go on. I'm listening." He lifts his thumb and forefinger up to his mouth, where he drags them across his bottom lip in a motion to zip them up.

Hot currents of indignation creep up my neck until my ears burn. "What's your angle, Owen?"

He shrugs. "I thought it was nice."

"You don't do nice."

"I'm plenty nice, but you—" He releases a low, sarcastic chuckle. "You just can't see it, can you? You're too set on making me the bad guy in your sweet little Addie show."

"I might be open to changing my mind about you if you didn't hate me, but I don't make a habit of going easy—"

"Whoa. Back up. What are you talking about?"

I jam my finger into the valley between his curved pecs and do my best to ignore how hard his chest is. They're just muscles, after all. It's nothing new. I've seen muscles before.

But his feel like more than just muscles.

They're the products of hard work and dreams come true.

He gained this physique from years of pursuing his passion in baseball, all before it was ripped away by his injury.

I respect these muscles.

My previously succinct trail of thoughts changes course, leaping into more of a zigzagging pattern as I stumble over what I want to say next.

He dips his head and inches closer, and my arm floats back to my side, my fingertips skimming the thin material of his button up.

His voice drops into a lower octave, one I feel in my freaking toes, as he says, "I don't hate you, Lockhart. I never have."

Time—and my heartbeat—sputters to a stop as the weight of his confession settles over me.

chapter
thirteen

OWEN

"Come with me," Addie whispers, then whirls on her heel.

I don't even register what she says before I put one foot in front of the other, flying next to her. I wouldn't have cared had she told me to shove my face into the ground—I would have fucking done it until dirt filled my nostrils, and I couldn't breathe.

My arm brushes against her shoulder, and something must jog loose in my brain. It's like two live wires in there, cutting off power and letting me function on autopilot.

I slip my hand into hers, but she swats me away, hissing, "Are you insane?"

"It felt like a hold-your-hand moment," I mumble. "My bad."

Ignoring me, she nods and smiles toward a few guests, and gone is the air of wonder I thought I saw in her eyes. A mask disguises her curious features now, and my easy steps falter.

Does she care about my confession? Does she believe me? There's a chance she wants to corner me just to interrogate me like she did over the dinner, as if I admitted the truth about never hating her in hopes of receiving something in return.

She drilled me, and she might as well have sunk her nails into my arms and clawed the shit out of me. It fucking nags at me to think no one ever does nice things for her for the sake of being nice.

At the base of the winding staircase, she pauses to check over both shoulders, then rips off the caution tape.

And my jaw drops.

She's the one who marked off the staircase for fear people would venture into the bedrooms upstairs and mess with the ornate figurines and objects that add to the historical value of this mansion.

But she's now the one tearing down the rules and climbing up the stairs.

"Where are you going?" I whisper, and the infrastructure of the walls carries my echo up to her.

With her hand on the railing, her fingers splayed over the side, she peers down at me with the same sparkle in her eye from before. "Care to find out?"

I trip over my feet in my attempt to reach her.

The paintings and patterned wallpaper are all a blur as we get farther away from the party, the music and chatter fading. In a flash of deep auburn curls and ocean-blue fabric, we disappear into a room. She grabs a fistful of my jacket and yanks me to the side in order to shut the door behind us.

Rays of gold and pink cascade over the bed through the window, and a shadow from the tree outside hides the rest of the room. The wallpaper is colorful and dizzying, with random shapes and what appear to be flowers. I don't think it'd help to turn the light on. I can already tell that the pattern is just too busy to absorb.

My eyes land on Addie. She slowly turns to face me and leans her back against the closed door. What's left of the sun catches the glint in her eyes and the sheen of her dress.

She's glowing like I've never seen her glow before.

I'm fucking captivated. I'm so lost in this trance that I almost don't catch her when she leaps into my arms.

Addie's mouth crashes into mine in a frenzied kiss, stumbling to take root like an anchor in the sea scrambling for enough ground to sink into.

I steady her in my arms, wrapping them around her waist until she's flush against me, my mouth slanted over hers as we melt into our own rhythm.

She tastes of champagne and mint, with a hint of something sweet. *What fruit is that?*

I open my mouth wider and delve my tongue deeper, determined to drink her in and identify what fruit lingers on her tongue.

I capture her moan, which echoes all the way down my body. The breathy, lust-filled sound travels down my bloodstream like a passenger, shooting straight south until my pants tighten.

"You..." she pants against my mouth and arches into me until her breasts nearly spill out of her sinful dress. "You are such a great kisser."

The hint of surprise isn't lost on me. Even so, pride soars across my stomach.

The room further dims as the sun reaches the end of its journey for the day, and we continue kissing, completely cloaked in darkness.

I'm kissing Addie Lockhart, and I never want to stop.

It's natural. It's right. It's... everything.

A loaded feeling of chaotic puzzle pieces finally falling into place worms its way into my fucking chest. Each burst of energy she elicits with every swipe of her tongue, every whimper and squeeze of her fingers over my arms, brings with it this question— why haven't we spent our whole lives kissing?

The change in the tides between us is almost too overwhelming.

I drag my lips away and finally decide the taste currently

dancing in my mouth is strawberry. She tastes of strawberry and mint, like she just enjoyed a mojito.

I press my forehead to hers and inhale, attempting to catch my damn breath. "I've wanted to do this for a while," I confess.

Her gulp bounces off the walls. "What's 'a while'?"

With the tip of my thumb and forefinger, I tip her chin upward until her blue eyes meet mine. They sparkle under the moonlight as if she holds the stars in them. "Longer than I thought," I whisper.

I guide her back to me, and I fuse my mouth to hers again.

Addie's hands slide from my arms up to my neck until she threads her fingers over my head, tugging on my hair and massaging my scalp. It drives me fucking crazy, and my dick is officially in pain.

"God, Addie..." I growl into her mouth as my hands slide from her hips and grip the underside of her round ass.

My thumbs skim her cheeks, and I nearly bust a nut on the spot.

I need this woman. I need her more than my heart needs its next beat.

"You're fucking gorgeous, Lockhart," I mutter as she nips on my bottom lip, her sighs and whimpers of satisfaction knotting my nerves into disarray.

"Addie, I..." I swallow around the lump in my throat as she drags her nails along my head before she cups her dainty hand over my cheek. "Addie?" I blink.

"Mmm?" She bites her lip.

And I blink again.

"Don't stop kissing me, Owen," she pleads.

"Wait." I grip her upper arms and shift backward, putting enough distance between us to help clear my head. "We're kissing. You and I are kissing."

"We *were*, anyway." She inhales, and her nostrils flare in the process.

"You and I don't kiss. Why are you kissing me?" I urge as normal function slowly resumes in my brain. "Is this some kind of elaborate prank? Bat your eyelashes and lick those pouty lips until I drop my pants, then you toss them out the window or something?"

"Not at all what I was thinking, but it's a solid prank for future reference."

"Cute," I deadpan. "What's really going on here?"

She tries to ease back into my embrace, but I tighten my grip and lock her in place. She drags her teeth along her bottom lip as her gaze zeroes in on my mouth. "I thought it'd be fun, just this once, to be unpredictable. To be anything but adorable little Addie who never changes."

"Who told you that?"

The corners of her eyes sink until they're frowning, and my stomach turns. "Everyone," she whispers. "Even my mom thinks I'm no fun. You heard her last night."

"She was kidding."

She throws her arms over mine and jerks away from me. "Of course, you'd say that. You think everything's a joke, but you don't know my mom. You don't know *me*."

"Is she the one you were talking about in the closet last night? The person you don't want to be?"

She combs her fingers through the ends of her hair and shakes her head. "Forget it. Forget this ever happened, okay? It was stupid."

"I don't want to forget it," I assert, moving toward her.

She glares, but it doesn't stop me.

Instead, I sweep my arms around her and tug her back into me. "Talk to me," I beg.

"I like kissing you."

"Me too." I lean my forehead to hers again as she traces indiscernible patterns on my chest with the tip of her finger. "And I want to keep kissing you, but I need to know what's going on."

"What's going on is that I want you. Right here. Right now. Just once." Her labored breaths fill the little space between us. "I can be unpredictable and spontaneous. Sleeping with you in a room we're not supposed to be in would cover both."

I cringe as her request skitters over me like tiny knives. What she's asking feels... wrong.

I'd love nothing more than to ease her onto this ancient bed and leave our mark in history by leaving my mark on her, but it would be for the wrong reasons.

"Not like this," I say, and the words are heavy, like my tongue is made of cement.

"What are you saying? Are you rejecting me?" She jerks back, attempting to wiggle out of my hold, but I just grip her tighter.

I hover over her, using my body to fill the space she's trying to put between us. Then I slide one hand up the back of her neck and spread my fingers, cradling her head in my large palm. "I don't want you for just one night."

"I thought that was your thing—one-night stands are in line with the Owen Conrad brand just like baseball and wavy hair."

I clench my jaw against the sting of her statement. It's not the first time I've heard something of the sort about me. People have always believed I'm the hit-it-and-quit-it type. That I hooked up with countless women while I played baseball, because I'm a flirt. Being a flirt and a professional athlete equals a serial dater to a lot of people.

But the truth is, very rarely did I ever go out with women, and when I did, it was with a girlfriend. I've always been a long-term kind of guy.

The gossip around town suggesting otherwise is largely misguided, but I've never felt the need to correct the rumors because they've been innocent enough.

Until now.

None of these assumptions have bothered me until Addie just tried to use me because of them.

My blood runs cold, and a chill skates down my spine. "I don't do one-night stands, especially not when I have feelings for someone, no matter how damn frustrating that someone is."

She purses her lips and tries to escape once again, but I can't let her go until she hears me out. This might be my only chance to speak my truth.

"I want you for more than just one night, Lockhart." I gather her hair into my fist and keep her face close to mine. "The next time I kiss you, I don't want it to be because you think you have anything to prove. I have no interest in being your dirty little experiment."

Her lips part, and she relaxes in my arms.

I grasp her hair until I'm sure my knuckles are white, and I tug her backward until her wide eyes lock onto mine. "The next time I kiss you, I want it to be because you beg for it. Because you ache for my mouth, my touch, my body, until you're fighting for air. I won't kiss you otherwise. And angel?" I dip my head low, my lips itching to connect with hers, especially now that I know how perfectly we fit together. "I can't fucking wait for that moment."

I tilt her upright until she's steady on her feet, and I exit the room with echoes of her arousing gasp washing over me, fueling the spark she just ignited.

This is far from over.

chapter
fourteen

ADDIE

"AND ANGEL? I can't fucking wait for that moment."

Phantom caresses dance along my bottom lip from where I felt Owen utter that sinful sentence. It was a promise and a challenge and a dare wrapped in one tempting package.

And the way his lips brushed against mine when the word "fucking" left his mouth was the bow on said package.

It was the only time in my life when I fully expected my ovaries to explode.

My phone releases its shrill alarm for the third time this morning, and I tap the snooze yet again.

I've never done this before. On a normal day, my alarm goes off once, and I shoot out of bed like someone tossed a grenade onto it.

But it's Monday, and I have no desire to kick off my morning routine with dancing in the shower to Taylor Swift, followed by enjoying a hot coffee while I get dressed for school.

Instead, I turn onto my back and blink at the ceiling while my alarm continues blaring as if I'm playing a game with myself to test how long I'm capable of enduring the god-awful sound before my eardrum bursts.

I tossed and turned for hours last night, and it wasn't because of the raging storm outside. The howling winds felt alive, shaking the foundation of my house. The rattling trees knocked against my window as if they were begging to be let in, like they weren't safe themselves out there.

None of the turmoil outside compared to the havoc inside.

All night, I was haunted by memories of Owen Conrad—*the asshole*.

I should've been taunted by the horrifying fact of knowing I came onto him, and he rejected me, but my subconscious was hearing none of that. No, my horny hoo-hoo wouldn't stop tingling to the mental soundtrack of Owen's growls, kisses, and scorching hot touches.

He pressed me against him until I could feel *all* of him, and dear, blessed Lord in heaven, what I felt between his legs was... huge.

And it was aimed right at me.

I miss the days when I didn't know such a thing about him. When I didn't yearn to feel his lips moving over mine. When I didn't wake up moaning his name and asking him to kiss me harder.

When I ran out of the room at the Buchanan House to rejoin the rest of the reunion, no less than three people asked why my cheeks were so red. Maren, the sweet saint of a woman, asked if the stress of the last week had finally gotten to me. She thought I'd exploded but didn't know it.

Maybe I did. Maybe that's the only reason I kissed my worst enemy.

Actually, my worst enemy at the moment is my aching, embarrassingly desperate core.

"Fuck Owen," I mutter, cursing him for the thousandth time since the reunion Saturday night.

I slap my phone until the alarm cuts off, and I toss the covers off me like a magician flips his cape around, as if to tell my bedroom "watch this trick." I kick my feet over and stand, ready to show up to school and act totally normal, my best feat yet.

With a huff, I square my shoulders and hold my head high as I launch into a shorter version of my morning routine, since I lobbed off twenty precious minutes from my schedule by stewing in bed.

Outside, leaves litter my front yard, along with random scraps and trash. A few cups caught onto my tall blades of grass at some point during the storm last night, and it's going to be a pain in my ass to clean up.

Next door, Scarlett climbs down her steps in leggings and running shoes, two pods nestled into her ears.

I make my way toward my car and toss up my hand in a wave, the cool morning breeze chilling my cheeks. "Was the storm really this bad last night?" I call out to her.

The young girl taps at her ear and pauses at the base of my driveway. "We got the best of it. Matilda's neighbor's flowers blew chunks all over her car. She DM'd me a picture of the disaster—it's a colorful massacre."

I snort. "Sounds like the name of a podcast."

"Are you using the mascara I brought over last week? Your eyes are on point today." Her swinging ponytail behind her head matches her enthusiasm.

Instinctively, I touch my fingertips to the corners of my eyes, heat flaring throughout my face. "I might've... tried it..."

"It looks great! Like you got a lash lift and tint without all the hassle, right? You should follow The Glamor Girlie on *YouTube*. She has all the best recommendations on makeup and hair products. I'll bring over some leave-in conditioner that'll change your life," she gushes, waving her hands in the air like they're the ones doing the talking.

"Do I need it?" I inspect the tips of my hair with newfound doubt and horror.

"Your hair is great and thick, but this magic just gives it a little *oomph*."

"We can never have too much *oomph*," I say and smooth my hair back into place over my shoulders, my tote weighing on me the more I stand here.

"You get it." With parting finger guns, she maneuvers around a large puddle and jets off onto her daily morning jog.

I slide into the driver's seat of my car and coo, "Please start for me today. You're a good car, yes you are."

Sweet-talking this lump of metal and leather has become part of my daily routine. As the gurgling engine crescendos to life, I check my makeup in the mirror overhead.

If Scarlett noticed the good mascara, so will others at work. Then again, it's possible she only commented because she's the one who gifted it to me. Plus, she's as prone to talking about such innocent things as she is gossiping about every racy scandal in town.

Why did I use the good makeup today? I always put my best foot forward when it comes to my appearance, but the fancy mascara might've been excessive for work.

But work isn't the reason I reached for the shiny new tube.

The real motive is more shameful than cursing in church or adding sugar to cornbread.

As I back out of my driveway, I grumble under my breath, scolding myself for trying too hard to get an irritating former baseball player's attention.

Suddenly, the obscene number of times I've cursed him doesn't seem like enough.

I turn onto Main Street and hiss, "Fuck Owen."

My shriek catches in my throat as I take in the current state of my classroom.

Last week, this was where dreams came to soar like butterflies, but right now, with a freaking tree smashed through the window and across one corner, the dream is dead—as dead as this innocent tree.

When I left my house this morning, I figured the worst thing that would happen to me when I arrived was running into Owen. I practiced and practiced my indifferent posture, along with my nonchalant expression, until confidence filled my bloodstream.

I did not expect *this*. This catastrophe is much worse than my situation with Owen Conrad.

"What happened?" I screech, my jaw unhinged. I scrunch my nose against the mix of smells ranging from the earthy scents to something like mold, and I blink rapidly to fight the dust filtering into my eyes.

Gemma places a gentle hand on my shoulder. "It's not as bad as it looks. It'll be an easy fix too, just a few weeks."

"*Weeks*?" My heart rate spikes as my mind races with different scenarios coloring my vision.

I'm dizzy.

A few weeks is a long time, and what if weeks become months? Where are we supposed to hold class during all that time? What about my freaking coffee mug shattered into a million pieces on my ceiling-tiled, powder-covered desk?

"Have any other classrooms been affected?" another teacher asks, but I don't turn to confirm who it is.

Gemma explains, "As it stands, only Addie's and my classrooms have significant damages, since this tree fell from hers to mine, but a few windows along the hall have been shattered too."

"Good Lord, the repairs we'll need." The other teacher lists the necessary electrical work, the new roof, and the paint. "That's not to mention the tree removal itself and the inspections."

Sable clutches a few folders to her chest as she rushes up to us and announces, "I've been on the phone all morning with the Rotary Club regarding supplemental funds. The school board president and our superintendent have already been notified as well, and we're working diligently to get someone from tree removal out here today to start cleaning up this mess. Resources are stretched thin, though, as many other sites around town have also experienced damages."

I open my mouth, but nothing comes out. I'm speechless as my gaze travels over my classroom. The tree cuts across one corner, with its branches cascading into Gemma's drama classroom. On its own, it might not have been such a disaster, but since the winds were so strong last night, materials have been strewn about like the storm ransacked the place for money.

My favorite posters of literary characters and classic quotes lie in ruins on the floor. My SMART board rests against my desk, a large crack down the middle like a fault line, and highlighters, markers, and notebooks are scattered around the room in disarray.

It's an absolute crime against education and English and—

"We have a plan!" Principal Weathers claps, and I whirl around to face him just as Owen strides up alongside him like a good little righthand guy.

The superintendent brushes past them, speaking sternly into the phone, and we garner an audience too. A few students pass by with their phones raised to capture the scene, hopping onto their tiptoes for a better look.

"Keep walking, please," Sable tells them. "There are glass shards and other debris you shouldn't be around."

They scurry off to the cafeteria, but not without sparing a few more glances.

I raise my hand but don't wait for Principal Weathers's acknowledgement before the words pour out of me. "Since it's my classroom that's suffered some of the most damage, I'd like to be involved in these plans."

Weathers clasps Owen on the shoulder. "I think you'll be pleased with the solution we came up with."

"You two came up with a solution?" I can't believe what I'm hearing, and we haven't even gotten to the details of this little plan!

But Owen's smirk is indication enough to know, without a doubt, that I'm not going to like this.

"Ms. Stephens, you'll set up in the auditorium. It only makes sense for the drama class to use the stage, anyway." He then turns to two other teachers with a smile, instructing one to use a section of the cafeteria and the other to share the music room.

I guess there has been more damage I wasn't aware of. Why didn't anyone call me to come in sooner? Actually, I would've arrived sooner on my own had I not spent an extra twenty minutes in bed, thanks to Owen and my annoying thoughts of his smoking-hot kisses.

I'm still lost in la-la-*disaster* land when Weathers turns to me, nudges Owen with his elbow, and proclaims, "You'll share the gymnasium with Coach Conrad."

My heart tumbles into my stomach, and if I thought my jaw was unhinged before, it's completely disconnected from the rest of my face now.

I raise a finger as my rapid breathing crosses the line into dangerous territory. "If I could say one thing, please."

"It's the perfect plan. We need to move on to other matters."

That's it? Is this really happening?

Weathers sidesteps me as he puts a phone up to his ear and maneuvers into the classroom, where the superintendent joins him and points to the ceiling. As he finishes up on the phone, Weathers turns to the remaining teachers, hands up with palm to palm. "I'll keep you updated with further news and instructions as needed. Thank you all for your cooperation."

Is he speaking English? I'm pretty sure he is, but then why don't I understand him?

"Hey, roomie!" Owen raises his hand for what appears to be a high five, but I dive underneath it and march straight past the office, tear across the lobby, and race through the cafeteria.

With my tote dragging across the dirty floor, I power walk past the blur of students eating their breakfast.

All the while, I repeat under my breath, "I am a professional."

I can share a space with Owen Conrad for a few weeks because I'm a damn professional. I care about my kids, and I will not let anything hinder their learning experiences, especially not someone like Owen.

I am a professional who can share a space with him without killing him... or jumping his bones.

The last thought skids into my mind as I wrap my hand around the handle of my car door, throw myself inside, and finally unleash the scream I've held back for the last two days.

chapter
fifteen

OWEN

"Where'd you go?" I spread my arms out to my sides as Addie stalks into the gym, her giant tote glued to her shoulder like an extra limb. Her steps sound angry as each one echoes across the empty gym, and the sounds only grow louder the closer she gets to me. "I'm thinking we celebrate the news of our arrangement with a drink at the Tap."

"I hardly think that's necessary." She frowns, but that's not what gets my attention.

Her eyes do. They especially pop today, with her lashes thick and curled around seas of clear blue.

"Did you do something different today?" I wave over her face. "You look amazing. I mean, you always look great, but today, there's something—"

She drops her tote by my feet with a thud, then gathers a fistful of my shirt in her hand, pinching the skin underneath in the process, and drags me into the Health classroom.

She only lets go to shut the door behind us and draw the shade over the window.

My smirk is too strong to stifle. It cracks through my poorly constructed façade, especially when her eyes instantly land on my mouth. A strangled breath heaves out of her like she's warring with herself, and it's the opening I need to close the distance between us.

As I tower over her, I lift her chin with my hand and rasp, "Ready to beg for that kiss yet? Because I've thought of nothing else since Saturday night."

"You're jonesing for far more than I can give you. I can't date you, Owen."

"Why's that?" I slip my hand along her jawline, inching my fingertips into her hair until I cup her cheek. I can't help but touch her.

It's more than a want—it's a damn necessity wrapped in desire.

"We're mortal enemies."

"A bit dramatic, don't you think? I figured you and wasps, or you and fun, would be mortal enemies. Not you and me." I stretch my hand until my thumb reaches her bottom lip, tracing it as memories of kissing her jolt my body awake better than the energy drink I nearly inhaled on the way here this morning. I'm too aware of being alone with her for at least a few more minutes before our classes arrive.

"Fine." She tears herself away from me almost in slow motion, like she hates the idea of not touching me—that makes two of us. She spins once and sighs. "Funny business aside, the truth is that we are wrong for each other. You and I are co-workers. We now share a freaking classroom. The whole school will know about us before we can finish the sentence—*peaches are the superior fruit in all the world.*"

"That's one thing we can agree on." I stuff my hands into the pockets of my sweatpants, restraining them against reaching out for her again.

It's as difficult as refraining from taking back my promise not to kiss her until she asks for it.

"I have far more things to worry about right now," she says.

"Such as? It's not like you're going to do the repairs yourself. Let the professionals do their thing, and enjoy your time at the gym. It'll be like a vacation." I wink.

"I need to make sure new supplies are ordered. I need a SMART board and... and... a new favorite coffee mug." She gulps, fidgeting with her fingers.

"A coffee mug?" Is she serious?

"Forget the coffee mug." She runs a hand through her hair. "My impeccable reputation would be ruined because this is the scandal—dating my co-worker—that I never asked for."

"You and your fucking reputation," I grumble.

"It's important to me. Things like that matter," she insists.

"You're serious, aren't you?"

The lip twitch I love so much subtly pops. If I weren't so close to her, I might've missed it.

"Look, Lockhart, dating each other is not against school policy. We're two consenting adults. Sure, the school and the rest of this town might whisper about us for five minutes before moving on to the next bit of gossip, but it's not a reason to fight this thing between us. And let's face it, your impeccable reputation doesn't keep you warm at night, does it?"

"No." She shoots me a pointed stare. "My weighted blanket does."

"Anything your weighted blanket can do, I can do better, and I can do more."

Strokes of deep crimson brush across her cheeks. I start to believe I'm winning her over, but then she pulls the damn rug out from under me.

"I want to be principal here someday. Future principals aren't floozies who jump into bed with their hunky co-workers."

"Hunky, huh?"

"Future principals don't get involved with the people they work with. They're ethical and responsible, and they don't give in to every urge just because that co-worker dropped off dinner for them once. We don't even have anything in common, Owen." She gulps, and I follow the movement with more focus than I ever did a baseball flying at my face. "We should forget my moment of insanity. Let's pretend I never kissed you, okay?" The final word leaves her lips on an exhale, and it resembles a pant. It's similar to the breathy sound she made the other night when she kissed me.

It drives me fucking wild.

"No can do, angel."

"Why are you being so difficult?"

"I'm being honest, unlike yourself."

As I step closer, she visibly steels herself like she's bracing her body against a strong wind.

I lick my lips. "Our kiss wasn't the kind of kiss you ignore. It was the kind you remember forever. The kind that's seared into your memory like a tattoo. So, you see, pretending it never happened is like trying to ignore ink engraved into your skin. It's impossible." I stop just short of her, my hands still trapped away. "And if you think I'm obsessed with you after a single taste... well, then, you're absolutely correct."

Her lips part as she angles her head to the side to peer up at me.

"You don't really want me to let this go," I urge.

"You're wrong."

I squint as I study her closed eyes and heaving chest. After a beat, I raise my hands, palms facing her. "If you really want me to forget, fine. I'll never speak of it again."

She blinks.

"Happy?"

Addie purses her lips and fidgets with her fingers.

I cock a brow.

"You're giving up just like that?" she demands. "What happened to wanting me to beg? To being obsessed with me? To being seared into your memory?"

One side of my lips lifts. "I meant every word. But I don't

make a habit of pursuing someone who insists they don't have feel-ings for me."

She shifts but makes no other effort to leave. This is her chance to turn around and walk away. To abandon the whole matter and any possibility of us in the privacy of this room.

But she continues standing here and staring at me, her chest heaving harder and faster as her pants fill the space between us.

"Unless I was right, and you don't want me to let this go," I venture, purposely toying with her. Her squirming is pretty fucking fun.

"I do. I mean, I don't... know. You're confusing me."

"It's yes or no, Lockhart. That simple."

She licks her lips. "Maybe." Her voice holds more of a question than confidence.

"I can work with maybe." I lean down and rasp against her lips. "I affect you. And you leave me no other choice but to show you how perfect we could be together."

I make my way out of the Health room, my head high as I whistle an upbeat tune to match my mood. If she protests to my promise or says anything else at all, it's drowned out by the bell and my racing mind.

chapter
sixteen

ADDIE

"I NEED a sixteen-ounce Fall in a Cup, please, plus all the iced pumpkin cookies you have left." I fold my elbows onto the narrow counter at Cream and Sugar, the breeze sweeping through the damp hair at the back of my neck.

It was so hot in the gym today, I couldn't stop sweating. It was totally because of the AC wheezing like it was on life support. It was not because the PE teacher was frequently running in sweatpants, which lit me on fire from the inside out.

My currently flustered state has nothing to do with the latter. Absolutely *nothing*.

Except I'm not even fooling myself.

Maren pokes her head out of the window, her cheek dusted with a flour fingerprint. "I don't have many cookies, but those left are all yours."

I rise onto my tiptoes and swipe my thumb across her cheek. "Don't know how long that's been there."

"Probably since this morning." Her sigh is weary, and I can relate. Aren't we a match made in heaven this Monday afternoon?

"You're the only person ever looking out for me, so thank you. Take all the cookies."

One by one, she packs up a few treats and slides the lavender box my way. Then she fires up the espresso machine for my coffee with the kind of ease and precision only learned through years of practice. At this point, I imagine every step of baking and brewing is a habitual sequence for her, unless she's trying new recipes.

I carry my box of goodies toward a picnic table, my back aching from the stress of today and launching a new era for my classroom—literature and critical discussions against the backdrop of dodgeball and screeching sneakers along the gym floor.

Stray tree limbs and gobs of leaves litter the park grounds as far as I can see. The walking path is obstructed by the debris, and the end of the seesaw on the playground is broken. Of course, the seesaw's demise might not be a new occurrence, but still. Together with the dark, heavy clouds still swirling the sky, it's an ominous day, for sure.

Seems like the storm touched us all in one way or another. Out here, there might be a few leaves, but they were going to fall eventually, anyway. The storm didn't ruin their lives like it did mine by destroying my classroom and tossing me into a ridiculous situationship with my enemy, who's not really my enemy and who's trying to be the opposite of my enemy.

And the truth of the matter is that I wish I could believe him.

"Order up," Maren chirps as she sets a cup in front of me, then slides onto the bench on the opposite side.

"Bless you and those magnificently talented and giving hands." I pop the lid off and inhale a whiff, gathering the notes of cinnamon like I'm hoarding them for later. My first sip consists mostly of foam, but it's enough to relax my tense muscles. It warms my hands and my insides like a relaxing bath.

"Long day?" She arches a brow.

"That's putting it lightly."

"Did it have anything to do with the storm? Because the few

people who have come by today all had some wild story." She scoots forward as I blow on my coffee to cool it. "Old Gus tripped over a big branch in his driveway, and he rolled into the street, from what his neighbor Octavia said."

I clutch my chest. "Is he all right?"

"Actually, according to his brother Karl, he's never been better. It's like his fall knocked his bad hip back into place. No limp or anything."

"You're kidding." I gape.

Old Gus benefitted in the strangest way from this storm—the lucky son of a gun.

She snaps her fingers. "Then there's Tanner Thomas. He found a whole mailbox on his front porch. It had been ripped right out of the ground, soil and all, but it wasn't his."

"Is that a bad sign or an omen?" I ask around the mouthful of cookie I devour.

"Not sure yet." She snorts. "He found out the mailbox belonged to a woman who just moved in down the street. From what I hear, they really hit it off. They're going out tomorrow night, so it could be a great thing, or it could scar them both for life."

"So cynical." I tsk.

"I just meant any undercooked meat at dinner can scar them, not love. I'm not a monster." She shrugs, but it's not so innocent. The small curve in her mouth confesses plenty. "Besides, I'm not the most cynical one sitting at this table."

I glance around, iced pumpkin cookie crumbs decorating the table like confetti. "Did I bring my imaginary anti-love friend again? For Pete's sake. I thought I left Patricia at home."

Maren's shoulders tremble as we both burst into laughter.

"Fine," I manage and inhale a steadying breath. "It's not that I'm cynical. I just haven't found the right guy who checks all my boxes."

"Oh, God. Don't tell me you have an actual checklist."

"I don't, and if I did, my mother would've burned it in a ritual in the woods to rid me of suppressing restrictions. Then she'd burn incense and ask the universe to drop several strapping young men into my lap because resigning myself to one guy is just too boring."

"Sounds like a fun Friday night," Maren jokes as she reaches behind her head to tighten her ponytail.

I put my own hair up around lunch. It reminded me of Rain gushing over how similar we look with my hair so long, and instantly, my stomach rolled.

But I had to tie up the strands. I couldn't take the heat any longer, but the relief was minimal and short-lived. I could breathe more easily once Owen disappeared into the classroom for Health. Without his eyes following me, I cooled off almost instantly.

The *ass.*

"We should get out there."

I blink toward Maren.

She toys with a piece of wood sticking up from the table, dangerously close to getting a splinter. "You haven't gone out with anyone since Stewart, and I haven't dated since like, the last swarm of cicadas took over Sapphire Creek."

"Do you think those bastards altered some kind of cosmic energy? At this point, such a ridiculous notion might be the only explanation as to why I haven't felt inclined to date anyone." I roll my eyes. "I mean, it's not a priority, but it's just... no one's made me feel all squirrelly and tingly."

"Or hot. No one's made me feel hot and bothered."

"Me neither, except for—" I swallow his name to the depths of my soul.

Owen's name nearly fell from my mouth, and I swear the sky grows darker, as if to warn me against such a colossal mistake.

"Except for Stewart?" she ventures, a doubtful arch in her brow. "There's no way he did much for you."

"He did *nothing* for me, if you catch my drift." I lift the coffee cup for a sip. I need to wet my suddenly dry throat, and it's a good thing this drink has cooled. The way I gulp it down could've really done some damage to my esophagus had it been scorching hot. "The guy was so selfish in bed. There was one time after happy hour when he was particularly frisky for some afternoon delight, and I literally didn't feel a thing."

If Maren were drinking anything, there's a good chance it'd be sprayed all over me. "How is that possible?"

"You tell me." I grimace.

That's how it was with Stewart. In hindsight, we weren't a good match for many reasons, but I ignored them all because I was tired of being alone. I especially overlooked our physical connection—or lack thereof.

We didn't connect on any level, and it took me six months to come to terms with that, although he did help matters. It was what he said the last day I spoke to him that sent me over the edge, and for that, in a way, I'm thankful.

I could've dedicated another six months to him, and what a tragic way to waste more of my precious twenties.

"Like I said, we need to get out there," Maren asserts. "I fear for my health. I'm experiencing the lady version of blue balls. Purple ovaries."

I snort into my cup and nearly sneeze with the assault of the cinnamon on my nostrils.

"Nate's moving back to town."

I freeze. "There's no way I heard you correctly..."

"That's what he wanted to talk to me about the other night." She breaks off the wooden piece from the table and turns it over between her fingers like a baton. "He wasn't just in town for the reunion. Evidently, he was here to arrange his return to Sapphire Creek later this month. He closed on a house—his *parents'* house." She flicks her dark gaze up to meet mine, and the gravity registers with a force of a shower of bricks falling over us.

"But that's next door to your house." I gape.

"Exactly." She blows out a heavy breath and chucks the miniature wood spear over her shoulder. "He and his daughter are going to be my new neighbors. Isn't that just as sweet as pie?" Sarcasm drips from her tone.

"What about his ex-wife?"

"I didn't ask, but even if I had, I wouldn't have heard his answer, given how loudly my ears were ringing."

"Maybe it'll be good for you? Somehow? Perhaps?" I offer with a wince.

"That's like saying stepping on knives would be good for me," she deadpans. "He is going to be right next door in all his dark, manly glory, and I can't be single. I'll be too tempted to fall into old patterns, and I just can't. I need to distract myself with someone—*anyone*—else."

My heart sinks a fraction. As much as I'd like to see Maren and Nate rekindle their romance in one of the greatest love stories in Sapphire Creek history, she doesn't believe it would be good for her, and I respect her resolve.

In fact, I agree, but it doesn't stop me from asking myself— why do we want the ones who are so damn bad for us?

"I kissed Owen at the reunion," I blurt.

Maren nearly leaps off the bench in rather dramatic fashion.

"I mean, it was this really stupid moment where I was like, really stupid." My heart races as I attempt to gather my thoughts— and fail.

She covers her mouth with one hand, but her smiling eyes give her away. Her clear enjoyment of my insanity scrapes a nerve.

"What are you laughing at? It was a horrendous mistake, and you find it hilarious?" I practically shriek.

"I knew it!" She drops her hands back to the table, flashing me a wide, satisfied grin. "I knew there was something between you two."

I scoff. "How dare you? I don't like him."

"Babe, you talk about Owen Conrad more than you do Taylor Swift or *Shark Tank*. You like him, even if you hate that you like him. Why else would you kiss him?"

"Because... because... there was probably something in the champagne, like freaking... delusion pills." I stumble over my words, further embarrassing myself, and my cheeks flame.

"Delusion pills?" She arches a brow. "I think the only delusional one here is you."

I slump in my seat with a huff.

"Is he a good kisser?" she asks in a hushed tone, the smile she wears still smug and irritating.

I can't lie to my friend. "He was phenomenal," I mumble. "I floated outside my body, Mar. I mean, I don't believe in magic, but his kiss may have altered my whole belief system."

She squeals.

I do a double take, since it's not something I've often witnessed or heard myself, but it's true. Maren Clayton actually squealed.

"That's bad," I state. "It's bad for me to entertain anything with him."

"Why? You said yourself that no one's given you any feels lately. Bond didn't do it for you, and he was a perfect gentleman. Maybe you need the opposite." She wiggles her brows. "Owen might not check your boxes, but he could show you a good time. Why not pursue it?"

Because I might like him.

I swallow that admission down. I'm not ready to confess as much to her—or to myself.

"I'm not fun." I frown.

"What are you talking about? You're fun as hell."

"I don't possess his level of fun. I don't wear tiny shorts and cheer from the stands at baseball games. I don't even watch baseball at home. I don't watch any sports."

"So?" This gorgeous, normally insightful human doesn't get it.

"We have nothing in common, Mar, and besides, he and I work together. There are too many reasons not to get involved, including the fact that the storm launched a freaking tree into my classroom like a rocket from Hell. He and I have to share the gym for *weeks*."

"Everything you just said makes all this that much more *delicious*," she says, hissing the final *s* with far more enthusiasm than I feel.

"It's beyond complicated, and I don't do complicated. I can't like him," I assert, but it doesn't come out as strongly as I intend. I lose my nerve halfway through, as I did the time I explained to my mother why I started dance lessons.

I told her it was because my father's new wife basically made me, but it was a lie. I started lessons in part because I simply wanted to, but also because I knew my mother would hate it.

And I eventually had to come clean, especially after she called my father in an outrage over how his new bimbo was treating me. What a fun ordeal that was for me—*not*.

But here I am, lying again, as if I didn't learn my lesson back then.

"What does Owen think about the kiss?" Maren asks, flipping her switch from amused to "let's get down to business."

"You leave me no choice but to show you how perfect we could be together."

Owen made a promise to win a challenge I never introduced.

And yet, the second he voiced his acceptance, I had to squeeze my freaking thighs together. My entire lower body clenched as if attached to the end of a string only he controlled.

The truth is, he does something to me. He makes me feel things I haven't felt in a long time, if ever. Kissing him made me realize I might not have felt true arousal in my boring adult life.

"What does Owen think about our kiss?" I repeat the question in rhetorical fashion. "Let's just say, if he's being honest, it's not something he'll be forgetting anytime soon." I chew on the inside of my cheek, a burst of undeniable excitement sizzling through my lower stomach. "And I can't confidently say I'll be forgetting about it, either."

seventeen

OWEN

"HOW BAD WAS the storm for you? Mom said her azaleas are completely wrecked." Whitney's voice sounds through my phone speaker as I pull up to the school. Huck makes noises in the background like he's playing. "You okay?"

"I'm great, actually," I chirp as I ease into my parking spot. "The storm did me a favor, to be honest."

"How so?"

"It opened a door, and I ran through it." I smirk as I find Addie walking into the school, her large tote bag in place as it is every morning.

"Super cryptic of you," she mumbles, and Huck's little *oohs* and *aahs* interrupt like he's trying to join the conversation.

"I'll tell you more at family dinner tomorrow night. You and Huck will be there, won't you? No poetry slam or class happy hour or arts and crafts with your neighbors or whatever the hell you've been up to this week, right?"

"Your imagination has no bounds, does it? As if I have the energy for anything more than half a cup of coffee." She coos, presumably for Huck's benefit.

Even though she can't see me, I grin. "I thought we agreed to live a little, sis."

"And I tried last weekend. I had a date set up and everything with a guy from my psychology class, but Huck came down with a fever. Instead of enjoying a meal by the river and making googly eyes over our forks, I was racked with pure terror from head to toe as I raced Huck to the ER, where of course, they said I was over-reacting."

"I assure you, you weren't."

"Thank you, but in hindsight, I definitely was." Her sigh mixes with a soft laugh.

"He's okay, though?"

"Perfect." She hums. It's the tune she usually hums when she rocks him, and I imagine her doing just that in the middle of her bedroom, Huck tucked into her arms.

I check the time. "I need to get going, but I'll see you tomorrow."

Once we end the call, I climb out of my truck and head inside, my muscles aching with each step. Yesterday's leg workout was nothing short of brutal, and I'm feeling it tenfold this morning, especially in my right knee.

At the door to the gym, I shake my right leg to the side in hopes of loosening it up, and I accidentally kick someone.

"What the hell?"

"Lockhart, shit!" I reach out to grasp her arm. Thankfully, it's not like I kicked her with the force I'd use on a punching bag, but still—it doesn't work in my favor to kick the woman I'm trying to win over.

"Are you practicing the moves from *Footloose*?"

"It's jujitsu, actually."

"Are you taking Keenan's class?" she asks, the shock worn off completely.

"I was just kidding." I give her a tight-lipped smile. "But does he have a jujitsu class here in Sapphire Creek?"

She nods. "He opened a studio recently."

Instinctively, my eyes fall onto her lips. They're a deeper pink color today than usual, and they're distracting as hell. "I'll have to try it out," I say absentmindedly.

"I'm glad I ran into you like this."

"Need me, did you?" I lean my shoulder against the door and flash her my best smirk.

"I did." She presents a stapled bunch of papers from the monstrous bag over her shoulder. "If this is going to work between us, we need itineraries, schedules, and rules. Otherwise, we're just in the jungle with zero food and supplies."

I reach a tentative finger out for the pamphlet. Is this about us? When I proposed she and I get together, I knew it'd be hard to navigate, but I didn't expect her to draw up a list of demands and rules.

Then again, this is Addie. She makes a list for everything, so I shouldn't be that surprised she'd go this far for a romantic entanglement.

I thumb through the stack and release a low whistle. "Is this a contract I need to sign?"

"It's not *that* extensive," Addie clips. "I expect to have yours by Friday, and it can be as detailed as you'd like."

"Are you giving me homework?"

She shrugs. "If that's what you want to call it..."

I tilt my head, studying her every delicate feature. Behind those crystal eyes and the easy dip of her top lip exists the spontaneous woman who came on to me last weekend. She kissed the fucking breath from my lungs like a swift kick to my stomach—and I liked it.

I like Addie, both the strict list fanatic and the wild kisser of the night, but if she's going to great lengths to instill structure into a relationship before it's even begun, it's hard not to think she's uncomfortable.

And I don't want to cause her any discomfort.

"Listen, Lockhart," I start, softening my tone from before as my eyes land on hers. I press off the wall and move toward her as I say, "We don't have to follow any kind of rule sheet. We can take it day by day and see where it leads."

"A little organization and boundaries never hurt anyone," she presses.

"No, and if this is what will put you at ease, fine. I'll have my details to you by tomorrow. But I just think defining this from the beginning will put too much pressure on us."

She jabs a finger onto the packet. "This is supposed to help alleviate the pressure. Trust me, it's a good idea, Owen."

"Is this really so hard for you that you need guidelines?"

"I've never done this before. Have you?"

"Not like this." I wiggle the chapter book, the pages flapping in the morning breeze. "But I guess there's fun to be had somewhere in these pages."

"This isn't about having a jolly good time."

"Then what's it about?"

"The kids. I want what's best for them and their future."

"Kids?" I blink. She won't even let me kiss her again, and now we're talking about kids? This woman is going to be the death of me.

Addie leans onto her heels, her lips pursed. "You keep trying to convince me you're more than fun, but all you do is prove you're not. This is all just a big game to you, as always."

She whirls around, her scent lingering over my senses as her hair flips over her shoulder with a vengeance. I'm so distracted by her that I don't immediately realize she's heading away from her new classroom.

"Where are you going?" I call out, which grabs the attention of other teachers and a few students milling about.

All I get from Addie in return is a flick of her wrist, shooing me off.

I thumb the edges of the papers, skimming over the top, and my heart plummets into my stomach like a batter diving for first.

What I thought was a love contract is absolutely nothing of the sort.

Rather, it's her class schedule, laid out with red tabs along the days of testing when she requests I take my class outside or use the Health room in order for her students to focus. I whip the packet open to the final page, which outlines her plans until Christmas break, just in case construction on her own classroom is delayed.

We were told it'd take no longer than a month, but she's right —a little organization never hurt anyone. I'd like to add foresight and preparation to said harmless list.

I just wish I would've realized what I was holding before I stuffed my size thirteens into my mouth and played right into what she thinks of me.

And we were making such good progress before this misunderstanding.

I lean on the door again as the bell rings, the shrill alarm practically shaking the ground beneath me.

Instead of entering the building, I stare after Addie as she disappears into Building A, her large bag nearly catching the door, but she saves it at the last second.

I'm so glued to her every movement when the door behind me opens and smacks into me.

"Oh! Sorry, Mr. Conrad." One of my students grimaces.

"It's fine," I assure him, then mumble under my breath, "I deserved it."

chapter
eighteen

ADDIE

My Wednesday evening has been reduced to a pile of sequined costumes at the dance studio.

At least the new costumes arrived in the correct color. The company finally got it right, and to make up for the inconvenience, they expedited shipping.

The fitting tonight went about as expected.

Five- and six-year-olds ran around the room, a blur of Christmas red, the matching headbands in their mouths.

The older age group wasn't much better. The number of complaints over itchy fabric and uncomfortable wedgies was off the charts.

Not to mention the decibel of moms, big sisters, and grandmas as they fought for attention. The mess would compete with a volcanic eruption.

Iris threw her back out trying to hold a younger dancer still while she pinned the costume in order to alter it for a better fit, so I insisted the poor woman go home, draw herself a warm bath, and relax.

Her niece and I cleaned up, and now I have the studio to

myself, much to my delight. After the week I've had, I need this alone time.

I shuffle the last of the costumes onto the table at the head of the studio, the bright Post-Its with names pinned to the various costumes. Green means they're ready, yellow means they need altering, and blue means they go in the pile of extras for future dancers. These are for the winter recital in a couple of months, and Iris and I have plans to reuse these costumes in the future.

I slump onto the chair next to the blues, my head spinning from echoes of the chaos of tonight's classes. I enjoy a moment to catch my breath, but there's no better way to alleviate some of the pressure in my body than what I plan to do next.

With a deep, steadying inhale, I retrieve my phone from my tote bag, open my music app, and click on a song. Tonight's choice is a fast-paced one—I need something uplifting after the last week I've had.

The beginning notes soon blast from the Bluetooth speaker, the trumpet of "Hips Don't Lie" by Shakira ringing out with passion. With a newfound zap of vivacity, I spring from my seat and glide into the center of the room by the time the song jumps into the first verse.

I mouth the words as I move my body with the freedom I never experience outside this studio. It's the reason my stepmom insisted I take dance as a girl—something to simultaneously help me loosen up and build my confidence.

This outlet worked so well I never gave it up, but nowadays, dancing is just a way to escape the colliding thoughts in my crowded head. When I'm moving like this, energy courses through me, clearing my mind and making me smile.

It's hard not to smile with this much fire blazing inside me through every bounce, shimmy, and twerk of my hips, the latter of which doesn't match Shakira's abilities in the slightest, but this isn't about accuracy or skill level at all.

This is my time. No scores or judgments at all. I'm just dancing for me.

And a surprising guest, evidently, as my head swivels to the side and catches movement by the door. My gyrations slow as I strain my neck for a better view through the glass—who is lurking out there at this hour?

The studio's been empty for half an hour.

With the song nearing the end, the trumpets softer now, I tiptoe toward my phone and turn it off, then wait for any sign of more movement. Another shuffle outside draws my attention, and I inch toward the door. Did one of the parents or guardians leave something behind? I yank on the handle, and the familiar face staring back at me is unexpected.

"What the hell?" I screech through a heavy exhale as beady eyes shine under the streetlight. "Why are you creeping around in the dark like a possum?"

Owen enters the light of the studio, his features more visible and prominent under the bill of his baseball cap. "A possum?" He scoffs. "There are much sexier animals to compare me to."

"This is about being creepy, not sexy."

"So, you admit I am sexy, then?" He lifts his chin, angling it to the side, and I nearly lose myself to the outline of his strong jaw.

The urge to trace every line, valley, and peak of his chiseled physique suddenly captures me in a chokehold. My imagination runs wild like a bull once its pen opens, bucking and kicking through my lower stomach.

Being this close to Owen hurls a hot current of desire for this frustrating man.

"You don't need to answer, but your silence speaks for itself." With a wink, he maneuvers around me, but he doesn't disappear down the sidewalk or cobblestone alley toward Bready or Knot and the rest of the square.

Instead, he enters the dance studio.

"Wait." I pick up my feet one after the other with great difficulty. "What do you think you're doing?"

He reaches his long fingers for the folder tucked underneath one bulging arm. "Two days early."

I place my hands on my hips and wait for an explanation.

"You asked for my class schedule, and I'm turning it in two days earlier than the deadline you gave me." His grin widens, transforming from an innocent one to something more smug. "Do I get extra credit for that?"

"Not quite." I accept the folder—props to him for using one. In my flustered state, I didn't think to use one for my own, and I appreciate his attention to detail. "You could've given this to me at school in the morning."

"I couldn't wait that long. It's a good idea."

"You didn't think so this morning." With the folder in one hand, I place the other back on my hip, my pulse slowing back to its normal rhythm after a quick dance.

"I just needed a minute to let the idea wash over me. Kind of like chocolate mousse. It's not really meant to be whipped like that, but once you realize it still holds the same flavor in a different, delightful medium, you agree it's a great idea."

"Do you ever get dizzy living in your own head with all those wild thoughts?"

"Do you?" he tosses back.

"Touché."

He presents a small bag dangling from his wrist that I hadn't noticed. "I'm also here tonight to give you this."

I don't immediately accept the black-and-white gift bag from Conversation Pieces, the *C* and *P* scrolled across the front in a vintage Victorian font.

"It's not going to burst with confetti the second you touch it. It's just a gift."

"Why? Are you trying to buy my affections?"

His exhale is one of exasperation, and seemingly losing

patience, he dips his own hand into the bag and retrieves... a mug. At least, that's what it appears to be. I've just never seen one like this, with its giraffe-printed stripes decorating the sides in diagonal patterns.

The frame itself doesn't stand upright. It's like the Leaning Tower of Pisa.

Leave it to Mrs. Marilyn to sell such a bizarre item at her store of wild and wondrous things.

Owen nudges it into my hand. "You said you need a new favorite coffee mug, so here you go. It's one less thing you need to worry about, which gives you more mental capacity to consider dating me."

My gaze snaps to his and travels over his face. Determination blossoms in his green eyes, and his Adam's apple bobs before he sets his jaw into a firm position.

Owen is completely, utterly, certifiably sober and very serious.

Did someone turn the heat up in here? Suck out all the oxygen like a damn crane just picked up the studio and planted it on Mars? Why can't I breathe?

I am speechless, but he breaks the silence for me. "What dance was that?" He wiggles his finger over the floor and levels me with his wide eyes, a glint in them that I don't believe I've ever noticed before.

I think he's impressed.

Pride swells in my chest as I croak, "One I made up."

"I had no idea you were a choreographer." He spins around. "Hell, I didn't know you worked here."

"How did you find me?" I ask as I place the items he brought me onto the table next to the costumes.

"Austin."

"He's busy with Caroline in New York!" I gape as I inch toward him again.

"He's never too busy for his best friend."

"*I'm* his best friend," I argue, my eyes narrowed.

"You were a lot more relaxed while dancing," he says, a light tilt in his smooth voice. Owen always seems at ease, and it draws me to him.

He lures me in with his peaceful presence without me even realizing it.

Just like now, I inch closer to him because I can't help myself.

"How long have you been practicing that one?"

I run my fingers through my loose ponytail, and my cheeks flush. "I actually just made that up. When I dance alone, I don't stick to a routine or calculated sequence. I only do whatever feels right."

"You, Addison Lockhart, don't have a formula or practiced sequence?"

"Not in here, I don't. This is a sacred space, like when artists go to the park and simply draw whatever they see or feel."

"Being an artist looks good on you."

I dip my head, reaching my hand behind my neck just to have something to hold onto. I might as well be thrust under a spotlight, splayed open for his scrutiny and curiosity.

He's so damn curious.

And it's rather intimate, especially when he looks at me with such intensity. It's like he truly sees me and can't get enough.

"I don't actually work here, though. I volunteer."

His eyebrows disappear under the shadow cast over his forehead from his hat.

"It's just that Iris is nearing retirement, and her niece will take over afterward. While she currently pays her to show the dancers their choreography, there's no money in the budget for a third helper, but they need more bodies around to wrangle these kids. They're like chickens."

His chuckle floats between us, effortlessly consuming the small space—and me.

"So, Iris and I came to an arrangement. She insisted she didn't feel right letting me volunteer, so I suggested she let me use the studio after hours for myself. Win-win."

"You dance a lot here alone, then?"

I nod and swivel my attention around the room, admiring the potted plants in the corner. They're flourishing, with the help from Iris's niece. The older woman and I agreed neither one of us could take care of a plant.

The rest of the floor plan is occupied by nothing but echoes of dancers past. The imprints of their leaps, plies, and pirouettes can't be seen, but they exist in here like the giggles and cheers from a job well done.

This warm space has become almost as familiar to me as my own home.

"You looked... serene when you were dancing." He says it so softly I almost don't hear him. "I've never seen you look so free, and I'm sorry."

A ball of emotions lodges itself in my throat. "Why are you sorry?"

"For interrupting."

chapter
nineteen

OWEN

"Please continue." I lunge toward a table at the back of the room and bypass the nightmare of red fabrics and blinding sequins stacked on top of it. I opt for the chair and find Addie gaping back at me.

"I'm not going to dance for you," she asserts, outrage coloring the tops of her ears the same crimson red as the material next to me.

"Pretend I'm not here."

"That's impossible." She shakes her head, then pauses with amusement flooding her eyes. "Unless..."

I sit up straight, on the edge of my fucking seat as I wait for the rest of her sentence.

"I will dance—"

I clap in victory.

"—if you dance with me."

My lips instantly tumble into a frown.

She sashays over, her hips melodically sweeping from side to side much like they did during her dance. And her hips aren't lying right now—she wants me to dance, if not more.

Dear God, please tell me I'm not imagining the devilish flicker in her eyes.

"Fine." I hop onto what I consider clown feet, especially compared to her graceful ones. "Let's go, angel."

I sense a blink of hesitation, but she shakes it off and steels herself. "Let's," she chirps and grabs her phone, using her pointer finger to scroll on her screen until music plays from a speaker.

"Is this Britney?" I venture as the beginning techno-like sounds of a synthesizer drown out my question.

Addie slings her arm through mine to lead me to the center of the room, and she immediately dips her body in front of mine, practically rubbing her ass on my junk.

I've never fainted, but my current lightheadedness comes fucking close.

With her confidence triple her usual level like she's cranked up a dial, she steps around me, circling me with slow, intentional steps.

Her heels hit the floor, and she bounces off her toes as she trails a finger across my chest and around my back.

It's sensual—she's beyond my wildest dreams.

And she never ceases to amaze me.

By the time she completes the circular pattern, I'm dizzy as hell, even though I haven't moved.

On the first note of the chorus from "Toxic," she jumps to the side and tosses her hands up. "Follow my lead!" she calls over the music.

I mimic her moves, throwing my hands into the air, then back down to my hips. I match her gyrations from side to side, and then we switch directions, lurching to the back, where we repeat the same moves.

I'm a few steps behind her.

At one point, she no longer dances to the beat, which is clearly for my benefit.

The truth is, I have great rhythm when it comes to catching, throwing, and hitting a baseball, but this is a different story.

I'd be more graceful in fucking scuba flippers.

I'm tripping over my feet left and right as she gives me a crash course on dancing, but it doesn't matter. I'm enjoying myself, mostly because she's obviously having fun.

Addie laughs, and it exceeds the volume and beat of the fast-paced song. It's a sound I wish I could capture, but even a replay from a recording wouldn't do it justice. The real thing is unmatched, with its airy release.

If I could assign a color to her laugh, it'd be pink—fun, light, and feminine.

It's the shade her cheeks adopt as she spins in my arms, her grip around my hand firm and strong. The way she hangs on to me borders on a cling, similar to the white-knuckled hold of an oar controlling a boat against a current.

But it's not me who's leading—it's her.

"Catch me." She gives me only a half second warning, then leaps into my arms, her legs spread into splits in midair with toes pointed like a pro.

The abrupt ending of the song is the complete opposite from how slowly she slides down my front until her feet flatten on the floor, but she doesn't back away.

Lingering in my embrace, she licks her lips and peeks up at me through feathery eyelashes, her cheeks redder than before. Her nostrils flare as her gaze travels down to my lips, and she shudders.

If I weren't holding her, I probably would've missed such a perfect physical response to me. I affect her, and it's just as well, because she affects the hell out of me.

My hands float to her hips and pause, my fingers skittering over the waistband of her skintight leggings. I'm in baggy sweats, but if she keeps staring at me like this, they're going to fit like leggings too.

She makes me so fucking hard without even trying.

I angle my head to the side, so the bill of my hat is out of the way. Then I dip it low with every intention of closing the distance between us, effectively losing my challenge to make her beg. It's worth the loss.

The tips of my thumbs graze a sliver of her skin beneath her flowy shirt as my nose brushes the point of hers.

I'm so damn close, but she squeezes her eyes closed and releases a heavy sigh. "I can't."

My muscles lock up worse than they do after a hard workout, and my chest sinks.

"I'm not ready," she whispers as she threads her fingers at the nape of my neck. "I want to be, but..."

"What is it, angel?"

"I still don't know if I can trust you." Her lips twist as if the confession tastes sour on her tongue. It's no fucking treat to hear it, either. "If we're going to be more than just a casual fling like you say you want, then I need to be able to trust you."

My swallow doesn't go down easily. In fact, none of this is easy.

If there was a particular moment in history that she could point to in order to tell me when she started hating me, then I could apologize, make things right, tear my heart out to show her how serious I am about us.

But without that, my plan to show her I'm a stand-up guy is going to take more time, and I was serious when I told her I'm a patient man.

Truth be told, I appreciate that we're on the same page. That if and when we kiss again, she agrees it's intimate and binding—a moment shared between two people who trust each other.

"I get it," I rasp.

She releases a humorless laugh that just twists the proverbial knife into my gut as she untangles herself from me. "Honestly, I still find it hard to believe you're not trying this much just to see how quickly I'll cave."

"This isn't a game, Lockhart," I assure her, my voice taking on a gravelly edge.

"It's not, which is why I can't give into you until I'm sure, no matter how…" Her nostrils flare even wider than before, and her pupils dilate as she visibly undresses me. "No matter how horny I am."

I cock a brow.

She holds a hand up and closes her eyes again, her shoulders high in a defensive position. "Please forget I said that. The last few days have been absolutely brutal, and I'm stressed, and clearly, I'm nuts. I've just been acting and talking all crazy." She finally opens her eyes and forces a smile. It's not the same smile from before while we were dancing, and it doesn't sit well with me.

As she attempts to brush past me, I reach out and slip my palm over her shoulder, urging her to relax. With her back pressed against my front, I bring my lips to her hair and speak low, as if we're not completely alone, when I affirm, "I'll be as attentive as your boyfriend as I have been as your enemy. I promise you that. I'm happy to fucking prove it to you, too, however long it takes."

Again, she shudders underneath my touch, and the vibrations are stronger than before.

Thick red specks blur my vision as lust fuels my brainwaves.

"What if…" She raises her hand to grip the back of my neck, and she arches into me, painfully gluing the curve of her ass between my legs.

Even though I can't see her face, I know the exact moment she feels me. Her arousing gasp echoes in my head, and there's no mistaking how much she likes what she feels against her backside.

"Tell me what you're thinking," I urge as I trail my fingertips up and down her velvet skin.

Only a whimper answers me, and her grip on me tightens.

"I can give you a taste, angel," I whisper as I loosen her ponytail until her hair is as free as her. Then I bury my face in the strands that cascade along the slope where her neck meets her shoulder. "I can give you a taste of what it'd be like to be mine. It'll show you exactly how fucking attentive I am."

She grows limp in my arms for a ghost of a second.

"Would you like that? I need to hear you say it."

Addie slowly pivots to face me. "Not here." She nods toward the less than private glass door, through which I spied on her like a possum, as she so lovingly called me.

She rushes to turn the lock on the door and returns with a leap. With my hand in hers, she leads me toward the back, where we disappear from any potential witnesses into what I can only describe as a private nook. It's half a hallway with a restroom nestled at the end.

Addie plasters her back against the wall and tugs me toward her, lips parted as her eyes roam over my face and chest. "Touch me."

It's a simple request, but it releases her sinfully supple lips as a dire plea.

My legs wobble as if the weight of the entire world rests on them.

I promised we wouldn't take things to the next level until she agreed she'd be mine and only mine, but I can't, in good conscience, leave her needs unmet.

She told me she's horny, and I'm only fucking human.

"Put my hands where you want them, baby," I growl along her jawline, the wisps of her wild hair brushing my cheek.

Without hesitation, she covers half my hand with hers and tucks it into the front of her leggings.

"Fuck," I hiss as she guides me between her legs until I'm cupping her wet heat.

And she is soaked.

Dear Babe Ruth and Joe DiMaggio—I'm in heaven.

This is officially what it's like to follow the light, and I don't regret being blinded by it and caving to her needs.

We're just getting started too.

I use the tip of my finger to tease her slit, and she slumps against me instead of the wall for balance, her moan a prayer on her lips.

My own body buckles as if I feel the satisfaction she feels, but I can almost guarantee I'm enjoying this far more than she is.

Her eyes fluttering closed, she takes one finger, then two. I press into her until I'm knuckle deep, and her chest heaves as she seemingly fights for her next breath.

I lick my lips, savoring the way she slowly unravels for me, succumbing to me.

Addie Lockhart is coming undone by my touch.

I hook my fingers, one at a time, and her eyes fly open, the yelp she releases echoing between us with fervor. "Owen!"

My hard cock pulses against her as I fist her hair in my palm. "I love it when you say my name," I rasp as I trail my nose along her cheek like I'm attempting to absorb her.

The grip she has on me tightens tenfold, her tiny hands clenched around my bulky shoulder.

I want to kiss her—a bruising, punishing kiss to show her just how damn agonizing it's been to *not* kiss her again these last few days.

When I slide my fingers out, she whimpers in protest and still doesn't let go of my shirt. Rather, she pinches my skin, and it turns me on even more.

"I know I promised you a taste, but it's me who needs the taste." As I lap her up from each finger like a popsicles in the middle of summer, I sink onto my heels, my knees at her feet as she watches me with desire swimming in her eyes. "May I?"

"Yes," she whispers and thrusts her fingers through my hair as I get to work on her leggings.

I slide the elastic material down each toned thigh until it's wadded around her ankles. She steps out of one side, but I don't make it to the next before she throws her free foot over and hooks her knee onto my shoulder.

Which is when I see it—a birthmark located inside her thigh.

It's in the shape of a heart, and I can't help but bring my lips to that spot.

Her body limps lower on the wall, and I use both hands to hoist her up as I nip at the birthmark, paying special homage to it.

My brain malfunctions.

Hot blood courses through me, lighting me on fire.

With her hand still in my hair, Addie jerks my face between her legs, and I growl. She needs me, and I fucking love it.

Almost as much as I love the sweet taste of her.

I squeeze the backs of her legs with both hands and bring her closer until my face is completely buried in the happiest place on earth.

Addie rocks into me, riding my tongue as I devour her.

Her previous moans turn into full-on cries of pleasure, thanks to me.

When her muscles tighten, and her body shatters, it's my name she screams.

And when I stand, it's my arms she melts into.

chapter
twenty

ADDIE

"There's more where that came from. All you have to do is say the word."

That's the last thing Owen said to me before sliding my leggings into place over my hips and walking out of the dance studio two nights ago.

And those words have been on repeat in my head ever since.

"Miss Lockhart?"

I hear my name somewhere in the back of my head as if I'm asleep, but really, I'm lost in Owen Land as he leads his class into a series of stretches.

He's touching his toes, his loose hair dangling over his forehead.

Many quietly mind his instruction, while some complain of soreness from running up the bleachers earlier this week.

To those, Owen says, "If your muscles are sore, that just means this class is working."

It makes me smile.

And the fact that his round ass is on display, with his black sweats stretched tightly across each curve, well, that just makes me bite my smiling lip.

"Miss Lockhart?"

I turn back to my students, wide eyes staring back at me from the bleachers. Their books and notebooks are open in their laps and on the seats next to them, the patterns staggered and a bit like a college auditorium–style room instead of the traditional rows of desks we had in my currently destroyed classroom.

"Hmm?" I blink, completely dazed and confused. *What in the world were we talking about?*

I struggle to force my internal compass to point north when something hits my back and practically launches me into the present again.

"I'm so sorry!" Behind me, on the other side of the volleyball net, a young girl covers her mouth as she visibly shrinks in embarrassment.

Owen jogs over, the short sleeves of his thin shirt nearly fused to his biceps as he pumps his arms forward and backward. He retrieves the ball at my feet while I continue staring at him.

Actually, I'm gawking.

I clear my throat and wave to the girl. "It's fine."

Owen holds up the ball, flashes a smirk that I feel between my legs, then jogs away, calling out to his class to focus on the placement of their strikes. "We're learning the skill of precision and coordination here."

My throat dries as his knowing eyes find mine.

He runs to the other corner of the court as the students resume their volleyball warm-up, and I can't tear my gaze away from Owen.

His hair is free from the confines of a hat, and the strands bounce with every stride.

Each time he lifts his hands to rest on his stocky hips or run them through his hair, thoughts of the other night in the dance studio transport me right back there—in the middle of my class!

Oh, Lord.

This is not the time nor the place to let this man rile me up, no matter how ruggedly, sinfully, frustratingly sexy he is.

"Miss Lockhart?" Mary Ellen raises her hand.

I nod for her to go on, and immediately, her words rush out.

"Cody is comparing Nathanial Hawthorne to some gamer nerd on *YouTube*. It's an outrage."

"It's symbolism," Cody shoots back.

Mary Ellen scoffs. "A video game has nothing to do with Hester's scarlet letter."

Hester Prynne.

Nathanial Hawthorne.

The Scarlet Letter.

It all comes roaring back as if I've emerged from a coma, and I release the hold my teeth had on my bottom lip.

We're discussing the scarlet letter Hester wore in the novel and the different symbols it serves, but my head drifted off to the PE teacher on the other side of this godforsaken gym.

Mary Ellen continues, "Comparing a YouTuber to one of the most respected authors in history is ridiculous."

"MadGamerMax is influential in his own time. Why do we have to talk about the sixteen hundreds? It's literally old news." Cody fist-bumps the kid sitting next to him.

I open my mouth to add to this conversation—aka do my job. After all, Cody poses an excellent question. It's one I'm frequently asked, and I always have such an insightful response.

But right now, nothing comes to mind except for the parallels between me and Owen to Mary Ellen and Cody. Those points smack me between the eyes.

The way these two go back and forth is excessively familiar, and suddenly, I'm thrust back into high school myself, where I'd often argue with anyone willing to jump into the metaphorical ring with me.

I dominated discussions in my English class with similar

passion as Mary Ellen, and Owen was only heard when comparing the pace of a book to the speed of a baseball pitch.

Looking back, he wasn't wrong, and neither is Cody, although I don't know this MadGamerMax person. This line of thinking just lies outside the box, and is that really a bad thing?

Chantal chimes in, "Actually, *The Scarlet Letter* is still relevant. Women are judged left and right for their sexuality and supposed sins. Dragged through the mud until they're blue in the face."

"Exactly!" Mary Ellen bursts. "But just like Dimmesdale, men hide behind their power, insecurities, and long history of escaping public criticism. They're never vilified for their indiscretions."

"Not until Taylor Swift came along to rip them in half." Chantal reaches up to high-five a proudly smiling Mary Ellen, and my heart soars.

This is the kind of moment that reminds me why I love my job so much.

My goal is to eventually progress to hold the coveted position of principal, but that's not to say it'll be easy. Missing these moments with these scrappy and mindful kids will be gut-wrenching, to say the least, which is why I rock back onto my heels and soak it all in.

I fold my arms over my chest as the students continue back and forth, and I only jump in when we veer off from a lively discussion and onto the cusp of chaos, as Cody brings up MadGamerMax's ex-girlfriend who may or may not cyberstalk the apparently famous YouTuber.

"All right!" I clap my hands, and their attention snaps to me in sync. "Let's stick to the novel, okay?"

For the rest of class, we keep the discussion focused without interruption from the volleyball game, and my eyes drift to Owen a total of six times for the hour, which is better than yesterday's count of thirteen.

By Monday, I hope to get down to three, until he's no longer driving me insane, but deep down, I know those goals might not be reasonable.

The quick blow of a whistle and the stampede of hurried footsteps that follow from Owen's class dispersing into the locker rooms to change alerts me—we have five minutes left.

It's been his MO all week. The first time he blew the whistle, I jumped out of my skin and threatened to flush the damn thing down the toilet.

It didn't stop him from doing it again and again. It's a habit, as he claimed, but I haven't brought it up again since the first day. The truth is, I surprisingly appreciate the last call, of sorts. It lets me stay present for the discussion without worrying about checking the time so often.

I don't need the clock when I have him.

"I think that's a good place to end what was a rather impressive discussion. Thank you all for participating." I pace in front of the bleachers.

I have just enough time to remind the students of their reading assignment for the next chunk of *The Scarlet Letter* when the bell rings, and my palms have never been sweatier.

"Good job today." I clap like this is the end of a show, and I internally roll my eyes at myself. I'm officially losing it.

Once the coast is clear, I shake my wedgie loose and smooth the front of my pants down, vowing not to pace again for the rest of the day. These high-waisted trousers inflate like I unleashed a parachute in them.

"Is this dance new?" Owen's voice sounds from behind me, and I snap upright, freezing as if he caught me with my hand *down* my pants. "I must've missed it the other night."

I turn around, using my finger to swipe the loose hair stuck to my lips. "I call it the bad-decision dance. Like it?"

He hums as he saunters toward me, and a glint bounces in his emerald eyes like a pinball. That irritating, mischievous twinkle makes me feel as if I'm on display.

"By the way, you promised to keep the ball on your side," I point out.

"Not my fault you got in the way."

I scoff. "I was teaching my class."

"Were you?" He stops a foot from me. "Because it seemed like you were doing an awful lot of staring at the PE teacher instead of discussing Hester Prynne and all... her... naughty ways."

"*Pfft.*" The sound slips from my lips more like a purr.

It was supposed to hold more indifference. I'm not supposed to react so easily to the way his words drip with suggestive innuendos, but his slow utterance just sent a heat wave through my nervous system.

"Don't worry—I won't tell anyone, Lockhart." One corner of his lip curls upward. "I'll simply add it to our growing list of secrets."

"The other night never happened," I draw out, but it's no use. At the moment, I couldn't convince anyone a tree's trunk is brown, not with my breathy voice full of weakness.

"If it never happened, then how come I can still taste you?" His tone drops an octave when he says *taste*.

It's sensual—so excruciatingly and tantalizingly sensual.

He whistles a tune as he returns to his side of the gym, while I stifle my urge to climb him like a freaking tree right here at my sacred place of work.

I've never entertained such a heinous idea, and I wish I didn't mean it.

Owen Conrad has turned my whole damn life upside down.

"Oh, my Lord, no," I mutter under my breath as I turn my car off and take in the pink-and-yellow van parked on the side of my house. "It's fine. She's probably dropping off Kin's green beans," I say, totally talking to myself because I've completely lost my mind. "It's fine. All is well."

With a deep inhale—followed by a second and a third—I finally step out of the car, tote in hand like a security blanket, and trudge up the steps.

Rain swings the door open, and it's not just Kin who's behind her; she's brought friends, as in *plural*.

I did not take enough deep breaths before walking in here.

"My baby's home!" Rain tosses her arms around my shoulders. "You were gone a long time today."

I sigh. "This is how long I work every day."

"No wonder you have those bags under your eyes." She studies me, then fluffs my hair. "But your hair is gorgeous. I love that we look so alike. What did Mr. PE say last weekend—that we could be twins?"

"He says a lot of crazy stuff."

"I like him," she says in an airy, singsongy voice. "He's good for you."

"It's funny how you remember what he said about us, but you don't recall that I told you we're not together."

Her eyes widen. "You two had sex!"

The strangers occupying my living room turn their heads, and I've never wanted to be a rug so badly. I'd actually prefer to be the paisley rug they're currently sinking their bare feet into.

I gasp. "No, we didn't."

"You let him sip from your sacred garden. I can tell." Kin winks at me.

"That's so—how dare—you have some gall—" I open and close my mouth, floundering like a fish on a hot sidewalk.

"I can tell too," Rain chimes in.

"You said we had sex, which we did not, so you were wrong."

"But Kin was right."

"That's beside the point."

"Aha! So you admit there is something between you and Mr. PE."

My cheeks are on fire. I'm dangerously close to needing to dunk my face into a sink full of water.

"Oral pleasure is still sex, baby," Rain adds. "Any physical, animalistic act that awakens our inner goddess—"

"Please stop." I hold my hands up. "I'll give you anything to stop that sentence. I'll give you this bag if you promise to never finish that sentence."

She grimaces. "This bag is rather gaudy."

"You can't have it, anyway. It contains my life." I angle my body away from her and pat my tote, as if she's hurt its feelings. Given how emotionally supportive this thing has been, I wouldn't immediately dismiss the notion, either.

"Your life should not be able to fit into a bag. Am I right?" Rain shifts her attention to her friends, then glances back at me. "Why do you chain yourself to such a small life in one place, with uncomfortable clothes and a single bag to show for it?"

"You know I didn't mean literally. It was a hyperbole." In the corner of my eye, I see Kin lifting his hand, and smoke billows over him. "Are you burning sage?" I cringe.

"I need to cleanse the negative energy in here. Otherwise, I'm going to hang in the van."

"There's a grand idea," I mutter and cross my arms over my chest.

"Go to sleep! You can wake up once we leave!" Kin calls out to the ceiling.

I turn to my mother, my nerves pinched between exhaustion and extreme irritation like a thumb and forefinger. "Is he talking to this supposed negative energy?"

"Of course. Don't you?"

"Well, I don't have any pets, so who else would I talk to?" I flash a sarcastic smile. "Speaking of leaving, when will that be exactly?"

"Don't tell me you're in a rush to get rid of us." Rain tsks. "That's no way to treat the person who gave you this house, is it?"

I purse my lips as my head spins. It's the same looney tune and fight with her each time she decides to pop in unannounced. When she was here for the chili dinner, she didn't stay here. I don't know that she stayed in Sapphire Creek at all.

But when she does stick around the house, her visit ranges from two days to two months. I never know with her.

The last time she showed up was probably six months ago, which was the longest stretch between overnight visits. I should've known this would happen, because why wouldn't it? This week has been full of surprises.

"I'm actually going out of town for the weekend, so the house is all yours," I announce.

"You are?" Rain pulls back, clearly shocked. "With Mr. PE?"

"His name is Owen, and no," I call over my shoulder as I shoot down the hall, mentally organizing a list of toiletries, clothes, and shoes I need to pack.

Oh, and I need to figure out where the hell I'm going.

chapter
twenty-one

ADDIE

Getting practically kicked out of my own house
couldn't have come at a better time.

Fixing my lawn mower and dryer can wait another week.
Besides, it's October, and the growth of grass has slowed. I don't
need to mow every week like I did over the summer.

My dryer will have to wait a few more days. With Austin's
absence from the auto shop, Judd's been slammed and hasn't been
able to get away. No matter—the clothesline has been working just
fine.

I needed distance from town, and Savannah is so close. Yet it's
far and big enough to feel like a whole new world. The truth is, I
would've driven all the way to Atlanta had I known my mother
and her wandering crew would've crashed my productive weekend.

I'm positive those "friends" are just random people she likely
met yesterday too, if history tells me anything, and they're definitely going to leave me a gift other than the lingering notes of sage
—a mess. They're going to leave a giant, irritating mess for me to
clean up, but that's a problem for future me.

Right now, I have a problem with my traitorous hormones, which are the biggest reasons I needed to hightail it out of Dodge.

The gym is the second largest space in the school, but it's still not big enough. Not when it comes to Owen Conrad and his stupidly sexy smirk. A whole ocean couldn't contain him or the feelings he makes me feel.

I drown in them.

Who even am I? I never daydream like I have the last two days, and it's all because of Owen.

IN MY DEFENSE, the guy's ass is round and strong. His sweatpants stretch over it each time he moves, and honestly, it should be illegal. It should be against policy to wear anything but business attire to school, even if he is the PE teacher.

No one should get special treatment because of their subject, or perfect ass.

Thirty-five miles away from Sapphire Creek, I drive into Savannah's city limits. I've been here a few times and know my way toward downtown, but I have no solid destination.

I need a hotel room, but a walk along the river sounds heavenly.

A drink at one of the many rooftop bars sounds even better.

But I don't do any of that. Instead, a bright sign with cursive writing catches my eye—a hair salon.

The ends of my strands tickle my cheeks as if to whisper encouragements for me to go in, and I turn into the parking lot.

Time to be spontaneous.

"TABLE FOR ONE, PLEASE." I nod toward the hostess and flash her an easy, bright smile. My fresh new look gives me all kinds of boss babe energy.

My new hair is light and airy, and it makes the rest of me feel the same, which I desperately needed after the last week. It's the little things, after all.

"Right this way." The hostess spreads her arm for me to follow her as we meander past a bar on one side and a few tables of two on the other. People are perched on teal stools at the bar, where they sip on fun cocktails in Mason jars.

She comes to a stop at a small table in the corner, and she sets a menu in front of the far chair, then lights the wick of the Mason jar candle in the center. "Your server will be right with you."

"Thank you." I toss my bag into the empty seat across from me, behind which the restaurant is spread, giving me a panoramic view of the rest of the crowd. There's a commotion from behind me, and I nearly fall from my chair trying to get a good look.

In the hall, a few girls wait for the bathroom, giggling with flushed cheeks.

Different smells of unique combinations of foods mix in the air around me, and my stomach rages with hunger.

As I peruse the menu, the letters jumble, and my mind drifts to Owen once again. It's like I'm staring at a word search puzzle, but instead of stringing along the letters to innocent words, the two jumping out at me are OWEN CONRAD.

Owen, whom I hated, but I let him do unspeakable things to me—and I freaking loved it.

Owen, who likes me a great deal.

Owen, who is my co-worker.

More than that, we share a classroom, and I was so distracted the last two days that I couldn't properly do my job. It's another reason I didn't want to get involved.

I definitely shouldn't have let things go as far as to ride his face like I was on a mechanical bull. Hell, I gyrated my hips into his face like a porn star. Who was I?

Up until Wednesday night, I didn't think I had anything in common with a porn star, and it was a simpler time.

The music overhead switches to a faster country song, and bopping my head along, I run my hand through my hair, long past the ends, which hover a couple inches above my shoulders. My fingers haven't grown accustomed to the new length just yet.

I haven't gotten used to the color yet, either, as I used the bathroom earlier and actually did a double take when I caught myself in the mirror.

I'm surprised I went through with my itch to be spontaneous. I didn't even call Caroline or Maren for their consultation. When the hairdresser confirmed they accept walk-ins, she asked me what I wanted done, and the request tumbled from my mouth so simply.

I continue skimming the menu, coming across outlandish combinations like PB&J chicken wings and a grilled apple pie and chicken sandwich. The drink menu with signature cocktails is just as delightfully unique, and I decide an apple cider mojito is just what I need.

After the server saunters away, my order scrolled across her notepad, I glance up and freeze.

Of all the cities, restaurants, and people, the guy in this establishment staring back at me is none other than the object of my thoughts and fantasies.

Am I seeing things? Have I lost my mind? I chopped my hair off and dyed it dark, and I'm dining at a restaurant whose menu makes no sense. This is it, isn't it? I've officially gone insane.

"What are you doing here?" I ask at the same time that Owen rests a large hand on the back of the empty chair across from me and says, "Lockhart, your hair..."

This is real—he's here. Owen is here in a long-sleeve thermal with the top button popped open, revealing a peek of his chest. But instead of wishing he'd undo the other two buttons to show off more taut skin, I'd rather slip my hand inside and explore his muscles for myself.

The front of his shirt is tucked into the waistband of his faded jeans, a hole ripped in the knee. His hat is firmly in place over his head, the bill of it casting a shadow over one half of his face under the glow of the lights overhead.

Instinctively, I touch my fingers to the short dark-brown strands, which the hairdresser called "chic and flirty as hell." She loved this look, as do I, and although I didn't do this for anyone other than myself, I suddenly find myself caring if Owen likes it too.

"I had dinner." He blinks and leans a second hand on the chair as if he needs to steady himself. "Your hair looks..."

"Majestic?" I finish for him with a smile.

His lips curl into a grin of his own as he continues staring at me. I can't look away, either. "It suits you," he says, and my heart flip-flops.

I tear myself away from his gaze, and around the sudden lump in my throat, I blurt, "I agree. It suits me rather well to look different than my mother."

He cocks a brow.

"She and I are total opposites, as you might've noticed. She's fun, and I'm boring. I normally pride myself on that, but today, I figured why not be neither? I opted to just be different."

His hum confuses me. It's a light, raspy sound with zero indication as to his intention.

Which makes me ramble further. The tips of my ears burn with each word tripping on my tongue. "I'm sure you of all people would love it if I were more like my mother, though," I say, and my mouth twists into a cringe.

My stomach churns with instant regret. Why did I open my big, stupid mouth? This is supposed to be my peaceful alone time, but two minutes with Owen Conrad, and I'm nosediving into an awkward pit of discomfort.

"Why would I want you to be anyone but you?" He angles his

head to the side, the shadow over his face shifting and revealing more of his eyes. The emerald abyss stretches far and wide in his blazing eyes, and my pulse spikes.

"The other night in the custodial closet, you called me boring," I whisper, my gaze stuck on his again.

Understanding drains the color from his face. "What I said doesn't make it true. It just makes me an asshole, and I'm sorry."

With great—or terrible—timing, the server sets my drink down and asks Owen, "Will you be joining her?"

I wait expectantly for his answer, hoping he accepts the invitation I should've offered myself, but I was too flustered for manners.

"I'd love to." Owen scoots the chair out, and I reach for my bag to set it on the floor. "I'll drink what she's drinking, please." He points to my short glass, inside which, mint leaves float around the light orange drink among the ice cubes.

"Good choice," I tell him as the server scurries away.

"You haven't even tried it yet. Or have you had it before?"

"No, but it looks good. Has to taste good."

"Can't argue with that logic." He gives my face a once-over, and his eyes darken, as if he's referring to something else entirely.

I clear my throat and shift in my seat. "I actually haven't been here before. I just remember Gemma talking about it, so I thought I'd try it."

"Same." He chuckles.

"The food is definitely different."

"Trying new and different things is fun." Again, it seems he's speaking in code. That maybe I should try new things—like him.

He would be new and different for me, for sure, and I can't confidently say I'd hate it. The small taste I've gotten of Owen screams that I'd love it.

"You are here alone, right?" He leans back, the gleam in his eye dulling.

"I am. What about you?" I glance behind him as if a third someone will pop out to join us.

"I just finished having dinner with my sister and her baby boy."

"You're an uncle?"

"The best around."

"If he's still a baby, he has several years before he admits to that," I tease and sip from my drink. The mix of sweet and minty works well together, and it complements my mood just fine too.

"He will, though. I'm going to teach him everything he needs to know."

"Bless his heart." I lick my lips, happily lapping up the excess drops of my drink when something very important occurs to me. "Wait. Do you come here to Savannah a lot to see them?"

He nods. "I help Whitney with babysitting and lending a hand around her duplex if her dishwasher's leaking or if the beam in her closet falls. My family's rallied around her to do everything possible so she's able to finish college."

The server arrives with Owen's drink, and he clinks it to mine.

I follow his bobbing Adam's apple with unnecessary interest, and my cheeks flame as my thoughts wander into fantasy land. I clear my throat again. "What about her baby's father? How does he fit in?"

"I'd like to think he'd be there every step of the way if Whitney had gotten his phone number or learned his real name. But instead, she came home from that summer vacation with far more than a tan and a hangover."

"Is that what's kept you so busy lately? Why you've missed things around school?"

He gives me a tight-lipped smile.

"Why didn't you say anything?"

"You never asked."

My mouth dries. "Well, then, that makes us both assholes."

"Two assholes sitting in a tree," he sings. "You know what

comes next, Lockhart. And you know exactly how to get it. Just say the magic words," he goads, and the cloud of lust in his eyes thickens.

A blush burns through my cheeks.

It would be so easy to give in—and it would feel oh-so good to be bad.

chapter
twenty-two

OWEN

HER EYES SPARKLE, and it's not just because of the candlelight reflecting in them.

She's enjoying herself. Addie Lockhart is having fun with me, and the more I get to know this side of her, the harder I fall.

I'm royally fucked when it comes to her, in ways I never saw coming, and I have no doubt she has feelings for me too, even if she won't admit it.

But the night is young.

"I am sorry about flaking, though." I frown. "I might've been helping my family, but I shouldn't have abandoned you. You had a lot more to do than I ever realized, and I was unfair to you."

Addie blinks at me over her fresh plate as I sip my surprisingly tasty drink. Yet another thing she's right about. "I'm sorry too. I shouldn't have assumed the worst in you."

We stare at each other like we're unsure about this new territory we're entering. I know I'm confused over what to do next. She and I just apologized to each other—and meant it.

And the sky outside is still clear. No Hell freezing over or pigs flying.

"Are you sure you don't want anything to eat?" Addie shifts in her seat, breaking the silence and our staring contest. "I hate eating alone," she says softly.

"Weren't you planning on doing just that before I crashed your evening?"

She rolls her eyes. "I hate being the only one at the table who's eating."

"Fine." I lift a finger toward our server, who happens to buzz by. "Can I please put in an order for mozzarella sticks with strawberry jam?" I ask her.

She nods, and with her departure, Addie squirms across from me. "You didn't have to do that."

"I did."

"Why?"

"Because you hate eating alone. You kind of made me order food."

"It's not—you are so—why did you even sit down?"

"I like annoying you."

She narrows her eyes, and I fight a grin. "Sorry to disappoint you, but my annoyance quota has already been met for the day by my mother and her unruly acquaintances."

"Sounds like the beginning of a really good story, but before you continue, I have one request." I drop my eyes to her untouched plate. "Eat."

"I'm waiting for your food. It's the polite thing to do."

"As I'm sure you've noticed, Lockhart, I don't care too much about politeness."

Her eyes darken, and the mystery swirling in them beg me to solve it. What is she thinking? Does she like the thought of me being impolite in private? I sure fucking hope so.

"You may continue," I say, my voice suddenly hoarse.

Between bites, she relays the story of her mother's whirlwind intrusion. She stabs a triangle-shaped waffle and jabs a piece of fried chicken onto the end, then shoves the whole thing into her mouth.

Impressive.

I stare at her lips as she talks, her free hand waving to the side with every new detail of some guy named Kin and what Addie refers to as his "asinine anti-negativity dance."

"I'm glad I left." She nods and pierces another piece of chicken with her fork with the intensity of what she'd likely enjoy doing to Kin's sage. "I much prefer the cozy room at the Riverview Inn and Suites. They have free Wi-Fi."

"That's hardly an amenity anymore. I'm sure Forsyth Park has free Wi-Fi now."

Her head bounces from side to side as she chews, and I take it as an agreement.

"They just took over your house, though?" I lift a brow.

"It's what Rain does—barrels into town like a storm and leaves all the evidence behind." Grimacing, she reaches around her half-eaten plate for her water and sips.

Our server arrives with my mozzarella sticks and a pitcher of water, which she uses to top off our glasses.

"It was a house she gave me, after all, and I'm so unappreciative any time I suggest she and her friends clean up after themselves," she clips, obviously repeating Rain's words. "Does she think I like finding wicker sandals in the garbage disposal? No. I really don't."

"Adding that to my list of things not to do to you, although I didn't know wicker sandals were a thing."

"Me neither, until I fished them out piece by piece, along with a picture of a black cat."

"Another asinine ritual, perhaps?"

"I didn't ask." She sighs. "I've thought about moving so many times, but I just can't bring myself to sell that house."

"Why not?"

"It's the house I grew up in, but it's more than that. It's..." She traces her bottom lip with her teeth. "I guess I just want to make sure my mom always has a place to come home to, and that's home for the both of us."

Her voice is thick with vulnerability, and my throat constricts.

"How do you do that?" She leans back in her chair.

I pause with my hand hovering over my plate. "Do what?"

"You make me say things. You're like a conversational ninja."

"It's a gift." I bring a mozzarella stick to my mouth and practically eat the whole thing in one bite. I would have, anyway, had Addie not lurched forward, her hand outstretched and eyes wide.

"It's too hot," she warns. "Are you okay?"

I chew, which proves difficult with the large smile spreading across my face.

"You probably have third degree burns on your tongue." She sits back, and I glimpse a dab of syrup on her chest.

When she leaned forward, her shirt must've dipped into the syrup on her plate, and now a stain the size of a quarter sets over her breast.

Instantly, filthy images of licking the sweet and sticky condiment off her naked tit slam into me like a punch to the gut.

I know what she tastes like, but I didn't get to explore the rest of her body the other night. My muscles have never been so tight. My entire body is so hard I'm in pain.

The rest of my fried cheese does not go down easily as I use every ounce of strength to purge the thoughts from my mind.

She drives me crazy.

"You did burn your tongue, didn't you? You're so red." She bunches a napkin in her hand and dabs the end of it in her water glass, then scurries around to my side.

I'm assaulted with her sweet scent as she brings the cool tip of the napkin to my cheek. "It's cute when you worry about me," I rasp.

"Someone has to," she jokes, and it's clear she has no idea how hard her seemingly innocent statement hits home.

"You should know..." I dip my gaze to her lips. "It's not the food that's hot."

"What is it?" She retreats, but she doesn't return to her side of the table yet.

I'm rewarded a few seconds longer with her close proximity, so I inhale extra whiffs of her perfume while I can. "It's the syrup on your shirt."

Addie glances down, but her expression is obstructed from my view by her short and wavy strands drawing a curtain around her face. "Great," she mumbles and slowly steps back to her seat, swiping furiously at the spot with the wet end of the napkin she just used on my cheek.

And the scene—for whatever unholy, pathetic reason—turns me on even more. She's gripping her breast, for fuck's sake.

I'm a mere pitiful mortal.

I clear my throat and shift, wincing as the pain from my stiffy jolts me. "Please stop. You're killing me," I manage.

"I have to get it out before it sets. Then again, it's syrup. It's going to take a lot more than water to clean it. I need dish soap or some—"

"I'll buy you a new shirt. Please just stop."

She finally glances up and idly sets the napkin down.

"You have no idea, do you?"

"About how to get a stain out? Of course, I do."

I shake my head, and the movement feels like it happens in slow motion, as if I'm moving through quicksand. "You have no idea what you do to me, Lockhart."

chapter
twenty-three

ADDIE

I COULD BECOME addicted to him.

Owen kisses like it's an art form. Each swipe of his tongue and caress of his fingers along my skin is special as he worships me.

I'm well aware of how in tune he is with my body, and I have the acute experience of how easily he made me come apart etched on my brain and body forever.

But more than that, I could grow obsessed with the way he looks at me. His eyes bore into me like he's seeing me through a tunnel. Like he sees nothing but me.

When he says romantic—sometimes even dirty—things and pairs it with this look, the wall I've built around my heart crumbles as if it's made of clay.

"How is everything tasting?"

It requires a beat for us to pause our staring contest, and in sync, he and I turn toward the server. "Great," he says, his voice strained.

"Perfect," I mumble around the lump in my throat.

"Saving any room for dessert tonight?" she asks, and her expectant gaze bounces from me to Owen and back again.

My stomach rolls with need, but it's not for dessert. Not of the sugar variety, anyway.

"I think that's all for tonight, don't you, Lockhart?" His eyes darken until they reach the most mesmerizing shade of forest green.

My words stumble over the ball of disappointment in my throat, so I nod, instead.

After all, this is my doing. He's made it clear time and again how much he wants this—how desperately he wants me—but I've asked him to wait.

I'm the one who's in control, and as much as I normally enjoy the responsibility, I'm tired of letting it keep me from what I want.

And what I want is Owen Conrad.

THE CARPET between the foot of the bed and the fireplace gets a workout as I pace back and forth in my hotel room, the scent of fresh linens filling my senses from the plug-in in the corner.

The color of the palm tree wallpaper on all four walls matches the forest green of Owen's eyes when I left.

He paid the bill, and I just freaking left.

Did I even say thank you to him? I'm really not great at that, as it turns out.

I pick up my phone, then drop it on the bed. After a few more paces, I scoop it back up again as Maren's words from earlier this week play in my head on repeat.

"You like him, even if you hate that you like him."

She was right. Liking him—and acting on it—will lead to nothing but trouble for me, but is the *what-if* worth it? Is not knowing what we could be worth the possible backlash at work?

"Shit," I mutter as I tap on my screen to make a call.

Owen answers on the first ring, and at the sound of his voice, I clench my thighs together, my skin sizzling with the rumble of his simple greeting.

I blow out an unsteady breath. "I'm ready to beg, okay?"

"What room are you in?" He follows his question with what I can only discern as a strangled grunt.

"Riverview Inn and Suites, room 115." I resume pacing. "Were you already on your way back to Sapphire Creek? How long will it take for you to turn around?"

Silence answers me.

"Owen?" I pull the phone back and realize he's ended the call. *What the hell?*

The man is simply incorrigible! He insists I beg, and when I tell him I'm ready, he disappears. What kind of game is that?

The no-good, frustrating giant with too-big muscles and an eye-twitching personality. How dare he be so—

A knock on the door sounds, interrupting the tirade of unsavory things I'd like to say to him next time I see him.

But when I open the door and find him leaning on the frame, I nearly swallow my tongue. My tirade won't be necessary after all.

"How did you get here so fast?"

"I've been waiting in the parking lot for your call." Owen steps into the room, and I move backward with every foot he eats up, matching him stride for stride. "And I'm damn glad you did."

"Really?" The word leaves my mouth in a squeak.

"I've been waiting for you for days—maybe even years, if I'm being honest with you and myself." He rams his fingers into my hair as my back hits the grooves of the fireplace, the mantel hovering above my head. "I'm a mess. I think about you nonstop. You're all I see during class. I don't know what you've done to me, Lockhart, but I fucking love it."

Gasping, I cling to his shirt until I dig my knuckles into his ab muscles.

"Beg for me," he says, but it's more of a plea too. "Beg for my mouth. My touch. The way I make you feel. Beg for *me*," he whispers, maintaining a firm twelve inches between our lips.

"Kiss me, Owen. Please." Did that come from me? I don't sound like myself. My voice is breathy and dripping with lust. "I need you to kiss me. I just... I need you."

I never thought the day would come where I'd beg Owen Conrad to kiss me... but here we are.

And I don't regret a single second.

"That's right, baby." His hold on my hair tightens on either side of my head, the extra tension heady. He's clearly hanging on by a thread—or a strand, in this case—and it's turning me on, hurling me into levels of horny I've never succumbed to. "Tell me how badly you need me to kiss you."

"So damn bad," I say on an exhale as he presses his body against mine. "Please. I can't take it any longer. I need you to freaking kiss me before I explode."

A low growl erupts from deep in his chest, and it vibrates between us. He shifts his hold on me, dropping his large hand to cup my cheek. "Finally," he rasps and leans in, but I don't angle my face to the side in time.

The bill of his hat hits my forehead, and I wince.

"Fuck. Sorry." He releases my hair and swivels his hat until it rests backward on his head, the bill out of sight and no longer a problem.

"You should wear your hat backward from now on," I say softly.

"Yeah?"

"That way, I can easily kiss you whenever I want."

"Done," he says without hesitation, and I believe him. He means it, and I don't think my heart could soar any higher without leaping from my body altogether.

"Kiss me already." My toes curl, and I bite the corner of my lip. "And Owen? Pull my hair again. *Hard.*"

He rams both hands into my hair, sweeping the short strands

away from my face, and he fuses his mouth to mine in a kiss so delicious, I see not only stars, but rainbows and unicorns too.

Owen kisses me with fervor until the small vase of pink flowers and the picture frame next to it rattle on the mantel above my head.

I sink into him, wrapping my arms around his waist, and he yanks on my hair until the sting trickles down my spine with pleasure.

He meets my request with flying colors.

"Do you want to know what else I want?" I manage between breaths and hot kisses.

"Tell me."

"I want you to make me scream like you did the other night at the dance studio, but..."

He drags his lips across my jawline, grazing his teeth along my skin, and my eyes roll into the back of my head. "But, what?"

I moan as his fingertips dance along the column of my throat.

My lips part in preparation for another kiss, but he keeps his mouth a few centimeters away. He's toying with me, and the sensations it produces flit through my core in small bursts of arousal.

"But, what, angel?" he presses.

"I want you to... make me scream, but this time, while you... fuck me." My eyelids flutter open.

His body jolts, and the hand at my throat slips to the back of my neck, clinging to me like I'm the only thing keeping him upright. "I fucked you with my mouth and fingers."

I fist his shirt and bring the tip of my nose to his. "Tonight, I want *this*." I drop my free hand between his legs and cup his large —and very hard—length.

"If you're sure..."

I meet his gaze. "I trust you, Owen."

His next kiss is all-consuming and hungry, and a zip of desire rips through my desperate core.

The items on the mantel rattle again as he wraps his arms around my waist and engulfs me. Turning us around, he drops his hands to cup my ass.

I'm so dazed, I don't immediately realize him literally sweeping me off me feet. I'm no longer on the floor. Instead, I climb higher and higher until I'm able to wrap my legs around him.

With half a step, he reaches the end of the bed and lays me down, his lips still locked on mine.

He's everywhere.

I'm wrapped in Owen, hot and safe and turned on.

His cologne, his hands, his mouth. It's everything I didn't know I'd been missing in my life.

He slides his hand down my stomach and inside the waistband of my leggings, my labored breaths echoing across the room.

The soft lighting from the lamps on each nightstand cast a glow over his features, and his lips twitch when he sinks a finger inside me. His body remains halfway on me as he quickly works me into a frenzy.

I gasp and moan as a second finger joins the first, and my hips buck into the air, the tension rising between my legs.

He increases his pace as I ride his hand. His body moves with mine, sliding up and down the bed as if he's chasing his own pleasure.

"Oh, Owen!" My eyes fly open as my stomach clenches just before my body trembles with release. In an attempt to hold on to him, I throw my hand around his neck and knock his hat off in the process.

That thing has been a hazard tonight.

I melt into the bed as my climax rocks my world, and my head spins.

"Loosening you up like this has become my new favorite thing." Owen kisses the corner of my parted lips.

"I'm definitely a fan, but don't you dare think for a second that

I'll go soft on you because of this." My words of warning would mean a lot more if I weren't still squeezing his hand between my legs or if I weren't so breathless.

"I wouldn't dream of it," he plays along, smirking.

He knows exactly what he does to me—he turns me into a puddle. A happy, satisfied puddle of bliss. A greedy one too.

"I think I need more loosening up," I say with a hint of a challenge. "I'm still... so... tense."

"You drive me crazy," he says against my lips, then works my loose shirt over my head.

With eager fingers, I jerk his belt loose.

Our movements grow hungry, our breaths heavy.

"And you—" I clamp my mouth shut as he slides down the front of my writhing body, my leggings in tow. "You surprise me at every turn."

"Better be a good thing." He chucks my leggings over his shoulder, leaving me in nothing but my pink-and-white bra and panty set.

"Definitely." I mean it too.

I've meant everything I've said to him tonight.

Each time I scream his name while I'm at his mercy, it feels unexpectedly right.

He rakes his hooded gaze over my body, and I use the pause to my advantage.

His appearance is wild and free, his belt unfastened and the zipper of his pants resting open in a V. Red boxers peek through, and my mouth waters.

"Get over here," I demand.

"Yes, ma'am."

As he finishes undressing, I unhook my bra and wiggle out of my panties. My racing pulse further spikes when he retrieves a condom from his back pocket, drops his boxers, and works the rubber over his solid cock.

He's huge.

My gulp is more audible than I intended, and his eyes snap to mine.

"You ready, angel?"

chapter
twenty-four

OWEN

I TEASE my covered shaft while she nods in answer to my question.

I'm throbbing. Aching. Desperate.

The urge to fill her—to feel her squeeze every inch of me—makes me dizzy. This woman is otherworldly. Special. Fucking Sexy, with a capital *F* and *S*.

I've never wanted anyone as badly as I want Addison Lockhart.

She scoots to the edge of the bed, her legs spread and giving me the perfect view of her swollen flesh. She's so damn soaked.

Addie responds so fucking well to me, and I'm as afraid as I am excited that I'll never get enough.

"You love when I touch you, don't you?" I whisper, almost daring her to deny the truth. "You've refused this for so long, and you regret it, don't you?"

"I don't."

I cock a brow as I keep my feet rooted by the fireplace.

Her gaze is locked on my fingers trailing over the head of my pulsing dick. "Waiting has made this week that much better." She gulps again and flicks her gaze up to meet mine. "More delicious, wouldn't you agree?"

"Fuck," I growl and kneel before her.

Unsurprisingly, she's right. The last several days of keeping my mouth off her have been excruciating, but it's that much more satisfying now. All the tension is finally going to break.

I kiss the inside of her thigh, nipping at the birthmark there much like I did the night at the dance studio.

She grabs hold of my head by my hair and tugs. I skim my nose along her smooth skin until I reach her quivering sex, where I enjoy a taste.

I need her coating my tongue.

"Oh," she pants and grips my hair tighter.

I place my hands on either side of her and slowly rise, nipping and kissing her stomach and ending with the valley between her breasts.

I'm so hard, my vision blurs. I'll go blind if I don't bury myself inside her already, but tasting all of her awards me a different kind of pleasure.

Addie lies back onto the bed, her legs still dangling over the edge. I capture a beaded nipple between my teeth and tease her until her back arches into me.

"Yes." She toys with her other tit in her hand, and I cover her fingers with mine while we play together. "Oh, yes."

Her pants reach my ears like my favorite music.

This is already an experience I can't describe, and I haven't even been inside her yet.

I suck on her nipple and knead her other breast, my palm still over her small, delicate hand, while my dick bobs in sensual pain against her leg.

After I release her from my mouth, I curl an arm underneath her and slide her up onto the bed. Then I nestle myself between her legs, my tip immediately finding her with ease.

"I need you, Owen. What have you done to me?" She smooths her hair back, then leans up to run her hand down my abs.

She places kisses across my shoulder too, and my chest stirs.

"I was just going to ask you the same," I manage.

When she drapes her hand over my cock, her jaw drops, and I cover her mouth with mine.

She eases back, taking me with her and lining us up.

Every muscle in my body strains to go slow. To make this good for her. To do this right.

I inch only the tip inside her before pulling out.

"Don't go easy on me now, Owen." She shakes her head. "Fuck me like you mean it."

My arms buckle, and most of my weight drops onto her, surely about to crush her.

She moans and writhes beneath me with her feet dancing up and down my legs, urging me to hurry.

"I'm going to fuck every reason you've ever hated me right out of you," I vow.

The kiss I give her is a punishing one. I kiss her hard until it's painful, and I surge into her wet, dripping heat until my cock is drenched in Addie Lockhart.

"That's it, baby." I thrust into her again, instantly drunk on the way she stretches to take me in full. "Take all of me. Just like that."

"Yes. God, yes." Her eyes roll into the back of her head as I slam inside her, rocking into the hilt of her over and over again, until I'm sure the sounds of our slapping bodies can be heard outside.

"This is how you want it, isn't it?" I grunt. "Deep and hard."

"It's so much." She licks her lips and whimpers, her fingers digging into my ass.

My muscles clench and loosen underneath her grip with every thrust.

"So fucking good, angel." I slide up and down her body with each movement, her hard nipples raking against my skin.

I'm going to explode. There's a good damn chance I won't even survive this.

There's nothing better after this, anyway. Nothing will ever compare, so I'd go out on top, that's for sure.

"Ride me." I flip us over and position Addie on top of me.

She squirms until she straddles me, and it's a good thing she's so flexible. With her being so small compared to my large frame, her knees don't even reach the bed on either side of me.

"You're so big," she says, shifting on top of me and digging her knees into my thighs in the process.

"Thanks," I toss back with a proud smirk. I think my dick grows even harder too, although I didn't think that'd be possible.

"I'm talking about your build." Nothing in her airy voice indicates my body size is what she's referring to.

"I know what you meant." I wink and grip her hips to help her onto my bobbing cock. It glistens from her wetness.

I adjust my hips on the bed, when I feel the dampness she left behind before we switched positions. She's fucking soaked.

Dear Jesus, she's going to kill me.

"Ride me," I repeat as she finally sinks onto me, swallowing every inch of my cock with ease. "Ride me until you come again. I want to feel you come on me."

"Oh-kay," she sputters as she uses my chest for balance, her nails clawing at my skin with desperation.

She goes slow, establishing a steady, easy rhythm, like she's acquainting herself with my size from this deeper angle. Her eyelids flutter each time her hips meet mine, and I keep my unwavering gaze on her every movement.

The lick of her lips.

The small beads of sweat between her full breasts.

The peek of her mound when she rises.

With each second ticking by, she ruins me more and more.

"Owen..." Her mouth falls into an *O* like she's about to say my name again.

I pulse inside her as she works her hips back and forth, slowing down further, and I snap. I need more. Faster. Harder. Everything in between.

"I can't... It's too much... I—" She loses her words to a drawn-out moan as she rises off me. Most of her weight settles onto her hands on my chest, instead.

My tip twitches against her thigh, begging for more.

I tighten my hold on her hips, so she doesn't go far. "You can do better than that, Lockhart."

"Is that a dare?" she says, and a twinkle sparkles in her eyes.

"If you want it to be."

She narrows her eyes, which are no longer lazily blinking open and closed. Without another word, she takes me again and rides me faster, just as I need her to.

I'm going to fucking combust.

Her tits sway sideways as she leans forward and jerks her hips up and down, the walls of her sex clenching around me.

"That's my girl," I whisper, and she must like the sound of being my girl, because her cry leaves her sinful mouth in a higher pitch than I've ever heard from her.

My words must fuel her, as she rides me like chasing ecstasy is her new profession.

I slide my hands up and down her bouncing thighs, refraining from stealing control from her. She's too mesmerizing like this. It'd be a crime to take it away from her.

Addie flips her hair back and gives me the perfect view of her face as her thighs hold me hostage, practically squeezing the life from my cock.

Then her orgasm bursts free, unleashing chaos with a mix of her strangled cries and quivering limbs.

I follow suit before my jaw comes unhinged and I break a

tooth. I clenched my teeth so hard to tamp down the urge to come, I was on the cusp of real damage to my physical well-being.

Addie glues her cheek to my stuttering chest, and I wrap my arms around her, holding her here just a little bit longer.

My next breaths don't come easily. I'm fucking spent.

"Well? Do you still hate me?" I manage.

With her head still on my chest, her words are muffled. "If I say yes, does that mean we can do that again?"

I chuckle, but it's a weary sound. "I'm nothing if not diligent when it comes to a promise."

"I've noticed," she whispers.

I'm dizzy with the whirlwind of this evening.

I'd only been at the restaurant because Whitney was desperate to be out in the world and away from her stuffy duplex, which she claimed was trying to eat her alive. According to her, the walls had been closing in on her earlier this afternoon.

I was happy to take her and Huck out, but what started as an innocent dinner turned into so much more after I ran into Addie.

This feels like the beginning of... something.

And while it's too soon to know what that something is, I'm excited to find out.

twenty-five

ADDIE

IN THE BATHROOM of the inn, I dig a tank top out of the bag I threw together just before I left. Had I planned this trip with more than a minute's notice, I would've made a list of things I'd need and crossed them off as I went.

At the very least, I would've neatly folded my clothes, but tearing them off the hangers and tossing them inside this bag was the best I could do with little time to spare.

I also would've packed something a little sexier than this old tank top.

Then again, this whole night has been unexpected. No amount of planning in advance could've prepared me for what happened with Owen.

Did I really ask him to fuck me like he meant it? And did I actually ride him like my life depended on it?

It was one of those moments in a journey of self-discovery that requires the top spot of a highlights section. Before tonight— before I climbed onto my co-worker and gyrated my hips like a hula dancer—I hadn't realized I'm still on a journey to find myself, but now that I've experienced such a phenomenon, it's hard to say I'm not.

Being on top of Owen, harnessing the power of my body and sexuality to suck him dry, was, in a word, *spectacular*. I felt things I'd never felt before—raw, thrilling arousal.

I was completely myself, and it seemed to hit all the right buttons for him.

He came while he was still inside me. He'd jerked and pulsed with so much vigor, it was a surprise he'd been able to walk just thirty minutes prior.

He'd turned red and feral, his eyes an even darker shade of green than they were at the end of dinner.

And he held me like I'd run away otherwise.

To be honest, I thought I might want to, but as I fluff my new hair and tame a few of the tangles, I don't have any itch to flee. There's no sense of dread in my throat or a wave of nausea through my stomach.

For once, my mind isn't racing with a million thoughts and responsibilities.

I'm at peace, like this was always supposed to happen between Owen and me. I don't know how to feel about that, but it's a contemplation for future me.

Over the last couple of weeks, I've come to realize I should take it day by day when it comes to Owen. He always surprises me, so it's useless to try and think ahead.

I use a damp washcloth to dab at the corners of my eyes for the runaway mascara, then apply a thin layer of lip balm before I exit, anticipation singeing my nerve endings as if the last few minutes away from him were enough for me to already miss him.

My heart thumps at the first glance of him.

Owen stands next to the bed as he tugs his shirt in place over his jeans. I catch him just in time for a glimpse of his abs, each hard muscle carved to perfection.

Once the fabric settles into place, I realize he's fully dressed, shoes and all. He's even wearing his hat, and while my chest warms with the sight of it on backward, just as he promised, my stomach drops.

He's clearly ready to go, while I stand in the bathroom doorway in nothing but my tank top and panties. "Are you leaving?"

He turns to face me. "Yes."

"Oh." I shift onto my bare right heel. "Right. You should go. Why would you stay in Savannah for the night? It's not like we should cuddle until the sun rises and enjoy French toast in the morning. You definitely don't want to come to the spa with me, either. Or maybe you do. Do you like facials?"

Owen rounds the corner of the bed and sits on the edge.

"Because guys can like facials. We all have acne and buildup on our faces. It's natural," I continue rambling. "Facials are for everyone."

Did my voice grow louder? I'm yelling, aren't I? Although I believe what I'm saying, I don't know why I'm saying it as if I'm on a soap box, enlightening a room full of judgy people.

"A facial sounds fun."

"You can come," I offer and fidget with my hands. "I might add a manicure to my appointment too. I've destroyed my cuticles over the last two weeks from all the stress."

"You deserve to relax," he says coolly, completely the opposite of how I'm feeling.

I should let him go. We did what we did, and it's over now. Cuddling and getting breakfast together are two things real couples do, and we are not one.

Or are we?

I've never had sex with anyone who wasn't my confirmed boyfriend, but it feels too neurotic and inappropriate to ask Owen "What are we?" right now.

Or is it very appropriate?

He's the one who insisted a single night with me wouldn't be enough. It wouldn't be totally out of line if I were to ask.

"I'll need to head back in the morning to help Lottie at the studio," he says, thankfully interrupting my emotional spiral. "She's hosting a special brunch event."

"A Boozy Brunch—I've seen posts for it on social media."

"That's the one."

"So, you're going to leave in the morning, then?" I lift a brow, internally cringing over how hopeful I sound. There is no subtle bone in my body right now. Owen turned my limbs to mush with his magic penis.

"If that's all right with you, angel." He threads his fingers together in his lap, again as cool as a slice of watermelon.

It's unnerving, but I try to muster a modicum, at the very least, of nonchalance. Shrugging, I simply say, "Fine."

His lip twitches, and I can tell he so badly wants to smirk.

"It's just that you have your hat and shoes on, so when you said you were leaving, I thought you meant right now."

"I did—I do." He rises and meets me toe to toe, his large frame towering over me. He captures my chin between his thumb and forefinger, and with his mouth hovering over mine, he adds, "I'm craving ice cream. I was hoping we could go get some together."

"Oh. Um..." I gulp. "I'll put pants on."

"Good idea." He winks, then plants a heavy kiss on my lips.

Heat spreads across my cheeks and down to my core. By the time he breaks our connection, I'm floating, and I forget what I'm supposed to be doing.

I forget all thoughts that don't involve stripping him naked and climbing on top of him again.

"Pants, Lockhart." He nods to his side, where my leggings landed after he tossed them over his shoulder earlier.

"I know." I stick my tongue out as I bend over to scoop them up. "Where do you want to go for ice cream? Leopold's is closed, but we could try somewhere else."

"I have somewhere in mind, if you like surprises."

"You'll have to tell me, because I'm driving."

"I can drive."

"I know you can—obviously—but I'll be driving now."

"This is my idea. Seems like I should drive."

I shimmy my leggings into place and bring my hands to my hips. "Then have fun with your idea alone. I'll wait here."

"You are the most stubborn person I know."

"Strong-willed and independent, you mean? That's okay. People mistake such qualities for stubbornness all the time." I flash him a sarcastic smile.

"Fine." He shakes his head. "You drive; I'll give directions."

"YOU COULD'VE JUST SAID Dairy Queen." I roll into the drive-thru. "It's hardly a hidden gem you needed to surprise me with."

"I like surprising you, especially with my huge—"

"Don't," I warn.

"—dick." From the passenger's side, Owen exaggerates an exhale. "Damn. Feels good to finally finish a dirty sentence like that."

Flashes of his very large appendage fitting so tightly between my legs in the best, most delicious way render my body hostage.

My skin tingles with remnants of his touch and his kisses.

He gripped my hips so hard I'm sure I'll bruise by the morning, and I ate up every second. For the first time in my life, I actually wish we would've recorded ourselves just so I'd have proof that it happened.

And so I wouldn't forget a single thing, not that there's any chance of that happening, but still.

A sex video? I'm wishing for scandalous sex videos now?

What spell does Owen have me under?

I pull the window down to prepare for our turn as soon as the sedan in front of us moves forward. "Doesn't relate to why this would be a surprise."

"Sometimes, it's all about the little things."

"You just said it's the huge things—or thing, in this case."

He throws his head back and laughs. The hearty sound echoes out my open window, drifting into the night, and I smile too. I don't remember a time when I've had that much of an effect on his funny bone. He and I don't exactly have a similar sense of humor.

"I knew you thought it was huge," he says as I assume the sedan's spot at the speaker, which crackles with static before a voice greets us.

"Order whenever you're ready," they say.

"What do you want?" I ask Owen as I scan the menu, contemplating what mood I'm in—fruity or chocolatey.

"If I said you, is that sappy, romantic, or both?"

"Now is not the time for such grand ponderings, Owen," I hiss, but my smile is natural. I can't stop it any more than I can stop my heart from beating so fast because of him.

"Fine," he draws out. "I'll take a cookie dough blizzard, please."

"I'm thinking strawberry cheesecake," I say, but it's mostly to myself.

With our orders in place, I curve around the path toward the window, where Owen reaches his long arm across my chest and hands the scrawny teen his credit card. Once the window closes, I shrug Owen off me and declare, "I could've paid."

"You're driving. It's only fair that I pay."

I tsk as the window slides open again. I can't easily reach the two cups, so I use my window to leverage myself and rise halfway out of my seat.

Which is when I feel a pinch on my ass.

Yelping, I nearly drop the sweet cargo onto the asphalt outside. "What do you think you're doing?" I whisper-scream toward Owen as I nestle the two treats inside my cupholders.

"Wasn't it obvious? Your ass was right there for the squeezing, and if you didn't think I'd take the opportunity, then you don't know me at all." He snorts and holds his shoulders high, clearly proud of himself.

He's ridiculous and goofy, but he's also safe and strong. I like the mix of qualities in him. They work as well as the wild combinations at the restaurant earlier tonight.

And I like that he can't help himself around me. How long has it been since I felt so desired? Since a guy just couldn't keep his hands off me?

Too long.

If I were told two weeks ago that Owen Conrad would be the one to end my dry spell, I would've cackled until tears streamed down my face.

But peeking over at him, even as he licks the melting ice cream off the edge of his cup like an animal, I'm glad it was him.

twenty-six

OWEN

"Who was your favorite teacher in high school?" Addie sticks her plastic spoon in her ice cream and holds a finger up. "And don't say Señora Gomez. She can't hear you, so there's no need to kiss her ass."

"She always gives me extra Spanish candies, though." Even when she was my teacher and not my co-worker, Señora Gomez would sneak me a few extra pieces because, according to her, I was *muy grande* and needed more food than the other kids.

She wasn't wrong.

"You brownnosing chump."

"You're one to talk," I toss back. "Weren't you voted teacher's pet four years in a row?"

"Someone had to take the title. Why not me?" She shrugs, completely unbothered by the superlative that others might consider insulting. "Besides, I was good at being the teacher's pet."

"I respect it." I use the back of my hand to wipe excess ice cream from my mouth.

"Use a napkin, for crying out loud." She reaches over to the nightstand, plucks a napkin we got from Dairy Queen, and hands it over. "Your favorite teacher—someone we don't currently work with."

"Coach Stevens," I say without hesitation.

"Your old baseball coach?"

I nod as I set my empty cup onto the nightstand on my side of the bed. "We still keep in touch. I even went to his daughter's wedding over the summer. In fact, he tried to set me up with her a couple of years ago. Said I already felt like family, and he'd be ecstatic to make it official."

"What happened there?"

"I guess I'm just not into women who are nice to me." I throw my arm around Addie's shoulder and give it a squeeze.

"Who is?" she teases back, playing along as voices drift in from outside.

Since we returned with our treats in hand, guests have roamed the halls, likely tuckered out from a day of exploring the history of Savannah and walking along the river.

In the parking lot outside our window, car doors click shut, and cell phones ring. The faint music from the room next door offers a quiet lullaby for us as well.

The world is still awake, thrumming with energy and a heartbeat of its own, as Addie and I come alive in here. We're getting to know each other in ways that have my blood pumping and my pulse skyrocketing.

I've never enjoyed the company of a woman like this, but then again, Addison Lockhart is no ordinary woman.

"Your turn in the hot seat." I follow Addie's tongue as she licks her bottom lip and stows her cup away, shifting out of my hold. "Is it true you once dated a professional zombie?"

Her eyes widen. "Where did you hear that?"

"Teacher's lounge. I hear everything in there. My secret is to pretend to make coffee so the others don't suspect I'm eavesdropping. They usually forget I'm even standing there."

"You're either an evil genius or you're ridiculous, but I'm confused because you've put me in some kind of sexy trance."

"All of the above," I proudly offer. "But talk of sexy trances will not get you out of answering this burning question. Did you or did you not go out with a guy who dresses up as a zombie every single day to go work at a haunted house year-round?"

"We did not date," she asserts.

"I heard they did pop-ups all around Georgia. Did all the traveling turn you off?" I playfully joke.

The tips of her ears turn red as she throws her head back and groans.

"Oh!" I snap. "Did he come to bed in full makeup and costume? Zombies don't do it for you, do they, Lockhart?"

"You are relentless!" She tosses her hands up. "Okay, here's the sordid story, and please don't make me regret telling you this."

I bounce on the bed, jostling her next to me, but I can't help it. I'm more excited for these details than I am the World Series.

"I met Drew at a convenience store in Atlanta during a school field trip to the CNN headquarters. He was wearing a suit and tie, and he was totally charming. We hit it off over our love of Skittles, and he asked for my number to keep in touch."

"Do zombies have phones?"

She glares. "Do you want to hear the rest of this?"

I make a motion with my hand to zip my lips tight.

"Long story short, he asked me out, and we went to dinner, where he cried over his divorce for an hour. As it turned out, he'd only been wearing a suit the day I met him because he was going to meet his ex-wife and attorney."

"So, what was the problem? He was single, at least."

"Being single is important, but it's not exactly the only criteria I need."

"What else do you need?"

"I need guys to not try to come to bed in their zombie costumes."

"I knew it!"

"For the record, I did not learn this detail about him first-hand," she reassures me. "Evidently, it was one of the reasons he and his ex divorced."

"Sorry that didn't work out for you. He sounds like he really needed a win." I stifle a laugh behind my hand, sure my face is red. Pressure builds behind my eyes.

Addie smacks my chest, and I lose the battle. My laughter rips from my throat. "It's not funny! This is my life," she bursts. "And to be honest, Zombie Drew might not even be the worst experience I've ever had."

"For the love of God, please tell me more."

"For your information, it's not polite to laugh at other people's misery," she clips, but I don't miss the twitch in her lips. She's enjoying this as much as I am.

"What did I tell you before? I'm not polite." I lay a clumsy kiss on her mouth, enjoying the faint strawberry taste on her tongue, until I work a giggle loose.

"Fine!" She pushes me back onto my side of the bed. "This is not exactly funny, so you'll be sorry you asked. I haven't told anyone this before, either, so give me a break."

The increasing gravity in her voice as she talks causes a stutter in my pulse, and my smile melts away like the remaining few bites of ice cream in her cup.

"My last boyfriend was Stewart. Things were okay between us, but it wasn't anything special. We were never going to work forever, but he cut the relationship short when he told me I should be more like my mother." She gulps and averts her gaze, her tone hesitant.

It's clear this confession is hard for her.

Hearing it is hard for me too.

"He told me I should be like my mom, who's more fun and less uptight. Maybe if I loosened up like her, he'd love me."

I furrow my brows, and the urge to demand his full name so I could throw my first uppercut is on the tip of my tongue.

But she laughs. It holds no life or humor in it like the one she let loose earlier, and I hate that this Stewart is the reason for it. "I guess he did me a favor in the end. I got out of that relationship much sooner than I'd expected, so there's that."

"He didn't know what he had, Lockhart. You're funny and kind and loyal. You're—"

"You don't have to do that." She waves me off. "I didn't tell you just so I could be showered in compliments. I guess I just told you because it felt like it was finally time to let that go."

"I meant what I said about you," I whisper. "And I'm glad to be the one to take this burden off you."

She meets my gaze, and the balls of her cheeks redden.

For the next few seconds, we stare at each other, both of us frozen.

Our breaths even sync up.

She has no idea how special she is, and I can't stand the wasted time I spent teasing and verbally sparring with her, when I should've been worshipping the ground beneath her. She deserves nothing less.

Then again, had we not been at each other's throats, we wouldn't be us, would we?

Arguing with her is one of my favorite things about us.

"I think we've talked about me enough tonight." She clears her throat and peers down at her fingers in her lap. "I want to know more about you. I mean, we've known each other for basically our entire lives, but I don't know that much about you."

"What do you want to know?"

"Is everything too much?"

I release a soft chuckle. "You won't be impressed."

"Try me."

"Two of my favorite foods are steak and peaches, not at the same time. I love being near water, whether it's in an ocean, river, or simply a glass." I shift on the bed, and she remains stock-still, her attention solely on me. "I enjoy helping my family with new babies, technology problems, or painting a new studio. And I'm happy to be teaching. It's exactly what I'm supposed to be doing with my life."

She drops her gaze and uses her finger to trace the scar along my knee. "You don't... regret not playing baseball?"

"Some days, I miss playing professionally. More than anything, I miss the team." A smile tugs on my lips as I recall too many good times to count. I'd need a year to relay them all to her. "But when I tore my ACL for the second time, and the doctor told me my career was over, I was relieved."

She arches a brow.

"Here's the truth—I only ever pursued baseball because I was good at it. It was fun, and it challenged me in ways I needed when I first started. When others told me I was good, I just listened and went where they suggested. I didn't stop to consider what I really wanted, because according to my dad, I'd be batshit to throw away all my potential. He was my biggest fan."

"Sounds like a lot of pressure from him."

"I think it was the only way he knew how to connect with me." My smile slips into more of a frown as I internally consider how far apart we've grown since my surgery. Without baseball, it's like he doesn't know what to talk to me about, so we end up discussing my sisters, Huck, or the lawn.

He taught me to rid my yard of weeds by spraying them with a mix of a gallon of white vinegar, a cup of salt, and a tablespoon of dish soap.

"Anyway." I sigh. "Being told I couldn't play anymore was like giving me permission to finally chase what I really wanted to do. I just didn't realize until that moment in the doctor's office that I was ever looking for permission." I dip my head and swallow, my pulse throbbing in my leg. "I've never admitted this to anyone before."

"Your family doesn't know?" Surprise is heavy in her question.

"They kind of assumed I was always too devastated to talk about it, so they tiptoed around the topic until it became old news, next to Whitney's unexpected pregnancy, Lottie's new studio, and Laurel's bright future in medicine." Another sigh escapes me like admitting all of this out loud is draining for me.

The truth is, I don't remember the last time I even talked this much about myself to one person. I'm more of a listener.

"Why don't you tell them the truth?" she asks, and her tone is so gentle. So free of judgment or any kind of demand. She's genuinely curious.

I open and close my mouth for a beat before I finally say, "It's never felt important enough to share the truth with them. Anytime we're together, there's always some other crisis, and at this point, it's been too long to clear the air now."

"I think I know what you mean." Addie places her delicate hand on my veiny forearm, her touch soft but firm all at once.

And I kiss her.

Each swipe of my tongue massages hers with gratitude and pleasure and everything in between. It's no ordinary kiss—none of my kisses with Addie have been.

It's like each one tells a story, and I'm not done exploring the next chapter.

chapter
twenty-seven

ADDIE

I BLINK ONCE, twice, three times until my eyelids are strong enough to stay open on their own. The sun poking through the blinds on the windows makes it difficult, though, as does the sinewy forearm draped over half my face.

Owen.

We fell asleep talking. We had a fierce debate over the episode of *Shark Tank* we turned on. As it turns out, he's a big fan too, and we spent over an hour betting each other on which Shark would make an offer.

Some time after that, I awoke with the moon high in the sky, and the world outside was quiet. The music from our neighbors had been silenced, and the surrounding guests seemed to have been tucked in for the night.

But I was wide awake, with one thing in mind—the thing rubbing against my ass as Owen spooned me from behind.

I couldn't sleep. I could barely breathe as heat flooded my core. My lower belly ached with lust for him.

And once again, he delivered.

His eyelids had lifted but remained at half-mast as he slid his hand onto my stomach and inside my panties.

It was electric—and loud. I was louder than when I hang upside down on a roller coaster.

Owen does that to me. He pushes all the right buttons in every sense, and he drives me crazy.

Next to me, he groans and flops onto his back. "Why are you awake?" he mumbles.

"You haven't opened your eyes. How do you know I'm awake?" I lift a brow, but he still doesn't look at me.

"I have many talents, as you experienced last night. Seeing through my eyelids is yet another skill I possess."

I squint, but he remains the same.

"I actually just took a wild guess." He pries one eye open and smiles a smile that reaches into my chest and tugs on my fragile heart. "I figured you'd be asleep until tomorrow. I wore you out pretty good."

I shift onto my side to face him, angling my body toward him like a flower rising toward the sun. "I'm in good shape."

"In that case..." He turns onto his side as well and trails his fingertips up and down my arm, leaving goose bumps in their wake. "Ready for round three? I shine in the mornings. Even before coffee, I'm damn good with my—*shit*."

I release the hold on my lip I had with my teeth as he peers over my shoulder and frowns.

With a sigh, Owen raises up, his frame nearly too large for this queen-sized bed. In truth, he'd probably make a king-sized bed look small. "It's almost nine thirty. I need to head back, or Lottie will have my ass."

"She could always set up, and you can take down." I slide the covers away from my body until I'm completely exposed. I've never slept naked before, but I might need to make a habit of it. It's quite freeing—or it just feels life-changing with Owen naked beside me too. "We could see about that third round..."

His gaze travels down the length of me, his eyes darkening more and more with each inch he drinks in.

"I could show you just how flexible I really am."

Something equal parts appreciative and sinister flashes across his expression. "You little temptress."

He draws me in for a slow kiss, and as I sink into him—as I start to believe I've won—he jerks back. I'm left with my mouth hanging open and my heart racing as he practically jumps off the bed.

"I need to... go." He holds his hands up, his chest heaving like this measure of self-restraint sucks up all his energy.

As he rounds the corner of the bed, his mumbled words are muffled. I'm too distracted by the bulging muscles in his arms and legs. His quads flex as he bends down for his pants, and when he faces me, his long, turgid cock points right at me like it's begging for me.

Excess saliva suddenly coats my tongue.

But once he's fully dressed, it hits me that he's not coming back to bed. He's leaving.

Owen is going back home to Sapphire Creek, where everyone knows us—where we work together. He's going back to reality, and I have to join him soon.

The same ball of dread settles in the pit of my stomach as it had last night when he was dressed, except he's actually leaving this morning.

Blood rushing to my ears drowns out the voices from outside. It muffles my own heartbeat as I consider our options.

"We have to keep this a secret," I blurt and hug the covers up to my chest, hiding.

I'm a coward, aren't I? Or am I being smart? Before last night, I knew the difference. In fact, I knew a lot of things, but after the night he and I shared, I barely know which way is up.

Owen blanches.

"I know how that sounds." I clutch the covers, and sweat builds on my upper lip.

"It sounds like I'm your dirty little experiment after all." His powerful shoulders sag.

I shake my head and lean forward, keeping the covers in place as I interlock my fingers around my legs. "It's not like that—believe me."

"Then what is it?" He sits on the edge of the desk and crosses both arms over his chest. He's only a few feet away, but right now, as he studies me with defeat clouding his eyes, he feels eons away.

"It's us exploring whatever this is." I point between us. "Owen, before I toss an explosive into the center of my life, I'd like to see if we could even turn into anything serious. I don't know if we even like each other that much. Do you? I mean, you could find you hate how much I ramble. You could find you're too turned off by my labeled pantry, or the excessive collection of soap in my bathroom. What if it turns out that you don't hold a candle to my obsession with Skittles?"

"I get your point."

"We need a test drive."

"I'm not a car."

I tilt my head.

He pushes off the desk, paces in a single circle, and sighs. "You're right, not about being turned off by anything you do, but the sentiment is compelling."

My exhale purges my muscles of tension, and a small smile spreads. "So, you agree to keep this a secret for now?"

He spreads his arms. "Take me for a spin, baby. I promise, I'm a smooth ride."

My grin is full-fledged as I throw the covers off and meet him at the edge of the bed, where we collide in a mix of heated kisses.

His hands roam over my bare body, squeezing and kneading and caressing like he's paying tribute to it.

Skin sizzling, I fall back and bring him down with me, but again, he flies upright with a drawn-out groan. "I have to..." He touches his lips, and I bite the inside of my cheek. "I don't know. I have to go... somewhere. Someone... needs me." His sharp inhale echoes across the room.

"Right." I trace my lip with my fingertip as I complete my hundredth perusal of him since yesterday.

"What, um..." He scratches the back of his head. "When is your spa appointment?"

"My what?" I hum.

"Aren't you going to the spa?"

I jump from the bed. "Oh! Oh my gosh. It's at ten thirty."

"Do you know where you're going?" He smirks.

I stick my tongue out at him and toss back, "Somewhere with someone."

"How mature."

"Oh, Lord. Less than a day with you, and I'm already stooping to your level."

He takes measured steps until he reaches me, and placing his thumb under my chin, he tips my head back to peer into my eyes. "It's much more fun down here."

With that, he sears a kiss to my lips, then backs away. His hand curls around the doorknob to leave, and I reach out to stop him.

"For the record..." I start. As many books and homework assignments as I've read, and as much as I normally talk, I'm struggling with words at the moment. "I don't hate your hair. I actually like it."

"I know." Sparks of amusement bounce in his clear eyes. "It was obvious how much you like it by how hard you pulled on it last night."

My next breath catches in my throat.

"See you soon—in secret—Lockhart." With a parting wink, he slips through the door, and I'm left with only my racing thoughts once again.

My mouth still tingles long after the door clicks shut. I tingle all over from him, and I don't know how I'll survive keeping my emotions in check when it doesn't feel like he and I are new.

It doesn't seem like we only just crossed the line, starting last Saturday. With Owen, it's as if we've been doing this all along, and the realization both excites and terrifies me.

My buzzing phone on the desk pulls me out of my stupor, and I cross the two feet to check it.

OWEN

Seriously, what spa are you going to this morning?

The Pampered Peach. Why?

I wait for the bubbles to show up to indicate he's typing, but they don't appear.

Once I'm dressed, I check again, but there's still no new message from him. I see an unanswered text from DeDe asking me to cat-sit Birdie. It might be the first time in history that I haven't immediately responded to a message, especially one asking for a favor.

But I still don't answer. Instead, I tuck my phone into my tote, sling the bag over my shoulder, and grab my key card on the way out.

Five minutes later, I arrive at the spa, and the moment I step inside the lobby, my body falls slack. I'm overtaken by the heavenly smell of peaches and soft sounds of nature, like a breeze rustling leaves and birds chirping. The sweet smell and relaxing ambiance speak to my soul—and aching bones.

When was the last time I pampered myself? When have I ever dedicated a whole weekend to myself?

This might be the first time in my life when I've truly, selfishly, proudly indulged, in more ways than one.

I just wish I would've sprung for the whole package. At the

very least, I should've added a massage with my facial, but baby steps. I'm new at this whole self-care thing.

"Good morning," the receptionist chirps. "How can I help you?"

"I have an appointment," I say as I slide toward the counter. "Addie Lockhart."

While she types on her computer, her flawless nails tick against the keys, filling the silence between us. "Ah, yes. You upgraded your package, correct?"

"Just a facial."

She taps some more, and her smile reaches her eyes as she says, "Your package now includes the works—facial, mani/pedi, and a hot stone massage. Already paid for."

"Paid for? There must be some kind of mistake." I fish my phone from my tote and pull up my banking app to confirm the purchase. With my lack of sleep this week, there is a solid chance I accidentally booked the wrong thing and paid in advance.

It sounds like something I'd do. Earlier this year, there was an incident where I found three boxes of wines and cheeses on my doorstep, only for me to realize I'd sleep-shopped. When more arrived the month afterward, I found out I'd even signed up for a membership.

"I don't think—" I'm cut off when a new message comes through.

OWEN

Enjoy a FULL relaxing day at the spa ;)

"He didn't," I mutter to myself, then glance up to the expectant receptionist, who's still smiling so wide her dimples nearly reach her ears. "I guess he did," I muse.

"Your man sounds like a keeper."

My heart flutters like the flapping wings of a thousand doves as I follow her through a door toward the lockers. I barely register her instructions for the waiting room, where I think I can I find cucumber water and snacks.

I float through the motions of undressing and tying a fluffy robe around my waist, my mind reeling with the idea of Owen Conrad being my man.

chapter
twenty-eight

OWEN

I DRIFT into the Tap and welcome the mix of woodsy smells in this rustic bar. Immediately, I'm enveloped with clouds of perfume from the older woman seated at one table, and to my left, Scarlett squawks with her customers, tapping her pen to her server pad to the rhythm of her animated tale.

I cross the scuffed and scratched hardwood floor, the marks evidence of years of local patronage, and I reach the bar as screeching bursts from the stage, where Matilda and Hunter set up the microphone.

It's karaoke night—a Sunday night tradition around here. I've frequented plenty of them since I moved back to Sapphire Creek, and they've mostly been the same. After the weekend I've had, though, this one feels different, and we haven't even started.

I'm lighter than I have been in a while, and it's all thanks to Addie.

A fucking feather isn't as light as me, and it's not just because my balls have finally regained their natural color from the choke-hold one woman had me in last week.

It's because Addie allowed me the space to open up.

I hadn't realized how badly I needed to before she asked me to tell her about myself. It's crazy to think of all the years we've known each other, and yet, Friday night felt like we were meeting each other for the first time.

It was special and freeing.

I dropped the funny-guy mask and was honest with someone for what might've been the first time since I cracked my first joke at seven—my origin story.

The goofy-as-hell joke I told back then got the entire dinner table howling with laughter. Even Whitney, who was only six months old at the time, released a squeal.

The joke wasn't even one I'd made up myself. A kid in my class had told it. I didn't know I'd remembered it until it fell out of my mouth, along with a few bites of mac and cheese. I followed it up by hiding Mom's reading glasses later that night, and the rest was history.

Until Addie.

She brings out a whole new side of me.

"If I have what Owen's having, will it put the same dopey grin on my face?" Nate slides onto the stool next to me, and he and Cole share a laugh.

I don't even remember sitting down or ordering a drink, but a full beer sits in front of me like it appeared through pure magic. I'm in serious fucking trouble here.

"What's going on, dopey?" Cole asks as he fills a frosted mug up with Michelob for Nate. "What deal did you make with the dirty Devil to be this chummy?"

"I'm always happy," I say.

"Happy, yes. Chummy, no." Nate wraps his hand around the mug and points it at me. "What's up, Chummy McGee?"

I turn between my two friends, who both stare expectantly at me. Cole even leans over the bar onto his elbows like he has all the time in the world for me to share my filthy secrets, but in reality, he has customers slowly occupying every seat along the bar.

Karaoke night is definitely popular in this town. There's not much else to do around here, especially not on a Sunday, as most businesses and shops close on this holy day.

I slide my fingers through the dew on my mug and grin. "I had—"

The truth instantly dissipates on my tongue.

"We have to keep this a secret."

Addie and I agreed not to tell anyone about us. Does that include our closest friends? Has she told Maren or Caroline? Knowing her, she's taken her oath extra seriously. She probably wouldn't even tell Pastor Eugene if he asked.

In any case, I promised her I wouldn't share what's happening between us, and my word means everything, even if it requires me to lie to my best friends.

"I've been drinking all afternoon, and I'm already buzzed." I tilt my beer toward them. "Wild what some bourbon can do to a guy's mood."

"That's what you're going with—bourbon?" Nate lifts a brow.

Cole squints. "I don't buy it. You're hiding something."

"I bet he's hiding a cartoon puppy inside him. There's no other explanation than this is not really our very own Owen."

Cole throws his hands up. "God, how it all makes sense now. Your puppy heart is the reason you slobber over every meal and wolf down meat like it's from the last cow on earth."

"Also explains why it took him so long to be potty trained." Nate straightens up and places a coaster under his mug. They got new ones around here, and I think Nate's the only one actually who uses them at the bar.

"I took a normal amount of time to learn to pee," I toss back.

"Not what your mom said." Nate snorts, and Cole fist-bumps him.

"I never thought I'd say this, but I miss Austin. The bastard's rude as hell, but at least he minds his own business." I roll my eyes and sip from my mug as the other two continue snickering.

Scarlett rounds the bar and places her hands on both hips. A pen is nestled behind her ear like a fifties diner waitress, her outfit complete with a collared shirt. She's just missing one of those pointy hats. "Every time I talk to my friends instead of working, you threaten me with kitchen duty with the funky smells." The young twenty-something girl scrunches her nose as she glares at us, dedicating a whole three seconds to each of us and ending with Cole. "What should I threaten you with, Mr. Big Shot?"

"Tell him you'll paint his house yellow. He's always hated that color," Nate chimes in. "Or better yet—paint his beloved truck!"

Thankful for the subject change before I blurted something I'm not supposed to say, I snap my fingers and tease, "Tell him you'll leave a turtle in the bed of his truck the next time he slacks off. He's scared shitless of those things."

"Are you serious? What adult is afraid of turtles?" Scarlett bursts into laughter as Matilda sidles up next to her in a matching outfit, only hers is pink to Scarlett's blue.

"What did I miss?" Matilda, the second gossip queen of the south, asks.

"It turns out, Mr. Big Shot is actually Mr. Scaredy Turtle." Scarlett shakes her head, her grin still wide and amused.

"What's with the matching getup?" Kenny, their boss and owner, interrupts, pointing between the two girls.

Scarlett holds her head high. "It's October, and we're celebrating Halloween all month long with different diner outfits."

"Let's cut the celebration short, shall we? They're too distracting, and they don't go with the culture in here."

"Oh." Matilda slumps her hip against the counter.

"You two are the most exhausting part of my job." Kenny sighs, then nods toward the crowd and clips, "Table seven needs refills, and Mr. Charlie is ready for his bill. Let's not keep our customers waiting, please and thank you."

Cole tightens his lips and busies himself with a new order. I imagine it's not easy for him to be bossed around by a younger guy, especially since Cole was a hotshot lawyer in Charleston before life and pressure chewed him up and spit him back out into Sapphire Creek.

It's why Scarlett calls him Mr. Big Shot.

The previously peppy girl taps at the screen of their POS system with obvious agitation, and once Kenny scurries away, a tray of drinks in hand, Matilda scoops ice into a glass and mockingly mutters, "*Please and thank you.*"

Scarlett mumbles back, "The things I'd like to say to that petty man."

"Why has he been such a dick this week?" Matilda hisses. "This *please and thank you* business just joined his vocabulary, and I am so not here for it."

"Same," Scarlett draws out and finishes the simple word with a groan. "He needs to get laid."

"You're not getting any. Yet you're not a dick," Matilda says over her shoulder toward Scarlett, who finishes up on the screen and tears a ticket from the machine.

"You know we're in a bizarre reality when Mr. Big Shot is getting more than us combined, even with his girlfriend living in Atlanta." Scarlett nudges Cole with her elbow.

"There's no reality where I will join this conversation." He holds his hands up, backs away from the bar, and stalks toward the stage.

Nate and I turn toward each other in sync. "Who needs TV when the Tap is so much more interesting?" he muses.

"That's just the tip of the drama-berg around here." I clap his shoulder and jostle him. "You'll get your fill of gossip within your first week of living here. If you actually stick around, that is."

"That's the plan. The sticking around part, anyway. Not the gossip." He swipes his mug and sucks back a gulp.

"You're probably already at the center of gossip, man." I shrug toward the few ladies making eyes at him from the corner. "The second you even thought of buying your parents' house and moving here, everyone knew, and they're ready to pounce."

He follows my gaze toward the women, who curl their fingers in waves at us, then turns back to me with a smirk. "I'm not dating anytime soon," he asserts. "I just want to focus on my daughter and me settling into a new normal."

"Where you're stuck in one place."

"You make it sound like I'm trapped."

"You're not, but do you think you are?"

"I'd only be trapped if I had no other options, but I do."

"But you're choosing this one. Is there a particular reason, or person, you're moving back for?"

"It's stable, and I want us to be around family." He shrugs. "Plus, my parents want to move to a smaller place across town, where my father can stop complaining about how much yard he has to care for, and my mom will stop going on about all the nooks and crannies she has to dust. The timing is perfect."

"And it has nothing to do with who your new neighbor will be?"

"Maren?" His laugh is sad, like he's forcing happiness right after his puppy was run over. "She doesn't even want to be my friend, let alone anything else."

"Is that what she said?"

"Not in so many words, but the obscene number of glares I've received is enough."

"There's a fine line between hate and love, man. Trust me." I smirk and toss the rest of my drink back as Cole grabs the microphone to kick off karaoke night.

After his quick greeting and introduction of the first singer, a short bob of dark hair by the door catches my attention.

Addie enters behind Maren, and she immediately finds me in the growing crowd, her twinkling blue eyes locked on mine.

My fucking heart thunders in my head.

It's the first time I'm seeing her since I left her naked in a hotel room. It's the first time since we agreed to keep things between us secret.

How am I supposed to tamp down the urge to scoop her into my arms?

chapter
twenty-nine

ADDIE

Owen rocks a gray Henley and dark jeans, and over his wavy strands, his hat rests backward, just as he promised.

Goose bumps erupt on my arms beneath my long sleeves. The hem of my flowered sweater sways across my waist as I follow Maren toward the bar, my high-waisted jeans loose around my thighs.

The dull ache in my legs reminds me of the way I unabashedly rode Owen to the moon and back the night before last, and I've craved that feeling ever since.

It was just two nights ago, but it feels like ages, especially now that I'm nearing him.

His gaze travels over me, following my every move as I maneuver through the crowd. I barely even register what song the karaoke star sings. It could be country, but it very well could be opera.

My heavy breaths muffle most of the noise in here until I'm standing right in front of Owen.

I blink. He blinks back.

Next to my leg, my fingers twitch with the electric need to

touch him, and when he shifts on his stool, his knee meets my upper thigh.

My legs feel like noodles. How is it possible to be turned on from such minimal contact?

"What're you doing in town again?"

I jolt in place and realize Maren's the one who asks the question, and she's talking to Nate.

"I was shooting nearby in a small Florida town, so I swung back by here to finalize a few things for the house and make sure Teagan's enrollment at the elementary school is set up."

My friend makes a noncommittal sound and waves for Cole's attention. "Can I get a Jack and Coke please?" She flicks her gaze to Nate, then adds, "Make it a double."

"That kind of night, huh?" Cole lifts a brow as he grabs a tall glass.

Next to us, Nate chuckles. "Pace yourself, Maren. You'll be seeing a lot of me soon."

"That reminds me." She sarcastically snaps her fingers, her fingernails painted black and deadly. It's like she's just waiting for an excuse to sink them into some pour soul, and Nate's the easiest target. "I saw plenty of For Sale signs on the other side of town. Maybe you'd be more comfortable there, and your parents can just keep being my neighbors for the rest of eternity. They're much better."

"I'd have to agree. My mom and dad are much better company." Nate folds his arms across his chest, and his lip twitches. He's clearly stifling a smile.

"I'll say," Maren grumbles as Cole slides her drink toward us. "Do you even know how to play Bridge? Because your mom and I are an unbeatable team. We have quite the competition going against the Hendersons from across the street, and if your mom quits, I'll have to suffer under the wrath of their smug smiles every week."

Nate's amused expression slips, and a frown replaces his earlier smirk. "You hang out with my mom?"

Maren shifts, her lips parted. "Sometimes. She makes the best scones around. I think she's the reason Mrs. Goodwin stopped selling them at Bready or Knot." The laugh my friend releases doesn't sound like hers. It's too high-pitched and fake.

She needs a rescue.

I turn again to face Owen, who's knee still rests along my upper thigh. "How was Lottie's—" I gulp back the rest of my question. I was just going to ask about Lottie's brunch event, but I shouldn't be asking him such pleasant things.

Secret. He and I are supposed to be *secret*.

"I mean, how did you ever see well enough to catch a baseball? Doesn't the fact that one eye is so much bigger than the other make it impossible?" I place both hands on my hips and practically lurch backward in order to break our physical connection.

A deep crease forms between his brows.

And I glare.

His eyes widen with understanding. "Look at you and your new haircut. Finally decided to live a little, huh?" he tosses back.

"I'd love it if you tried shutting up, but you just love the sound of your own voice, don't you?" I snap.

"No one loves the sound of their own voice more than you." Owen narrows his eyes.

"I was wondering when you'd start in on each other," Nate says.

Maren points at her Apple watch. "We were here a whole three minutes without you speaking a word. Must be a record."

Nate finishes his beer and slides off the stool. With a wave of his arm, he offers, "Take a seat, ladies. We'll get out of your hair." He pins Maren under his intense gaze and adds, "There's enough room here for all of us."

And I have a feeling he's not just talking about The Tipsy Tap.

"What a gentleman," I say sarcastically, then tell Owen, "Why am I not surprised you didn't think to give up your seat for a lady?"

Owen rises to his full height. In the process, he leans in until his nose grazes my hair, and he whispers, "You weren't a lady the other night."

"Meet me in the bathroom in five minutes," I whisper back, then jam my elbow into his side. "Have you ever heard of personal space?" I burst.

After I settle onto the empty stool and order a drink, I catch Owen's gaze as more and more people occupy the space between us.

His arousal is undeniable. Dark shades of desire lurk in his eyes, and I could practically melt onto the floor under his heated expression.

It's risky asking him to meet me in the bathroom, but I have to get him alone. I can't stand this charade, and it's only day freaking one.

But I can do this. My job and reputation are at stake. I'm more than equipped to do whatever it takes to meet my professional goals, even if it means secretly making out with my co-worker in a bar bathroom.

Which is what I want right now more than any delicious cocktail.

Of course, it's more than my professional life at stake, isn't it? But that's not something I can face right now. It's karaoke night.

Another singer takes the stage, and I immediately recognize her voice.

"I'll be singing one of my favorites tonight," she says.

Daphne. She hardly ever comes to karaoke night, let alone volunteers to sing, but when she does, it's truly something special. Her voice was made for the stage, although her taste in fashion does wonders at her boutique as well.

God just gave some women countless gifts.

The bouncy notes of "Man! I Feel Like a Woman!" echo across

the room, and Daphne dives right into the verse, without even looking at the screen for the lyrics.

Maren and I toss our hands up to cheer as loudly as possible—Daphne deserves the praise.

Many women open a space in the middle of the crowd in front of the stage. They grab their friends and dance to the fast-paced song, shaking their arms in the air and bumping their asses against one another.

"Should we?" I ask, hooking my thumb over my shoulder.

"Not even if I'd had three of these," Maren deadpans and holds her glass up.

"Fine. I'll just dance right here." I shift from side to side on my stool, bopping my head along to the fun beat and sipping my drink.

On the other side of the dance floor, Owen and Nate laugh with a few women I strain to recognize from my seat.

I nearly slip off my stool in order to get a better look at their faces, and Maren catches my arm. "Dancing a little too hard, don't you think?"

"Yes. Dancing. I was definitely not spying." My laugh trembles out of me as I toy with the straw in my drink.

Maren nods toward Owen. "How is it going with him?"

"Going? *Pfft.*" I shake my head. "Nothing's going on with him. We share a classroom, and that's all, unless you count the fact that a student sent a volleyball flying right at my head last week. That was super fun."

"Right," she draws out. "You totally knew what I meant, though."

I swallow around the lump in my throat.

She sweeps her long locks over her shoulder, leans in, and whispers, "Any more kisses with the enemy?"

Why did I have to tell her I kissed him? Lying to her now would be so much easier if she had no clue about us.

But how can I lie at all? Maren's one of my best friends in the world. She was the one who saved me when I started my period while at school. I started several months before she and Caroline did, so none of us were prepared.

But Maren jumped into action. She discreetly asked the nurse for a pad, which she snuck underneath the bathroom stall door, and she waited for me to come out so I wouldn't be alone.

She didn't tell anyone. Not like Yvonne, who wouldn't shut up about another girl in our class and the red stain on her ass. The monster told everyone she came into contact with.

A bump on my shoulder distracts us, and when I lift my eyes, I find Owen. "Sorry. Didn't see you there, Lockhart."

"How could you? When all you seem to notice are beer and tramps," I shoot back.

He cocks a brow and nods his head toward the bathroom. I study Maren to make sure it's a subtle gesture, but her attention is on something over my shoulder.

If I had to guess, I'd say she's spying on Nate.

"I have to go to the bathroom," I blurt, and a few heads swivel our way. Guess I said it louder than necessary. "Be right back," I say at a lower volume and scurry toward the back, where Owen just disappeared.

I catch him just in time before he enters the one on the right.

His timing couldn't be better, as he definitely rescued me from having to lie to Maren about us. Evading is totally not the same as lying.

Daphne draws out the final note long after the music ends, and the crowd goes wild with hoots and hollers. Many of them chant, "Encore!" before she's even taken a breath.

With most of the bar preoccupied, I quietly slip into the bathroom, where two strong hands and a chiseled body press me against the back of the door.

Owen locks it, and with the echo of the click drifting over us, he covers my mouth with his. "We've been here for all of thirteen minutes, and I haven't gotten to kiss you. It should be a crime," he mutters between kisses as his fingers skate up my arms.

As he buries his hands in my hair and pulls on the strands, he kisses me harder, stealing my breath with each swipe of his tongue.

He hardens against me.

And right as I trace the buckle of his belt with my fingertip, fully prepared to yank it off, he lunges backward. "I can't. Not here." He swipes at his mouth. "Too many people out there."

I hold my hands up as if to show him I'm unarmed. "You're right. That would be reckless." I nod as the noises of reality quickly filter back into my foggy brain. A slow song begins, the melody soft and barely audible in here. The voice is loud enough, though, and as Owen and I face each other from two feet apart, it feels like the singer is serenading us. "What should we do then?" I whisper.

"If we were out there, I'd dance with you." Owen removes the distance between us with a single stride and sweeps me into his arms, one around my waist and the other tugging on my hand. "I've always wanted to dance with the prettiest girl in the room."

I fight a smile. "I'd be a lot more flattered if I had more than a toilet to compare myself to."

He nuzzles his nose into my neck.

And as we dance next to said toilet, it's the most fun I've ever had at a karaoke night at the Tap.

"So, tramps, huh?" I feel his smile spread against my shoulder, where my sleeve has drifted over it.

"Not the best word choice for those women you were talking to." I wince, thankful he can't see me or any insecurities written on my face. "I'm sure they were perfectly pleasant women."

His chuckle washes over me with warmth. "If you must know, they were my sisters' friends. They just wanted to tell me how much they enjoyed Lottie's brunch yesterday and how good it was to see Whitney, who ended up attending too."

"Oh. I'm sure that's all they wanted." I roll my eyes.

"Are you jealous?" He pulls back a fraction to peer into my eyes.

My mouth flounders open and closed. "I don't get jealous, especially not over hot young things with skintight clothes and heels."

"But if you were jealous, I'd say..." He dips his head until his lips reach my burning ears. "I like it."

Lust fogs my brain again, rolling in to distract me from seeing clearly. "I, um..." I lick my lips. "Of course, you like it," I croak. Then I shake myself out of the trance and add, "Your ego can't survive without a continuous stroke of compliments."

"That's not it at all." His sober expression reaches deep inside my chest as he says, "I just know jealousy means you care. It means you want me, and I like the idea of you claiming me. Because, angel..."

"Hmm?" My teeth sink into my bottom lip as I hang on to his next word.

A knock on the door breaks us apart.

"What were you going to say?" I urge.

A smile appears on his face, but it's not one I've seen before. It's almost shy. That can't be right. Owen Conrad is never shy.

Another knock sounds.

He gives me one more kiss that leaves my head spinning and rasps, "To be continued."

"I've never been a fan of cliffhangers in books, and they're even worse in real life."

"Real life awaits, baby."

I blow out a frustrated breath, glance toward the door, then back at Owen. "I'll distract them while you sneak out behind me."

I inch the door open, and through the sliver, I find Iris's niece on the other side. "Hey, Cheyenne!" I slip into the hall and loop my arm through hers. "I've been meaning to call you about the messages I've gotten about the dance costumes. I'm sure you've gotten them too."

"Oh, tons of messages." She squeezes my hand. "Aunt Iris had to start taking medication for her high blood pressure, and I'm not sure it wasn't because of the dance moms—God bless them."

As I lead her away from the bathroom, I glance over my shoulder and catch Owen peeking through the sliver of the cracked door, his eyes locked on mine.

He winks, and tiny supernovas explode in my chest.

Keeping him a secret might be the hardest thing I'll ever have to do.

chapter
thirty

OWEN

"THIS PATIENT SUFFERED from a left temporal hemorrhage and started speaking with an accent. It's called Foreign Accent Syndrome," Laurel says as she sets the bowl of salad in the middle of my dining table.

"That's what happens to me after three tequila shots." Whitney snorts as she shifts Huck onto her shoulder and pats his back to burp him.

"French, right?" I ask Whit as I set silverware on either side of every placemat.

"How did you know?"

"You used it on me a few years ago, although you were too young to drink then, which makes me wonder..." I narrow my eyes.

But she shrugs, humming along to her own rhythm.

"Why do I bother? You guys don't get it." Laurel huffs as she stalks back into the kitchen to help Mom with more dishes.

"Relax," Whit calls out. "It's family dinner. We're just trying to have some fun."

The front door shuts, and Lottie whisks into the dining room.

"What did I miss? I saw Laurel's car outside. Is she already into it with y'all for not listening on the edge of your seats to her riveting tales of medical crises?"

"How did you know?" Whit's eyes widen in awe.

"We spend too much time together, don't we?" I muse.

"Nah." Lottie waves with her free hand, a covered dish in the other. "It's just that Laurel's too predictable."

"You say it like it's an insult," my third sister returns with a platter of stuffed mushrooms and a basket of breadsticks.

"It's not a compliment," Lottie teases. "I'm surprised you're even helping set the table. Isn't that beneath you, Doctor Conrad?"

"As the oldest daughter, it's my responsibility to help." Laurel raises her chin with pride.

"You're older than me by a minute!" Lottie bursts.

Huck burps, pulling all of our attention toward him as if he just knew he needed to break the impending explosion.

Even from this young of an age, it's clear the kid possesses a talent for being the funny guy, just like his favorite uncle.

I'm the first to chuckle, and the rest of the girls follow suit.

"It's great to finally hear you all laughing." Mom rushes into the dining room, an apron tied around her waist and oven mitts over both hands. In her grasp is the world's greatest smelling lasagna.

The cheese still bubbles on the top—she obviously just pulled it from the oven.

I inhale another hungry whiff, and as I finish setting out the napkins and silverware, the doorbell rings.

"That's probably your father," Mom says and pats my shoulder. "He said he'd be running a little behind."

"He never rings the doorbell, though." I leave a question hanging in the air, but all I get in response are a bunch of shrugs.

Lottie does nothing but swipe a stuffed mushroom, and Laurel slaps her hand. She really takes her role as a-whole-minute-older sister so seriously.

I make my way toward the front door, and my cautious confusion comes to a screeching halt as I swing it open.

Shoulders grazing her ears, Addie steps off the top step when I join her on the porch. "Where are you sneaking off to?" I lean against the doorframe.

She spins on her heel to face me, chewing on the inside of her cheek. "I thought you might be busy. There are a lot of cars in your driveway. Or are they all yours? Do you like cars? I didn't know this about you."

A pair of headlights flash us as my father pulls into the spot behind Lottie. "I have no real attachment to cars, no."

"Interesting," she chirps, but it sounds forced. She's nervous, and it makes me so deliriously fucking happy that I affect her so much.

"Those are my family's cars. They're all here for dinner."

She blanches underneath the porch lights. "Oh my God. I knew this was a mistake, but I was trying to be spontaneous and fun. And I'm even wearing slutty lingerie. I don't know what I was thinking."

My cock twitches at the image of the kind of lingerie she might be referring to, and I'll be damned if I don't find out for myself. "Stay," I urge as Dad saunters up the path toward us.

Addie's eyes bug out of her head. "I can't meet your family," she hisses.

"Hey, son." Dad climbs the steps and claps my back. "Who's this?"

"I'm his co-worker," Addie sputters. "I just came by to... to... let him know I had a change in my schedule and will need him to take his classes outside tomorrow."

"Forecast says it's going to rain, though." I fold my arms over my chest.

"Is it? I didn't, um, see that." She fumbles down the porch steps. "I'll go back to my original plan, then. Okay. Take care."

As Addie marches back toward the driveway, I squeeze my dad's shoulder and say, "We'll meet you inside."

Addie's short strides are no match for my long ones, no matter how quickly and purposefully she makes them, and I catch up to her before she reaches her car at the end of my driveway.

I lurch in front of her and cut off her path. "You're not naked under there, are you?" I point to her peacoat. It's buttoned down all the way to her upper thighs, which are bare. Her lean muscles blink as she shifts from one boot to the other.

"No!" she hisses, but her outrage is instantly replaced with hesitation. "Why? Would that have been sexier?"

I hook my finger under her chin and tip her head back. "Everything you do is sexy." My growl is mixed with a raspy chuckle. "I'm just happy you're here. How did you know where I live?"

"Same way you got my address."

"Austin," I muse, but something hits me. "What did you tell him you needed it for?"

"He didn't actually ask, and I don't suspect he cares at all about why I needed it." She shrugs. "But I told him you left your hat at school, and I just wanted to drop it off in your mailbox."

"Sounds about right." I slide my fingers up her cheek and into her short wavy strands, untucking the locks she had hidden behind one ear. "Hey, Lockhart?"

"Hmm?" She bites her sinfully red lip and peers up at me, her eyes sparkling like the stars in the evening sky.

"Can I kiss you already?"

"You better."

She barely completes her smartass response before I crush my lips to hers. She tastes extra sweet tonight.

Maybe it's because she's been torturing me from afar all week, showing up to work in heeled boots and leggings. She always looks professional, but I've suddenly been distracted by all the ways her outfits are sexy.

Mainly, I imagine it's midnight, and I fling each article of clothing across the gym floor, then have me a taste with her sprawled across the free-throw line.

We've survived four days of classes and secret glances from across the gym.

It's obvious she's been tortured too. Why else would she surprise me at my house tonight? God, this fucking woman will be the end of me.

She moans in my mouth, and my mind drifts into dangerous territory, filling itself with filthy images of spreading her across the porch steps and having my way with her. My neighbors are far enough away, given my house sits on fifteen acres. There'd be no witnesses other than the fireflies and fish in the creek cutting through my property.

But a burst of laughter from inside rattles my brain and reminds me we are not actually alone right now.

"Come on," I whisper, my voice hoarse.

She slips her hand into mine and squeezes, but our connection breaks when she starts toward her car, and I walk toward my house. "What are you doing?" she asks.

I take her hand in mine again and nudge her back down the pathway toward the porch. "You're joining us for dinner. Knowing you, there's zero chance you've eaten tonight."

"I mean, you're right, but I can't come inside!" She digs her heels into the cement path, but she's no match for my strength—or determination. "Unhand me right this second!"

"I've already met your mom, and now, I'm returning the gesture."

"That was an accident," she argues. "Trust me, if she hadn't shown up to the chili dinner, you wouldn't have met her for a very long time, if ever."

"We're having lasagna tonight. You like lasagna, right? And

breadsticks. They're the garlic kind." My mouth salivates, and my stomach growls as I bring her along. "Then we'll play some Jenga, and after everyone leaves, you'll show me this elusive lingerie."

"You're out of your freaking mind," she whisper-screams as I drag her up the steps. "I'm not going in there to meet your whole family. That's insane!"

"What would be insane is allowing you to drive all the way out here and letting you leave with an empty stomach." I pause with my foot on the last step. "Letting you leave unsatisfied would be a terrible disservice."

"You're off the hook. I don't need to be satisfied in any sense." She attempts to free her delicate hand from my wolfish grip yet again, but it's no use.

"Then why did you come here?"

"To get my fill of the countryside," she deadpans.

It makes me chuckle, and her gaze follows the rise and fall of my chest before I spin back around, my hand still holding onto hers as I tug her the rest of the way toward the door.

"Owen Sylvester Conrad!" she bursts.

My laugh tears out of me with gusto, and the echo scares the birds from the trees in my front yard. "My middle name is not Sylvester." I pause again right next to the door—so fucking close.

With my guard down, she yanks her hand free. "Well, I don't know what it is."

"And your best guess is Sylvester?"

"You look like a Sylvester." A small smile dances on her lips.

"What are you afraid of, angel?"

"A lot of things—spiders, seaweed touching my leg in the ocean, and my woven blankets unraveling. Oh, and right now, I'm afraid of how totally casual you are about introducing me to your entire family." She folds her arms over her chest and shrinks. "It's very serious, and you don't seem to realize that."

"I do realize it."

"And you don't care?"

"I do care. As a matter of fact, I care a lot. It's why I want to hold your hand, walk inside, and eat together with my family."

"What happened to keeping us a secret?"

"My family doesn't count."

"They are people with eyes and ears—they freaking count."

With a sigh, I twist the knob and head inside, leaving the door open for her to make a choice. I've said my piece, and the rest is up to her.

"Where are you going?" Her voice carries down the narrow entryway and over me.

"I'm going to eat—I'm starving," I say over my shoulder.

ADDIE

I HAVE a million things waiting for me at home to tend to, especially since Rain practically turned my house upside down. She and her friends finally left last night, and the house is currently in shambles.

With her departure, a singed bra hung over the fireplace, several new candles lined my counter, and one of them tore down my clothesline on the back deck. Her *marvelously classy* friends even scared off Judd, who attempted to come by for my dryer for the hundredth time—I've lost count. According to Judd, a tall man in nothing but cargo shorts told him they were in the middle of an orgy.

Had I been there, I would've erupted like the air from a whale's blowhole, so it was probably best that I was at the dance studio.

I turn to leave—more like, flee—when a round of laughter drifting from inside gives me pause. It lures me in like a whimsical promise of a worldwide eutopia. I could use some blissful whimsy, especially after the week I've had.

With a huff, I shove my hands into the pockets of my peacoat and storm inside, following the muffled voices into the dining room like it's the freaking yellow brick road.

The heels of my boots thudding across the wooden floors slows as I reach my destination.

The pearl color of the walls gives the illusion of a larger room than what it is, especially with the sparse décor. There are only a few pictures of Owen's family on one side, a window framed with pale green curtains, and a leafy plant in the corner. The arched entrance from the kitchen is high, and it makes me feel small.

As do all the eyes staring back at me.

Everyone's here—his parents, three sisters, his baby nephew, and Owen. I didn't want to believe they were actually all here, but they are. My perfect vision doesn't lie.

This is a mistake!

"Hi there." Owen's mom is the first to smile, and it's a warm, comforting one that immediately puts me at ease. It's one I've never seen my own mother wear.

"Hi," I practically squeak.

I've stood in front of classroom after classroom of teenagers for years. I've given countless speeches and introductions at dance recitals and pep rallies, and I've even completed a few presentations for the school board too.

I never shy away from the pressure of an audience, but nothing compares to this moment.

A pool of sweat doubles in size at my lower back, and my stomach tightens.

Owen's mom scoots her chair back and waves me over. "Come on in, and take a seat, darlin'."

I find Owen stuffing a forkful of lasagna into his gargantuan mouth as he stares back at me. I've never seen anyone look so smug while eating, but he accomplishes it far too easily.

"This is Addie." He points his fork in my direction, then waves it over the rest of the table. "That's our father, Bill, and our mother, Dorothy. These are my sisters, Whitney, Lottie, and Laurel, and the stud on the end is Huck."

"It's nice to meet you all. I'm so sorry to intrude," I say, managing to find my voice through the panic seizing my chest. "You've already started eating, and I'm being rude. I didn't even bring a covered dish or a bottle of wine—I don't know if any of you like wine or drink alcohol at all," I ramble. "I don't have a gift, either."

"We don't need any gifts. We're just happy for you to join us." Mrs. Conrad throws her arm over my shoulders and leads me to the empty seat between her and Owen.

"Is it not someone's birthday? Or another special occasion, perhaps?" I glance around the room. There are no decorations, cake, or any other indication of a party, but why else would the whole family gather around this enormous oak dining table on a weeknight?

"No," Whitney says, but the simple syllable ends on a high note like it's a question. She shakes her head slowly, as if she's unsure of a special occasion.

"We get together once a week or so for a family dinner." The one across from me, Laurel, shrugs, like this is normal.

They all rearrange their schedules and get together that often... just because? I thought this sort of thing only happened with fake families on TV.

"But I can't make it next week," Laurel says to the rest of the group. "I have to get more serious about studying for Step 1 this spring."

"You're studying for something that's not until spring?" Whitney gapes. "I didn't even start studying for midterms last week until the night before!"

Her mother shoots her a stern glare as she takes her seat, and I drape my peacoat over the back of my chair, freeing my flowy top from its cage.

"I mean... not midterms. I meant to say... grocery shopping. I

don't grocery shop until the night before I need something."
Whitney shrinks, then points across Lottie to their other sister.
"Good for you for being so diligent, Laurel. Go get 'em."

Mr. Conrad's smirk catches my attention, and it's not because
it's the only movement made after Whitney basically outs herself.

It's because the mannerism is so familiar. This is exactly where
Owen got his smirk. The two men are very similar in appearance,
although his father is far smaller in size.

Mrs. Conrad holds up her hand. "We haven't even gotten to
dessert yet. Let's discuss next week after that."

Huck stirs in his highchair, and while the attention shifts to
him, I take advantage of the distraction and pinch Owen's leg. His
knee bumps the table and draws his mother's eyes toward him, but
he waves her off.

"You are unbelievable," I hiss in hushed tones. "You lured me
in here with delicious food—cheap tactics."

"You're the one who came to me, baby." He winks as he sips
from his glass of water, and I'm suddenly so hot, I'd love to pour it
all over me.

"Addie, darlin'—what would you like to drink?" Mrs. Conrad
gently pats my shoulder and jolts me.

"I, um…" I pause to catch my breath and slowly rise on trembling knees. "I'll get a water from the kitchen. No need to
get up."

"Nonsense. Make yourself a plate, and I'll be right back." She
pats my shoulder again and scurries away while I blink at the
spread in front of me.

Where do I even begin?

My stomach growls, but no one seems to hear it, other than
Owen, anyway.

He reaches for the lasagna and sets it next to my empty plate.
"Eat before your stomach eats you." Pointing to a corner piece, he
whispers, "I'd recommend that one. It's the biggest cut, and you'll
need your strength for what I plan to do to you later."

I clutch my chest, almost to ensure my heart is still, in fact, beating underneath.

This guy is straight trouble.

Mrs. Conrad returns with a glass of water, and her timing couldn't be better. I down nearly half of it with my first gulp.

"Hang on..." Lottie pushes her food along her plate, but her focus is solely on me. "You're *the* Addie? As in, Addison Lockhart?"

I nod. "You probably saw me running around the homecoming parade a couple weeks ago. And I went to school with Owen."

She shakes her head. "You're also the one Owen couldn't stop staring at during the chili dinner."

Owen slows his chewing, and when he swallows, his Adam's apple bobs with seemingly great difficulty.

Lottie snaps her fingers. "Bond was talking about you, and our big brother got so squirrely."

"When has Owen ever been squirrely?" Whitney teases as she reaches over to wipe drool from Huck's chin.

"When there's a pretty girl at stake," Laurel tosses.

"No way was I squirrely," Owen says with a wide grin. As he turns to look at me, amusement flits across his green eyes. "At the chili dinner, Lockhart and I weren't even *friends*."

"Well, we're co-workers," I quickly add. "I teach English at the high school."

"Oh?" Bill raises a brow. It's the first syllable he's uttered since I sat down, and I can't tell if it's a good thing.

"English was my favorite subject," Mrs. Conrad gushes. "I was such a big fan of *Wuthering Heights*. I think I read it three times in high school just for fun."

"Wasn't that the one with Heathcliff?" Laurel ventures.

"Wow. I'm surprised you know anything other than the name of a disease or a bone," Lottie teases.

"I'm not surprised you can't chew and talk at the same time."

Laurel swipes at the sleeve of her shirt. "You got tomato sauce on me."

"Relax. What do you even need real clothes for? You live in nothing but scrubs."

"When I'm a doctor, I'll wear mostly scrubs, but there are so many things to do before then. I have to—" Laurel holds up her fingers as if to start listing all the things, but Lottie and Whitney cut her off.

"Please don't start." Whitney groans. "I did not sleep enough last night to hear your long list of words I've never heard of."

"Besides," Lottie cuts in. "We've heard it all before. I'd rather hear from Addie." She pins her gaze on me.

"Hmm?" I swallow the last bite of my lasagna after having inhaled the delicious dish with the gusto of three sumo wrestlers. I was positively starving.

"Do you like to paint?" Lottie asks.

"I've never really painted, unless you count the finger-painting assignments we were given as kids." I smile.

"What about pottery? Do you like pot?" Whitney pales. "Oh my gosh—I didn't mean that. I was just—"

"We know, sweetie," Mrs. Conrad says, swooping in to put her youngest at ease.

"I haven't tried that, either." I frown.

"What do you do for fun? Gardening, perhaps?" This comes from Mrs. Conrad, and I stare a beat before I realize I don't have much of an answer.

"I've never had much of a green thumb, not like my mom. When she stays in one place, anyway." I clear my throat and quickly bypass my unintentional mention of Rain. "I guess I don't have much time for fun. I'm always busy grading papers and volunteering at the dance studio."

"She's a phenomenal dancer," Owen announces.

"That's one skill I so wish I had," Lottie laments.

I smile softly. "I do like to dance, but I mainly just practice once a week. I used to do it more, but like I said, I guess I just got busy."

"Busy is good." Laurel nods. "I am happiest when my schedule is packed. Makes me feel productive and useful."

"You have no life," Lottie jabs, then widens her eyes at me. "Not that you don't have a life, either."

"You're kind of right, though." I shrug and attempt to appear unaffected, but in truth, I am. It's not because of Lottie's joke, but because my life has been loaded with appointments and opportunities to get myself to where I'm going professionally.

What about my personal life? What about fun? I hang out with my friends and attend karaoke nights on Sundays, but those aren't hobbies or pastimes just for myself.

The only thing I've done for myself recently is book a spa appointment out of town and sleep with my co-worker, neither of which I regret.

I should do more of those things, but I should also adopt a hobby.

As the conversation continues, I drift into the rhythm of their back and forth, as if I come to all their family dinners. Mrs. Conrad insists I call her Dorothy, and Mr. Conrad shares stories of my own father.

According to him, they were friends in high school, but I've never heard my dad mention him. It's not too surprising, though. When we do get together, which becomes rarer and rarer every year, Dad mostly asks about me and my life. He'll occasionally mention what new hobby his wife has undertaken and conquered, but he keeps his personal life under lock and key.

After we all devour a slice of pumpkin pie, I rise, my stomach full and satisfied. "I'll get started on the dishes," I offer, but Dorothy playfully swats my hand away.

"You'll do no such thing." She holds a finger up. "The Conrad Rule is that I cook, but the host washes the dishes."

"And if we're eating at Mom's, Dad's in charge of the dishes," Whitney adds.

Bill takes a mini bow in his seat, and I nudge Owen in the shoulder, my smile widening as I say, "I like this rule. Lucky, lucky Owen."

"I'm about to get lucky," he whispers, coughing on the last word, and I glare.

I skim the room to confirm no one heard him, then mouth to him, "What is wrong with you?"

"Where to begin," he mumbles with a smirk.

"Jenga?" Lottie claps.

Laurel checks her watch. "I have time for one round, and no cheating!" She directs the last part to Whitney. "Just because you have a baby doesn't mean you get five free passes."

"Tell that to Dad," Lottie says. "He's the one who lets her get away with it."

"She's the youngest. What can I say?" Bill shrugs as he stands from the table and shuffles into the living room.

"Addie, you in?" Lottie asks. "We can add your name to our ongoing scorebook."

"Sure," I answer without hesitation, and I feel Owen's eyes on me. "How exactly long is *ongoing*?"

"For the last fifteen years," Whitney chimes in. "I was almost seven when Mom and Dad decided they needed more ways to occupy all of us since eating and running around the yard weren't enough."

"The rain put a real damper on their tempers," Dorothy explains. "We needed an inside game, and Owen suggested Jenga."

"It was the only thing on our shelves at the time," Bill adds with a good-natured grin.

"Aside from peppermint snowball cookies at Christmas, Jenga is our longest-standing tradition." Laurel maneuvers around the table in the direction where their father disappeared.

"I love traditions," I whisper as a pang of sadness mixed with jealousy spears my chest.

This family might make their playful jabs at one another, but they're wholesome and loving. They're kind and inclusive and welcoming.

The Conrads have traditions in their homes, and they value them as much as I do.

As a kid, my parents established plenty of them—camping in the yard with s'mores on the first night of fall, movie nights with bowls of Skittles every Sunday, and more. These nights brought us closer together as a family. With every laugh, moments of juice spewing from our noses, and comparisons of rainbow-colored tongues, we were tied together.

But once my parents divorced, almost all of the traditions stopped. The one that remained was chili dinner with my mom.

From then on, I relied so heavily on the traditions of the school, especially those of homecoming. It's why I'm so adamant —and desperate—about upholding the importance of such annual activities.

"We're ready!" Laurel calls out, and the rest of us filter away from the dining room.

Owen and I are the last ones out. With his family far enough ahead of us, Owen squeezes my ass, and I yelp.

"Are you okay?" Whitney's head whips around, Huck cradled in her arms.

"Thought I saw a... spider. Just a fly." I force a smile, and when I turn around to scold Owen, his red face tells me all I need to know.

He's not sorry one bit. In fact, he's rather proud of himself as he watches me with a twinkle in his eye. It's the kind of look people have when gazing at the stars or drinking in a sunset over the ocean.

It's a look of awe.

And I'm deliriously happy to be on the receiving end of such a look from Owen.

chapter
thirty-two

OWEN

"Next time, bring your losing hat because you're going down." Laurel wags her finger at Addie, then shrugs her jacket over her shoulders.

"We'll see," Addie taunts back.

"You are trouble." Laurel shakes her head, then flicks her gaze toward me.

I only shrug, but my throat thickens.

Addie just spent the last hour dominating in Jenga. Laurel is the most competitive of us all, and she was so irate over the first loss, she agreed to play again... and again.

She lost each time and wanted to play another round, even though she'd originally insisted she couldn't stay long. My sister is the sorest loser of them all.

We would've played more, but Whitney needs to head home. With Huck in her arms and a diaper bag strapped to her back, she swivels in front of the door to say her goodbyes. To Laurel, she chirps, "I'll see you when I see you. Feel free to call when you're not studying for the Step Up."

"It's Step 1," Laurel corrects. "*Step Up* is a dance movie."

Whitney rolls her eyes as Laurel bends to kiss Huck on the back of his fuzzy little head. "Just... good luck studying." Laurel then busies herself with Mom and Dad, and Whitney leans into me to whisper, "Nice job getting a life."

I follow her nod in the direction of Addie, who makes her way down the hall toward us, her knee-length skirt sashaying from side to side.

My parents leave right behind Whitney, but not before my mother takes me aside, a million questions in her eyes as they bounce from me to Addie and back. All she says is "We should chat soon."

I figured she'd be curious about Addie since I never bring girls to family dinner, but Mom hardly ever wants to chat with just me, which means she's far more than simply curious.

This is damn serious.

Lottie joins the remainder of us by the front door and loops her arm through Laurel's. "We're still going shopping this weekend, right? I need to get a dress for Theresa's wedding next month."

"Your old college roommate? She's getting married?" Laurel asks as she retrieves Lottie's coat from the rack for her.

"Yes!" She throws her head back. "I've told you this a zillion times. She's having an outdoor wedding in a heated tent. I told you the whole debacle about the initial scam she almost fell victim to, but then her mother's friend from Tampa personally knew a guy whose brother had a connection with a legit heated tent company."

Laurel tilts her head. "You really think I remember all that? I have far too many other details to worry about at school."

"You could at least remember that she's getting married," my other sister mumbles.

"I'll write it down," Laurel deadpans.

"Goodbye, big brother." Lottie throws her arm around my shoulders, and Laurel waves to Addie.

"It was nice to meet you, and I'm serious about the rematch."

"Name the time and place." Addie juts her chin up, her eyes a mix of amusement and challenge.

As they tug the door open, Addie raises her voice when she tells me, "Before I leave, I just need to go over some details with you about class tomorrow."

Laurel and Lottie share a knowing glance, and I can tell they don't buy Addie's stiffly delivered lie. I wouldn't, either, but I let her have this.

"Yes. Very important stuff," I play along for the sake of our agreement to keep things secret.

My sisters are not that gullible, though. My whole family knows something's up with Addie and me—I didn't have to say it. They're a smart bunch, but there's also the fact that I've never introduced them to a woman before, except for Vice Principal Sable. I ran into her when I was shopping with Lottie at the grocery store, but that's the extent of such introductions.

I'm sure my sisters will have loads of questions too. We'll see how long it takes before they explode with them all.

But right now, I have one person and one thing on my mind.

Once they disappear through the front door, I'm finally left alone with Addie.

I'm more aware of the silence now that everyone's gone, and more than that, I'm aware of her. Everything about her screams at me—her blue eyes are soft tonight with the lightest touch of mascara, both cheeks are tinted crimson, and her lips are pale from licking them all night.

She enjoyed the lasagna and the pie. That much was obvious, given she was the last to sit down with a plate and the first to empty it.

I also got the impression she doesn't experience this a lot with her own parents, if ever. I knew big gatherings weren't in her wheelhouse since she's an only child, but I didn't expect to witness how big of a deal it is.

She appreciates tradition, and I just inadvertently hurled her right into the middle of several of them.

And I'm glad I did. Otherwise, I wouldn't be rewarded with this wistful expression she gives me now.

"Then there were two," I say and inch toward her until we're toe to toe.

She lifts her eyes up to my hair. "No hat tonight."

"I can put one on, if that'll make you kiss me faster."

"I'd rather just kiss you." She flings her arms around my neck, tugs me down, and fuses her mouth to mine.

My hands skate to her backside and cup her ass, my grip firm and desperate.

We're not fucking close enough.

She tangles her fingers in my hair as I walk us backward, stumbling around my house like I've never been here before.

I'm dizzy and crazed—damn insane for this girl.

We somehow find our way back into the dining room, and I swipe the table, vacating a spot from silverware and a couple of glasses. The next to go is the bowl of salad, and lettuce flies off the surface like confetti. They all tumble onto the carpet in a chaotic mess.

"What are—"

I cut Addie off with a hoist of her hips up and onto the table. "It's my job to clear the table, isn't it?" I wiggle my eyebrows, then steal another kiss.

"This is hardly clearing it," she murmurs against my lips. "But I'll help."

She reaches back and grabs the can of whipped cream from when Whitney went back for her second slice of pumpkin pie. Addie squeezes a swirl onto the tip of her finger and brings it to her mouth, but at the last second, she's smears it onto my own lips.

"You're the best helper," I joke as my nerves run haywire.

She hums and sinks into me, lapping up the whipped cream

from my face, and I about lose my damn head as the sweet and sexy taste of it all turns my brain cells to mush.

I lick my way south, sliding her loose shirt into a *V* on her chest until I bury my head between her breasts. I only pause there for a beat before I kneel in front of her and unzip each boot, which I chuck to the side.

As I stand back into my previous position between her legs, she yanks her shirt over her head, revealing a black mesh bra lined with lace in the shape of flowers. The way the cups press her tits together makes my mouth water. On top of that, the material is transparent, and it gives me the perfect view of each beaded nipple.

This bra is enough for any mortal to go into cardiac arrest. How am I supposed to stand a fucking chance?

"You're trying to kill me. You're torturing me for being such an ass for the last ten years, aren't you?" I manage over the erratic beating of my heart.

She tucks her bottom lip under her teeth and slowly shakes her head. "I've already forgiven you, but if you want to earn bonus points, I can think of a few ways…"

I growl into her neck, then skim the tip of my nose up the column of her throat and cover her mouth with mine. I shove her skirt up to her waist and slide my fingers along the fabric of her panties.

I curl the barely existent material in my fist and jerk down.

Addie gasps into my mouth, and my dick jerks against the denim of my jeans.

With a lift of her hips, I rid her of the panties, and I rest on my knees again to free them over her ankles.

Instead of standing up again, I position each of her knees over my shoulders and rise up until I'm eye level with her sweet, wet flesh.

Here's to the second round of dessert—I've always been a glutton for something sweet.

My mouth waters as I find the birthmark on the inside of her thigh and kiss her there first.

Then I swipe my tongue up the seam of her, and her hands slam to the table with a thud as she leans back.

Clinging to her thighs, I work her into a frenzy in the way I already know drives her wild. With every lick and nip, I strive to outdo myself from the last time. What new noises can she make?

"Be loud, angel." I spread her legs farther apart and thrust my tongue deeper into her before pulling out again. "I want to hear how good I make you feel. If you want more, I need to know how crazy you are for me."

"Yes, yes—whatever you want, Owen." She delves her fingers into my hair and shoves me back into position. "I just need more. Give me more. *Please.*"

"That's it," I whisper, then blow cool air onto her heat.

Her hips buck. "Oh, God!"

"That's exactly it." I smirk and get back to the relentless strokes of my tongue, savoring every taste and sensual sound leaving her parted lips.

Her quick breaths grow in volume and speed, like she's just finished a marathon.

Her legs clench around my head.

"Oh, oh, oh!" Her moans rival that in any adult film I've ever watched.

Addie's sensational as a long cry rips from her throat, and her climax coats my tongue and chin. She keeps coming, her body writhing on the dining table, and her hand slips to the side, knocking over a water.

Neither of us moves.

Not until she's finished.

By the time she straightens her spine again, her bra has shifted to the side, one nipple halfway exposed.

The side of her head is dotted with sweat.

Her nostrils flare with satisfaction, but there's a glint of desire still lingering in her blue eyes—that, and mischief. She's definitely not finished with me, which works out magnificently.

Addie claws at my shoulders and arms, urging me to stand. I rise as she drops onto her feet, and when I open my mouth to ask what's next, she renders me completely fucking speechless.

She cups me between my legs, clutching my throbbing cock in her palm. "My turn to feast."

chapter
thirty-three

ADDIE

I ROTATE US AROUND, spinning on my heels like I do while dancing with a partner, and I push him back until he rests against the edge of the table.

Then I sink onto my knees in front of him, grabbing hold of his zipper on my way down.

Owen's sharp, echoing inhale feels like a megaphone captured the sound of it, and it fuels my movements.

I move faster as desperation colors my vision.

I've only ever done this to one other guy before. I've never had much of a desire to do it, especially since most of the guys I've been with were hardly generous in return.

Not like Owen.

He's always selfless. He's equal parts tender and firm, and I suddenly have the overwhelming urge to make him feel as good as he makes me feel.

Once he springs loose from his jeans, drool threatens to dribble from my mouth.

"Is this seriously happening?" he whispers under his breath, as if he's talking to himself.

But I answer, anyway. "Almost." I narrow my eyes as I reach for the can of whipped cream by his foot. It must've fallen off the table when I was previously on top of it.

I pop the top off and squirt it on him, beginning at the base of his veiny shaft and drawing a line up to the tip, where I swirl a healthy dose.

"Oh, fuck," he breathes, and his cock twitches, just begging for me.

I toss the can aside, where it joins the rest of the mess, and I take my sweet time licking the whipped cream off him.

Owen shudders beneath me.

I place my hands on both of his hips to steady him—not that I have that kind of strength, but at least I can anchor myself. This is just as titillating for me as it must be for him.

It's addictive being in control like this and entrancing Owen in such awe.

I cover his tip with my mouth, savoring the last of the dessert topping, and then I take as much of him as possible.

I don't stop until he hits the back of my throat and tears well in my eyes.

"Jesus, that's so fucking good, baby." Owen caresses the top of my head as I bob slowly, easing him in and out of my mouth.

The lingering sweet taste of the whipped cream mixes so deliciously with his natural taste, and I lose myself in the moment.

We're much like we were in Savannah, except we're not out of town this time. Here, we're in Owen's house, only a few miles from the school. But it doesn't matter to me.

Right now, I chase the feeling of ecstasy that only he offers. I chase it like I'm the fastest freaking woman on earth.

I quicken my pace and suck him off as if this is the last thing I'll ever do.

He repeatedly hits the back of my throat, harder and harder as he thrusts his hips into me and rides my face.

And I can't get enough. Tears stream down my face, and still, I happily moan and practically gag on him.

It's so unbelievably *hot*. I'll later be adding this to the list of things I never thought I'd say before Owen.

"Okay, okay," he pants and pulls a fistful of my hair back, separating my mouth from his pulsing length. "I can't come like this. Not yet. Not before I get inside you."

"Then what are you waiting for?" I challenge as I swipe at the corners of my eyes and rise to my full height.

His hooded gaze bores into me as he thrusts his pants the rest of the way off. Owen steps out of them as I shimmy out of my skirt. Then he walks us backward until I'm pressed against the wall.

"I have condoms upstairs," he says, his length prodding against my stomach.

"No. Here. Now." I nod. "I'm on the pill, and I have checkups regularly. You know I have a whole color code for that, so I can stay on top of my health."

"Mine's not that extensive, but I've also been tested recently." He uses one large hand to smooth hair away from my face. "Are we really doing this?"

I nod again, but this time, it's more emphatic. "Hurry."

With one arm around my waist, he lifts me up the wall, and I wrap my legs around him, sinking onto his erection with ease.

My eyes roll into the back of my head as he stretches me so perfectly. I grip him between my thighs like a vise as he propels me up and down, my back sliding on the wall.

He plunges into me with vigorous, hungry strokes, ramming his hips into me like he's trying to make us both one with the wall.

We practically shake the foundation of the house.

My body vibrates with another orgasm, and he pulses inside me.

Owen clenches his jaw as I unravel, his name a breathy whisper on my lips. He abruptly pulls out, sets me onto my feet, and flips me around.

Hot spurts of his release decorate my back and ass. I glance over my shoulder to find him pumping his shaft with the rest of his climax.

A line of sweat skids from his neck down to his chest, his cheeks flushed like he's been in the sun all day.

He's positively captivating.

His groan is drawn out before he utters, "That was..."

"Majestic." A smile dances on my lips as he kisses my shoulder.

"Don't move."

I do as he says and wait for him to return with a damp washcloth, which he uses to delicately clean me up. The warmth, plus his soft circling motions, soothe my back, and my eyelids flutter. They're suddenly heavy with elated satisfaction.

When he pauses, I glance behind me, where he sinks onto his knees. "What are you doing?" I ask, my voice a silky whisper of contentment.

His teeth sink into my ass cheek in answer. "Fuck, I've been wanting to do that all damn week."

OWEN

ADDIE EXITS MY BEDROOM, and my next breath gets lodged in my throat.

She's wearing only a shirt and panties, and as if that image weren't hot enough on its own, the shirt is mine.

She spins on her heel, graceful and beautiful, flashing my last name printed across the back of the shirt. It's one I used to wear during workouts and practices when I played baseball.

It looks like it belongs to her, and my chest stirs for the hundredth time this week.

"If you still played baseball, I'd wear this to your games," she says as she sashays toward me and wraps her arms around my waist.

"No way." I shake my head. "I'd miss the ball every time because I wouldn't be able to take my eyes off you."

"You're too charming for your own good, you know?" She rests her chin on my chest and peeks up at me. "It's just as well—I don't know anything about baseball."

"Unacceptable," I say hoarsely. As assertive as I would've liked to sound, such a thing isn't possible when she looks at me like this.

Addie's gaze is so pure and comforting. A thousand other

descriptions come to mind too. Her eyes just make me feel things I've never experienced before.

I dip my head for a slow kiss. With a deep breath, I nod over my shoulder. "How about a glass of wine on the deck?"

"Perfect." She links our hands, and I lead her toward the kitchen.

With full glasses perched in our grip, we settle onto two cushioned chairs on my back deck, the three-quarter moon bright tonight. On my phone, I pull up my app and turn the surrounding lights on, dimming them to a romantic setting.

The hot tub buzzes with the jets, which are on a timer, and Addie hooks her thumb toward it. "Nice hot tub."

"We can get in later if you want."

"I don't have a swimsuit."

"You don't need it." I wink, and this earns me a mischievous grin. Unable to stand even the three feet between us, I jerk her chair closer to me.

She nearly spills her drink, but she doesn't complain.

"How was your day?" I ask, my voice low.

"You want to know about my day?"

"I want to know everything about you."

"Well." She licks her lips, and I follow the movement with my gaze. I'm completely consumed by her. "It was uneventful, for the most part," she says with a shrug. "A couple of students were out with a stomach bug, which sucked, but I wasn't hit by a dodgeball or basketball this time. That's one good thing. But the PE teacher I share a classroom with was wearing sweatpants."

"What's wrong with those?" I cock a brow.

She lifts her darkening gaze. "They're too distracting, especially when they're paired with wild hair and devilish smirks."

I fight one of those smirks right now, hiding behind my glass of Pinot Noir. "It sounds like the trouble I'm having with the perky English teacher I share a classroom with."

"Oh?"

"She bends over a lot, and it's hard not to picture leaving teeth marks in that ass. In fact, the first chance I got, I did just that."

Her gulp is magnified by the silence of the night. "And what did you think?"

"All I can think about is doing it again," I rasp and lean over for a wine-soaked kiss underneath the stars with the woman who's completely taken over my body, mind, and soul.

~

IT'S BEEN an hour of talking and drinking, but we're doing less of the latter now that both our glasses are empty. I should've brought the bottle out here with us. I had every intention of retrieving it from inside, but twenty minutes have passed, and I still haven't moved.

I'm too hooked on Addie, and all we're doing is talking about family and friends.

Such innocent topics are somehow far more interesting when she's the one I'm chatting with. We could talk about rocks and I'd be captivated.

She curls her foot under her other knee and twists to fully face me, her glass abandoned on the table on the other side of her. "It's wild that our dads know each other, right?"

"I had no idea, but it makes sense. Everyone around here knows one another." I shrug. "Did you say your dad lives in Louisiana now?"

"Just outside of New Orleans in my stepmom's hometown."

"Do you get to see them much?"

"I used to visit a few times a year, but it's been a while now since my last trip out there. He's so busy with work, and I've had a lot going on too—I'm actually a lot like him with the routines and lists and organization." She sighs as a smile teases her lips. "When I do visit, it's always the best time. We go to Café du Monde for beignets and coffee, stroll through the

French Quarter, and enjoy the museums. Once, we ran a marathon through the city together, and it was a blast. My stepmom made us matching shirts and cheered us on from the sidelines—she opted to ride her bike along our route instead of running."

"She sounds supportive."

"Very." Addie nods, then snaps her fingers. "Another time, I met them in Pensacola for a beach trip, and we found some baby sea turtles. It's all I could talk about for months, and my dad started calling me 'sea turtle.'" She balances her chin in her palm as she rests her elbow on the chair. "We've made a lot of good memories since the divorce."

"What ever happened with your parents?" I ask, but then I think better of it. "You don't have to tell me. I don't mean to overstep, but you saw my family. We hardly have any boundaries."

"I want to share with you," she says, and her tone is almost shy as she tucks her hands back into her lap. "If you can believe it, my mom wasn't always the way she is now."

"How do you mean?"

"For one, she was Mom and not Rain. She had a full-time job as a receptionist at a local dental office, and she and my dad were happy... until she saw a psychic during a girls' trip with some of her friends right before I turned ten."

"A psychic?"

Addie's lips tighten into a frown. "One hour with a psychic, and my mother was a different person. She'd somehow been convinced that she needed to clear my father's trust fund to make donations to various charities, and we should all become vegetarians. That we should all be closer to the earth. On my tenth birthday, she even tried to convince us to sell the house and travel the country in a van, where she'd educate me on the world by being one with it."

"What did your father say?"

"He thought it was some kind of phase she'd grow out of. That maybe she was having her midlife crisis sooner than most people, but the *phase* took on a life of its own."

"What do you mean?" I scoot to the edge of my seat and lean both elbows on my knees.

She twists her lips this way and that, pausing before she blows out a frustrated breath. "She sort of maxed out all their credit cards with donations to environmental charities and organizations. Her thought was that my father would have to pay one way or another, but what he did instead was serve her divorce papers."

I swipe at the corners of my frowning lips.

"He stuck around in town and helped with our financials for a while, but eventually, Rain and I filed for bankruptcy. Dad made sure we kept the house, but then he packed up and moved to Louisiana, where he met Henrietta." She offers a sad smile that cuts through me when she says, "He found his happy and never let go."

My stomach churns.

While I can appreciate the sentiment of clinging to joy—it's a beautiful notion—he left his daughter.

He moved away and started a new life without Addie.

The underlying sadness in her voice suggests she might feel the same, but I don't press her on it. Who am I to tell her how she feels?

"Maybe that's one thing we don't have in common." Her laugh is unsteady and hesitant. "He at least figured out how to be happy."

"What would make you happy, Lockhart?" I urge, peering into her eyes, which glisten under the bulbs of light strung around my deck.

Her expression softens as a slow, wicked smile spreads. "Right now, a little dip in the hot tub would make me happy."

I clap and stand. "Beat you in there."

"You're on!" She jumps to her feet and wiggles out of her

clothes, nearly stumbling with her panties around her ankles on her way to the hot tub.

I race past her, fling my shirt off, and climb into the hot tub, grateful I already slid the cover off earlier this afternoon for some maintenance.

This is perfect hot tub weather, and the soak works wonders for my knee, not that it's at the forefront of my mind.

What's more important is the naked fucking angel dipping into the water next to me.

"Hey!" Addie sinks into the hot water until the steam rises around her flushed cheeks. "You didn't win. You're still wearing shorts."

"The rule was to beat me in here. We didn't specify with or without clothing." I chuckle as the wheels in her head clearly turn for a rebuttal.

Guess she doesn't have one, but she does pout. Her bottom lip juts out as she splashes me with water.

I splash her back, lunging toward her and cornering her.

Addie's wet hair and dripping breasts call to me.

As I capture her mouth with mine, I cup her tits in each hand and tease, knead, and pluck her nipples.

Even in one-hundred-degree water, she shudders under my touch, and I savor every one of her moans and whimpers as the cool breeze nips at my shoulders.

She pulls my shorts down, which go easily with the water, and she urges me backward until I hit the opposite corner.

The jets massage my back as she floats over me, straddling my hips while she continues kissing me. I'm hard underneath her, and I grunt as she positions me right where I need her.

She sinks onto me, and my relief is immediate, like I'm lost when I'm not inside her.

I dig my fingers into her slippery skin as she rises and falls, and her head lulls to the side with each movement.

Her hair falls over her face, and I slip my fingers through it until I gather a fistful of her strands at the back of her head, tugging on them just as she likes.

This earns me a heavy moan.

And I grow even harder inside her as she rides me faster and wilder, the water sloshing over the edges next to us.

My head spins as I give myself to her yet again, hoping like fuck that I can be the one who makes her happy for days, weeks, and months to come.

And beyond.

chapter
thirty-five

ADDIE

"Meet me in the Health room in one minute, or your ass is off to detention."

Owen saunters past the row of bleachers, whistling an easy tune as I gather my thoughts—and ovaries.

I had two coffees this morning, but they don't compare to the energy boost his scandalous request gives me.

Scanning the gym, I confirm we have no witnesses, not that they'd be in here this early. We still have twenty minutes before first period.

I scurry toward the Health room and check once more over my shoulder, my paranoia nagging at me. With the coast still clear, I inch the door open and lock it behind me.

Owen slams his mouth to mine, both hands on my cheeks as he devours me with his kiss.

Last night was a dream. At least, I thought it was when I woke up.

I startled awake in my own bed after a particularly naughty dream of Owen and me in the hot tub, but it was real—so very wickedly real.

He'd insisted I stay the night with him, but I knew it was a bad idea. I wouldn't have been able to get up this morning to make it to work on time, not with a naked Owen sprawled across the bed.

With an enormous helping of self-control, I drove myself home, lost in a daze.

I danced in the bathroom while I got ready earlier, and I used my best mascara too, which has earned me several compliments all week.

I tear myself away from Owen and straighten my sweater back into place, then fluff my hair. "I think that'll do, Mr. Conrad."

"Oh, fuck. Don't call me that. Not unless you want me to hightail it out of here with you bent over my shoulder." He adjusts himself and groans.

I lick my lips, fantasizing about him doing just that, when a nutritional poster behind his head catches my attention. It's not because a group of cartoon fruits and vegetables stares back at me, either. It's a reminder.

We're at school.

This is our place of work.

We are professionals, who definitely did not have sex in a hot tub last night, and we're sticking to that story.

I need to get out of here!

He wraps his arms around me again, but I swat him away and smack his chest. "We need to be more careful, don't you think?"

"Fine." He holds his hands up.

"Wait two minutes to leave," I whisper as if someone might hear me, then turn toward the door.

And he squeezes my ass, his breath hot on my ear when he says, "You look beautiful today."

My heart stuttering, I take a deep inhale, throw the door open, and force one foot in front of the other until I reach my side of the gym. Soon afterward, I hear the Health room door shut, and he waltzes out, whistling the same tune from before as he gathers basketballs onto the rack.

"Good morning," Sable chirps, appearing seemingly out of nowhere.

My shoulders jump to my ears as I spin to face her. "Hi," I croak as I hear what sounds like Owen dribbling a ball behind me.

"Just wanted to come by with an update on your classroom." She wiggles her shoulders in a mini celebratory dance.

"My classroom?" I blink.

"The damage wasn't as extensive as we thought. In fact, the repairs on the roof are almost finished, then we'll paint, and you'll be ready to move back in sooner rather than later."

Instinctively, I glance back at Owen, whose shirt lifts as he shoots the ball from the three-point line and makes it.

"I'm actually surprised you haven't asked about it."

I turn back to Sable. "I'm sorry?"

"I expected you to be more involved with your classroom, to be honest." She giggles. "I imagined clipboards and itineraries for the remodel, and I was definitely prepared for daily briefs or something."

Oh, crap.

That does sound like something I'd do. What doesn't sound like me is quietly letting the professionals do their jobs without intervening just so I could make eyes at the PE teacher every day.

"Well." I swallow as another dribble sounds, but this time, it's much louder. It's like the basketball bounces inside my head, pounding against my brain. "I'm a team player," I manage. "I didn't want to overstep. I'm good at a lot of things, but construction is a whole other beast."

We share a laugh, after which she nudges me with her elbow. "I appreciate your patience, and I'm so thankful for how well you've made this new arrangement with Owen work."

"Just doing my job," I say with a jut of my chin upward.

"You should see what's going on with the other teachers who needed to team up. Revenge plots, broken thermostats, and missing tea bags." She shakes her head. "We should have coffee this weekend. I'll tell you all about it, and maybe I could even pick your brain to see how you've managed to be so successful. I mean, you and Owen have it all figured out. You're a great team."

"We're just co-workers," I blurt.

Her phone screen lights up with an incoming call, and she touches my elbow as she says, "Keep up the great work, and oh—I know I've said it before, but it's worth mentioning again. I just *love* your new hair."

She strides away, and I clutch my stomach as a wave of nausea rolls through it.

This is the first time I don't experience an adrenaline rush from her kind words about me.

Am I sick? No. I'm fine. She was simply complimenting me—it's nothing new. She doesn't suspect a thing between Owen and me.

From the sounds of it, I'm just making her life easier with these temporary classroom assignments, and that's all.

No need to panic.

Except the nagging urge to throw up doesn't leave me the entire morning. During the middle of second period, I even have to rush to the locker room to hurl into a toilet, but it's a false alarm.

My pale complexion is real, though, and it isn't because of the fluorescent lights above the bathroom mirrors.

I'm just having a minor crisis, but it's nothing I can't handle. I've basically trained my whole life for easy decision-making and an obscene amount of pressure. I can handle what comes next with Owen and me, no matter what it is.

When the bell rings for fourth period, and the students shuffle out of the gym, I take a seat next to my large trusty tote and retrieve a protein bar. One bite, though, and I'm ready to vomit again.

It's my favorite snack, but right now, I couldn't want it any less than if it were a bag of dirt.

I wrap up the end and stick it into a baggie in my tote, my shoulders slumping. It takes everything in me not to slither to the floor and lie down. To my surprise, nothing sounds better than a nap on this disgustingly dusty floor.

But students file in and pull me out of my weird trance. I have a job to do. Now is not the time to fall apart just because my fantasy life and reality are colliding.

After a quick greeting, I open my textbook to the short story of the week to break up the long reading assignments since we finished *The Scarlet Letter*. I use my pointer finger to trace the title at the top of the page and say, "'The Tell-Tale Heart' by Edgar Allan Poe." I swallow with great difficulty like I'm trying to force down a cotton ball. "Unreliable narrators. Voice. Tone."

The students blink back at me from the bleachers, expectant expressions mixed in with bored ones too. Nothing out of the ordinary, but my thoughts are jumbled. It's as if I've forgotten to speak in full sentences, with a subject, verb, and transitions.

"Let's start with the narrator." I cough into my palm, but it does little to alleviate the pressure in my throat. "How would you describe him?"

I nod toward the first kid to raise his hand. "Delusional."

"And what gives you that impression? What examples could you use?" I press.

"He says in the story that he's sane, but he also kills an old man in his own bed," he answers, his eyes wide.

"Good. Good." I pace in front of the bleachers—bad idea. It feels like I'm rocking on a boat, and my sea legs haven't quite matured. "Let's dive deeper into this narrator."

Owen's whistle from the other side of the gym makes me cringe, and the echo of it doesn't immediately wane as it normally does.

The distraction takes me a second to gather my wits and remember the lesson I have planned. I've already done this three times today. I shouldn't have any trouble successfully completing it a fourth.

"What do you make of the narrator's specific details and hypersensitivity to his surroundings in the scene?" I pose.

Thankfully, the students do a wonderful job of discussing the complexity of Poe's character as they dissect and analyze pieces of the short story.

One student raises a hand and asks, "Does this guy have a name? I don't remember reading one."

"Excellent observation," I say. "He does not give a name in the story. Do you think it's a deliberate choice? If so, why?"

I take a seat as they bounce ideas back and forth regarding the universal relatability of a character with no name, while some students argue it was a lazy choice to leave out the name.

At one point, their conversation is lost in the game Owen's leading, and my stomach squeezes. I don't know how long I remain frozen as the room spins around me.

"Lockhart?"

When I glance over, my head moves in slow motion, and my eyes don't immediately focus on Owen.

"Hey, are you okay?" He kneels in front of me, one comforting hand on my knee.

"I, um, don't know." I slowly blink, my eyelids heavy.

"What exactly are you feeling?"

I wrap my arm around my stomach and take a deep breath, but it does nothing to settle the increasing nausea threatening to commandeer my body. "I'm going to throw up."

"Now?"

"I'm going to throw up," I repeat more emphatically and use his shoulders for balance to help me stand.

With his assistance, I reach the locker rooms just in time.

I collapse onto my knees in one stall and hurl this morning's breakfast into the toilet, tears streaming down my face as my stomach clenches in agony.

Owen calls out to me from the entrance of the locker room, but I barely comprehend his muffled words over the throbbing in my temples.

Torture. This is absolute freaking *torture*.

I slump against the wall of the stall, and my lungs squeeze as I fight for breath. Several minutes pass before my pulse finally steadies, and the nausea subsides.

I press my back into the wall and hoist myself onto my feet, straighten my sweater, and blow the hair out of my face. Once I wash my hands and touch up the smeared mascara in the corner of my eye, I exit the locker room, dragging my feet like I just got off a ten-hour flight.

And when I pause, it's not because I can't walk any farther. It's because Owen is addressing my class. His own class is alternating between running up and down the bleachers and shooting free throws.

I'm within earshot, but he doesn't immediately notice me.

He points to Mia. "You said this song is so bouncy and catchy, but it's actually really sad. Most of us would agree, yes?"

Some students don't move or otherwise respond, but many others nod.

"Why do you think Taylor put such a fast-paced tune to sad lyrics? Why the juxtaposition?" Owen asks my class as I study the scene.

What exactly is going on here?

Students look left and right at one another as if looking for answers written on their foreheads.

"Could it be because it's yet another way she's doing this with a broken heart? It's in the lyrics, right?" Owen poses. "She puts on a happy façade, like the song, but she's also sad inside."

"The song *is* her," Mia supplies.

Owen throws his hand up and spreads his fingers in a mic drop gesture. He swivels his head toward his class, who's making much less noise, and calls out, "I see you! Get back to work, people."

His eyes land on me.

My smile is instant. It couldn't be contained were my mouth sealed with duct tape.

His eyes slowly crinkle in the corners as his own grin spreads.

And for this split-second moment, we're the only two people in the building.

OWEN

THANK FUCK, Addie's okay.

She looks great in anything and everything—I've said it before, and I'll say it a million times more—but green is not a comforting look for her face.

She scared the shit out of me, but she returns from the locker room less green. Her eyes are red, though, so I'm not completely at ease just yet.

The bell rings for lunch soon after she approaches me, where I stand in front of her class, and all the students file out.

"Awesome class," one girl gushes as she sidesteps Addie and me.

"Taylor for the win," I say back, spreading my arms to my sides. Once we're alone, I give Addie a once-over and ask, "How are you feeling?"

She rubs her stomach. "My throat's a little sore, but I think I can manage the rest of the day. Hopefully."

"Why don't I take you home? Sable or a sub can fill in for your class."

"Or you could." She points to where her students were just previously scattered. "Were you analyzing Taylor Swift lyrics?"

"Her song 'I Can Do It with a Broken Heart' has many levels. We didn't even get to the half of it."

Addie appraises me with what appears to be a mix of awe and disbelief. "You've actually listened to Taylor Swift?"

"Duh." I scoff. "I have three sisters—I'm an honorary Swiftie who knows most, if not all, the songs. Just try me. I dare you to quiz me."

She holds her hand up and giggles. "I think I believe you. I'm just... I need a minute to process this new information."

"Take your sweet time, baby. I'll wait." I wink.

She starts to smile, but it quickly transforms into horror. Her hand flies to her mouth, and she bolts for the locker room again.

"Shit," I mutter.

The stomach bug has been going around. Could that be what she has? If that's the case, I should be worried too, considering how close she and I got last night—three times.

After the hot tub, we continued the party in the shower, and I could've died a happy man in there, complete with the suds of my men's Dove bodywash.

I touch the back of my hand to my cheek to confirm I don't have a fever. Truthfully, I couldn't be in better shape right now. No fever, nausea, or headache. I feel great, but it doesn't mean I'm in the clear.

She could also have food poisoning.

As soon as she exits the locker room, her eyes redder than before and makeup smudged, I'm waiting for her right outside the door and ask, "What have you eaten in the last day or so? Anything out of the ordinary?"

"Nothing I can think of. You think this is food related?"

"Could be, but the stomach bug could also be at play." I don't miss the relief in her exhale. "Do you think it's something else?"

"Sable said something this morning that I thought I might be freaking out about, but, um, never mind."

What could Sable have said to set her off?

Addie groans into her palms.

"I'll take you home," I offer.

"My classes." She lifts a limp hand, doing her best to gesture over her makeshift classroom on the bleachers. "The students. I... What..."

I guide her to sit. "You can barely stand or form complete sentences. You need to get some rest at home, with a bucket next to you at all times."

"I actually didn't make it to the bathroom that time." She winces. "I had to throw up in the sink."

"That settles it. I'm calling Sable and taking you home."

"What about your classes? They'll... Who..." She clutches the side of her head in her hand and squeezes her eyes closed.

Addie's in no condition to drive or be left alone for long, but she's right about my classes. It'll be a lot simpler to fill in for one teacher at the last minute, but two might be a lot to ask.

"I'll figure something out," I reassure her. "Right now, we need to get you home."

I gather Addie's textbook, notes, and pens into her tote, then throw her coat over my shoulder as I call Sable and inform her of the situation.

"I'll be right over," she says.

The next call I make is to my mother. I didn't have all the details ironed out before I called, but with four kids and a grand-baby, she's no stranger to all kinds of ailments. She jumps into caretaking mode and gives me all the answers I was hoping for.

More than that, I'm relieved she's able to help. I almost didn't call, given how busy I know she is with her part-time job at Dad's pharmacy, plus Whitney and Huck.

Sable arrives with a brown paper bag in one hand and half a

sandwich in the other. She stops to check on Addie, who takes one whiff of her food and gags.

As she rushes to the locker room again, Sable turns to me with a frown. "Not the best day to bring a tuna salad sandwich with me."

"It's not you. It's whatever virus or food poisoning she has."

"You'll make sure she gets home safely, right?" she asks, concern etched in the crease between her brows.

"I'm on it." I muster my best smile. "I'll be back before my next class, but if for some reason I'm not—"

"I'll handle it," she reassures me.

I thank her, fling the tote bag over my shoulder, and grab my keys from the Health room, after which I meet Addie back in the gym, her arms wrapped around her stomach.

My chest hurts to see her in pain like this.

With my best mask of confidence I can force, I guide her outside, where I place a kiss to her temple. "Let's get you home."

"I HAVEN'T HAD time to clean up since my mom left the other night," Addie croaks. "I'll get to it."

"There will be plenty of time for that later." I put her water bottle in her hand and urge her to sip as I say, "Right now, your only jobs are staying hydrated and resting."

She winces as she swallows, and it's obvious the water doesn't go down easily.

The only time I've been to Addie's house was the night I secretly dropped off dinner for her two weeks ago, but I didn't come inside.

I'm not sure what I expected, to be honest. Matching curtains and throw pillows, or perhaps labels for glasses, coffee mugs, and plates stuck to her cabinets. Part of me imagined Taylor Swift posters and *Shark Tank* merch, but I'm not ruling them out just yet; they're probably hidden away in glass cases.

In any case, I didn't expect the mess.

It's absolute chaos in here, and guilt eats at me as I guide her to the only empty seat on her couch. How can I leave her here and go back to work for the afternoon? I need to help her. To at least clear the laundry and snack wrappers off her couch.

"Where might a bucket or a bowl be?" I ask her.

"I'll get it." She starts to sit up, but I place both hands on her shoulders and nudge her to stay where she is.

"Just point me in the right direction, please."

"To the left of the kitchen sink, there should be a few mixing bowls."

As her head falls to the back of the couch, I launch my search of the mixing bowl. The kitchen sink is halfway full, and the counter is littered with used forks and napkins. The refrigerator is bare and nothing like the one at my mom's, which is covered in baby pictures of Huck, plus wedding and baby shower invitations.

Addie's cabinets are not labeled, but the pantry is. Once I located the biggest bowl of the four immediately available, I check the Cs in her pantry and find an open box of crackers.

Supplies in hand, I return to her side. "Eat a few of these, and use the bowl as needed. I'll be back to check on you later."

"You're leaving?" Her eyelids flutter open, and her scared gaze shoots me right in the chest.

"I have to get back to my classes, but I won't be leaving you alone. I promise."

This seems to put her at ease as she sinks back into the cushions.

I pull my phone from my pocket and find a text from my mom. The one above it was one I sent with Addie's address.

MOM

I'll be there in fifteen minutes.

This gives me all the relief I need. If I can't be the one to look after her, I'm glad it can be my mom. She's the best person I know, and Addie will be in good hands with her until the final bell rings.

"How about we get you into comfier clothes? Maybe even lie down in bed?" I ask.

She barely lifts her head, but I think the sound she makes is a yes.

I dip low enough to wrap my arm under hers and hoist her onto her feet, leaning most of her weight onto me. We make it out of the living room before I realize I don't know where I'm going.

As if she reads my mind, she points to the end of the hall. "That one."

Her bedroom is sparsely decorated in florals and a few picture frames of her, Maren, and Caroline. There are a couple with her parents from when she was younger, and there's a more recent one of her with sea turtles at the beach. It must be from the trip to Pensacola to visit her father that she mentioned last night.

Everything in this room is tidy and in its place. Did she chain this room off during her mother's stay? How else did she manage to keep everyone else from destroying it like they did the rest of the house?

Addie rests on my shoulder as I peel back her comforter and help her slide inside. With a sigh, she says, "You're pretty good at taking care of me."

"This is nothing," I whisper, but I can't be certain that she hears me.

She drifts off to sleep with a soft snore, and it gives me another moment of relief. She'll be asleep when my mom gets here, but when Addie wakes up, she'll be happy to know she's not alone.

I stay with her for a few moments until my phone buzzes.

MOM

I'm here.

I kiss Addie's temple, my nose tangling in her wavy strands, and then I tear myself away to let my mother in.

"I didn't want to ring the doorbell in case she'd fallen asleep," she says and kisses my cheek in greeting.

"How did you know?" I ask as I grab some of the grocery bags from her hands.

"Like I said on the phone, this is not my first time. I've seen it all, including sleepwalking and attempting to learn French from the exhaustion and delirium of throwing up. Virus or food poisoning—either way, she's got to be drained."

"Should I take her to the doctor?" I ask.

"Her symptoms are consistent with one of the two, and a doctor is only going to tell her to rest, drink water, and eat soup and crackers." Mom points to the bags. "I brought everything I need to make soup, and there's a box of saltines in there too. There's also a small case of water out in my car, if you could please bring it in and set it next to her bed. That way, she won't have to keep refilling a glass."

"You are a saint. Thank you so much for this." I give her another hug, then jog out to her car for the water.

By the time I return to the kitchen, she's already set a pot on the stove, and she's measuring out rice for the chicken and rice soup she always used to make us when we were sick.

Addie is definitely in good hands, and some of my earlier guilt dissipates.

"I'll come back in a few hours to clean up in here, so don't worry about any of that," I say. "Just keep an eye on her, please."

"I've got it from here, son." She gives me a warm smile as she rounds the counter to give me another kiss on the cheek. "We still need to have our chat too."

"Right after you tell me who tried to learn French," I tease.

She winks, and I thank her again as I back away toward the front door.

Outside, I race down the porch steps but stop. Scarlett freezes practically mid-jog and stares, her mouth wide enough to fit half a cheeseburger. I almost don't recognize her with her hair piled underneath a ballcap and not a stitch of makeup on. She usually works the Tap like she's ready for her closeup on camera.

She yanks her earbuds out. "What are you doing?"

"I could ask you the same."

Scarlett points a long finger to the house next door. "That's where I live. Your turn." Her eyes widen. "Wait. Are you here to finally off Addie?"

"What? No. We're not…" I clear my throat. We're pretending. Addie and I are still pretending, and that includes lying to Scarlett, or at least treading the fine line of the truth with vague answers. "We don't even hate each other that much."

She twists her lips. "Over the summer, you tried proving she's European and living in this country illegally just so you could get her deported."

"She'd somehow convinced Kenny to replace Sunday specials from the good beers to some bullshit light IPA." I scoff and meet her on the sidewalk.

"Seems like an appropriate response to such a travesty," she deadpans.

"Addie's done and said a lot worse," I say with a snort.

"Oh, for sure. The latest being how badly she wants to chop off your microscopic balls and feed them to you like M&Ms."

I lift a brow. "What did I do to earn such cruelty?"

Scarlett shrugs. "Just a typical Tuesday afternoon, which is why I'm still not convinced you're not here to bury her body and clean up after yourself." She points to the minivan in Addie's driveway. "Why else would you bring such a hideous monstrosity? It must be filled with bleach and body bags."

"That's my mom's."

"You called your mom for murder cleanup?"

"You listen to too many true crime podcasts," I shoot back. "Shouldn't you be at the Tap? It's happy hour."

"Exactly." She rolls her eyes. "I needed to get away from David's impatience and Lisa's whining over her less than stellar cocktail that 'tastes like a toddler mixed it,'" she grumbles, tossing up air quotes. Guess it's a common complaint from the Tap's resident high-maintenance cougar. "Plus, Kenny's had a stick up his ass for two weeks now, and I can only take so much. I asked off and didn't really wait for an answer."

"Smooth."

"Gotta go after what you want, Conrad," she says with a shrug as she walks backward toward her house.

"You most certainly do," I mutter under my breath as I take another look at Addie's house, fantasizing about last night—the whole last week, really.

And I want more of that.

chapter
thirty-seven

ADDIE

I WAKE up from my deep slumber in a daze.

My head pounds, and my stomach aches.

Chills rack my limp body as I heave myself into a seated position against the headboard.

The sun's still shining, so is it safe to assume it's still Friday? Or did I sleep for twenty-four hours? Either one could be true.

I rub the sleep from my eyes, then find water on my nightstand. At the sight, I smack my lips and realize how dry my mouth is. It's like I've spent the last two hours sucking on cotton balls.

The few sips instantly soothe my scratchy throat, and I throw my feet over the side of the bed, only to land in a bowl—my puke bowl.

Owen.

He was here, in my house, taking care of me. He was gentle and comforting, and—

"Oh no." I cover my mouth as I gag, my stomach recoiling in wild discomfort. I hoist the bowl up to my chin and race to the bathroom, only to find it's a false alarm.

With a sigh, I return to my bedroom, weak from head to toe.

I'm so out of it that I don't even flinch when a head pokes into my room, although at any other time, I would've shrieked and grabbed the lamp from my desk to use as a weapon.

I have no strength for all that right now, but I am surprised to find it's not Owen.

"Mrs. Conrad?" I squint.

"Now, now. I asked you to call me Dorothy." She pushes the door farther open and enters, a tray in her hands with a steaming bowl in the center and a glass vase of two pink flowers in the corner. "I thought I heard you stirring. You should try to eat something, darlin'. Some soup and crackers should help settle your stomach."

What is happening? Am I hallucinating?

"Come and sit." She gestures toward the bed, where the covers are thrown back from my nap. "Sit, sit," she insists.

I do as she instructs, settling back into my previous position on the bed and pulling the covers up to my chest. It's at this point that I realize I'm in mismatched pajamas—I'm wearing a green-and-white Christmas top and shorts decorated in raspberries. Did a monkey dress me?

"This is chicken and rice soup. I make it for my kids all the time." She props the tray onto its legs over my lap, and the smell is actually very pleasant. "Not to brag, but Whitney says it's magic."

I blow on a spoonful and take a bite, although it's mostly chicken broth. I close my eyes and savor the warm, soothing soup. "So good," I whisper and dunk my spoon back in. I'm only one bite in, but I already know this is going to work wonders on my throat.

"Eat some crackers too, and drink plenty of water."

"Mrs.—Dorothy," I correct myself. "Not that I'm not super grateful, but what are you doing here?"

"Did Owen not tell you I was coming?" She tilts her head.

"I don't think so, but then again, my head's a little fuzzy."

Which probably explains the outfit. It's possible I thought this combo matched in my disoriented state.

"Owen had to get back to work, but he wanted to make sure you're taken care of. That's where I come in." She spreads her arms.

I lower the spoon slowly as what she says resonates in a puddle of goo in my chest. "That's very... thoughtful," I whisper.

"That's my son for you."

"I hope I didn't intrude on your day. I'm so sorry. If you need to go, I'll be fine," I assure her.

In truth, it's more so for my benefit. I'm not great at accepting help from my own friends, let alone someone I've only met once.

I hate being taken care of—this is actually my nightmare—but I meant what I said about the thoughtful gesture. And I'm too weak to stand my ground.

"Oh, don't be silly. My boss is very understanding." She winks.

"I don't get it."

"I work for my husband, darlin'." She giggles, and it all makes sense. "Now, you eat up while I clean the mess I made in the kitchen right quick. I'll be back to check on you."

Through the fog hanging over my mind, I latch onto the word *kitchen*.

My mom.

The disaster.

So much mess.

"I'll clean up, Dorothy!" I croak as I plop the spoon into the soup with a splash and a clink.

She stops with her hand on the doorknob. "You will do no such thing. You're going to rest and pay no mind to anything other than that. I'm here to help, so let me help."

Her tone is so strong, her words punctuated with finality. My overwhelming urge to protest still lingers, but arguing feels futile and even a little disrespectful.

I sink back into my seat, but my guilt and self-consciousness don't dull.

Dorothy returns thirty minutes later to take the tray away, and my eyelids feel heavy again. My stomach is a little less queasy, thanks to the soup, but I'm still fatigued.

"Food poisoning," she says.

"Excuse me?"

"That's my best guess for what you might have. You're sweating, and your symptoms are far too abrupt and severe to be a stomach virus." Her confidence alleviates my uncertainty, and I nod. "Which is a good thing."

"How so?" I slide farther into the covers to lay my head on the pillow. I'm not normally so comfortable, even under these conditions, when relative strangers are around, but Dorothy makes it easy to let my guard down.

It's probably where Owen gets it. As similar as I believed him to be to his father, he's actually a lot like his mother.

"It means my son's in the clear." She smiles. "Stomach virus is contagious, but I don't believe I need to worry about him."

My mouth dries again, but it's not because of my ailment. "He's not... I mean, we're not that close. I wouldn't have gotten him sick. I work all the way on the other side of the gym from him," I say as quickly as my feeble body allows.

She waves me off. "No need for any of that, Addie."

Any of what?

That's what I'd like to ask, but nothing comes out of my chapped lips.

"Now, any idea what you might've eaten to cause this? I know it was not my lasagna from last night." She holds a finger up.

"Definitely not your lasagna. That was perfect in every way," I gush, clutching my waist. More cramps amplify across my stomach, and I shift uncomfortably. "I suppose it could have been the eggs I made this morning? I didn't check the date on the carton, as I was in a rush, but I don't think they've been in my fridge that long." I sigh. "I had chicken salad for lunch yesterday that might've been past its prime as well. I should really keep better track of that stuff. I'm normally great at it, but lately, I've had my dang head in the clouds."

She tilts her head, and amusement bounces across her features.

I clamp my mouth shut, then backtrack. "I just mean, I've been taking some time for myself after a busy summer and start to the school year."

She hums. "I'm going to whip you up some toast."

My stomach rolls, and the cramps worsen as a lump climbs up my throat.

"You know, I've never seen him this happy," she muses wistfully right before she disappears through the open door.

I revel in her admission and what that means for Owen and me for only a moment before I need the bathroom to throw up for the sixth time. Or is it the ninth? I've totally lost count.

THE GUZZLING cry of a mower prompts me awake.

I must've dozed off again after my last fit. Puking my guts out really takes it out of me. I've never had food poisoning before, and it's exactly as bad as I always thought it would be—and worse.

When does it go away?

I check the time on my phone, noting it's almost six. Next to my phone, I find a plate wrapped in aluminum foil and a note that just says, "Eat me."

I opt for the water to wet my sore throat, then close my eyes again.

I have the weirdest dreams. One starts with Owen standing at the foot of my bed, his cheeks dotted with dirt and flakes of grass. He kneels beside me and dabs a cool, wet washcloth along my forehead—it's refreshing.

Then he kisses my temple and disappears.

I want to call out to him and beg him to stay, but my voice doesn't work. It's like my lips are sealed shut. My heart aches for him to come back, but everything darkens again.

In another dream, he holds my hair back while I hurl into the toilet. I'd be embarrassed in real life, but since this is a dream, I feel free to do what needs to be done.

And he doesn't say anything. Rather, Owen simply rubs circles on my back, and when I'm finished, he carries me back to my bed, where he gently lays me down. How can he be so gentle? He's a muscular giant with the strength of freaking Captain America. Yet his gentle caress along my forehead is like that of a feather.

"I've got you," he whispers as he smooths my hair back.

All the dreams end the same too, with him walking away and me desperate to call out to him, but I don't. Nothing ever leaves my mouth, and the ache in my chest vibrates with sadness throughout my whole body.

chapter
thirty-eight

ADDIE

I TRUDGE out of my bedroom and down the hall, feeling worse than I ever have after any hangover or flu combined.

Rubbing my eyes with the heels of my palms, I run into the wall, disoriented after fifteen hours of sleep and odd dreams.

In the living room, I smell fresh linens. Am I imagining it? It definitely smelled like sage and burned pancakes yesterday morning when I left for work.

I blink several times, then scan the couch, coffee table, and rug. They're all clean. Everything is spotless.

My jaw drops as I take in the fluffed throw pillows and the stainless corner of the rug. Before my mother left, she informed me of a tea spill and that it was bad luck to clean it up, so she left it.

It's become obvious to me over the years that she makes shit up, and it's mostly because she wants out of responsibility.

But there's no tea stain. No trash or dirty cups strewn about. No sign there were rowdy, ill-mannered people here at all.

I rub my hands up and down my arms, which no longer tremble under the curse of chills and body aches. Right now, my skin just crawls with a different kind of feeling—one I've never been keen on.

Chewing on the inside of my cheek, I cautiously meander into the kitchen, and sure enough, it matches the living room. The sink is free of any dish, drop, or mark. The stove and counter sparkle, and the windows have been wiped down too.

The only difference in here is that fresh flowers sit in a vase in the center of the breakfast table. It's a beautiful arrangement, with greenery interspersed among pale yellow, white, and orange blooms. Those definitely did not come from my property.

Which means *someone* got me flowers.

It's probably the same someone who brought a box of muffins from Bready or Knot. The yellow-and-white striped box is tucked under the flowers, and I open the top to take a whiff, testing the strength of my stomach for the day.

The smell is heavenly, but I'm not feeling a fresh muffin quite yet.

Brows furrowed, I peek through the window above the kitchen sink and admire the freshly cut grass. Even the hedges are trimmed.

When I thought I heard a lawn mower yesterday afternoon, I figured it was one of the neighbors. It was not. It was my yard.

How much of my dreams were actually reality?

"Good morning!" someone chirps from behind me, and what's left of my stomach falls to my knees.

I whip around, expecting to find Owen, but it's...

"Bo?" I ask, and two innocent eyes stare back at me. The not-even-twenty-year-old was in my English class a couple years ago, and he now works with Austin at the auto shop.

While I do know him, it's not well enough for him to be standing in my kitchen.

This was probably Owen's doing. He brought his mother to cook for me last night, and now he must have Bo up to something too. Did he enlist the whole town to help me, the incapable, puking damsel in distress?

"What are you doing here? Did you mow my lawn?" I ask.

"No. I fixed your car." He shrugs as he wipes his hands on a dirty rag.

A freshly showered—and dripping—Owen appears over his shoulder. Water droplets from his wet hair splatter across the top of his T-shirt, and his eyes shine like crystals catching the sun's rays.

"How did you know it needed fixing?" I ask, and it's directed more toward Owen, who seems to be the mastermind since it's clear the kid is just the messenger.

"It took you three tries to start it in the school parking lot the other day. Figured it was a starter problem, so I called in an expert." Owen holds his chin high with pride.

"I was going to fix it. It was on my list for next week," I say, hugging my gurgling midsection.

"Now you don't have to. It's done." Owen's innocent smile doesn't reach me as it did yesterday. Right now, it makes my blood boil.

I turn toward Bo. "I didn't know you made house calls."

"I do for three times the pay."

I gape at Owen again.

Bo cringes. "Sorry, dude. I forgot I wasn't supposed to say anything."

"Next time, I'll wait for Austin to be free."

Bo grumbles, and I level Owen with my stare. "Why did you pay him so much for *my* car?"

"What? I have money."

"And I don't?"

Bo shifts, his discomfort radiating in waves between us.

"That's not what I said, and it's definitely not what I meant. It's just that I have baseball money."

"I don't care if God Himself gave you stacks of gold. You have no right to go and spend it on me. Let me pay you back." I scan the counter for my tote, but it's not there. It's not at the breakfast table, either, and when I rack my brain for the answer as to its whereabouts, I come up empty.

Then again, it could be right in front of me, but it's hard to see past the red dots blotting my vision.

"I don't want you to pay me back. How do you still not understand the concept of an act of kindness?" His jaw sets. "Here's how it works—you let someone mow your lawn while you're sick, and you let that same someone get your car fixed, and you don't pay that someone back. You just say a simple thank-you, which I don't think you've ever said. Do you know how?"

My eye twitches. This is not happening. Not returning a favor is like not saying "excuse me" when I sneeze or leave the table. It's rude. And I especially can't leave things with Owen like this. There is no scenario I can live with where I'm in Owen's debt.

He's done too much for me, and the feeling of weakness creeps up my spine. This is why I don't ask for help. It's why I take care of everything myself. I hate being a burden to anyone, and I hate owing anyone anything.

"Why are you acting like saying two words is figuring out how big the universe is?" Owen folds his arms over his chest.

"If you don't care about getting anything in return, then why do you insist on a thank-you?"

"It's good practice for you," he shoots back.

"You cleaned my whole house!" I throw my hands up. "Not just that, you got other people involved too." I point to Bo, but he's nowhere to be found.

He must've snuck out during yet another one of my ridiculous squabbles with Owen.

"Bo and your mom," I continue. "Did you ask Leon for advice on the lawn too? I'm sure he was *so* happy to hear from you. He just loves weirdo do-gooders knocking on his door unannounced."

"What is your problem? Do you need to go back to sleep? Clearly, you didn't get enough rest last night."

"I'm perfectly capable of taking care of myself, Owen," I clip. "I don't need you to fix me."

He jolts backward, a frown etched into his face in the most unnatural way. Only grins and smirks belong there, but I've put a damn frown in their place.

"I know you can't help yourself, but I can handle this on my own," I assert.

"Can't help myself?"

"I never thought I'd say this, but you help too much. Your sisters, your nephew, your parents. When do you ever do anything for yourself?" I pose.

"That's what this is about?" He releases a humorless laugh. "I didn't realize lending a hand to those I care about is a crime, but thank you for clearing that up for me."

"It's not, but don't you ever get sick of being taken advantage of?" I ask, lowering my voice. "I don't want to be yet another person you need to drop everything for. I just want..."

"What do you want, Addie?"

I cringe at his use of my first name. No Lockhart, angel, or baby.

Just *Addie*.

And it drips with disappointment.

What is my problem? Am I seriously mad because he's so considerate and caring? That his heart is as big as this freaking town?

Or do I just not understand it because he actually does it out of the kindness of his soul and not because he's seeking praise? Not like me.

"I want to be more like you," I whisper.

His expression drops into one of shock.

He looks as surprised as I feel by my answer. Where did that come from? Is that why I'm upset—because he's making me realize I'm a compliment whore?

I lick my lips, acutely aware of the words as I speak them. "I don't want to care so much about the give-and-take of good deeds. I wish I could just appreciate the favor and let it rest."

The tension in his brow eases, and one corner of his mouth curls upward. "You can start that journey by saying *thanks*."

I shift uncomfortably in place as years of habit come to a head. "I dreamt that you held my hair back while I vomited." I wince.

"That was real."

"And carrying me to the bedroom?"

"Also real." He nods, his expression frustratingly unreadable.

"You mowed my lawn too," I say, and this time, it's more of a statement since I already know the truth.

He mowed my freaking lawn while I practically wasted away last night. I hate that I'm partially upset over my existential crisis, but also that I didn't have the chance to witness—and gawk—at a sweaty Owen, who might've been shirtless, engaging in physical labor.

I bet the sun glistened off his muscles, and I missed the whole thing.

But that's not the important part.

"This is hard for me." I blow out a heavy exhale, my head fuzzy and overwhelmed. "I've been severely independent since I was a kid. When my parents divorced, I was suddenly ten going on thirty. I had to be the adult in our house, and not once did my mother thank me. Do you know what she did? She criticized me for being too responsible and making perfect decisions. She said I should be outside playing in the dirt with the rest of the kids in our neighborhood. Can you believe it?" I scoff.

"It shouldn't have been that way for you," he says softly. "Nothing about that was fair."

I swallow the lime-sized lump in my throat, thankful for the validation. It's a relief, to say the least. Why have I never talked about this before? I could've freed myself from the burden long ago.

I wring my hands in front of me. "I guess it's why I'm so

desperate for praise. I never got it from the two people who always meant the most to me, and in turn, I never learned how to offer it when someone does nice things for me. And you, Owen, have done the kindest things of all."

He dips his head, scratching the back of his neck, and when he raises up again, his cheeks redden. The shy blush squeezes my heart.

Owen has proven time and again that this is just who he is. This isn't a game, and he's not working an angle. He's just a kind guy.

And I don't deserve him.

I shake my head as I lament, "I've said such terrible things to you and about you—over ten years' worth."

"Right back at you." He chuckles.

I round the counter and stop a foot from him, inhaling deeply as if to try and absorb some of his confidence and all-around good-ness. "Thank you." And for some unknown reason, I poke his chest with the tip of my finger.

He lifts a brow.

The tops of my ears burn. "I don't know why I did that."

He full-on smirks as he covers the spot I poked with his large hand. "I'll cherish it always."

"You really didn't have to do any of this, but I'm very grateful."

"You are welcome," he says, his voice thick with sincerity. "And I'm very glad you're feeling better."

"It was scary there for a while." I slide my fingers into my hair, which gives me pause. "Oh, God. I look like shit, don't I?"

"Never."

"Don't lie to me."

"Never." He cracks a grin and pulls me in for a hug, his arms easily swallowing me. He rests his chin on my head and sighs. "Did I mention how glad I am that you're feeling better?"

My smile spreads against his chest as I breathe him in, thankful he's here.

"And..." He pulls back. "Is this a good time to let you know I also fixed your dryer? Judd was here to help until Mary reminded him they were supposed to be with their niece and nephew, so I did it alone."

"That's it." I shake my head and separate myself the rest of the way from his embrace.

"What?"

"That's the last straw." I throw my hand up and round the counter toward the stove. "I thank you for all you've done, but I'm making you pancakes for all your troubles. That'll make us even."

As he takes a seat on a stool at the counter, he teases, "It's bad luck to reject pancakes."

thirty-nine

OWEN

ADDIE LAUGHS as I finish vacuuming up the pile of pancakes into my mouth.

I catch a runaway blueberry from the side and pop it into my mouth as I bask in the light sound of her laughter. It's much better than the sounds she made last night.

She was right earlier—it did get scary there for a moment. I hated that she was in so much pain and discomfort, but I can breathe a little easier now that more color has returned to her cheeks.

The tops of her ears get even redder after I kiss her.

She nibbles on her single pancake, but she mostly munches on a few crackers.

"Still not able to eat, huh?" I wince. "And I'm a jackass who just devoured five pancakes."

"I did tell you to, so you're just being a good boy."

"You know I can't resist it when you're bossy." I wink as her easy smile sends shots of relief throughout my nervous system. I push the bakery box to the side. "Lottie sends her love with the muffins. I was supposed to ask for your favorite, but you were still asleep. She grabbed one of each."

"I'll have to send her a thank-you cobbler."

"A text is fine."

She rolls her eyes. "What are you doing today?" she asks over her glass of water before she sips.

"Nothing planned. You?"

"In light of recent events, I'm going to take it easy, especially now that I don't have a whole house to clean and disinfect."

"Movie marathon?" I suggest.

"You'd be okay with watching movie after movie on a sunny Saturday?" She arches a brow.

"If it's with you, yes." I push my plate aside and fold my arms over the table in front of me. "Besides, I'm a bit of a controlling nurturer and would like to keep an eye on you to ensure you're actually going to take it easy today."

"As long as you don't strap an ankle monitor to me, you can stay," she teases and rises to put away our plates.

Once I thank her for breakfast again, I hold my hands up. "I'm going to wash these bad boys. Got a little crazy with the syrup."

I waltz out of the kitchen, easily making my way around her house after only a day. We got extremely acquainted yesterday as I tried to tackle the things that needed to be done around here.

In the bathroom, I change the Band-Aid on my finger from where I cut it on the lawn mower as I installed a new spark plug. It was me against the wily beast, and while it got its jab in, I came out on top and was able to fix it in order to cut down the jungle in Addie's yard.

I exit to find Addie chewing on her thumbnail as she paces the living room. "What's wrong? You getting sick again?" I ask, my instincts jumping into emergency mode yet again.

"What happened at school yesterday?" She pauses and stares blankly at me. "Because if that other stuff wasn't all a dream, then neither was the fact that you brought Sable to my class or that you gave me a ride home. Not just that, but you invited random people to my house, where you showered and made yourself comfortable." She waves her hands around.

"Did you really think I was going to let you drive home by yourself? You were in no condition," I reason.

"Owen, Sable—our freaking boss—saw you give me a ride home."

"So?" I blink, completely lost on her zigzagging trains of thought today. She's definitely disoriented, and I don't blame her, not after the horrendous fucking night she had.

But I thought we were done with her analysis of the events.

Addie paces again, throwing her head back to look at the ceiling. "Who else saw you giving me a ride? And what about Lottie and Bo—who are they going to tell that you were here? Can they be trusted not to tell anyone about us?"

And there it is.

Her sudden panic makes sense.

She's worried about our relationship, which is supposed to be a secret, but I've opened a can of worms, apparently.

"They're not going to tell," I say as I stuff my hands into my pockets, my shoulders heavy.

"Did you ask them not to? Did they reassure you they wouldn't?" she presses.

"I thought asking them not to would be suspicious, so I didn't. Besides, you had dinner with Lottie the other night. Her dropping off muffins is hardly a reason to panic."

"Great," she clips. "This is just *great*."

"What's going on, Lockhart?" I ask on a sigh. "What's the big deal?"

She gapes. "The big deal is that our personal life is about to be aired out all over town like a freaking tornado siren." She snaps and points a finger up, a lightbulb flashing behind her eyes. "Unless we get ahead of it. I'm supposed to have coffee with Sable this weekend. I could call her to meet now, where I play off some story of you and me together as a rumor, and I can nip it right in the bud."

"Or, you could tell her the truth," I blurt.

She snaps her horrified gaze up to mine.

And I freeze.

I hadn't meant to say it, but now that it's out there, I'm glad I did.

"Are you insane?" she squeaks. "We can't tell her the truth. Not yet."

"You like me, and I fucking like you. Why put off the inevitable?"

"We're not there yet."

"What will it take for us to get *there*, Addie?" I urge. "Because I'm fucking there."

"What are you saying?"

"I more than like you," I say on an exhale. "I never stop thinking about you. I never stop wanting to make you happy. You're my favorite, and I don't just mean my favorite woman, teacher, or even dancer. You're my favorite... everything."

Her eyes well with tears as a deep blush floods her cheeks.

"I don't want to keep you a secret anymore. I want to hold your hand while we walk around the square downtown. I want to dance with you at karaoke night at the Tap. I want to tell the world about us because you're the best fucking thing that's ever happened to me. You're too amazing to keep a secret, and I never should've agreed to do so to begin with."

A tear slips down her cheek, and her lips part.

I brace myself against the back of her couch, my heart lurching over and over again like runners clearing hurdles on a track.

Addie worries her lip between her teeth, and her silence is complete torture. Then she shakes her head, and my stomach sinks. "I can't. Not yet. It's not the right time."

"The job will be the job, no matter the time."

She scoffs. "I don't expect you to understand. You don't care about things the way I do. You just cruise through life with a joke and a grin, and everything works out for you. But that's not the reality for the rest of us. We have odds stacked against our character."

"What does that mean?"

Her face twists. "My mother's made quite the name for herself around here. She's unreliable, flighty, and loose, to name a few poor qualities of hers. Sleeping with a co-worker is something she'd do—and has done plenty of times. When she's held a job for more than a week, that is." She shakes her head, and her voice is unsteady when she poses, "Do you know how hard it's been to detach myself from her? To prove I'm nothing like her, not only to myself but to this town? This is complicated, okay?"

I blow out a frustrated breath, attempting to absorb what's really been going on here. It's not just about the job, the school, or the future.

It's her mother—the one who's been holding Addie back for years.

From where I stand, she's let her mother control her and her actions for so long. I just never thought I'd be caught in the crosshairs.

Disappointed doesn't even begin to cover the feeling creeping its way down my spine.

Shaking my head, I stalk toward the front door, with her hot on my heel, and I jerk my jacket from the rack. I whirl around to her and point around the wadded-up jacket in my hand. "I care about things. I care *a lot*. There's nothing more I can say or do to prove that to you or to show you that I care more about you than my career or reputation or anything else. You clearly don't feel the same, so we should stop wasting each other's time."

"You're ending this?" She freezes with her eyes wide, and the surprise and regret mingling in her blue irises slice through my stomach. "You know I like you, Owen," she says, her lips trembling. "I wouldn't have put myself out there like I have the last couple of weeks if I didn't feel big things for you, but it's not so simple."

"It could be."

"There's so much to figure out."

"All that matters is how we feel."

"So, what then? I either tell the school and everyone else in town about us, or we're done? Is that it?" She purses her lips and juts her hip out, challenging me like she's done so many times before.

But this is something else entirely.

This is the moment of truth—the difference between despair and happiness.

"As a matter of fact, yes." I widen my stance and stand my ground.

Her mouth falls open. "Are you seriously giving me an ultimatum right now?"

I step into her space, glad she doesn't back away. "Feel free to make a pros and cons list to help you out."

Addie shoves me backward, or at least she tries to. I don't budge, but she continues her feeble attempts, anyway. "Get out!"

"As I've said before, I'm a patient man, but don't take too long to decide. I'd hate for you to lose too much sleep over this."

"Leave. Now!" She gives me one last push, and I let my feet stumble backward for her benefit.

"Talk soon, angel," I call over my shoulder as I disappear through her door and march down her steps, my stomps heavy like I'm crushing spiders.

I flinch against the late-morning sun in my eyes, and the fall breeze cools my flushed skin.

I'm hot. Seething. Frustrated.

Addie likes me. She didn't have to explicitly say it for me to know it's the truth, but it's not enough. Not when she insists on hiding me away like I'm a shameful mistake.

Her job and public moral grounds are important to her, and I respect them.

But I also respect what we have, and I can't stand by while she stows us away like a dusty old trunk under the bed.

My mind's reeling as I drive around town. I could go home, but it's so empty. I'd go crazy.

Without thinking, I find myself driving toward my parents' house, antsy for that chat my mom promised.

chapter
forty

ADDIE

I throw my car—my newly perfectly functioning car—into park in front of a bustling Cream and Sugar.

Great.

I need Maren's undivided attention, but it doesn't look like I'll get it.

Still, I climb out of my car and stand in line. This is better than staying at home with my warring thoughts.

Three minutes later, the group in front of me moves as one, which is when I realize it's the Carmichael family of eight. I was so distracted by my fight with Owen that I didn't even recognize their faces. They were all just a blur.

Maren pokes her head out of the coffee truck and greets me, but it's not her usual friendly face. "What's wrong? You look like you haven't slept in days."

"I was up all night with the Devil wrangling a bull in my belly."

She squints.

"I'll explain later."

She hooks a thumb over her shoulder and says, "I have new coffee cookies I want you to try."

My fingers twitch at my sides as I make a noncommittal sound.

"I'll grab a couple of those, and then do you want your usual Fall in a Cup?"

"Thank you, but I don't want anything right now. Can we talk?" I nod toward the free picnic table under a tree as the Carmichaels disperse toward the park with their goodies in hand, and quiet descends.

Maren wipes her hands on her apron and steps aside, revealing she's not alone today. Tonya waves at me, and I think I wave back. I try to, at least.

I pace in front of the picnic table as Maren takes a seat and asks, "What's going on? You never turn down cookies." She waves a hand over me as I tap the outsides of my thighs to a nervous, off-beat rhythm. "I haven't seen you this worked up since they discontinued your favorite index cards."

"I'm with Owen," I blurt. "I mean, I was."

"Oh," Maren draws out, and her easy smile surprises me.

"What?"

"I already knew." She shrugs.

"How?" I screech.

"Scarlett was here this morning, babbling about Owen being at your place all night."

"That little... Wait." My eyes widen. "Did anyone hear her babbling?"

"Just me. And I gave her half a dozen cinnamon sugar cookies and a gift certificate to Daphne's to keep quiet."

"You dirty little saint."

"Tell me everything."

I pace by the picnic table as I relay the aftermath of our reunion kiss, the naughty special at the dance studio, and the filthy weekend in Savannah.

More than that, I share the significance of what he's done for me.

"I put off cleaning my house after my mother torpedoed it just so I could go to Owen's for a spontaneous visit." I throw my hands up. "I never drop responsibilities like that unless it's for work."

"That's a good thing, right?"

"It is. That's what I'm saying." I lick my lips. "He makes me... calm. I'm easygoing with him, but I'm still myself. I can be everything with him, and he's like, fine with it. More than fine, really. He likes me for all that I am, and he said so many wonderful things. Then I—*ugh*." I bury my face in my hands to hide my heated cheeks.

"What happened?"

I look back at my friend and twist my lips. "I kicked him out."

"Why did you do that?" Maren gapes.

"He gave me an ultimatum. Said if I wouldn't tell the world we're together, then he and I would no longer be together."

"Wow." She leans back, the frowning lines around her lips smoothing into shock.

We remain silent for a few loaded seconds as more customers line up at the truck. Maren perks up when someone asks for a coffee cookie. She's clearly pleased with her new concoction, and after I clear up this mess with Owen—and eat more magic soup for my queasy stomach—I'll devour her new masterpiece too.

"So, what's the problem?" Maren lifts a brow toward me.

"An ultimatum is so unfair."

"Is it, though? You're not willing to openly admit how important he is to you, so I'd bet he feels slighted. Why would he stick around if he's unwanted?"

I blow out a breath and finally take a seat.

"What's the real problem?" she prods.

"My job, Mar. What happens to my job? I'd be putting my professional career in jeopardy and my personal life on display. It's so not like me."

"Doesn't mean you can't do it."

"Fine. Say I did all that, aired my business to the whole town that I've been intimate with a co-worker, and it doesn't work out between us? I'll be the laughingstock of the century."

"Why wouldn't it work out? Have you detected red flags?"

"If you count mowing my lawn without telling me a red flag, then yes." I snap my fingers. "Oh! And get this. His whole family gets together once a week to eat dinner. They don't do it to celebrate a birthday or something, either. They do it just because. Who does that?"

"Sounds more like green flags to me."

"Okay, so there have not been any real red flags—not yet. But there will be."

"Why are you so adamant that there will be?"

"Because that's what happens, isn't it? It's what happened with Stewart and every other guy I dated before him."

"Stewart was not a real possibility for you and your future. He was a pastime, at best, and when you realized you deserved more than to settle, you did the mature thing and broke up with him."

"The point is, love doesn't last, Maren." My shoulders slump. "Just ask my parents. Better yet, ask yourself. Look what happened with you and Nate, and you two were the real deal, even at such a young age. It was so obvious to everyone, but it exploded in a matter of minutes."

She dips her head, but not before I glimpse her frown.

"I am so sorry." I squeeze her hand in mine. "I didn't mean to bring up ancient history. I know it's painful, and I'm way out of line."

"I'm over Nate," she asserts. "But this isn't about your parents or what happened ten years ago with me. It's about you."

I exhale in frustration.

"If love isn't real, what would you say to Caroline and Austin?" she challenges. "Who would've thought Austin Kyle, of all people, would turn his life upside down for anyone? I never would've guessed he'd find a way to be happy with a woman, but here we are. Those two fell for each other in less than a week."

"They're different."

"Why?"

"They're the exceptions. Every rule has them, just like the stupid *i before e* rule. It's not always the case."

"That's not the entire saying." She snorts. "It's *i before e except after c*, and you know it. Which brings me to my point—you see what you want to see. Try looking at the whole picture here."

"What if the whole picture is scary?" I whisper.

"Then you take a deep breath, count to five, and face your fears head-on. It's the only way to overcome them." Maren sits back. "I think it'd help to talk to Rain."

"You want me to talk to my mother?" I gape. She can't be serious.

Except she totally is.

With a stone-cold expression, she pins her brown eyes on me. "She could offer some clarity into your skewed perception of love."

"She'd tell me there's no such thing."

"Has she ever actually told you that?"

"She doesn't have to. Her entire life is an homage to the senti-ment." I roll my eyes.

Maren holds her hands up. "All I know is that when I brew a flat coffee or bake a sour cookie, I don't blame the espresso machine or the mixer. I go to the source—me. What did I do? Did I confuse the ingredients? Measure the wrong quantities? Perhaps the recipe simply wasn't a good one. Whatever the case, the mystery isn't going to solve itself."

"You paint quite the picture."

"I try." She pats my hand. "I have to help Tonya, but call me if you need anything. I have more colors with which to paint." With a snort, she hoists herself off the picnic table as more noise drifts from the truck.

Several more people have crowded the window, one of which is none other than Nate McAllister. Has Maren caught sight of him yet? She's about to be pissed.

I stick around for a beat to ensure I don't need to stand in for backup. I'm at my weakest at the moment, but I could still do some damage, if needed.

Besides, I'm enjoying the fresh air after a long night of doom and gloom. It's going to take a lot more than nature's sweet offerings to rid my skin of such clamminess, including at least twenty showers, but this is a good start.

My other issue is not off to a pleasant start, though.

Talking to Rain? Discussing someone I care about with *Rain*? She's going to tell me to dump him—I just know it. She's going to list all the ways it's not worth it to dedicate my heart to one man and tell me that I'm too young to do so to begin with.

None of that is what I want to hear.

It's not what I want at all, but how can I make this work? It's asking too much to have it all, isn't it?

forty-one

OWEN

"ARE you ready for our chat yet? Because I could use your advice," I plead.

Smiling warmly, Mom ushers me inside. "You take a seat. I'll get us some sweet tea."

"Thanks," I call over my shoulder as I power walk toward the living room, where I make myself comfortable on the couch.

Except there is no such thing.

I could lie down on a bed of fluffy puppies, and I still wouldn't be at ease, not with Addie and me in such a fucking mess.

Mom returns with a tray, on top of which she's arranged two glasses, a pitcher, and a ceramic bowl of cut-up lemons. As she pours us each a glass, I clear my throat and say, "Thanks again for helping with Addie yesterday. I couldn't be there myself, and it was a relief to know you were there."

"Of course, darlin'." She squeezes my chin between her thumb and forefinger, wiggling my face this way and that as if I'm twelve again. It's what she always used to do, following it up with, "What a handsome boy you are."

I know Dad's proud of me for the most part, but Mom has always been my number one fan, no matter what.

"I'm actually surprised you were free to help. I know you have your hands full." I shift on the couch as I sip from the glass.

"I'm never too busy for my favorite son."

I chuckle. "I'm your *only* son."

She sinks onto the other end of the couch and lifts a brow, her lip twitching. "I'm surprised you asked for my help to begin with. You never do."

I angle my large frame toward her, swallowing most of the couch. "Sure, I do."

"You have always been fiercely independent, son. When you had surgery, I offered to come up and help you around the house, but you'd hired *strangers* to clean and cook for you. When you moved from Atlanta, none of us knew you'd already packed and sold your house. You told us after the fact, per usual. It's like you don't want to give us the opportunity to lend a hand, but that's what family does. We're there for one another."

"I couldn't agree more. It's why I was happy to move back here. I love being here for the girls, and for you and Dad."

"What about you, dear? Who's there for you? Because you don't want us to be."

"That's not true." I shake my head and set the glass onto a coaster on the coffee table. "I know you're all busy with a million things, and I don't want to make your lives harder."

"How come you let us make yours harder? It's not fair, is it?"

"You're not making it harder, Mom. How could you say that?"

"How could you say it about us?" she shoots back with a glimmer in her eye.

"Point made." I crack a sad smile as guilt swims through my stomach. Sighing, I lean forward with my elbows on my knees. "Sometimes, I feel invisible," I admit quietly, my voice a lower octave than usual. It's almost like it doesn't belong to me. "Like I'm just the funny guy everyone wants around for a laugh, but that's it. That's all I'm good for, plus household repairs and babysitting. Sometimes, I think if I didn't help so much, you all would forget about me entirely."

Mom places both hands over her heart, the hurt in her eyes a stab in my chest.

"You didn't do anything wrong, Mom," I reassure her. "It's me. It's my own insecurities. Please don't feel like I'm blaming you for anything."

She swallows, and the thick sound indicates it's not so easy. My pulse spikes—and not in the good way like it does after a particularly rewarding day of students overcoming their individual obstacles and accomplishing goals.

It's in the antsy way like after I swerve my car on the road to narrowly miss a deer.

Why did I say anything? This isn't why I came here. I came to talk about Addie, not the relationship with my family.

"You should blame me—all of us," she says softly.

"It's not you. I'm not mad at any of you."

"You should be," she asserts more firmly than before as her tone grows in weight and gravity. "We've dropped the ball, and I'm sorry for that. I'm sorry we've asked so much of you, and I'm sorry I didn't try harder to be there for you, even when you said you didn't need me. You're my son, and I should've known better than to leave you be. I just never wanted to push you too much. I didn't want to push you away."

I dip my head like it's too heavy to hold up.

Mom laughs, but it holds a lot of sadness. "I think the strong ones are often overlooked, and you're one of the strongest people I know. It's not always obvious when the strong struggle, and we need to do better about that, starting now. Tell me what's on your mind, Owen, and don't you dare say everything's fine." She holds up a finger. "I won't have it. I'm not going to let you leave until you tell me everything."

"What? Are you going to tie me to the fridge?" I tease.

"There's an idea." She smiles back. "But how about I just bribe you with sweet potato pie?"

"You know the way to my heart."

She stands and pats my shoulder. "Walk with me, darlin'."

I slide onto a stool at the counter while she pilfers through cabinets and drawers for plates and silverware, my body heavy as I absorb her apology.

It was important to share my truth with her, after all.

When Addie had asked me last weekend if I thought it would help to talk to my parents, I'd said no. I didn't think it would change anything, but I was wrong.

I've been quietly strong for most of my life. I've been a rock for my family—one that comes with countless jokes in my back pocket.

But I don't always have to be, do I?

Although it's too soon to tell, and I should probably also air things out with my father, it's already obvious to me that my mother and I are headed down a new path.

She meant what she said.

"Spill." She waves a fork for me to talk, then grabs a silver pie spatula to ease a slice from the whole.

"I've been secretly seeing Addie."

"And?"

"I thought you'd have more of a reaction."

"It was hardly a secret, son. You two were obviously together. The way you looked at her was like Laurel looking at her medical textbooks. Give me a little more credit." She tilts her head.

As she sets a plate of pie in front of me, I blow out an exhale as I pick up the fork and toy with the crust of the slice. "The truth is, I never wanted it to be a secret at all, but I agreed because she's scared of putting our jobs in danger."

"And you're not scared?"

"Not enough to stop..." I choke back the word—the four-letter word I haven't even uttered to Addie herself.

I can't tell my mother before I tell her.

"Loving her?" Mom finishes, anyway.

Guess she will *know before Addie.*

I definitely should've given Mom more credit. She knows me better than I thought.

And no matter who learns it first, it doesn't change the fact that it's true. I'm in love with Addie. She makes me crazy, and I actually love how strongly I feel things when I'm with her.

She grounds me when I'm lost.

With her, I'm seen.

With her, I'm a much better person, and it's because of Addie that I'm even here having this pivotal conversation with my mother. Had she not kicked me out of her house, I wouldn't have ended up in this scenario now, or maybe ever.

I simply nod as my heart jumps into my throat.

"She feels the same way—I know she does," I insist.

"That much is obvious as well." Mom takes a bite of her pie and shrugs, as if it's as strong a fact as the sun being bright.

"I gave her an ultimatum." I hang my head and nudge my pie away. I don't fucking deserve it after what I did. What was I even thinking?

"You did what?" She freezes with her fork midair.

"I told her if she wouldn't disclose our relationship to the school administration and this town, then she and I were done," I grumble.

From the other side of the counter, she grabs me by the chin, but this time, it's not so cute and comforting. She jerks it like she's pissed. "How could you put so much pressure on her like that? Surely there's a better way to solve this with a compromise—one that's fair for you both."

"It's either we keep hiding or tell Principal Weathers and everyone else. What compromise is there?" I yank my chin from her grasp and stand to pace behind the row of stools. "And if we keep hiding like she wants, for how long? To what end? Won't we just be making it worse the longer we keep pretending there's nothing going on between us?"

"Does your need to share this relationship with everyone have anything to do with your concern that if you don't lock her down now, she'll leave? That she won't stick around for longer than just a laugh—isn't that what you said before?"

My own mother using my words against me should be criminal.

I stop dead in my tracks and place my hands on both hips. Like it or not—and I really don't fucking like it—she's right. I'm afraid Addie's having fun with me now. That she's letting loose for the first time in her life, and she's attracted to the wild ride more than she is me.

But the good times won't last. What happens when the laughter stops?

"Darlin', that girl is crazy about you. We spent one night with you both, and we all knew it was the real deal. Your sisters haven't stopped talking about it."

"You all have been talking about my personal life behind my back?" I level her with a firm glare.

"Your personal life is all our business, just as the girls' lives are too. That's how it is in this family. You know that." She scoffs and gobbles another bite of pie, calmer than the still air before a storm.

"Unbelievable," I grumble.

"As I was saying… She's serious about you, and not just for the fun." She rounds the counter and stands in front of me. "You realize that she didn't have to come in the other night and meet us all, right? She knew we were having a family dinner, and she joined us, anyway. Whether she's old-fashioned or a more modern woman, in any case, meeting family is a big deal. And she strode in with shoulders high and shot the shit with us the entire night. People don't go to such lengths for a meaningless fling."

"I want to say you're right."

"Then just say it." She shrugs again, but this time, she has a twinkle in her eye. "Son, actions speak much louder than words. Like this pie, for instance."

"Pie?"

She points to my slice of sweet potato pie, which I've abandoned. "Your aunt Ruth goes on about me not liking her recipes, and she never believes me when I tell her I do. She's always thought the worst of me."

I arch a brow. This is the first I'm hearing of my father's sister not liking Mom. She definitely isn't obvious about it, but it could be a Southern thing. Everyone's polite, even in their rudeness.

"But I make her recipes for pie, casseroles, and even stuffing for Thanksgiving, and I always credit her when I'm complimented. Actions mean everything." She pats my cheek, and already, I feel better.

Not that I'm out of the woods just yet.

"You've shown her you love her, haven't you?" Mom asks, but the serene clarity in her eyes indicates she knows as much.

I confirm, anyway. "What do I do now?" I whisper, fucking desperate for her ideas.

"For starters, you have to take back the ultimatum. Nothing good ever comes of one."

"I can do that. I can take it back." I nod, but the uneasy feeling from this morning comes rushing back.

Will she forgive me for being such an ass about this whole thing?

chapter
forty-two

ADDIE

I PACE MY LIVING ROOM, wearing a hole in the heels of my fuzzy socks.

I should grade papers, adjust my lesson plans to account for my abrupt absence from yesterday, or stock my fridge. I should be productive, but instead, I'm thinking about Owen. I'm always thinking about him.

And I like it. I don't hate that he's a distraction from my responsibilities and goals. I don't hate that he makes me laugh and feel light.

In truth, it's one of the many reasons I like being with him—I love who I am with him.

I've spent the last few hours stewing over soup. Every spoonful I slurped reminded me that Dorothy made it.

Owen called his mom and asked her for a favor, which as I've learned, is hard for him to do. He's almost as terrible at asking for help as I am, but he did it for me.

How many times has he shown me how much I mean to him? And what have I done in return? I kicked him out of my house.

I didn't want him to leave. I wanted to beg him to stay. I

wanted to promise I'll come clean. That I'll plaster it on posters down at the Tap and hand out "Addie loves Owen" buttons at the door.

But I froze when panic seized my body.

If I let myself truly be with him, I'm putting more than my job at risk. I'm putting my heart on a chopping block and daring him to carve it in half for the whole town to witness. These people relentlessly dissect and gossip about the new specials at Gordon's Pizzeria—they'd have a field day with Rain's daughter following so closely in her mother's footsteps.

How can I take that kind of risk?

I mull over Maren's advice, swirling it all around in my head like a blender until the perfect concoction forms.

But it's not what I expect.

I reach for my phone, scroll to the name I need in my contact list, and pause.

I can't do this, can I? I'm going to call, and say what—how dare you? Why did you abandon me when I needed you most?

"I could, actually," I say to no one but myself.

After all, that is what happened. I've never admitted it to anyone except to myself, but I always pushed it aside because the truth was too hard to face.

It was too scary.

But I take a deep breath, count to five, and face my fears head-on, just as my friend suggested.

My heart thumps like a fist banging against a door, the reverberations nearly numbing my entire body as I force myself to press the name.

I need to do this. Not for Maren or Owen or anyone else. I need to do this for me.

Dad answers on the first ring. "Hey there, sea turtle."

The nickname might as well be the twist of a knife in my chest.

When Maren suggested I turn straight to the source, it wasn't my mom I needed to talk to. It's my father—the first man to ever break my heart.

"Do you have a second, or a few?" I ask, hesitation weighing my voice down.

"Sure. What's on your mind?"

"This is going to sound... odd. Maybe a little out of the blue, but... I think it's been a long time coming."

"Should I be sitting down for this?" His chuckle crackles through the speaker, and my stomach sinks.

Out with it.

"I'm mad at you," I blurt.

Any other sign of amusement fades, and the line is filled with silence, plus my heavy, labored breaths.

"Dad, I know you left because of Mom, and I don't blame you. I'm not saying you should've stayed and put up with all her weird, often insane, ways, but you didn't just leave her. You left *me*," I choke out, gaining momentum the more I talk as I finally release years' worth of agony. "You moved out of the house, and as if that wasn't far enough, you then packed up and moved three states away. I haven't seen you since last Christmas, and that was only because I came to you. I always come to you. I've invited you over countless times, and you're always too busy."

"Addie, sweetheart. It's far more complicated than that."

"There's nothing complicated, Dad. I'm your daughter. You should've tried harder. I waited for you to try harder until I convinced myself that I actually respected you for doing yourself a favor and getting away."

"I had to get away," he says faintly. "There's so much you don't know."

"Yes, there is. I don't know the circumference of the Earth, how to replace a spark plug in a lawn mower, or how to completely love someone no matter how badly I want to," I deadpan, although the final item has tears stinging the backs of my eyes.

"I... I had no idea." His tone is loaded with surprise and disappointment.

I release a humorless laugh and squeeze my eyes closed. "The funny thing is that I've always admired your busy, jampacked routine. I've admired *you*. I've mirrored my own life to yours so I could be stable and smart and sensical in order to be more like you and less like Mom. But it's bullshit. It's all... bullshit." My eyes fling open.

I've never cursed in front of my father, and I've certainly never cursed *at* him. I've always spoken as respectfully as possible to him and my mother both, although Rain often makes it nearly impossible.

Still, they're my parents.

"I'm sorry to be so rude, but—"

"You're right. I deserve that and far worse, to be honest."

My sharp inhale fills the silence of my house, and time seems to stop. This feels like one of those moments I'll look back on years from now—a turning point.

I just hope it's a good turning point.

"I'm a coward, sea turtle," he says, and his raw voice is loaded with vulnerability. From the other line, a sniff comes through, and my gut clenches.

He's upset.

"I should've made more of an effort to be part of your life, Addie, and not just the vacation dad. I'm so sorry."

His words wash over me, but the tension in my body doesn't subside.

My heart doesn't soften.

My eyes aren't freed of tears threatening to spill.

I don't feel better, but what did I expect? Did I really think a single apology would repair years' worth of damage?

As if he reads my mind, Dad adds, "I know that doesn't change anything right now, and I can't take back the way I hurt you. But I want to do better. I hate that you've been mad at me for so long."

"Why, Dad?"

"Why, what?"

"You said you're a coward. Is that all you've got?" I press. "It's not an explanation, and it most certainly is not grounds for a new future."

"I know. You're right." His sigh is heavy and strong through the speaker, and I almost feel it weighing on me. "It's just that your mother... well, she... Can we please have dinner this weekend? I could take a few vacation days from work and come to Sapphire Creek. I can be spontaneous like that for my daughter."

I sink onto my couch, my wary knees tuckered out for the afternoon.

"I'd really like to talk in person," he says, but it's more of a plea. "I'd like to see you. It has been too long, and I shouldn't have let this much time pass without making more of an effort." His tone is sincere, and I melt into the couch, my limbs mere noodles.

"Okay," I whisper. "I'll see you next weekend."

His sigh of relief brings a smile to my face, and after he promises to text me with an update on his itinerary for the week-end, we end the call.

But I don't move. Nothing but a warm pair of pajama pants and a sweater sound good—maybe even a glass of wine too—but I remain seated, my mind a muddled field of debris.

I faced my father. We're not finished, but I took the first step. It was scary and ballsy and overwhelming, but it's the move I needed to make. No matter what comes of it, I took a leap, and that's a big freaking deal.

I don't know how long I remain frozen like this when the lock on the front door turns, and my mother springs into the house with a cheery, "Honey, I'm home—again!"

Oh, good grief.

Do I really have to confront yet another parent tonight?

"Rain." I throw my hands up and stand, mustering the energy

for this reunion. "Two visits in less than two weeks. To what do I owe this surprise? Is Mercury in retrograde?"

She tilts her head in a way that lets me know she's not amused.

That makes two of us.

I peek over her shoulder through the open door to see if her friends are parking and caravanning up the porch, but nothing happens. No one enters, other than a couple of flying critters.

"I see you've had time to clean up the mess we left." She shuts the door, further confirming no one else will be joining us, much to my relief, given the aforementioned mess.

But I don't miss the disappointment in her words.

"Why do you say it like that?" I ask.

"No, no. I expected nothing less than for you to break out the hazmat suit and douse the house with bleach."

"For your information, I didn't clean it. I've been a little busy." I saunter into the kitchen for a glass of wine, and she follows.

"With Mr. PE?"

"With work and friends and dance." I shut the cabinet and set the glass onto the counter, where I pour from a bottle of red until the surface reaches a millimeter from the rim. "Wine?" I offer her.

"Sure." She shrugs. It's rather nonchalant, but I don't buy it. There's something in her eyes. It swims and dances with a life of its own in her blue irises, and I know the rest of this evening won't be easy on me.

I set a full glass of wine in front of her, clink my own to it, and sip.

"You've been busy with that guy. Why can't you just admit it?" Rain presses.

"Is that why you're here? To pry into my personal life for God knows what reason?"

"As a matter of fact, yes."

I freeze with the rim glued to my lips.

"You seemed so happy last week. Your aura was glowing like a thousand stars were hugging you. It was the kind of glow only good and groundbreaking sex offers."

"Please, not that again."

Her lips curl into a wistful, almost proud smile. "You didn't even get onto us about the mess this week, and I think I saw you dancing in the kitchen one morning."

"I like to dance. I dance a lot, as you might remember."

She levels me with a stern glare. "You dance at the studio, where no one can experience your talent. You hide it away, when you should share it with the world."

I gulp and lower my glass to the counter, my hand trembling. What is with everyone and sharing everything with the world? Can't some things just be kept private for the sake of humility and grace?

"What's going on with you, Cloud?"

"You haven't called me that in years."

"Not since you yelled at me to stop."

"It's because..." I sigh and meet her gaze head-on. *Truth.* It's time for truth and perspective. There is no room for deflections anymore. "I'm sorry I ever yelled at you. I shouldn't have."

She folds her arms, her mouth falling open and closed. She clearly didn't expect me to apologize.

I hold a finger up. "You deserved to be yelled at, though. It was the only way to get through to you."

"Until you basically stopped talking to me altogether."

"You don't get me. You never have."

"I get you better than you think. It's why I'm here."

"What's that supposed to mean?"

"Your aura is now full of weeping willows dripping with shame and regret, which can only mean one thing. You blew it with Mr. PE." She says it as a statement, with zero sign of a question. There's not a single ounce of hesitation in her voice that might suggest she feels she's wrong.

"It wasn't completely my fault," I whisper.

"I'm here to help you fix it." My mother nods in the direction of the back door, gesturing for me to follow her.

And I don't know why, but I do. My feet move in heavy steps as I grab a jacket and step onto the deck, where I sit next to her on the outdoor couch, my wine tucked into my lap like a security blanket.

"You're scared of love, and I think your father and I are to blame," she says.

"What—how did you..."

"Like I told you before, I know a thing or two, honey."

"Fine." I tug on my jacket with one hand, bracing myself against the breeze. It's chilly tonight, but the air feels good in my lungs. "Tell me why my issues are your fault."

She heaves her legs onto the couch and crosses them, seemingly comfortable in her light layers. "We were your role models. Our marriage was your first introduction to love, and when it shattered, it was the only lens you'd ever view love through again."

I gulp for the second time, and I fear it won't be the last. She's coming in hot with the punches tonight, isn't she?

Rain clears her throat and toys with the stem of her glass, averting her gaze. Is she nervous? That can't be right. She's never skittish or shy. The woman parades around the country in a van, mostly without shoes.

She's not afraid of anything.

Instantly, my guard shoots up.

"I've never told you this, but when you were almost eleven, I tried to convince your father to take me back. Our divorce hadn't been finalized yet, and I went to him on hands and knees to beg him for forgiveness."

"Really?" I whisper. I had no inkling of such a thing ever happening. Dad didn't say anything, either, nor did I ever hear it from anyone else.

She nods. "I told him I'd made a huge mistake and that I was so sorry for my lapse in judgment. That I hated my life without him and us as a whole family." She sips from her glass and blinks rapidly at the yellowing sky like she's fighting tears. This is a side of Rain I've never witnessed before, and my heart clenches as it does for a kitten in a storm.

It's not easy to experience a force of a woman like her crumbling this way.

With an unsteady, watery voice, she continues, "I was honest and raw, but it wasn't enough. He said I was too dangerous, too unpredictable, and he couldn't live in a constant state of caution over what I might do next. And he was right." Her soft laugh holds devastating sadness that fills the air around us.

And although I don't disagree with Dad, as I've often felt the same about the chaotic clouds of outlandish ideas floating around her, I'm sad to hear it from her perspective.

Rejection stings in all forms, especially when it comes to love. My mother made a mistake in driving Dad away, and when she apologized—when she bared her soul—he still said no.

I imagine such a wound doesn't heal easily.

"I never got over him," she confesses in a low, haunting whisper.

"You're still in love with Dad?" I squeak.

She slowly nods, and my throat clogs with empathy and even more sadness for her.

All this time. All those guys. All this mumbo jumbo about marrying nature and living in the world as a free bird.

Has it all been lies? Cries for help? Madness?

For so many years, I've criticized her, when I should've been asking for what was really going on. Guilt reaches like a hand inside my chest and squeezes my cold, selfish heart.

"It's why I bounce from guy to guy without another thought. No one's ever measured up to your father." Rain brushes her knuckles across my cheek. "I blew it with him, but you don't have to make the same mistakes I did. I don't want this curse for you."

Curse.

That's exactly what my situation sounds like, and the word covers me like a bad omen, chills racing up and down my arms.

A curse is exactly what I'll fall victim to if I don't make this right with Owen. I'll be cursed to watch him from afar without being able to touch, kiss, or wrap my arms around him.

How can I never experience another one of his ass grabs?

There's something I never thought I'd say, and here's another—Owen Conrad somehow went from someone I couldn't stand to the one person I don't want to be without.

"Tell me what to do." I lift my teary gaze to meet hers. "And please don't tell me to perform some voodoo ritual and cut off more of my hair. What's a normal thing to do in this situation?"

"Normal—who the hell wants normal?" She cracks a grin. "I hate that you cut your hair, by the way."

"You've mentioned it once or twice." It's been eleven times, to be exact. I counted.

"You can't just tell him you're sorry. You can't tell him you care or even that you love him, even though you totally do."

"What? Love? No one said anything about love." I lean back like she smacked me, and my wine sloshes in my glass.

"Then how do you feel about him?" She lifts a brow and waits expectantly, but the slow wicked grin spreading from cheek to cheek says all I need to know.

She knows the answer, as do I.

Because love is the only word that sums up my feelings. Nothing else encompasses this massive explosion of happiness and caring and excitement I feel for Owen.

I don't answer, but I guess my silence is enough when Rain says, "You have to show him, honey. Don't just tell him. Don't do what I did. Maybe if I would've shown your dad that I meant what I said and that I'd changed, he would've considered saving our marriage, but it's too late for us. It's not too late to show Mr. PE what your heart is made of."

When I got off the phone with Dad earlier, I was still uneasy. My stomach tossed and turned like a restless toddler.

But as I talk to my mom, I'm relieved. Dare I say, I might even feel peace coming on.

How did she do that? How is it that my mother, of all people, is the one who puts me at ease like this?

As she runs her fingers through my hair while we talk, I realize it's because I've never pretended with her, not like I have with Dad just to keep the peace. It's easier to keep the peace with someone I hardly see.

But with Rain, I've never been anything but myself, even though I know she doesn't agree with my philosophies. She and I have butted heads plenty of times in my life, but we've always been honest and real with each other. That's what always matters the most when it concerns our relationship.

That's not to say I haven't been wrong about her, because I totally have in many ways.

She knows me better than I ever thought she did, but I am just now beginning to understand the core of her in return.

And through the biggest plot twist of my life, she's going to be the one to help me win Owen back.

ADDIE

Owen's late this morning, and the only thing at the forefront of my overactive brain is that it's because of me.

He doesn't want to accidentally run into me before class.

I don't know if he was at karaoke night last night. I didn't go, since Rain and I enjoyed a mother-daughter movie night for the first time in years. I wouldn't have opted to stay in with her on any other night, but yesterday was different.

She made me realize my relationship with her needs love and attention too.

But did Owen go to the Tap last night? Did he stay out late? How much did he drink?

And who the hell did he share a dance with?

I incessantly tap my pen to my notebook, my knee bouncing beneath it as I stew alone in the gym.

I don't know how long I keep this up until the door creaks open, and I pop onto my feet as graceful as a ballerina, although I don't feel so collected on the inside. My stomach is in absolute turmoil.

Owen rounds the corner of the bleachers, and when his eyes

find mine, his steps falter. He doesn't stop, though, not until he's a foot from me, his hands tucked into his pockets.

"Hi," I whisper as my heart stumbles over its beats.

"Lockhart, listen." He frowns, and I hold my breath. "About the other day..."

"Good morning, dream team!" Sable emerges into the gym, her heels clicking across the floor with far more pep than I can muster. Even with most of my strength restored from my bout of food poisoning, enthusiasm is not currently in my arsenal.

I haven't talked to Owen since Saturday, and it's been torture. I haven't been able to sleep, knowing he's angry with me and it's my doing.

I've been unfair to him, and I have to explain myself.

But with Sable's interruption, I'm not going to get any relief from our debacle. Not yet, anyway.

I force a smile like I do when trying new foods, which is my least favorite thing to do. "Sable. Hi. How are you?"

"I'm great, but I'm more curious about how you are. Are you feeling better?" she asks, concern laced in her tone.

Owen gives a tight-lipped smile as I assure her, "Definitely. I had a rough go of it, but I'm feeling a hundred percent today."

Except for the whole I'm secretly dating my co-worker, and it blew up in my face bit.

"I'm sorry I couldn't make it to coffee this weekend," I say. "After the whole ordeal with food poisoning, my mother came to visit, so it's been a busy couple of days."

Owen's eyes brighten at the mention of my mother, and my lips wobble with confessions bubbling up my throat.

Sable waves me off. "I completely understand. No need for apologies."

My gaze instinctively drifts over to Owen, who starts to back away, but before he gets too far, Sable reaches out to stop him.

"I also came by to give you both good news," she announces.

"Addie's classroom is almost finished. You can start moving back in there at lunch today, in fact."

"Today?" I squeak.

"A few good Samaritans from around town pitched in to help over the weekend. Wasn't that so nice?" Sable tilts her chin up, pride coloring her features. She loves this town almost as much as I do for its generous people—and delicious baked goods, among other things. "So, we're all set to get things back to normal."

"Normal," I repeat, but the word doesn't hold the same meaning as it might've last month.

Nothing will ever be "normal" again, will it? It can't. I don't think I even want things to go back to how they were when I had my own classroom—before Owen.

I won't see him all day, every day anymore. He'll be on his side of the school campus, and I'll be on mine.

I clutch my stomach, which rumbles like it did over the weekend, a wave of nausea rolling through it. It's not from any food poisoning, though.

"That's, uh... great," Owen says, but his tone falls flat.

A few of his students filter into the gym, and echoes of their laughter bounce off the walls. Owen hooks a thumb over his shoulder in their direction and parts from us with a brisk goodbye.

Sable nudges me aside and quietly says, "I'm glad you're okay. I was so worried about you. I wasn't the only one, either."

"Huh?" I blink back at her.

"Owen was a wreck. He was paler than you and out of his head with worry."

"Oh. He... well, he was probably concerned about taking on two classes at once for a minute. You know him—he's not a great multitasker." I frown.

A month ago, I would've let a jab like that roll freely off my tongue, but right now, the insult tastes more sour than a bad apple.

It's not right.

"Actually, he's become a good… friend." I peer over at him as he animatedly chats with his students before class.

My heart aches as if there's a whole country between us instead of just a basketball court.

"Is that all he is?" Sable lifts a brow.

I whip my attention back to her, gobsmacked as my tongue suddenly feels too big for my mouth.

"There's something going on between you, isn't there?" she ventures.

"Why would you say that?" I laugh nervously and twist my hair, my fingers itching for something to do.

"We've known each other a long time, Addie." She smiles, and it's warm. There's no hint of anger or judgment in her demeanor or tone, which puts me at ease, but it's only a fraction. "I even consider you a friend, and as your friend, I just ask that you be honest with me."

Tears sting the backs of my eyes.

This is it.

This is the moment. There's no way around it. It was one thing to pretend it's not true, but it's another thing entirely to lie when Sable's outright asking me about it. The latter would be a sin in my book.

I have to tell her, and I haven't even prepared for it. Then again, how does one prepare for such an occasion? Wear all black in mourning? Wear sneakers for an easy getaway once embarrassment takes over?

I don't even have cake or ice cream to wallow in once I get home.

But this is what I need to do. If I'm going to win Owen back, I need to come clean about our involvement, and this is my opening. I won't get another chance this perfect.

Besides, it might not be as bad as I've imagined over the last few weeks. I've been told on multiple occasions, especially by my mother, that I can really let my thoughts get away from me. I always assumed she just never took anything seriously, but after this weekend, I'm inclined to believe she might have a point.

Only one way to find out...

I clear my throat and manage, "Owen and I have been seeing each other, but it's new. It's not like we've been sneaking around for a year. Of course, he hasn't lived in town that long, but you know what I mean. Right?"

Her smile widens.

"You're not mad?" I cringe.

"Why would I be mad?" She rubs her hand up and down my arm. "Addie, I love seeing you happy, which you have been lately. It's all I want for you."

"Are you saying that as my friend or my boss?"

"Both."

Even though this is off to a decent start, I don't let my guard down. It's too soon to tell if this will end well or not.

"But as your boss, I must also say this."

Here we go.

I raise my shoulders higher and brace myself for impact as if I'm in a car headed straight for a brick wall.

"I just need you both to disclose your relationship to the administration, which sounds ominous, but really, all you need to do is sign a waiver. It's just so we can cover our asses." She squeezes my arm and adds, "That's all for the legal and official case of the matter, but the rest is possibly going to be more complicated."

"The rest?"

"The rest of the faculty." She offers a sympathetic smile, one that does not reach her brown eyes. And is it me, or does her big hair lose a little volume? Even her hair is sad for me. "There will be gossip, curious looks, whispers—you name it. They might give you a hard time too, but you have thick skin. You can handle it."

I nod, but I barely register her words.

"When the students catch wind of it, which they will, they might make a few jabs themselves. You know how kids are, but again, you can handle them until they latch on to the next piece of gossip. It's how the whole town works. It's nothing new to either of us."

Dread fills my stomach like buckets of oil, but still, I say nothing.

The kids.

Their reactions didn't cross my mind. I was so focused on my future at this school and my reputation across town that I didn't take the students themselves into consideration. How could I let that happen? I love my students. I want what's best for them, and that doesn't include a distraction by their scandalous teachers.

It'll be all they'll talk about for a while, at least. They do tend to sink their relentless claws into new rumors daily, so it would only be a matter of time before they forgot about Owen and me.

It doesn't make the consequences easier to swallow, though.

Sable exhales, intertwining her fingers together at her waist. "But when it comes to a promotion in the future, you shouldn't worry. Dating someone you work with isn't against any policy, so it's not like you broke a rule."

I finally perk up when she says the word *promotion*—the main reason I wanted to keep my relationship a secret to begin with.

"Maybe no rules were broken, but I know such a thing can be severely frowned upon. I don't want anyone to take me less seriously," I lament.

Her eyes droop in the corners with a solemn frown. "This is a small town. Optics are important, but they're not everything. You put your heart and soul into every part of this job, and it has not gone unnoticed. That counts for a lot." She checks her watch. "I need to get to a meeting, but we can discuss this more over lunch this week."

"I'd like that." I swallow and glance back over to Owen, but he's not there anymore. He's nowhere in the gym, and I suddenly feel alone, like I'm the only person on an island.

I need him.

I need the comfort only he can offer.

Sable starts to turn but stops. "Switching hats again and speaking as your friend, I know this career is important to you, but we can't control the future. Whether you get a promotion or not is never a sure thing, even if you hadn't gotten involved with him, but Owen is real right now. I'd hate for you to walk away from someone who makes you so happy simply for a *what-if*. Some things in life are worth the risks."

"Thank you," I whisper as gratitude fills my weary body.

She didn't freak out or give me the disappointed twist of her lips as she does when students are sent to the office.

I didn't die under the crushing weight of the possibly horrendous outcome.

I'm still standing, even if it is alone.

I've been alone a lot in my adult life. When I was a teenager, I often felt alone. I've always had the best of friends, but having Owen in my corner was like fulfilling some destiny written in the stars for me.

It's been one day with my mother, and I'm already talking like her.

Except this is true. He did fill a void I didn't know existed.

Owen's true right now, and if I don't grab destiny by the shoulders and shake it, I'm going to end up cursed, just as Rain warned.

chapter
forty-four

OWEN

MY PHONE FLASHES as I take a pull from my beer. It spills down my chin as I hurriedly reach for it, only to be disappointed it's not from Addie.

NATE

You going to the Halloween party at the Tap tomorrow night?

I'm not in the mood for festivities. For once, I'm not in the mood for a good time.

Don't think so. No costume.

Don't you wear a costume every day, or is that just your face?

"Ass," I mutter with a chuckle. It's not a hearty one, but it's better than the frown I've been wearing for the last few days.

I suck back another fizzy pull and sigh.

I went by Addie's house last night after family dinner at my parents', but she wasn't home. According to her social media—a moment of stalking I was not proud of—she was celebrating Caroline's move back to Sapphire Creek.

Addie and I haven't had any moment alone at school this week. I've barely seen her at all, since she's been busy organizing her classroom. She's never in the teachers' lounge when I'm in there, and her car always sits empty in the parking lot at the end of each day.

School wouldn't have been the most appropriate place to air out our issues, anyway, but at least I could've told her how much I fucking miss her.

It didn't help that my family stared at me during the entirety of dinner last night like I'm a hopeless loser.

A knock on the door lifts my damn soul, and again, I spill my beer on my shorts as I tear it from my mouth mid-sip.

Swiping at it with the back of my hand is futile, but I still do it as I saunter toward the door and open it.

Little eyes blink back at me, and my chest warms as Whitney blazes inside, Huck on her hip.

"I need to pee." She passes the baby over like a hot potato, slings the diaper bag against the wall, and races toward the bathroom.

"I'll have to teach you better manners than your mom's," I say to the little man.

Bouncing him against my shoulder, I walk us to the couch, and he twists my shirt in his tiny fist. The sounds he makes are incoherent, but I can tell he can't wait to talk.

"You'll be speaking in full sentences before we know it," I whisper. "All in good time. No need to rush. You're young and carefree."

What I want to tell him is to stay this little and innocent for as long as possible. It's what I've thought with each pound he gains, because time is moving too quickly.

"What are you saying to him?" Whitney plops onto the couch

next to us. "You better not be telling him anything about love, because that's not your strong suit."

"Never said it was," I toss back. "Wait. Why are you jumping to love so quickly? I could've been telling him about the burrito I had for lunch. It was one of the best I've ever had."

Whit studies me, her tongue in her cheek. "Plausible, but I'm sticking with love, especially after last night."

"Nothing happened last night."

"Exactly. You made no joke about Lottie's orange highlights, which she did seriously and not ironically for Halloween. She looked like a prop at a haunted house."

The idea of zombies at a haunted house reminds me of Addie's date she'd told me about during our night in Savannah. Everything fucking reminds me of her.

"I was being supportive," I argue, but my voice isn't as strong as I'd like.

"Is that why you didn't chime in when Dad let me win at Jenga? You hate it when he does that."

"He does it so often, I figured it was time to let it go." I give her a sarcastic, tight-lipped smile as Huck taps his fist to my cheek.

He and his mom are bringing on the punches, aren't they?

"Why are you here?" I ask and immediately regret it as her face falls. "I didn't mean to sound like I don't want you here. It's just that you never drop by unannounced."

"Maybe I should do it more often." She dips her head and fidgets with her fingers in her lap, her black sweater and scarf both extra thick like she's preparing for an ice storm. "I'm sorry I haven't been a very good sister to you."

"What are you talking about? Whit, you're an amazing sister." I furrow my brows.

"I always ask so much of you, and you're always there without complaint. I never return the favor."

I squint over at her as she continues to fidget. She doesn't meet my eye, and my skin crawls. "You talked to Mom. She told you everything I said, didn't she?" I shake my head.

"Of course, she did." Whit finally looks up at me. "We're a family. We should all know what's going on with one another, and actually—" She rises from her spot and smacks me in the back of the head, knocking my hat onto the floor.

"What the he—" I peer down at Huck, who stares at me with wide eyes. "I mean, what the *heck* was that?"

"You deserve it." My sister drops back onto her ass and bends her knee onto the cushion. "I shouldn't have had to hear that stuff from Mom. I wish you would've told me."

"What did you want me to say?"

"That you're unhappy with us."

"But I'm not," I assure her. "That's not at all what I said or meant."

"Don't lie to me." She narrows her eyes, and I hold Huck a little tighter. When he's older, his mother's stern glare is going to chill his bones. "You have every right to be mad at us. I call you anytime I need a babysitter, Lottie sends you 911 messages when she breaks a nail, and Laurel, well, she might not actually need anything from you, but I'm sure she calls you to complain about her workload like she does to the rest of us. And that is definitely something to be pissed about."

"I'm not pi—" I peer down at Huck again. He seems to be listening so intently, it's hard to imagine he doesn't understand much right now. "I'm not *peeved*."

"Then what are you?"

"I'm just... I feel invisible sometimes," I finally confess much like I did to Mom last weekend.

I halfway expect her to laugh and point out how many times I've been on TV. How often I still get tagged by random baseball fans I don't know on social media. How a meme with my face was trending online three years ago.

I steel myself against what I imagine will be a long monologue of all the ways I'm so popular around town too. That she doesn't even live here anymore, but she knows how well-liked I am.

But she doesn't do any of that. She doesn't even move or change her hard expression at all.

"I'm really sorry, Owen," she whispers, and her features darken with obvious guilt. Her lips droop into a frown that drags even the corners of her eyes down.

And while her apology is appreciated, I'm not sure the look on her face is worth it.

"I'll do better, okay? I promise." She squeezes my shoulder, and my stomach tightens.

"I'll do better about letting you in," I say in return. "After talking to Mom, I realized I might not be the easiest to help since I don't always ask for it."

"So, you're asking for it now, right? Because I have thoughts." She wiggles in her spot, tucking her ankle under her knee.

A deflection is on the tip of my tongue, but that's exactly what I just told her I wouldn't do. She's here to try, and I need to do the same.

Instead of diverting the conversation to something that removes the spotlight from me and onto her, I fight my natural instincts and relay the details with Addie—the important details, anyway.

Halfway through, I've barely taken a breath when a new message lights up my screen. I'm embarrassingly relieved to find who it's from.

"It's her, isn't it?" Whit scoots closer and peers over my shoulder. "Open it, open it!"

My pulse spikes.

"Well? What does it say?" Whit urges.

I read the message again. "To check my doorstep."

My sister flies off the couch as if I dunked ice water onto her. She's the first to the door, but she stops herself before throwing it open. "You should probably do the honors." She bites her lip, and it's clear she's trying to hold herself—and a squeal—back.

With Huck on my hip, I stare at the door for a beat before I open it, inhaling deeply in preparation to see Addie, but she's not there. Nothing's on my doorstep except for a large gift bag.

Whit jumps out and grabs the bag. "Were you expecting a present?"

"Not so much. Not after the ultimatum I gave her."

She freezes with her mouth dangled open.

"I haven't gotten to that part of my story, have I?" I grimace.

"You need a lot more help than I thought." She waves for me to follow her back into the living room, where we resume our previous spots, and she folds her hands in her lap.

"Should I be lying down for this?" I ask, only halfway kidding.

"Explain yourself, big brother," she says and sets the gift bag aside as if I can't be rewarded until I tell her the whole truth and nothing but the truth, so help me God.

With a frustrated exhale, I recount the rest of the unpleasant details, bouncing Huck on my knee to distract me from the weight of it all.

At the time, I thought the ultimatum was the best idea, but it was done out of fear. Hardly the right reason.

Defeat settles over me until I can't take the anticipation anymore, and I set Huck in the playpen I keep here for when I babysit, then wrangle the gift bag from my wily sister. "It's mine," I insist.

"I haven't decided yet if you deserve it!"

I rip the corner of the bag as I tear it from her surprisingly strong grip. "Whether I deserve it or not, it's mine," I repeat.

Once it's in my possession, I freeze before I look inside.

"You know she's just scared too, right?" Whit offers. "We say and do crazy shit when we're scared, but it doesn't make our feelings any less strong or real. Give her time to handle her fears like you're handling yours."

I swallow as Huck passes gas, which he follows up with a cry as if it scared him.

"He might need a diaper change." She gathers him into her arms and disappears to tend to him while I sit with my thoughts—and the gift bag at my feet.

It's almost as big as an average duffel bag.

I've lived a full life with glamor and risks. I've driven an IndyCar in a friendly race with other baseball buddies, the speed of which would terrorize many people, but I found it exhilarating.

I've been stung by a jellyfish.

And I've been hit in the face with a baseball more times than I can remember.

I shouldn't be afraid of a plain blue plastic bag.

With my heart racing, I pry through the tape and open the top, then dig into it for... fabric. There's a lot of orange fabric.

A note is pinned to the front in Addie's perfect scrawl as if she took her time with each letter—she probably always does—and my breezy laugh holds none of the weight or hesitation I felt before.

Immediately, I grab my phone and text Nate.

> On second thought, I will be at the party tomorrow night.

ADDIE

"This is corny, isn't it? I should go home and change. This was the dumbest idea since low-rise jeans." My palms sweat as I jump in front of Caroline and Maren to stop them from getting any closer to the Tap.

"I could not be happier that high-waisted pants of all kinds are trending." Caroline tips her red cowgirl hat at me with one hand and uses the other to point to the high-waisted bell bottoms she's strutting in. She makes a damn good Lainey Wilson.

And I'm so freaking happy she's finally moved here so we don't need to resort to missed FaceTime calls and sporadic texts anymore.

I know Austin is more than happy too.

But none of that calms me down right now. I'm too busy freaking out about Owen to enjoy the return of my oldest friend.

I smooth out the round edge of my red costume and continue, "He's not going to show up, and if he does, he won't be wearing his costume. He'll think it's too embarrassing."

Maren places both hands on my shoulders and levels me with a sincere stare. "It's the cutest idea since your homecoming float for

Caroline last month. The half-city, half-Sapphire Creek idea was inspired, and this one is brilliant too. He's going to show up dressed appropriately and tell you how much he loves it."

I nod along, but I don't release the breath I'm holding.

"If not, I'll punch him in the junk, then buy you all the shots your gigantic heart desires," Maren promises. That's exactly what it is—it's not a joke or a clever way to make me laugh, but a promise.

Her dedication to ruthlessly backing me up does help me relax, if only a fraction.

"Owen's funny. He'll appreciate this," Caroline adds.

"Well, he's more than just funny," I say.

"Of course," Maren chimes in. "He's also a really good kisser. What did you say about him—that he's phenomenal? That he made you believe in magic?"

"*Whoa.*" Caroline's wide eyes land on me like she doesn't know me. "I need more of these details, ma'am."

"Right now, we need to focus and hope for a stroke of magic," I say, completely serious, because this will either be the best night of my romantic life so far, or it'll be the worst.

Austin approaches us, his costume tragically uninspired, as he arrives in simple coveralls dressed as a... mechanic.

"Great costume. How long did it take for you to come up with that?" I ask sarcastically.

He barely cracks a grin as he gives me a once-over. "What are you supposed to be—friendly Satan?"

"That's not what this *S* is for." I gesture over the front of me, but he's stops listening before I finish my sentence. Instead, he nuzzles his nose into the crook of Caroline's neck.

They're blissfully in love, and a twang of jealousy hits me square in the chest.

I want that. I could've had that had I not been too scared.

I'm still scared, but there's a difference now—I'm not going to let fear and the unknown stop me from being happy.

Rain and my father have helped me come around. Rain left a few days ago, singing about her work being done here, and as promised, my father visited me this weekend. His flight left for Louisiana earlier this afternoon.

He was serious about making amends. He even arrived without my stepmom. I love her, but in hindsight, Dad often uses her as a buffer, like he needs a crutch to hang out with me. Without her around this weekend, he and I were able to connect in ways we used to before the divorce.

It left me feeling much better than our previous phone call.

The lightness in my chest is what stops me from running for the hills right now.

Sharply inhaling, I hold my head high and loop my arm through Maren's. "I'm ready."

"I don't think I am," she mumbles as Nate high-fives Austin, then adjusts the suspenders over his shoulders.

He's a fireman, and if Maren stares at him any longer, there might be a real fire to put out when she combusts. She's practically sweating.

"Hey," I say, nudging her to stay behind as Nate, Austin, and Caroline lead the way inside. "If you're serious about meeting someone new, this is your night. You are so hot in this Wonder Woman costume."

"You don't think I'm trying too hard, do you?" She adjusts the headpiece higher into her hair. "It's not too hot, right?"

"There's no such thing as too hot. It's perfect. Now go get some." I smack her on the ass and gesture for her to go inside.

But she doesn't immediately budge. "I'm not going to sleep with anyone all willy-nilly tonight." She scoffs.

"I was talking about some numbers and dates." I shrug, feigning innocence.

"Right," she draws out and slowly saunters inside.

Once she disappears, I freeze as Owen takes her previous spot.

My instant frown reaches every part of my body, carrying with it the gloom of a hundred rainy days.

He's not wearing the Skittles costume I left on his doorstep last night. He's not wearing any kind of costume, and I'm a big red dope.

"Hi." His small smile throws me off. Does he think this is funny? Is he laughing at me?

"If you thought this was too embarrassing, you should've just told me beforehand. You didn't have to come here to mock me in person." I fold my arms over my chest. I try to, anyway. The costume is ridiculously wide.

I could easily disappear inside of it like a turtle, but I won't give him the satisfaction. I'm done hiding.

"I'm not mocking you, Lockhart," he says, his sober tone washing over me with comfort.

"You didn't think the 'Two Skittles Walk into a Bar' note was too cheesy?" I tilt my head and squint for any detection of mockery in his solid façade.

"I loved the note." He inches toward me with the cool demeanor he seems to always possess when I'm in turmoil. His calm and collected persona will be the end of me.

"If that were true, you would've dressed up." I back away as he swallows every foot I set between us.

More people filter inside, a parade of superheroes, zombies, and cheerleaders. My thundering heart nearly drowns the commotion and music from inside, which grows louder each time someone yanks the front door open.

Owen glances over his shoulder as if to check for lurkers and eavesdroppers, then grabs my hand to lead me between two cars until we're tucked away from prying eyes and ears.

"I'm not dressed up because I don't want you to make a statement about us to everyone," he says. "I don't want you to out us until you're absolutely ready. I don't want it to be because I pressured you into it. That wasn't fair of me to demand in the first place, and I'm sorry."

I wiggle my hand from his grasp. "Don't do that. Don't let me off the hook so easily."

"There's no hook." He rams his hand through his hair, no hat on his head tonight. "There's no ultimatum, either. It was wrong of me to force you to do anything that makes you uncomfortable. I should've been more patient, but I was scared."

"You were?" This is news to me.

Owen is such a confident person. I didn't think anything could scare him, but if I've learned anything this week from my parents, whom I'd previously and naively believed were indestructible, it's that we all get scared. It's just part of being human.

"I'm not scared of my feelings for you. I'm not scared of us," he says, easing my hand back into his. "I'm scared of losing you."

My lips part as everything starts to make sense.

I squeeze his hand. "I'm sorry I ever gave you a reason to doubt my feelings."

"You didn't do anything wrong."

"But I did." I lick my lips, likely smearing the pale red lipstick Caroline gave me for the night. "It was never just about the job, and I should've been honest with you about that. I was afraid to tell everyone about us, but more than that, I was scared of trusting you with my heart."

"Angel, I would never take such a thing so lightly."

"I know." I cup his cheek in my small palm, loving the five o'clock shadow he's sporting tonight, and tilt my head. "The biggest wrongdoing of mine is letting you leave my house last weekend without telling you how important you are to me. I let you leave without saying how beautiful those things you said to me were. Worst of all was that I let you leave at all, and I'm sorry."

He shifts his face into my palm and places a kiss on my wrist. It's the softest touch of his lips on my skin, and it's enough to launch a tidal wave of emotions through my chest.

I melt against him like a current pulling me, and I can't fight against it, not that I want to. Not anymore.

"What I should've said was that…" I gulp. I've read countless romance novels and watched even more romantic comedy movies. I've swooned over so many grand gestures and heartfelt monologues, but none of those are enough. "You're infuriating," I blurt.

His good-natured chuckle makes me smile, especially since he doesn't release his all-consuming hold on me.

"You're sloppy and impolite," I continue as my smile grows wider. "When I'm with you, it's pure chaos. No rules or manners or logic. And I absolutely love it."

When he kisses me, the stars above us blur into magnificent streaks of bright lights as my eyelids flutter closed.

His kiss is firm and heated, yet loving and tender, and the bubble we previously resided in expands. It feels like it covers the whole world around us.

This is how we were always supposed to be—open and free.

"I love you," he whispers against my lips, and I gasp.

I thread my fingers through his hair and rise onto my tiptoes. "I love you too."

Owen Conrad loves me, and I love him. If that's not proof of magic and miracles, then I don't know what is.

"I want to take you home—now." He growls against my neck, but a burst of cheers from inside makes me jump back.

"There's one thing we have to do first." I shake my head, but the haze of bliss remains. "Well, two things," I correct myself.

"Name them."

"First—you need to put on your costume. Did you bring it?"

He slowly nods, clearly confused.

"Second—we need to go inside."

"We do?" He doesn't hide disappointment well.

"It'll be worth it, I promise." I give him another slow, sensual kiss to shamelessly entice him.

And it works.

"I just need two minutes," he rasps, then races to his truck as I make my way to the front door.

He wasn't kidding about the two minutes, although it seems he gets dressed in less.

"Ready?" he asks, his orange costume with the big *S* down the middle matching my red one.

"Almost." I slide my hand into his and grin. "Now I'm ready."

"Are you sure?"

"Positive." I punctuate the simple word with a jerk of the door, and we walk in together.

I'm not sure what I expected. Part of me thought the room might freeze, with the music screeching to a halt. Maybe I thought everyone's head would turn in sync to gawk at us in disbelief.

But none of that happens. Everyone simply carries on laughing with friends, dancing with loved ones, and chatting with new faces. Candy wrappers litter many of the tables around us, adding splashes of bright colors to the browns and neutrals of this rustic bar. The music is loud, and the energy is buzzing as people in masks and clown makeup mill about for drinks and appetizers.

I'm almost disappointed that my relationship with Owen isn't more of a grand announcement. I've been troubled for weeks—a dramatic display of reactions would've been more satisfying.

As if she reads my mind, Gemma from the school stops short of us, gapes, and points at my hand in Owen's. "Wait. Are you two..." She glances between us, curiosity coloring her eyes.

"We are together," I say at an unnecessarily loud volume, and it's not just because of the music.

Squealing, she pulls us in for a hug, and I accidentally knock off her princess crown.

"Sorry!" My hand flies to my mouth.

"Don't even worry about it." Gemma scoots the crown back into position. "My toddler helped me pick this out, and oh my gosh—I need to call my mother to see how they're doing."

Once she bolts outside, Scarlett fills her spot, followed by her friend Matilda. They're dressed in tame costumes, donning only black midi dresses and cat ears.

"I figured you two would've shown up in something shinier than Taylor's Eras Tour outfits put together." I point to their bland getups.

"This is what Kenny approved." Matilda rolls her eyes.

"Forget Kenny." Scarlett waves her off, then points at us. "You two are together, and I freaking knew it! Where's Maren? I need to tell her it's out in the open now, and I'm no longer sworn to secrecy."

"You knew, and you didn't tell me?" Matilda smacks her friend's shoulder. "I tell you everything, including the dream I had the other night where I was a cartoon tiger with a crush on a flower."

Scarlett pats her arm and forces a smile. "You should really keep some things to yourself."

As they get back to work, a few more familiar faces approach us to ask about our relationship. We haven't even made it three feet from the door.

This is more like what I had in mind, but Owen and I haven't gotten to get a drink or enjoy our first big party as a couple.

I'm asking for far too much, aren't I?

When the music cuts, Cole moves the mic and greets the crowd. "Welcome to the Tipsy Tap's Topsy Turvy—you know where you are." He waves off the guests, who share a laugh. "Just wanted to remind you all that we have several specialty cocktails tonight for you all to try. Witches Brew, Candy Corn Cocktails, and more. Live a little, okay, Sapphire Creek?"

Everyone whoops and hollers, and one woman even tosses her pointed witch's hat in the air like it's the end of graduation.

"I have an idea," I tell Owen. "Wait here."

I race up to the stage before the music comes back on. Right as Cole steps down, I climb up, stopping him in the process to say, "I need the mic for just a second."

"This isn't karaoke night. I don't have the machine set up."

"I know that." I scoff.

With the mic in place by my mouth, everyone's attention turns to me. I find Owen in the back, but he moves forward, slowly meandering through the crowd while keeping his eyes on me.

"Hi, everyone." I laugh nervously, wringing my hands in front of me as butterflies erupt in my stomach like they might if finally freed from a cage. "I'd just like to add to the drink specials for the night. The Candy Corn Cocktail looks amazing, in particular. Oh, and Owen Conrad is my boyfriend. We're dating. Enjoy the party!"

Claps and cheers echo across the bar as I nearly stumble off the stage on wobbly legs.

On my way back to Owen, I lock eyes with Sable, who lifts her drink in a silent toast. I grin back with appreciation and continue moving through the crowd and their pats on the back until I leap into Owen's arms. Another round of cheers serenades us as I plant a big kiss on his mouth.

"You are crazy!" he calls out to me over the noise.

"You made me this way!" I shoot back as he sets me onto my feet.

A mid-paced song starts, and he nods over my shoulder. "Come on."

"Where are we going?" I ask as he pulls me toward the opening in the crowd.

He tugs me to his chest, lifts my hand in his, and sways to the beat. "I want to dance with the prettiest girl in the room."

epilogue

OWEN

Three weeks later...

"What am I looking at here?"

A noodle hangs from my mouth as I peer over at Addie, who leans against my kitchen counter. I gather the noodle the rest of the way into my mouth to chew it and set the pot into the sink. "Don't worry. I waited until the pasta cooled off before I dove in."

"That's exactly what I was worried about and not the fact that you're slurping noodles right out of the pot." She shakes her head as she sashays the rest of the way into the kitchen.

I turn to face her, drinking in the way her green dress dips into the valley of her breasts. Her cleavage is extra naughty these days. That, or I just fall harder every fucking day. Could be both.

The hem of her dress flows right above her knee, and the heeled booties she wears adds two inches to her height. She doesn't need to stand on her tiptoes to kiss me with those on.

She's been coming to my house frequently over the last two weeks, ever since the Halloween party, and she just... fits here.

This place is more complete with her in it than any of the furniture or dishes.

We filled out the paperwork as soon as we got to school on the Monday morning following the Halloween party. We signed it all and forged our love in ink, and "the earth still spins on its axis along the same path it's been on for billions of years," as Addie put it. She also followed it up with the fact that she could feel a little pep in the earth's spinning, though.

She's right about that.

And tonight, we're hosting our first dinner party. When I'd asked her why she wanted to do this, she answered, "Just because."

I couldn't think of a better reason.

Plus, with some of our friends traveling for Thanksgiving next week, it'll be nice to get together to see everyone in one place before they disperse for holiday chaos.

I wipe my chin with the back of my hand, and she thrusts a paper towel at me. "You feeling okay tonight? You've been in the bathroom for a while."

"I'm fine. Really fine, actually." The blush in her cheeks matches the red tips of her ears as she steps into my embrace and rests her temple on my chest.

"What's going on?" I angle her face up so I'm able to see all of it. She's hiding something in the oceans of her eyes.

"It's just that I was... well, I am..."

"What?" I study her expression, and although she's smiling, I can't help but be on guard. I hate being out of the loop.

"Owen, I'm late."

"That's not true." I point to the spread of food on the counter, all wrapped and ready to be served. "We're done in here, with a few minutes to spare. Everyone should be arriving in the next—"

"Not that kind of late." She laughs, and tears well in her eyes.

"What?" I freeze.

"I took a test—a few, actually—and... I'm pregnant."

My lungs shrivel as those two words and all the possibilities suck the oxygen from my body.

"I need to make an appointment with the doctor, of course, but four positive tests don't lie." She bites her smiling lip and rubs her hands up and down my back.

"You're... we're... going to have a baby," I whisper like I'm testing the fact on my tongue.

And it's amazingly awesome in a sense I can't wrap my fucking head around.

"I'm going to be a dad," I say, but it's more of a question, as if I still don't wholly grasp what she's saying. Can it be?

Could I be so damn lucky to be having a baby with the girl of my wildest dreams?

"You're going to be a dad, and I'm going to be a mom." She laughs into her palms, and tears stream down her cheeks, her mascara staining her complexion.

I tighten my arms around her and spin her around once, twice, and three times, my laughter bursting from me in hysterical fashion.

Her own giggles ring out with an echo, mixing with mine in a manic celebration, until I rest my chin on her forehead.

My heart rate slows as the pieces of my life continue floating right into place.

"This is the best news I've ever gotten." My brain short-circuits and switches on my fight-or-flight reaction. "Wait. How are you feeling? Do you need anything? You shouldn't be on your feet. You should be sitting with a glass of cold water and snacks. I definitely shouldn't spin you around like a psycho."

She squeezes my hands. "We have guests coming any second."

"Guests?" Oh, right. The dinner party. "We'll have to cancel. We can't crowd you and stress you out. You need rest."

"Owen." She cups my cheek in her small, delicate hand. "There will be plenty of time to take care of me over the next few months, but right now, we're going to enjoy a night with our family and friends."

My breaths are suddenly labored.

"We should probably wait to tell them, if you don't mind. I'd like to keep this just for us for a little bit longer."

This eases the abrupt tension pulling at my muscles. "I'd like that. Just our little secret."

She winks. "We're good at keeping secrets."

"Damn right."

With the ring of the doorbell, she tears herself away from me and stops on the other side of the counter. "Catch," she jokes as she blows me a kiss from her palm.

I raise my hand and exaggerate catching it, after which I tuck it into my pocket.

"That's why you're my favorite," she says.

Thirty minutes later, many of our friends and two of my sisters mill about my dining room, laughing and swapping stories. They have no idea just how much we're celebrating tonight and what this day means to Addie and me.

On my way to grab more drinks, Addie emerges from the opposite direction. I catch her by the waist and whisper, "I can't wait to get you alone later to properly ring in this new chapter for us."

"I'm going to hold you to it, Mr. Conrad."

A low growl vibrates from my chest, but it gets caught in my throat. "Wait. Is sex a good idea when you're, you know? I need to Google it. Or I'll call Laurel. She'll be happy to talk medical shit."

With everyone out of view, Addie cups me by the balls and says, "Sex is definitely a good idea."

I throw my head back with a groan. "Can I toss everyone out now?"

"Not before dessert. Mama wants dessert."

Mama.

I fucking love the sound of that.

"I love you." I kiss her cheek and use an ungodly amount of strength to walk away for more napkins, forks, or drinks—I can't remember.

Thankfully, Nate is in the kitchen filling a pitcher with ice water. He's on top of it.

"I still can't believe you and Addie, man." My old friend chuckles as the water runs. "Didn't she threaten to sue the school when you two were voted *The Cutest Couple Who Never Was*?"

"She did. Isn't she adorable?" I snort and lean on the counter for support until he's done, after which we walk out together.

I'm empty-handed, because again, I have no clue what I'm supposed to be doing.

My head and heart are both absolute puddles of bliss. People shouldn't be allowed to be this happy, right? It's too good to be true, but when I look across the dining room and find Addie's eyes glimmering under the light fixture above, I know it's very real.

And it's *ours*.

~

Thanks for reading! For more of Owen and Addie, check out the **free bonus epilogue**, using the link below.
https://georgiacoffman.myflodesk.com/ttoybonus

Curious about the rest of the books in the **Sapphire Creek series**? Check out *The Charm of You* for Austin and Caroline's swoony grumpy/sunshine romance today! And stay tuned for Maren and Nate in *The Chance of You*.
Learn more - https://mybook.to/SapphireCreekSeries

~

To be the first to hear about new books, sales, and freebies, visit
www.georgiacoffman.com

acknowledgments

There were so many times when I didn't think I'd finish this book. It was a challenge, as any book has always been for me, but this particular one took the meaning of challenge to a whole new level.

But I loved this story and these characters with my whole heart. I couldn't let them down. Their HEA was calling, and the pull was too strong to ignore. I wanted to do them justice. Anything less would've just been a crime.

Writing, editing, and publishing *The Thought of You* just proves how strong we truly can be. When we want something badly enough, we make it happen no matter what, and it's extremely beautiful. The reward is so worth it.

A huge thank-you to all the readers picking up this book and giving it a shot. Thank you for your support, reviews, messages, posts, and shares. I couldn't keep living this dream without you.

To Kate—you've created cover perfection for this series, and I am in constant awe. Thank you for sharing your creativity!

To my betas—Jennifer and Heather—thank you for your feedback. I love getting to see what resonates early on in the writing process.

To Nancy and Amanda—thank you for helping me make this book shine! I don't remember how I ever wrote a book before we connected. I appreciate your valuable insight.

A boatload of gratitude goes to my mom for teaching me many, many things. You're the reason I ever dared to dream big to begin with, and it means the world that you've always believed in me.

To my husband, my partner, my biggest cheerleader... You keep me motivated every day to do and be better than the one before. On the hard days, you remind me of all the good, the possibilities, the magic. You keep me going, and I love you, forever and always.

Official

A Gift Like This

about the author

Georgia Coffman is an author of over fifteen steamy contemporary romances. She has a Master's in Professional Writing and loves the TV show *Friends*, as well as shopping. She and her husband enjoy working out and playing with their two pups. Georgia loves to connect on social media or through email, so feel free to reach out with any questions, your fave book recommendations, or even a funny joke!